The Unforgiving

CHARLOTTE CORY
The Unforgiving

faber and faber

LONDON · BOSTON

First published in Great Britain in 1991
by Faber and Faber Limited
3 Queen Square London WC1N 3AU

Phototypeset by Wilmaset, Birkenhead, Wirral
Printed in England by Clays Ltd, St Ives plc

A CIP record for this book is available from the British Library

ISBN 0–571–16232–0

For Bob Cory

ACKNOWLEDGEMENT

I wish to acknowledge the unstinting editorial contribution of Fiona McCrae at Faber and Faber. And thank her, and also Barbara Burnett-Stuart of Daviot, Inverness, for their kind help and encouragement.

C.C.

Contents

I ORDER

1 Sweetest Sugar & Bitter Dregs   3
2 Puff-Adders   13
3 Brick Palaces & a Book of Scraps   19
4 The Power of Food   28
5 A Fading Photograph   37
6 Stolen Handkerchiefs   47
7 The Despised & the Despicable   58
8 A Matter of Chance   68

II DISRUPTION

9 Stretching the Salmon   81
10 The Girls have Yet Another Piano Lesson, Mrs Preedy
    Organizes, Mrs Glass Asks Questions and Mrs Curzon Starts
    a New Campaign   100
11 A Quarrel Patched & a Favour Asked   112
12 Strange Meetings   119
13 Knick-Knacks, Seed-Cake & All the Horrors of the Universe
    Contained in One Chapter   130
14 The Aftermath   144
15 Pasha, I Presume   158
16 Truth (Not Tooth) Extraction   168

III DESTRUCTION

17 Item Thirty-five: A Sealed Envelope   183
18 Enter Valentine Birtles   192
19 Desperate Dancing   203
20 An Everlasting Kiss   215
21 An Entrance & an Exit   227
22 Her Majesty's Ear   242
23 Milla Reflects   260

IV CHAOS

24 *Arcanum Arcanorum* – How, or What, on Earth? 277

25 1929: To Every Question an Answer 291

26 1941: A Resurrection 300

27 Never the Same Twice 307

28 Tea-Cakes 323

I

ORDER

1

Sweetest Sugar & Bitter Dregs

'Such delightful children, Edward!'

The scene is set. For an unforgettable occasion, perhaps – but perhaps not – there's no way yet of telling. 'Nothing ventured, Nothing gained!' Drily Mrs Cathcart entertained the glib phrase her erstwhile husband would have uttered on occasions such as this. Not that there had ever been any occasions like this exactly; and surely, not in the whole history of the world could this occasion in all its uniqueness and indeterminacy ever be replicated, let alone exactly? Elizabeth Cathcart quibbled with herself inwardly as once she had felt obliged to quibble with her erstwhile husband; and husbands do not come more erstwhile than poor Henry now!

Poor Henry, indeed! What nonsense was this? She had eaten her fill. It was time to raise the subject. 'Now or Never!' She braced herself firmly, mentally crossing her fingers for luck, as any minute now – *unless she herself were to make something happen* – she would have to rise, thank the man for inviting her, compliment him on a most palatable tea and then ask him to summon in the parlourmaid with her cloak and gloves. And that, presumably, would be that; her host might accompany her to the door, but even if he did, it would be too late to speak. It must be Now or Never, and only the one chance: *faites vos jeux!* Mrs Cathcart delicately cleared her throat and said out loud, with almost too much of a rush: 'Such delightful children, Edward!'

Edward Glass inclined his head. He did not betray himself by either frowning or smiling. Had he asked this widow to call him 'Edward'? He could not, in truth, recall, but the scene had undoubtedly shifted, the action was moving on fast. How readily and with what alarming zest this woman had entered into the spirit of their encounter! He watched her detachedly like a man at the theatre, but to his surprise he could not sit back and simply enjoy himself. He too was up there on stage, part of some performance that was even then unfolding, only too rapidly.

'Oh yes, the children, yes!'

As a fellow-actor rather than a high-handed critic, Glass wondered at Mrs Cathcart who sat before him in his drawing-room, playing her tricky part with such fluency and poise that he almost conjectured whether there wasn't, in fact, some script? But no, they had no plan to refer to, fall back on and, in the event of disaster, blame. No draughtsman in this drama to seek out and sack. He thought of those slapdash architects who, hastily scurrying with too much work, had buildings of four storeys *actually under roof* – the floors only held in place by temporary stays – before they decided on the layout of the interior or the style of their façades. Edward Glass, of course, did not work this way and yet here he was, and here also was Mrs Elizabeth Cathcart. Glass shifted in his chair. Yes, he admired a woman who knew so well what she wanted.

Mrs Cathcart paused, sipped at her coffee and, after a poignantly reflective smile to command his attention and engage his sympathy, she appeared to find the courage to resume. Her bravery in the face of such hazard was remarkable while her earnest, careful enthusiasm made her seem disarmingly vulnerable. The pitch of her voice was probably overdone, a risk he could see she must take. Edward Glass found himself, in spite of himself, willing her now to succeed.

'Such darling little faces, all three of them, the same. So full of life – Stacia, Milla and Helen! Tragically motherless as I, once . . .' (her voice fell modestly; he was startled then by the eyes she raised to meet his, sparkling bright in suspended frenzy. She was over the brink and brisk, almost businesslike) '. . . that is long past. They are the ones suffering now, poor darlings! How I long to help! If only *I* could assist in some way, Edward . . .'

Bravo, bravo! How could he match that? Out of habit, probably, he wondered if he would ever dare kiss such determined lips. Quickly he dismissed the thought, this was clearly his cue. But what were *his* lines, what was *he* meant to say?

The servants did what they could, but it wasn't easy. Mrs Curzon, the elderly housekeeper, probably tried her best, but clearly the place and the children were too much for her without Sarah there. He himself, Edward Glass, Architect, could not deny that he was at a loss between these four walls, in this structure he'd bought but not built.

What, other than this, was to be done with three not-so-little girls,

Stacia, Milla and Helen, the daughters of whom he found it impossible to think himself fond? The woman was trying to make it easy for him. She had said her difficult lines most convincingly. Glass sighed. This was not the kind of problem Edward Glass was used to. What fresh adjustments to the calculations or clever shift in the loadings could deftly solve this one? This was a wife's province, these daughters, Mrs Curzon, this large dark house in unfashionable York Street – but Sarah had abandoned her responsibilities and left without notice, leaving him to it. He too would like nothing better than to get right away. But something would have to be done first. Prompt action was desperately needed before the entire construction crumbled completely, some new mainstay must be lodged in place without delay. Yet still Edward Glass, the Architect, hesitated.

Belying her outward calm, Mrs Cathcart sipped noiselessly at her coffee-cup and giddily pictured the wheel spinning – how long must she endure this agony, what *was* the man thinking about? She gripped her only prop and tasted the bitter dregs fearing lest she snap off the delicate china handle and choke while holding her breath and not being seen to do so.

In his mind's eye, Edward Glass saw an iron girder being fixed in a panic and with great difficulty across the dome of an over-ambitious cupola. It was raised, lowered, twisted and then bolted into position. It looked magnificent! An inspired, unelaborate solution that miraculously appeared afterwards to be a deliberate, flamboyant feature of the design. The girder had secured more than a cupola; where would his Reputation be now if that wretched cupola had cracked or toppled and his first extraordinary building had been, as it very nearly might have been, a complete and expensive disaster?

Instead, he had won the Illustrious Gold Medal, received from the alabaster hands of the Prince Consort himself. 'The first of many I am, yes, confident in believing,' young Prince Albert had politely prophesied in broken English. '*Arcanum Arcanorum*?' he had been overheard asking an official: 'I do not comprehend what is this *Arcanum Arcanorum*?' It was a question Glass had enjoyed repeating, recounting the event, making much of the German accent: 'I do not comprehend what is this *Arcanum Arcanorum*?' He said it to himself. He'd repeated it mockingly when underlings asked him questions, or playfully when women tried, as women will, to extract promises and pin him down.

Poor Albert! The pale fellow from Saxe-Coburg-Gotha found England somewhat confusing. Obscure architects, using furtive *noms de plume*, confirmed his suspicions that it amused Victoria's loyal subjects to club together and deliberately make life complicated just for the sake of it. *Arcanum Arcanorum* – the most *secret of secrets*, indeed! Prince Albert made no secret of his own continual confusion. So many Royal sentences had begun 'I do not comprehend . . .' that if Albert had been a music-hall *farceur* this might well have caught on as his catch-phrase. As it was the young Prince looked the young architect straight in the eye and allowed him to overhear his question, 'What is this *Arcanum Arcanorum*?'

Funny to think of those countless Albert Memorials *Arcanum Arcanorum* had later had a casual hand in. From civic bodies all over the Land there had come ardent entreaties: 'Sir, Consequent on our Nation's sad Loss . . . our dear Queen's sorrow . . . our Beloved Prince's demise . . . to be funded by Public Subscription . . . prominent City-site being sought . . . And who better . . .'

Who better, indeed? Edward Glass had been up-and-coming, the 'genius of the future' they'd said, needing a young architect to say it about, and Edward Glass was as likely as any. How full of himself this had made him! Other architects would have leapt at the chance (Albert, though German, had been popular, his decorated Christmas trees had caught on and the craze for Memorials was an opportunity to show off at the expense of a subscribing Public) but this 'genius of the future' had refused to waste his time and his talents on such politic trivia. The money on offer had been good though, so Edward Glass dashed off a drawerful of flimsy sketches in a careless confusion of styles: appropriate memorials to the Consort's confusion, he'd laughed, signing his name with an expensive flourish and instructing an assistant to send them out on request. The accompanying invoices had received rather more care and attention. Young and brash though he'd been, Glass knew even then that no Artist can ever be sufficiently established in his field that he can afford to insult City Dignitaries with mean and paltry bills. The invoices were unflorid but quite unequivocal.

That was a long time ago. Few of Edward Glass's Albert Memorials were ever actually built: the sketches had baffled the builders;

the loyal Public had subscribed, but only enough to cover the cost of commissioning such prestigious designs. And yet the Illustrious Gold Medal had indeed been 'the first of many'. So it was the resplendent precarious cupola and not the reliable girder Edward Glass usually recalled whenever he thought about his first important success.

But now, sitting opposite Mrs Elizabeth Cathcart, a respectable impoverished widow, he remembered how that sturdy iron girder had saved him and how the Prince Consort's subsequent demise had been a lucrative business for Glass & Co.

'I do not comprehend what is this *Arcanum Arcanorum*?' Glass said the old words to himself and, like a man at the theatre again, but one whose attention has wandered, he looked abruptly and guiltily back at Mrs Cathcart. He wondered how he came to be entertaining such a plain-looking specimen, but then he noticed the sorry way she was clutching her cup which must by now be empty. He seized a plate of fish-paste sandwiches and thrust it towards her.

Mrs Cathcart, aware she had already overstretched the proceedings and long since eaten that most personal of things, her 'fill', leant gingerly, gratefully forward and helped herself. If she had more shame she would rise, thank the man, compliment him on a palatable tea, etc., but instead she sat eating indigestible sandwiches in the hope that he might speak. She had no shame for she had no choice. It was Now or Never, though only she knew it.

Curious how the woman lingered, giving him time, pinning him down. She had an artistry about her that a woman who relied on her looks alone would have lacked. A curious woman altogether. Curious too, Glass thought, how the housekeeper had decided sandwiches (sandwiches!) were called for.

He had deferred other things, not just the tiresome domestic chores Sarah had occasionally endeavoured to involve him in. It seemed to him sometimes he had spent his whole life deferring, putting off till later for fear that there might be nothing left, nothing more after. Deferring too the project he dreamed of, the building he'd one day set on this earth that wouldn't be the compromise architects usually make between what they can imagine creating and the budget set aside for the job. This construction would disregard all the ordinances, conventions, regulations, costs, illustrious medals and implacable critics – petty considerations that fettered the imagination and tripped up and confined the fantastic. For once in his life, just once if need be – and as soon as possible – *Arcanum Arcanorum* would construct something true that soared deep from his hidden, most inner reserves. Glass thought how Sarah had left only this behind her, this inconvenience. If he were ever to be free to effect that masterpiece he must surely speak to Elizabeth Cathcart at once.

Edward Glass glanced out of the window. I know nothing about the woman, he thought. I knew little enough about Sarah.

Child-bearing, or rather child-loss (Sarah lost more children than ever survived), had altered the Sarah Edward had once known. William had been their first born. The long gap between him and the next surviving, Stacia, could be accounted for by a succession of coffins of varying little sizes. Sarah had steadily lost interest in life and then – wholly unlooked for – Stacia, Milla and Helen had arrived and survived. All girls, unfortunately, but each time Edward came home they still seemed to be in the house and then William had quarrelled with his father and gone away and Sarah Glass had taken to her bed. The little girls thought of her as 'Poor Mamma', someone Mrs Curzon ushered them into the dark to see, warning them to keep quiet and not to touch anything or cause a disturbance. Sarah lay in her airless, darkened room, unable to care whether the three girls lived or choked themselves into three more satin-lined coffins. She was unmindful also of their happiness, yet because she was their mother, but without enthusiasm, she ensured they were clothed correctly and sent to school. Lying in bed, propped painfully on cushions, she let them see the effort their continued existence caused her but she hid from them, as she hid from Edward when he visited, the true weariness inside. A weariness beyond any weeping.

Edward rarely came and Sarah did not blame him. There was nothing to encourage him to come. They were strangers to each other, and when occasionally they met they had no reason not to exchange, or to exchange anything other than, a polite but meaningless greeting.

Sarah's last illness was undramatic and not unwelcomed by her. Edward called one evening to say 'Good evening!' but she responded with a deliberate, if constrained, 'Goodbye!' Her certainty, her quiet finality dawned on him afterwards as he stood beside their lively daughters at her funeral, Milla and Stacia giggling.

Theirs had not been the most fortunate marriage, Sarah had concluded, watching her husband walk from her room that last time. She no longer knew what she had once expected, but it had not been this: living alone in this joyless house with a permanent headache, an overbearing housekeeper (mentioning wills every time she had a relapse) and Stacia, Milla and Helen. When she looked at their eager young faces she knew life could only let them down. The thought of this worsened her worsening headaches and hastened her approaching death. As she unregretfully breathed her last, alone in the cold still hours of an unremarkable morning, Sarah Glass wondered briefly what would become of her three small daughters when even she, who had done so little, was no longer there.

Edward Glass lived for his work and for the great masterpiece he intended to produce one day. The rest of life, Sarah, their home, his other interests, were entirely incidental, and of this, unlike the configurations of his buildings, he made no secret. Sarah had been a loyal quiet wife. Her unexpected death was the only major inconvenience she had ever caused. She had been all that a wife should be. He had no reason to suppose Mrs Cathcart might not be the same.

It was Edward Glass's turn to clear his throat: 'Mrs Cathcart . . .'

He had her attention; she nibbled at her sandwich, her free hand adjusting the modest frills of her widow's white muslin collar. She was nervous but she was prepared. 'Please,' she pleaded with him fearfully, eagerly, silently: 'Get it over with, *rien ne va plus*, Now or Never, once and for all!'

'Elizabeth, if love is said to be the salt of life, we may surely call wedded love its sweetest sugar . . .' A perfectly appropriate speech, and one he rather thought he had read in a book.

Elizabeth Cathcart had read the same book. In her nervousness she almost smiled at the peculiarity of this recollection. She had read the book on a bookstall, skimming its pages bemusedly – impoverished women like herself were surely the curse of all bookshops! The benign bookseller had watched her, resigned, until she'd felt uncomfortable beneath his silent gaze, put the book down and moved away. It had been a kindness, his saying nothing. It generally is. Elizabeth of late had become a recipient of and recognized such kindnesses clearly. People lent her books, sometimes she got to read

9

other women's magazines; the costume she was now sitting in had been borrowed from a friend. Well, not a friend exactly – women in her position did not have friends – an interested acquaintance then. Lent out of pity, so that the pin which held a big tuck, just under her armpit, dug into her flesh like a sharp and timely reminder. The borrowed dress had been taken in – though who was ever taken in? – and a widow's white muslin collar discreetly tacked around the neck. She had wondered, standing at the bookseller's counter while he said nothing and she skim-read the speeches, what sort of person would actually purchase such a book: *Speeches for Any Occasion*, was it? *Speeches to Make when Speech Fails You*, perhaps, or *The Speech: that which is spoken Unforgettably on Occasions* . . . You would have thought a clever man like Glass would not need a book to refer to, fall back on and, in the event of disaster, blame. Was he so clever that he conserved his cleverness, whereas she must direct any cleverness she had towards this end? This 'occasion' she had made to happen? As unique and indeterminate as other occasions she had somehow brought about in the past. A past Edward Glass knew nothing about . . .

'I am growing silently hysterical,' Elizabeth warned herself sharply, sitting there being herself and yet also seeing herself sitting there; feeling the pin pricking painfully, and yet glad of the reminder. She looked down at her feet, at her shabby old shoes. He could not know that she knew he had learnt this speech from a book, but to doubt what Glass knew would be to underestimate the man and Edward Glass was obviously not someone to be estimated lightly. He spoke earnestly enough and presumably books of speeches were written to be spoken earnestly on unforgettable, otherwise speechless occasions such as this.

'What am I letting myself in for?' Elizabeth contemplated the question with rather an outsider's interest since whatever the outcome it could not possibly be worse than the last time: 'Henry James Cathcart, I thee take . . .' What a silly romantic girl she had been! If what she was embarking on now was foolish or rash, at least her expectations were realistic and her circumstances desperate enough to warrant the risk. She could no longer remember what she had ever seen in Henry Cathcart, a smooth-tongued young man who'd certainly have scorned a book of speeches. *He* had been ready with his words – if precious little else.

She glanced up and saw how Edward Glass was speaking straight to the wall behind her, the thin winter light from the window falling dimly across the concealment of his face. The day before, behind with her rent, driven by despair but bearing the infinite possibilities of this afternoon in mind, Elizabeth had stood on the landing and murmured something to the landlord's wife: not a lie, but not altogether true. The landlord's wife had gripped the balustrade and taken a decent step backwards, away from the edge of unpleasantness: '*The* Edward Glass? *You*?' She had slightly altered her manner, for she had heard of the architect's wife's untimely demise, but she could not resist adding, in tones the trade had hardened her to adopt sometimes: 'Well, Mrs Cathcart, I find *that* hard to believe, to be sure!' Nevertheless the immediate problem of the unpaid rent had temporarily receded and here, those same circumstances that had driven Elizabeth Cathcart to regretful, wishful invention were even now being turned inside-out. No wonder she felt her self split in two, her old self watching as her new self took over.

Elizabeth fancied she saw a hint of her own difficulties reflected in this sad shuttered face before her and, though the fire blazed in the grate, she shivered. Which of them was more to be pitied, he speaking borrowed words or she in a borrowed costume, tucked and tacked?

Then the speech (which Elizabeth, having read it already, did not attend to and Edward scarcely heard himself making) petered out, such speeches having no natural conclusion and ending in books with a row of printed dots . . . The hearer may respond to a question-mark if she so chooses. Elizabeth duly chose. Elizabeth smiled.

'Of course,' she said and, as if to leave no room for doubt, she repeated herself: 'Of course, dear Edward, I'd be delighted.'

Only too delighted. *Fait accompli*! There was a pause. Then Mrs Cathcart asked with wifely consideration and the new confidence to be expected of her: 'Shall I ring for a fresh pot of coffee? You must feel thirsty . . .'

'Thank you, er – my dear! I'm sure Mrs Curzon will be happy to see to it.'

While they waited for the housekeeper to answer the summons, Elizabeth Cathcart and Edward Glass looked calmly at one another. They were both exhausted but relieved that the heady performance was over; the wheel had stopped and yes, she supposed, she *had* won. The pay-out was evens – something unforgettable, but something they would neither of them choose to remember, had undoubtedly taken place.

'I told you so!' Elizabeth jubilantly clinched her inward quarrel as if with the erstwhile Henry. 'Unforgettable, completely and utterly unique, as the wheel spins, as occasions go!'

'As soon as possible, I think,' Edward Glass said. Having made a decision, he was impatient to see it implemented for, like the late Sarah Glass before him, he wished to be gone from this house. 'In fact, the sooner the better . . .'

'Of course,' Mrs Cathcart assented again. How the landlord's wife's disbelieving eyes would bulge: *Mrs Edward Glass*! She smiled at the man across the room, but if the distinguished architect saw her he did not particularly respond. She looked down at her shabby old shoes and resolved on the immediate purchase of a new pair. 'The sooner the better, certainly.'

2

Puff-Adders

'Well,' said Milla excitedly, 'things *are* hotting up!'

Earlier that same afternoon the girls had watched Mrs Elizabeth Cathcart arrive. They stood at the window on the upper landing from which vantage-point they often spectated on comings and goings below. This same woman had called a day or two back when they'd watched her go off with their father in a hired cab. And now, here she was, arriving again.

'Her again!' Stacia was disappointed. 'Who is she?' She screwed up her nose. Mrs Curzon had said 'a nice lady' was coming and to Stacia's eye there was nothing nice-looking about Mrs Cathcart. 'Her clothes are all wrong,' she observed, wondering why Mrs Curzon should have been so insistent: faces and hands to be scrubbed, hair brushed, best clothes to be worn. And, what was more, sandwiches had apparently been made downstairs. All this just for *her*!

Mrs Curzon had left the maids preparing refreshments and panted her way up from the kitchens specially to 'have words'. *Come unto Me all ye that Labour under impossible conditions and are Laden and Laid Low; I will give you Rest and a glass of Rum.* Repeating an unauthorized version of the Bible uniquely her own, Mrs Curzon fortified herself against what she might find in the old nursery. She found the girls half-dressed and idling.

Milla, perched on a bed, was reading aloud from an adventure book, her voice squeaky with mock-excitement: ' ". . . there, coiled up on the stump, with head erect, and body swelled with rage, was a gigantic *puff-adder*. It looked an embodiment of furious venom as it turned its seething head this way and that, ready to lash out and spring . . ." '

Mrs Curzon appeared in the doorway: 'Get up at once, the three of you! Scrub your dirty hands and filthy faces, brush your hair, put on your best clothes. See if you can look pleasant.'

'Oh, good!' exclaimed Milla, slamming her book shut and sensing that something must, at long last, be happening.

13

'Enough of that, young lady!' *The Lord will put down this foul pestilence* . . .

'I only meant . . .' Milla began, but it was no use. Mrs Curzon's mind was already quite made up.

'Stacia, you are to take your sisters downstairs, lead them into the drawing-room, smile politely and introduce youself in a sensible fashion . . .'

'Introduce myself? A sensible fashion?'

'You will say "Good afternoon, Madam . . ." '

'It's a lady then . . .'

'Yes, a nice lady – and do stop interrupting, Miss Stacia! There isn't the time. Ah yes, smile politely: "Good afternoon, Madam! I am Stacia Glass and these are my younger sisters Milla and Helen." Milla and Helen, you are also to smile. Then all three of you come straight back up here, *immediately*.'

'How very peculiar!' Stacia said.

'Who is she?' Milla asked.

'Never you mind!' snapped Mrs Curzon. 'If I catch one peep out of you, Milla Glass, there'll be no sandwiches . . .'

'Sandwiches?' Helen repeated.

'I dare say there'll be some left over from their tea, but . . .' she glanced pointedly at Milla, 'any nonsense down there and I'll let the sewer-rats . . .'

'But supposing she speaks to me?' Milla asked.

'Why should she?' Stacia retorted.

'Well, she might and what if . . .'

'Speak if you are spoken to but keep it short – we don't want you putting her off, not after all my hard work.' Mrs Curzon paused again, wondering if she had said too much. She had prayed long painful hours on aching knees for the Lord to send the Master some new wife to bring order to the chaos into which the household had descended since Sarah Glass's death. All her hard work could be swiftly undone by just one clever remark from Milla Glass.

'If Milla puts her off there'll be more sandwiches left over for us to eat,' Helen said. 'It would be a shame to let sewer-rats . . .'

Mrs Curzon stared briefly at the neat little Helen. 'That's enough. As though I didn't have other things to do and nothing dusted, the tea to make ready and . . . Snap to it – she's expected any minute and since the Master in his mercy has only just seen fit to inform . . .' Mrs Curzon grumbled her way back downstairs to inspect the plates of sandwiches.

'Puff-adder!' exclaimed Milla and immediately reopened her book: ' "All poisonous snakes suffer inconvenience when their poison-bladders become bloated with excess poison. Thus snakes are at times anxious to bite *anything that moves* and will sometimes rise up and attack without provocation . . ." '

'Milla!' Stacia made a grab at the childish adventure book. How could she lead her sisters down and introduce them sensibly if Milla didn't get herself ready at once? 'Your turn with the water.' She pushed Milla towards the washstand and as she pulled on her stockings she mused at the task before her. 'I wonder if I am expected to curtsey?'

Milla, obediently scrubbing her face, paused to remark that if the 'nice lady' arrived wearing a diamond tiara perhaps they should all three of them curtsey.

'You two don't know how!' Stacia scoffed.

Later, watching Mrs Cathcart arrive, the three girls agreed there was no need for anyone to curtsey. Stacia was disappointed; she had spent long hours in front of the mirror perfecting her curtsey. She would bestow her polite smile instead.

'I wonder why we've got to go down?' Milla asked.

'We just have!' Stacia told her. Milla looked a mess but she said nothing so the visitor would notice how she was the elegant one, the eldest, the one in charge. Stacia timed it carefully. Time for the lady to take off her cloak and gloves, chit-chat about the furnishings, sit down, have coffee poured, take a sip and eat a sandwich. And then perhaps another.

Mrs Curzon lay in wait for them, hovering in the hall-way outside the drawing-room. It was too late now, they would have to do. She rapped on the door and signalled the girls to enter. As Milla passed by she dived at the child's untamed blouse in a hopeless attempt to tidy her up and she gave the girl a sharp warning shove. Then the housekeeper stood back, like a theatre manager watching his hired cast's performance from the wings. She had done all she could. Surely she deserved that glass of rum?

Stacia duly smiled her polite smile, withheld her practised curt-sey, and concentrated on her lines. She did not look at her father or at the ill-dressed lady but she scowled down at their feet and made her speech. 'Good afternoon! I am Stacia Glass and these are my sisters – er, my younger sisters, Milla and Helen . . .' She faltered.

Milla watched Mrs Cathcart taking a deep breath. Their father across the room was clearly impatient with the spectacle and only supposed the tableau to be a necessary part of an irritating enactment. He fixed his eyes and his attention out of the window, tapped his fingers on the side of his chair and waited for the little show to be over.

Elizabeth Cathcart, however, raised a dutiful if perplexed smile and Milla saw her wondering what she could possibly say. Mrs Cathcart scanned the three eager faces, and then looked directly at Milla.

'Are you Milla, or Helen, then?' she asked.

'Milla,' Milla responded encouragingly, 'I'm Milla . . .'

'And what are you busy doing this cold afternoon?' Mrs Cathcart enquired after a slight pause. She herself had had a chilly journey coming.

'Nothing much – you know how it is!' Was it *cold*? Large fires blazed in every grate – all the usual economies had been neglected in the weeks since Poor Mamma's death – it had not felt like a 'cold afternoon'. What had they been doing? She could hardly say they'd been brushing their hair and scrubbing their faces, but the lady was trying to be friendly so Milla said: 'Actually, I've been reading to the others about puff-adders . . .'

'Puff-adders?' It was so unexpected a reply that the nervous Mrs Cathcart burst out laughing. Edward Glass turned back to the scene. He had not heard what Milla said and was surprised it could have been amusing, although he knew this particular child had a way of provoking laughter.

Milla opened her mouth to explain further about swollen poison-bladders. Catching Mrs Curzon's eye in the doorway, she looked hungrily across at the plates of sandwiches set before her father and this visitor. Milla did not like being laughed at but she did not want the sewer-rats to get all the left-overs, so she shut her mouth again tight. Edward Glass glanced at her impatiently, seeing only a tiresome child who wanted to speak but who had nothing even she thought worth saying. He hurriedly waved the girls away. Stacia,

16

Milla and Helen knew themselves dismissed; they tripped quickly out of the room and chased each other upstairs.

Mrs Curzon lingered long enough to overhear Elizabeth Cathcart applauding: 'Such delightful children, Edward!'

'The merciful Lord is merciful indeed for the children of the house are miraculously considered *delightful!*' Mrs Curzon announced on returning to the kitchens for her well-deserved rest and glass of rum.

'Thank goodness for that!' Mary Ann rolled her eyes to the ceiling and winked at Cora. Whatever next? A funny business, and no mistake.

Upstairs Milla had lost interest in both the lady downstairs and the slow-moving puff-adder adventure.

Stacia, however, was seething venomously: 'You're a little snake yourself, Milla Glass!' she declared, pushing her sister into the room. 'Why did you have to go and talk about puff-adders, showing off like that as if you were the one . . .'

'I hardly said anything . . .' Milla protested.

'I was the one who was meant to speak . . .'

'The lady spoke . . .'

'I was the one . . .' Stacia was hot with annoyance and almost in tears. It had been her scene, she was the eldest, and Milla had grabbed the spotlight. 'I told her which of you was which. She didn't have to ask as if I hadn't introduced you in a sensible fashion when I did . . .'

'You introduced us very nicely,' Helen said.

'Anyway,' Stacia went on, 'her dress was all horrid and bunched up at the sides. And did you see the state of her shoes?'

'No.' Neither Milla nor Helen had noticed the lady's shoes.

'Worn through,' Stacia told them. 'Worn worse even than Cora's . . .'

'Goodness!' said Milla.

'Shabby!' said Stacia.

'I wonder when we'll get the sandwiches . . .' Helen said.

'Why were there sandwiches?' Milla asked. Mrs Elizabeth Cathcart had not looked like anyone special enough for specially made sandwiches. 'Why was Mrs Curzon so keen to bribe us? What's in it for her?'

'Yes.' Helen liked the notion. 'What *is* in it for her?'

'Oh, who cares?' Mrs Curzon making a fuss over a woman with

downtrodden shoes worse than a heavy housemaid's was no more peculiar than anything else that had happened since Poor Mamma's death. Stacia, however, could not forgive Milla: 'I was the one who was meant to speak . . .'

3

Brick Palaces & a Book of Scraps

Several days later Milla glanced out of the landing window and spotted their father and Mrs Cathcart returning arm in arm to the house. Arm in arm! She called her sisters to come and look. 'You've got to see this!' she yelled.

'Oh, not her again!' Stacia grumbled and again was disappointed, although she noticed that the visitor was somewhat better dressed than before.

'Do you two know what *I* think?' Milla asked gravely after a moment's pause.

'No, we don't!' Stacia replied. It was a dreary afternoon with so little to quarrel about they almost missed going to the silly school where they learned nothing but at least their days were filled.

'What *do* you think?' asked Helen to oblige Milla.

'I think – ' Milla peered below – 'I think they've got married.'

'Married!' Stacia and Helen stared at Milla incredulously, but when they glanced back out of the window their father and Mrs Cathcart must have come indoors. Stacia narrowed her eyes suspiciously; from the quick glimpse she had caught, the woman *had* looked pleased with herself, licking her whiskers and patting her paws – 'the cat that got the cream' as the parlourmaid might say.

'I suppose it *is* possible,' Stacia conceded. Helen nodded.

'Anything's *possible*,' Milla laughed uneasily. Even this? Could their father and that awkward anxious-looking lady really have gone and got married, unexpectedly just like that, this afternoon?

'I wonder if there'll be sandwiches again?' Helen asked.

'There ought to be cake!' Stacia declared.

'Yes!' Milla agreed too enthusiastically. 'With white sugar-icing on top.'

The business of getting married now over, Edward Glass handed keys for York Street to Elizabeth. Banishing thoughts that this same bunch had only a month before belonged to a bedridden Sarah, he decided to show his new wife the famous diary which was kept in his study. They stood side by side at his desk as he turned the heavy gold-edged pages displaying the programme of building work which was scheduled to keep Glass & Co. occupied for the next ten years. Elizabeth had not been in his study before and she, for her part, showed herself mindful of the honour.

'Surely nobody plans a full ten years in advance!' the second Mrs Glass gasped appreciatively. She could hardly contain her emotions, ranging wildly between admiration and horror. 'So much work. So many entries. Such an enormous diary!'

Here, indeed, was the substance Henry James Cathcart had always lacked. A diary filled, not idly bespattered with pencilled-in balls, hunts, and club-meetings that one might or might not have the funds to attend, but heavily inked with commissions, secured by non-returnable registered deposits, names and addresses written out unambiguously in full. Here was income guaranteed to under-pin the decade ahead. She had never seen a volume like it; such volumes were surely not standard items, purchasable like books of speeches from booksellers' stalls?

'Wherever did you get such a splendid diary?' Elizabeth asked.

'A book-binder makes them specially,' Edward Glass told her, glad this new wife was sensible to what was before her. He folded back the covers to display the gold tooling driven deep into the plump red leather. Elizabeth extended a gloved hand and ran an appreciative finger over the scrolled initials 'E. G.', elaborately embossed in the centre of the cover. They were her initials too now, she thought, as she began to turn the diary's pages one by one, letting him see how impressed she was.

Glass followed her eyes and then, because of her evident amaze-ment and interest, he too looked afresh at the diary's contents. Mr Eames, Edward Glass's young assistant (young, but considerably older nevertheless than the new Mrs Glass) would continue coming to the house regularly to up-date the diary. And also to deal with correspondence and matters arising. The closely packed entries that filled the diary were largely in the hand of this same Mr Eames: Burnley, Plymouth, Birmingham, Bournemouth, Manchester and Newcastle – all on the same page for, likely as not, this was work to be carried out simultaneously. Glass knew he spread his energies too thin. He was well respected in the profession, and outside it too, but he'd never shown what he was really capable of. Why, even

John Ruskin failed to scoff; Glass longed to be added to the list of architects it pleased that opinionated wine-merchant's son to rail against.

'I trust the man implicitly,' Edward told Elizabeth, telling her now about the useful Eames. Glass rarely had to think about York Street when he was away, and he intended to get away again almost at once. 'If ever there is anything urgent, Philip Eames will deal with it. He has access to substantial funds. I will instruct him to see that you never go short, for I am grateful, Elizabeth.'

'Oh!' Elizabeth faltered and felt herself colouring horribly. To deflect anything unfortunate, and perhaps undeserved, she said quickly: 'I am grateful too, Edward, very grateful.'

Husband and wife stood before the awesome diary and the sprawling handwriting of the operative Eames, as an hour ago they had stood before the Register of Births, Marriages and Deaths, but now they were alone and Glass could only think to talk about Philip Eames. He had not meant to mention anything so awkward as gratitude.

'Eames will arrive *punctually* at three o'clock every Friday – I require my staff to be punctual,' Edward told her. How could buildings designed to stand for all time not have an architect who insisted on exactness in exactly this matter? Posterity and punctuality, architects and their assistants, were they not somehow inextricably linked?

Deciding that a man possessed of a substantial diary and making substantial funds available for her use could perhaps be excused his pomposity, Elizabeth meekly attempted now to say something light about glass houses, (Glass houses, you see) but Edward soberly informed her that he built factories chiefly – enormous palaces in red brick where the wealth of the Empire was sweatily forged – magnificent hotels, railway stations, churches, municipal buildings and civic offices. Anything, it seemed, but houses. She had not known this.

'I have nothing whatsoever to do with housing, Ma'am,' Edward Glass remarked with more disdain than he'd intended.

Edward Glass and his new wife left the study and returned to the drawing-room where Mrs Curzon was waiting with due congratulations and coffee set out as before. I know as little about him as he does about me, Elizabeth thought. There were no sandwiches this time and the housekeeper blithely enquired (as though a dozen loaves and fishes stood ready on a shelf in the empty pantry) if any were required.

'I think not,' Glass said abruptly. What have I gone and done? he wondered as he brusquely instructed that the children should be fetched down.

'Oh, yes, do ask them down,' Elizabeth added appeasingly.

'It's not my place to tell you your business . . .' Mrs Curzon began.

Glass sighed. Elizabeth said sharply. 'No, it isn't your place, Mrs Curzon. But I shall be grateful for any assistance, at the right time.'

'The girls haven't been going to school,' Mrs Curzon continued.

'Never mind that for now,' Elizabeth said firmly. 'I will see to it that the house is ordered at once, starting first thing in the morning, Mrs Curzon.'

Mrs Curzon accepted this. The Master was not to be troubled, which was as it should be. This new Mrs Glass who had appeared from nowhere would take things in hand. The housekeeper retreated proudly – the Lord had answered the grumbled prayers of this His humbled servant: 'I am lifted up and set down like a blackened kettle bubbling on the hob . . .'

Edward Glass watched Elizabeth pour. What a charmingly practical woman she was. And indeed, poor creature – for a moment his eye alighted on the cheap gold band he had yesterday sent Eames to fetch; it was too large for her finger, she would probably lose it – she had merely been a practical measure, a quick solution for dealing with the problems of this house and three motherless daughters. An expedient. A mainstay. She handed him his cup and saucer and he decided that, being a practical woman, she likely as not understood this without anything needing to be said.

Edward Glass stirred sweet sugar into his coffee and considered how he liked things understood, but unpronounced. It was something of his hallmark he supposed. The buildings he designed, though obviously complicated structures, intricately contrived, were so unboastful – secretive, some said – about their means of construction, that even other architects (never mind Marmaduke Blockhead gawping up from the street) could be forgiven for wondering that his wonderful fabrications ever stood up. Glass smiled; time now to get back to work.

'I leave everything in your very competent hands, Elizabeth!' he said. 'If there is *anything* you need you have only to ask Mr Eames – three o'clock, Fridays, I'm sure you will find him useful – and I'm sure the girls will be quite delighted . . .'

He had rather forgotten about the girls.

'I'll take good care of them – and the house,' Elizabeth was quick to understand the arrangements. It suited him, it certainly suited her. 'With a diary so full . . .' she added admiringly, no wonder Edward would be so little at home.

Mrs Cathcart, now the second Mrs Glass, liked to describe herself as 'nothing, if not practical'. Henry James Cathcart had seen to this, marrying her as he had, with his circumstances left deliberately vague. She knew now with the benefit of that most costly of commodities, experience, that she herself should have checked up on things. She should never have been so trusting, letting her father and the unknown Cathcart settle her well-being between them. Her father had liked Mr Cathcart, a convivial fellow one could enjoy a glass of something with – and that had been testimony enough.

Her father ought to have been more thorough in his pre-nuptial investigations, more searching in his pre-betrothal enquiries, but her father had not had the heart for it – literally, for he had died. He'd not been well at the wedding and by the time she'd returned from a drizzly week on the Isle of Wight the disease had got a firm grip. Had he seen her honeymoon postcard from Ventnor and perceived the misgivings she had tried to convey behind her tight words: 'Ventnor is not as I expected'? Had he understood the rebuke and, alarmed by what his own negligence had brought about, gone into a rapid decline? She could not know. She still blamed her father bitterly – she had never had the opportunity to confront him with his carelessness. She remembered him lying on his deathbed wasted and self-pitying and the memory angered her. It was she he had wasted and who'd deserved his pity. He was an old man and death was inevitable, whereas her life was just starting and should not have been blighted. His daughter's happiness should not have been left to the vagaries of chance and Henry James Cathcart.

Elizabeth sipped rather guiltily at her coffee and supposed it only natural after this wedding to think so heatedly of that other. Elizabeth did not mind that there was to be no honeymoon now; the subject had never arisen and hardly seemed appropriate. On the Isle of Wight, in the rain and the dustiness of the cheap hotel, poor Elizabeth had quickly discovered that the grandiose financial affairs Henry had described to her father over that convivial pre-nuptial drink existed nowhere beyond the sprawling confines of the man's vivid imagination. Henry James Cathcart had been that most dangerous of undomesticated animals, a cheerful optimist.

Elizabeth had suggested quite sensibly that they might move to the more salubrious end of the bay, but Henry had laughed, he liked it well enough where they were. After many similar evasions, his steady resistance to expenditure made Elizabeth realize that it was as much as Henry could do to hire their deck-chairs each day on the beach. Even this he had tried to avoid: it would most likely rain and the hire-charge be wasted; why didn't they walk along the promenade where fresh air at least was provided free of charge. Elizabeth had pouted and insisted on deck-chairs and, as they sat side by side in the cold with the canvas flapping and Henry, hands in his empty pockets, waiting for the rain to fall and prove his point, she had tried to probe a little. She had asked reasonable questions and soon she'd deduced that all the 'dead-cert' race-horses, bonds and shares, ingenious schemes, prospectings, dividends and interests he'd boasted of to her credulous father were nothing more than idle longings and vaguely preposterous gambles. She saw too that Henry would never admit as much even to himself, let alone, of course, to her. And he never had.

Those long few years she had spent with Henry Cathcart had been as overcast as the honeymoon. Elizabeth tried hard not to think of them but how could she ever forget them?

One weekend Henry was thrown from a bolting horse and H. J. Cathcart's sudden and unexpected death had revealed (as only death can) an extraordinary tangle of dubious financial dealings which there had not been the money to unravel. In the end, after countless pointless confrontations with creditors, lawyers and an assortment of unsavoury individuals who had claims they wanted heard, Mrs Cathcart's very widowhood felt fraudulent to her. She had worn the requisite black but could not feel any of a widow's regret, not for Henry or even for herself. What she had lost had been lost long before. She was too desperate either to indulge in extravagant mourning or yet to enjoy her regained freedom. 'I am nothing,' she told herself firmly as she rented a miserable room and then set out to find a means of existence, 'I must be practical.'

'. . . she is to be your mother,' Glass concluded.

The girls stared from one to the other. They had noticed at once that there was no sugar-iced cake, nor even any sandwiches that could be remaindered later. This afternoon the sewer-rats stood no chance, Milla thought, looking at the over-large, over-shiny plain ring on Elizabeth's left hand.

'That's nice!' faltered Helen, for one of them ought to say something.

Stacia had no intention of wasting her special curtseys or rehearsed smiles, so she folded her arms and raised her chin. What was there to say?

'I could show you my scrap-book,' Milla offered.

'Your scrap-book?' Elizabeth asked. She wondered what Edward could possibly have been saying. Once, in the distant days of her girlhood, she too had kept a scrap-book, filling it with pictures of dogs and ponies. To show it to anyone had been to bestow a great honour – as great an honour, perhaps, as an architect displaying his packed diary – so she smiled at the twelve-year-old Milla and said with an enthusiasm that surprised even herself: 'Why, Milla – or are you Stacia, or Helen, perhaps? – I'd love to have a look. How kind of you to offer! I might even be able to find you some scraps. What fun it'll be to sit down together and cut them out and arrange them. There is nothing I love so much as a pair of sharp scissors, a big pot of glue and a scrap-book . . .'

Edward Glass raised his eyebrows. How alarmingly young his new wife appeared to him then. The same age, he realized with a curious pang, as the girls' older brother, his absent sole surviving son, William. He would have to tell the woman about William, he supposed, or perhaps he could leave it for Milla to tell her when they sat together pasting paper-scraps. They were, it seemed to him now, rather more of an age. Still, it was too late to start questioning the design, and an Illustrious Gold Medal or unequivocal invoices were hardly at stake. The sooner he left York Street the better.

Milla stared at Mrs Cathcart, or rather, at *another Mrs Glass*! The replacement their father had found for them as a mother, but not like step-mothers in any of the books *she* had read. Beautiful and evil, someone to contend with – but this one was dull and boring, even Mrs Curzon had said she was a 'nice lady'. And how old she was; too old to be as passionate about paper-scraps as she tried to seem. Milla did not want interference. She did not know why she had mentioned her scrap-book at all, and to this stranger – 'are you Stacia, or Helen, perhaps?' Was there no difference between the three of them that the woman should think they were so entirely interchangeable and not somehow themselves?

Stacia coughed indignantly. 'I am Stacia,' she said emphasizing every word.

'And I'm Helen!' Helen squeaked.

'And that obviously leaves me,' Milla thought. There was no way *she* was going to join in and say 'I'm Milla!' She watched Elizabeth colour slightly.

'Well, now . . .' Edward Glass mumbled something about need-ing papers from his study and hurriedly left the room. Outside in the hall-way he picked up the faded photograph of his absent son. He must dictate Mr Eames a letter informing William, as his previous letter had informed him of Sarah's death, of the marriage to Mrs Cathcart. 'Elizabeth is a good and sensible woman' he would write (although he could never be sure that his son would receive the letter). He would not mention what he had just realized, that Elizabeth was the same age as William – a woman who loved nothing so much as a pair of sharp scissors, a big pot of glue and a scrap-book. 'We still keep your photograph on the hall-table . . .' he would add, a concession to the sort of thing Sarah might have wanted him to say.

'I told you so, didn't I?' Milla gloated. They were back upstairs, for immediately Edward had gone, Elizabeth yawned. 'I won't keep you,' she said with a smile, indicating they also could, and should, go.

'It was obvious,' said Stacia. 'She was wearing new shoes.'

'Was she?' Milla had not noticed.

'Expensive ones. What a shame Mrs Curzon didn't let you put her off, Milla,' Stacia said. 'You did your best, the puff-adders . . .'

'I hardly mentioned . . .' Milla began.

'She's our step-mother,' Stacia said as if it were Milla's fault.

'Like in Snow-White,' Milla nodded sadly, for it was disappointing: anyone less likely to give you a poisoned apple and turn you out of the house was hard to imagine. 'She'll live downstairs, and be called Mrs Glass like Poor Mamma . . .'

'And send us back to school,' Helen added.

'Well, if *she's* downstairs *I* will be glad to get out of the house.' Stacia dropped an elaborate curtsey in the mirror.

'It won't affect us that much, having her downstairs . . .'

'Oh, I wouldn't be too sure . . .'

4
The Power of Food

'The Lord is working His purpose out!' Mrs Curzon announced.

Mary Ann, loading a tray with used breakfast things, smirked and glanced quickly across at the new mistress. Down in the kitchens they were accustomed to such pronouncements; only yesterday Mrs Curzon had told Cora to humble herself 'before the righteous rebuke of the pudding'.

If Elizabeth was at all startled she did not show it. This may not be how a young bride might expect to be greeted by the housekeeper at her first breakfast in her new home, but Elizabeth had long since accepted that nothing in life was ever as you 'might expect'.

'The Lord has delivered you up unto us!'

Elizabeth looked at Mrs Curzon wearily but she continued her oration unperturbed: 'Life has been difficult for everyone, not only the Master; I have had tradesmen pestering me at ungodly hours with cuts of meat and species of fish not mentioned anywhere in the Book of Genesis, and then the three girls . . .'

Elizabeth determined to put an end to this – had not Edward said he was leaving everything in her very competent hands? Involuntarily she glanced down at her hands, so spoiled in recent years: 'Now, Mrs Curzon, let us waste no time in idle chatter! Fetch me a folio of writing-paper. We have much to organize and there's no time like the present . . .'

Elizabeth enjoyed making lists. Dreadful long lists had had to be made of Cathcart's effects, his debts and liabilities. Lists as endless as Cathcart's promises, his unredeemed irredeemable pledges, unresolved disputes and unpaid bills. In the end Elizabeth had had to laugh . . .

Cathcart's bankers had not laughed however. 'We've taken a ducking, Madam . . .' one of them told her gravely, observing her levity over the lists and deciding the young widow could have no real grasp of what her late husband had done. Henry James Cathcart had managed to keep two steps ahead of the law and when at long last they thought they were on to him, he'd outsmarted them once and for all by dying. A penniless mangled corpse could hardly be arrested for fraud and there'd been a whole house-party of witnesses to the nasty accident. This light-hearted wife, he noted with pleasure, had not been among those present: Cathcart had managed to keep two steps ahead of this woman, also. 'Let me tell you, Madam,' the banker told Mrs Cathcart sternly, 'men go to prison for upwards of twenty years for any single offence on these lists. Lucky for him that he died when he did.'

Elizabeth had laughed even louder – to think the chancer had had some luck then, in the end. What an incorrigible man poor Henry had been!

This female must be simple-minded, the banker decided. He asked Elizabeth what she intended to do: he knew she had no funds, women in her position did not have friends, he wondered if there mightn't be some interest in it for him after all? Uncompounded.

'I'll find something, don't concern yourself about me!' Elizabeth turned quickly away. The eagerness behind the banker's grim face amused her then but later, in her desperation, she had even had to consider returning to him for help. Fortunately this had not proved necessary and here she was now, through her own endeavours, the second Mrs Glass, sitting at a fine mahogany dining-table in front of a fresh stack of paper. She would stress the *second* to tradesmen and other acquaintances for this *second* Mrs Glass was 'nothing, if not practical' and wanted no misunderstandings. She craved only a straightforward life, free from further embarrassment.

Elizabeth set about her new set of lists this morning with a new enthusiasm. As soon as the house was properly ordered she'd be able to sit back and rest. She listed the tasks each servant was to perform daily, then once a week and then once a month. Annual tasks were entered on yet more lists.

Mrs Curzon stood helplessly, wonderingly by. Her prayers had been answered; this was as it should be, and as it had never been, even years ago when Sarah Glass might have been up to it. Elizabeth made out a list of jobs to be done that very morning. An advertisement must be placed at once to find someone to take charge of the children.

'The housemaid Cora goes up there,' Mrs Curzon objected to the extra expenditure.

'They must have a governess,' Elizabeth firmly asserted.

'But they go to school,' Mrs Curzon persisted.

'They need a governess to send them to school. Really, Mrs Curzon . . .' Edward had promised substantial funds. Someone to supervise the children and keep them out of the way was obviously an urgent necessity.

'The Master . . .' Mrs Curzon began.

'Where was I?' Elizabeth cut her short. 'Ah yes, *your* province, Mrs Curzon – provisions. Let me say right now that I do not like to see waste.' Coffee had been provided at *tea* and far too many sandwiches for two.

Mrs Curzon could hardly explain that she had had to bribe the children. She stood behind the new Mrs Glass and wondered at the woman as she scribbled page after page of itemized instructions. By what inner purpose, what stony resolve was this young woman that the Master had found, that the Lord had sent to deliver them, so determinedly driven? The housekeeper appraised the new Mrs Glass's cold set features as if she were examining an iced crème Cora had made, but here she found nothing slovenly to criticize. Was not this what she had been praying for? What she had made sandwiches for, and had organized the three children to make themselves pleasant for? Wherefore now did she stand weak-hearted?

All her life Mrs Curzon had been meekly beseeching the Lord for help of various kinds. Sometimes He'd listened to her, though often He'd seemed not to hear. Never had her prayers been answered as swiftly and efficiently as this. Mrs Curzon sighed: *My flesh trembleth for fear of Thee and what Thou mightest do next, for I am afeared of Thy Judgements* . . .

Mrs Curzon had had a trying time. A housekeeper can do without the Master coming home and moping about his house, not to mention unfettered children truanting from school and getting under her frantic feet. Sarah, for all her sins of omission, had at least seen that the girls were sent to school, and the Master rarely stopped at home. Sarah Glass had been ill so long that her death was a sudden surprise. Mrs Curzon's joints had stiffened, she sensed new pains in her neck and back. She huffed and sweated and went to church, praying angrily on painful knees, certain that He would be indignant on her behalf, which reinforced the righteousness of her own indignation: The Lord see-eth not as man see-eth, and the Lord would see-eth how overburdened, unrewarded and taken for granted a poor rheumaticky housekeeper had become, and the Lord would be angry. Then the Lord had sent Elizabeth Cathcart, a woman who could make out marvellous lists. Mrs Curzon marvelled at what had befallen them.

Mrs Curzon had first been employed by Edward Glass a quarter of a century ago at the time of his betrothal to Sarah, and for the last twenty-five years she had served the household thoroughly if unremarkably, attending every one of the babies' funerals, growing old and carefully saving her wages. She undertook far more than most housekeepers, Sarah having been so constantly indisposed, but this had not properly prepared her for complete responsibility.

'We keeps ourselves to ourselves,' Mrs Curzon would say when comment was unavoidable, as it had been when a woman came to lay out Sarah Glass. With Mr Glass so much away from home it could have been otherwise, but it hadn't. She had never known what Sarah had thought about anything.

It seemed to Mrs Curzon now that she had never known Sarah Glass at all, she had never taken much notice of her mistress and was unable to remember anything that could particularly recall the woman to mind. When she had gone in to examine the laying-out she'd been shocked not to recognize the pallid, shrivelled corpse lying on Sarah's bed. She would not have known who it was except that it lay where Sarah Glass had died and loosely wore clothes she herself had chosen from her mistress's wardrobe.

Try as she might, Mrs Curzon could not pray this sight out of her mind. Here was the guilt – a transgression that could not be hidden from the Almighty as it was hidden away from all earthly view, nailed down in a coffin buried deep in the wintry soil. Mrs Curzon had lingered in this dread duty, standing in front of her mistress's wardrobe of clothes and deciding not to send in any of the garments she herself hoped – for she and Mrs Glass were much the same size – to be given. Thus it was that Sarah Glass had gone to her last resting-place in an old mauve taffeta that no one would miss, Mrs Curzon herself did not want and Sarah would never have selected for the outing. *Thou shalt not escape the Consequences of thy dark deeds.*

Mrs Curzon pondered whether Sarah knew she was going to die. There had been no will. It did not occur to Edward Glass to offer Mrs Curzon any of his wife's belongings, as was customary and also expedient – what good were they locked in those large dark cupboards for someone to find one day and cause distress? Mrs Curzon could not help feeling that by dying intestate, by dying at all, Sarah had deliberately set out to show how little she cared for her housekeeper. Twenty-five years of service and then: nothing! No little gift, no treasured brooch, no legacy. Not that Mrs Curzon looked for reward on earth exactly, but it was upsetting all the same.

The death of a mistress of twenty-five years should mean more than this disappointment over a wardrobe of old clothes and the disorder and increased burden of work and the difficult decisions regarding the household's requirements. Mrs Curzon had none of Elizabeth's natural aptitude with lists. One day she ordered too much meat and another day not enough butter. Coffee quite unnecessarily had been served at tea-time. She was sharp with the parson and the housemaid left (a false accusation involving the parson) and had had to be replaced in a hurry by the useless, pudding-like Cora. The parlourmaid, Mary Ann, kept out of the way and did little to help. There was dirt everywhere, dust had got out of hand.

'There is dust on the ornaments,' Elizabeth was saying. 'I noticed it the first time I came to the house . . .'

Mrs Curzon nodded her head in delightful misery.

The second Mrs Glass added dusting to the parlourmaid's list. 'Item 73: . . .'

The harder Mrs Curzon had tried, the worse the confusion had become in the pantry. People trained to have Lords and Masters shouldn't be expected to decide between fish of the sea and fowls of the air; they needed clear instructions. Her resentments had magnified as she sat brooding each day over her menus and receipts. She was barely polite to Edward Glass whom she blamed for not noticing the shabby mauve taffeta. If only he had said in time: 'Certainly not, Mrs Curzon – the mauve taffeta is old and shabby. I'm sure Sarah herself would have chosen the lace-trimmed apricot organdie . . .' Or better still, he could have accompanied her to the wardrobe and discussed the garments in which Sarah would have liked to meet her Maker. Then he might have been induced to add, on an impulse: 'Take whatever else you like for yourself, dear Mrs Curzon! Poor Sarah would have wanted *you* . . . And, how about a little memento, the diamond brooch I gave her when dear William was born? What a happy household we were that day, do you remember?' But the man

32

had never gone near Sarah Glass's wardrobe. He'd entrusted this important job to his housekeeper and Mrs Curzon had succumbed to temptation.

'Vanity of vanities!' Mrs Curzon sighed regretfully. 'I am but a poor wretchedly deprived sinner, unworthy to kneel in my old apparel at your feet; I have coveted what was not mine but could have been mine, it is more than I can do to repent.'

The weeks following Sarah's death had been an unhappy time for both Mrs Curzon and Edward Glass. Edward Glass, Architect, much in demand all over the country, prowled about the house in York Street, glowering and glaring at Mrs Curzon as she glowered and glared back at him. He complained of the cold so Mrs Curzon, in defiance of her own natural sense of economy, had enormous fires lit in every room – never mind the expense, let the Old Misery pay!

Glass felt like a zoo-animal, futile and ferocious in an overheated cage with only feeding-times and the possibilities of escape to contemplate. The food had been intermittent and awful: watery blancmanges, tasteless meats, butterless sauces, dry salty fish, nearly all silver bones. Sitting alone over these miserable meals and within days of her funeral he was uncomfortably and distractedly blaming Sarah for the untoward disruption. Death was only another way she had found of attempting to keep him from his work.

It was Mr Eames, his competent fastidious assistant, who had interrupted a dictation to suggest a sensible solution: 'Sir, do you remember Mrs Cathcart?'

'Mrs Cathcart?' Edward Glass could recall neither the name nor the lady.

'At that dinner the other evening . . .'

'Ah. What of the woman, Eames?'

Eames explained himself, Glass nodded his head and a letter to Mrs Cathcart had then been dictated – or rather, Glass had said to the useful Eames: 'Write whatever you think fit . . .'

The first time Elizabeth Cathcart came to the house (and went to the Café Royal in a hired cab with Edward) Mrs Curzon had felt her leadened spirits lift. The next time she heard Mrs Cathcart was coming she had been ready at short notice with plates of sandwiches which Stacia, Milla and Helen were later allowed to empty.

'When I grow up,' Milla vowed, taking advantage of an unexplained lightness in the mood of the house to sit on the kitchen-table and wantonly swing her legs, 'I'll eat fish-paste sandwiches *all* the time.'

'When I grow up,' Milla Glass added in her thoughts, 'when dear William comes home, I'll keep dogs and do as I please. And I won't just have sandwiches – there'll be buttered tea-cakes every afternoon . . .'

'When you grow up, young lady,' Mrs Curzon retorted, but for once not entirely without good humour, 'you'll wish you were a silly little girl again, with none of the cares and tribulations, fish-paste or no!'

'I doubt that,' thought Milla, biting another sandwich.

'When *I* grow up,' said Stacia, scoffing at the tameness of Milla's ambitions, 'I'll have a dining-table fifty feet long and butlers and periwigged pages and enormous golden candlesticks and parties all through the night with Chopin and mountains of food on silver salvers . . .' Her imagination ran out.

Mrs Curzon sighed at the recollection. Those fish-paste sandwiches which the little girls had greedily crammed into their mouths afterwards had done the trick. Even if the bread had been a day or two old. This confirmed Mrs Curzon's belief in the power of food and made her all the more eager to slough off the responsibility she had assumed upon Sarah's death a month ago. Let the new Mrs Glass make out the pantry-lists, for had not those sandwiches (a Miracle of Loaves and Fishes which no one had ordered but which she had verily been inspired to prepare) ensured that the young Mrs Cathcart had become the second Mrs Glass, and with all speed?

'Everyone must stay in their own part of the house, Mrs Curzon. From now on, only venture elsewhere for a particular valid purpose. I shall inform the children's governess, when I have appointed her. Each morning after breakfast you and I will confer *very briefly* and after that I expect to be left in peace . . .' Elizabeth wondered if she had been too forthright. She hoped she had made herself clear.

Mrs Curzon admired the second Mrs Glass's brisk efficiency. Her youth would ensure there could be no question of familiarity between them, so there could be no disappointment. She would probably be an easier mistress than the difficult Sarah Glass, God rest her shabbily clad soul!

'I think that is everything, Mrs Curzon,' Elizabeth concluded, handing the housekeeper the lists.

Mrs Curzon hung her head in grateful submission and held the lists aloft like Moses descending with his tablets from Mount Sinai. She trembled in her fear and elation, the skin of her face shone and she remembered Sarah Glass's wardrobe. 'Well, there was just one thing . . .'

Elizabeth was already speaking, 'That is all for now. You can have a light luncheon ready for me at one o'clock and until then I do not wish to be disturbed.'

Still Mrs Curzon lingered. 'Er, Madam . . .'

'Yes?' Surely they had covered everything?

'I was wondering what you proposed, um, the er . . .' The housekeeper faltered; it is often hardest to speak what is uppermost on the mind.

'About the former Mrs Glass's room upstairs?' Elizabeth sensed immediately what the housekeeper hesitated to mention. Elizabeth had risen early from her solitary marriage-bed to explore the large dark house for herself. She had taken advantage of her step-daughters being half-asleep, telling them to get up at once and get off to school.

'Have you come to see my scrap-book?' Milla asked sleepily.

'What? Oh no, not now – show me later. We mustn't neglect your education . . .' A governess must be sought and taken on speedily. Downstairs again, in Sarah Glass's room she was surprised to find everything had been left untouched. Her predecessor's personal effects had not been given to the servants. Her clothes – and the woman was evidently much the same size as Mrs Curzon – still hung in the wardrobe. You could understand Edward withholding the customary favours from this tiresome housekeeper and naturally Elizabeth had no desire to go against her new husband's wishes. Besides, *she* certainly did not owe this Mrs Curzon anything.

'Her effects? Her clothes, are they what you are referring to, Mrs Curzon?'

The housekeeper gawped. Only Divine Intervention could have made the second Mrs Glass understand so quickly without anything needing to be said. Or was her transgression over the old mauve taffeta not buried away as deeply as she liked to think? Surely Mrs Glass could not see as the Lord see-eth? The stern young woman who had been sent to send the Master back to work and the children off to school was clearly endowed with powers even more remarkable than her list-making.

Elizabeth waved an impatient hand – this was just the petty grubbing about a second wife might expect. 'Let it all stay as it is. I see no reason . . . I will instruct you in due course to instruct the maids. I have precise ideas . . . There are more immediate tasks, Mrs Curzon, itemized now on those lists you are holding and waiting for you, I dare say, downstairs.'

Mrs Curzon could have wept for joy. 'The Day of Judgement is closer at hand than you think,' she warned Mary Ann and Cora. 'We will all be destroyed in our beds . . .'

5

A Fading Photograph

'You heard her,' Milla said. 'You heard how keen she was.'

'It was only in front of Father,' Stacia said.

'No, there's *nothing* she likes better than a pair of sharp scissors and a big pot of glue,' Helen reminded them, as if Milla needed any reminding; she had thought of nothing else all week. 'You mustn't disappoint her, Milla, it wouldn't be fair.'

'I only said it as something to say. How was I to know she's so keen on scrap-books? Next thing, she'll be taking it over. I've had the scrap-book for years, I made it myself.'

'Well, that should teach you to show off, Silly!' Stacia was impatient. It was Milla's own stupid fault: if she hadn't piped up there wouldn't be a problem. 'I don't see what the fuss is about, it's only a silly old scrap-book.'

'No, it isn't! It's mine!'

'Show it to her then, if it's so precious – she is your step-mother, after all!' Stacia flounced out of the room. Milla and Helen looked at each other blankly. Milla decided to be gracious and allow Mrs Glass to have a look.

They had hardly seen Mrs Glass all week. 'You're to stay up here when you're not at school,' Cora had been sent to tell them. 'It's the new rules . . .'

'Rules?'

'Yer, you've got rules and we've got lists . . .'

On Saturday morning Milla tapped on Elizabeth's sitting-room door, and got no response. Milla tapped again a little louder and when there was still no answer she bent down to look through the key-hole. She could see a wakeful Mrs Glass lying on the couch, thinking about something and patently ignoring Milla's knocking at the door. Milla was uncertain what to do next.

It was in this unfortunate position that Mrs Curzon found her, eye to the key-hole, hesitating. 'Just what do you think you're doing, young lady?'

'Oh, I . . . er . . .' Milla squealed.

Mrs Glass heard a commotion and opened her door to discover Milla on her knees and Mrs Curzon gripping her trophy by the ear.

'Are you two praying out here?' Elizabeth laughed at them. Milla shook herself free.

'She was spying through your key-hole, Madam. I caught her in the act!' Mrs Curzon said indignantly.

'*Spying*? On me? I *am* flattered!'

'No, no, I . . .' Milla protested, but neither Mrs Glass nor Mrs Curzon took any notice.

'Spying through the key-hole! Milla, kindly step inside . . .' The second Mrs Glass beckoned the girl through into her room and then she said briskly, 'I shall be interviewing a prospective governess, this afternoon, Mrs Curzon. A Miss Emily Housecroft. I require you to show her round the house and answer any questions. Oh, and by the way,' she added as the housekeeper turned to leave, 'what were *you* doing up here? We have had our conference – anything else should wait until after breakfast tomorrow.'

When Mrs Curzon had grunted something almost apologetic and gone, Elizabeth lay down again on her *chaise longue*; to Milla it was as if she had somehow been spirited with her scrap-book through the key-hole of the closed door like some genie materializing – whoosh! – from an old brass lamp. She smiled. Mrs Glass found the smile disconcerting.

'Were you spying on me, Milla?'

'Mrs Curzon always thinks the worst . . .'

'Yes, I had noticed. Now then . . .' Elizabeth and Milla looked at each other. 'Was there something, Milla?'

Milla held out the scrap-book she'd been clutching to her chest. 'You said you wanted to see it,' she said, opening it up so that little bits of paper flew all over the place and had to be retrieved. 'You said you might have some scraps.'

Elizabeth watched Milla scampering around. Where in the few small bags she had brought with her could the child imagine there'd been room for scraps? It was a long time since paper-scraps had seemed to Elizabeth to constitute one of life's necessities. She suppressed a giggle: 'Oh, did I? Yes, I rather think I did. Sometime, Milla dear . . .'

'It . . . doesn't matter,' Milla said hastily, getting up off the floor and cramming the cuttings back into the book. There had been no need to expose her private scrap-book when she didn't want to anyway. Stacia had been right – that was the worst of it. Mrs Glass had clearly forgotten the foolish promise.

Elizabeth looked at Milla who stood on one foot like a crestfallen imp, her unbrushed hair tucked back on one side behind a bright red ear, and she felt unaccountably sorry for her lack of interest in this funny child. She patted the seat beside her: 'Sit down, Milla, why don't you. . . '

Oh dear, this was not Elizabeth's idea of a scrap-book at all! None of the nice printed scraps her aged aunts used to buy her. The aunts who kept up appearances whatever the cost – and a ha'penny a sheet those paper-scraps had cost for they were heavily printed, fretted with gold and imported from Germany. They had given her an expensive album with a leather cover, the word 'Scrap-Book' embossed diagonally across the front. What could have become of it? Lost like a lot of other things a long time ago, Elizabeth supposed.

The aunts would sit the infant Lizzie-beth on their starchy laps and, while they and her father bemoaned the family's descent in the world, Elizabeth had been obliged to carefully cut out and stick down all the costly little doggies and ponies from Germany.

'No, not there . . . over here, Lizzie-beth! That's better . . .' It had been an odd early education certainly, this careful arranging and sticking down of scraps.

Elizabeth's mother had died young. The aunts had never understood why their impetuous brother had chosen his wife in much the same way that a careless man might thoughtlessly buy a cheap pair of shoes. You get what you pay for in this world and, what with her feeble constitution and her having even less money in the bank than he, it was hardly surprising that the stitching had ripped and the sole come away. He'd got a bad bargain, left then with the child Elizabeth to feed and educate. 'She'll have to marry well if she's to have pretty shoes on her dainty feet,' they'd agreed – the one thing the old aunts had ever agreed on.

Elizabeth, with Milla sitting beside her, glanced down at her nice new shoes, so comfortable and unworn.

'No, that nice little doggy wants to be on a *blue* page,' an aunt had shrieked, seizing hold of the scrap Elizabeth was pasting. Then, like rooks in a nest overhead, the old women had squabbled ferociously over whether the heavily printed creature was an overfed Orkney shepherd's dog or a woolly St Bernard without the barrel.

Yes, that was it! That was the dreadful smell she had been trying all week to place – it was the ancient rooks' nest of crawrring aunts she'd been reminded of in Sarah Glass's shut-up room upstairs. A nauseous admixture of camphor, naphthalene, liver-salts, Water of Violets and rose-hip syrup.

The elderly aunts had died off one by one during her childhood. Every time an aunt departed this life, Elizabeth had difficulty remembering which of them had gone missing. There was little she could see to distinguish the ragged black rooks, yet how offended they became when she'd muddled them up. It was this she had been uncomfortably reminded of when the Glass sisters had put her right so huffily – 'I am Stacia'; 'And I'm Helen' – it was just the same huffiness as all those years ago.

The aged aunts had subsisted all their lives on annuities their wealthy industrialist father had left them. As young women they had been rich and well able to please themselves (pleasures that had not included the acquisition of husbands) but with the passing of so many decades the value of these annuities had dwindled. In the end there had barely been enough money left to cover the costs of a funeral. Each death placed a heavier burden on surviving members of the family. Dying off had resembled some macabre party-game – musical-chairs: catch-as-catch-can; dying-off – where the rooks left behind in the nest when the music stopped were obliged to pay up. The art of winning had been *to die off first*. Eventually, when only Elizabeth's father was left, the loser had craftily pulled an unknown newcomer into the game. Responsibility for Elizabeth had been hastily handed over to a Mr Henry Cathcart.

Elizabeth turned back now to Milla's scrap-book – a few sheets of badly folded, rather coarse paper with an untidy assortment of snippets from yellowed newspaper stuck down higgledy-piggledy all over the place. What a haphazard child! Where glue had oozed over one page it had removed the surface from the print on the next. Some of the scraps had come loose and some had never properly stuck. There was, however, pasted in pride of place, a poor pencil drawing.

'William sent that,' Milla said proudly. She had slapped it over something else.

'William?'

'You know, dear William . . .'

'No, Milla, I don't know. You'll have to tell me.'

So Milla told Elizabeth Cathcart who had married her father only the week before about her brother, dear William. William, who had set out to seek his fortune – and supposedly that of the family too for it was somehow assumed that William would return one day and share this fortune – seven years ago when Milla had been five years old. She had no recollection of the day William left, nor any true recollection of William, so talking about dear William was rather a jumble and something she treasured. Just like the pages of her scrapbook. A fading photograph of her brother, taken the summer before his departure, had stood on the hall-table ever since. From time to time, Milla studied what was left of the picture but every time she looked the photograph had faded a little bit more.

'I wondered who that was,' Elizabeth had studied the photograph also and noticed the old-fashioned frame needed replacing. It was altogether rather curious, finding herself step-mother to a photograph – a barely discernible photograph, at that. Yet even this, the second Mrs Glass suspected, was probably not as curious as playing step-mother to Edward's three dull daughters.

Dull? Were they dull? Or was it that they were another woman's offspring and so, quite naturally, they bored her? Elizabeth glanced sideways at Milla and encouraged the girl to chatter.

News from William had always been scarce. You had to ask if a letter had come. Usually it hadn't, but even when it had, details were never forthcoming. This absence of definite information made Stacia bored with the subject, Helen had never had much interest in it anyway, but Milla thrived on the gaps left wide for her to fill in. For some reason Edward and Sarah Glass did not like to talk about their son. Milla however liked nothing better. 'I think it annoys people when I ask questions,' Milla said wistfully.

What *do* you expect? Elizabeth wondered. Out loud she enquired: 'Where did he go, this brother, William?'

To the United States of America – Milla had looked in an atlas at school. He'd taken a boat from Liverpool . . . Milla traced a map in the air for Mrs Glass's benefit. 'He must be homesick, don't you think?'

'I wonder why he left, then,' Elizabeth said, although she wasn't particularly interested. Anyone might expect Glass & Co. to become Glass & Son, in time, but Edward had never mentioned a son. Cathcart hadn't been forthcoming about *his* liabilities, either.

'I don't really know,' Milla admitted. 'He set out to seek his fortune . . .' She repeated her words and Elizabeth understood this was what the child had been told. She noted the 'dear', conferred in such a way that you knew this William was not dead and being talked of like the aunts who had caused hardship by dying off and needing the expense of funerals. Dear Alice, Maud or Whoever had always been said with the sorry sigh of the impecunious obliged to fork out.

To Milla the 'dear' of dear William meant something resplendent that conjured up a bright green parrot and a great heap of gold spilling out from a seaman's chest. 'When dear William comes home' was a much repeated phrase, not necessarily spoken, of course. For a long time now there had been no letters. Except in Milla's imagination, William had altogether faded rather like his photograph.

'Ah well!' Mrs Glass said, tiring of the subject. This was obviously something she was going to have to put up with along with the rest.

'I wish dear William *would* come home,' Milla said yearningly.

'Do you?'

'Yes . . .' Milla hesitated. Before Elizabeth could think of a way to forestall her, she went on: 'You see, I hardly remember him . . .'

'We all forget things . . .'

'Yes, but if you clearly remember people, and things that have happened,' the child said insistently, 'then they haven't gone away, have they? The things aren't over. They're still there really as though they *were* still there . . .'

Elizabeth looked sharply at Milla. Milla was blinking back tears.

'He sends presents home, does he?' Mrs Glass asked softly, wondering how this conversation had got started and how it could be ended without undue upset.

'Well, no . . .' Milla sniffed, nothing they knew about except this crumpled drawing of an ill-defined landscape which Milla had smoothed out and appropriated for her scrap-book. She looked intently now at the smudged pencil lines that Mrs Glass was looking at and thought how there was more in this scrap of paper that had come from across the Atlantic than her step-mother could possibly see. Things took on the value *you* put on them, a value outside that only *you* saw, which lasted only as long as you and gave you a value also . . .

Elizabeth Glass shifted uneasily. But for the fading photograph in the hall and this poor sketch initialled 'W. G.' that must have come from somewhere, the story of William Glass might have been a children's fairy-tale: Once upon a time, full seven years ago, our brave Hero set out on a bold adventure . . . Milla at five, scarcely more than a baby, while she at eighteen had not yet encountered Henry James Cathcart, the dubious young man who would remove the shiny wrapping-paper and leave her holding an untied ribbon. She smiled indulgently down at Milla and showed the girl she did not believe a single word. She wished she had some present though to give her.

'Now then,' Elizabeth said, returning to the real world, 'I've got a visitor coming, a prospective . . .'

'Ah!' Milla closed the scrap-book and stood up.

'Thank you for showing me,' Elizabeth said quickly when the girl was already at the door.

'That's all right!' Milla grinned – she did not know why she felt so sad.

'I hope dear William has found friends over there,' Sarah had fondly mused. It was one or other of the girls' birthdays with Edward on a rare visit home and dear William was – because Milla (always Milla) had raised the subject – under discussion. One day, Sarah thought, the girls would have to be told. The quarrel had been Edward's fault, let Edward tell them.

'Of course the boy's got friends!' Edward Glass barked impatiently from the other end of the table. He looked again at his watch, and then at Milla, whose tenth birthday it had been and who sat wearing a paper birthday-hat.

Milla regarded it as her birthday treat to discuss dear William. She spoke up now, defending her mother, thinking about her brother and most of all, not wanting her favouritest subject pushed aside just yet: 'Not necessarily! It can be the loneliest thing, leaving home and going all across the world on your own. I think dear William must have been very bold and brave . . .'

Edward laughed outright.

43

'How would *you* know?' her mother turned on her curtly. 'How could you, *a spoilt little girl who has never been anywhere*, possibly know what it's like?' Sarah Glass had had a struggle to get up and dress. The strain of seeing Edward and the sight of all the lurid birthday-party food on the table made her short-tempered and queasy.

'Milla overheard Mrs Curzon,' Helen said explainingly, biting into a lemon puff.

'Yes, Milla likes listening to the servants,' Stacia joined in.

'I can imagine it!' Milla insisted shrilly. 'I may have heard Mrs Curzon but I *can* imagine it.'

'Of course you can't!' Stacia said.

'You can, can you?' Edward laughed.

'Yes, I can!' Milla, a gaudy orange and gold party-hat perched foppishly on her unkempt hair, stared defiantly back at her father who sat at the end of the table laughing at her. They had not expected him that afternoon.

She had heard her mother at the front door saying in a tone of surprise: 'Edward! How nice! It's Milla's birthday, you know . . .'

'Is it?'

'She's ten today.'

'Is she really? How quickly time passes . . .'

'Does it?' Sarah sounded weary.

'Well, of course it does.' Edward was impatient. 'When you're busy! There are some papers I need from the study . . .'

'It must be nice to be busy and need papers. You haven't come for Milla's birthday, then?'

'Well . . .' Edward Glass faltered.

'You must stay for tea – Milla's birthday tea . . .'

Milla heard her father groan.

'For Milla's sake,' her mother pleaded. 'If not for mine . . .'

Edward Glass had stayed. Milla saw him look furtively and frequently at his watch as the tea things were passed round and now he was laughing. Milla thought it rude to laugh at someone on her birthday. Her tenth birthday.

She opened her mouth to speak but her father cut in loudly: 'Go on, Milla, birthday-girl! Tell us what it's like the other side of the globe. Most of us have never been privileged to pass beyond Britannia's windswept shores.'

'Well . . .' Milla couldn't think where to begin.

44

'We're waiting!' Glass jeered at his ten-year-old daughter the way he sometimes made fun of a draughtsman in front of the others, reducing the man, making him unable to speak.

Milla carefully repositioned the paper hat on her head and then opened her jelly-stained mouth: 'It depends where on the other side of the globe you go. The manners and customs of the Uncivilized World vary considerably – now, take the Argentine, for instance, someone might find themselves . . .'

For a moment Edward Glass stopped laughing. Sarah scowled fretfully at the daughter who had let her down, making a nuisance of herself in front of Edward. Stacia's eyes opened wide. Helen gazed uncomprehendingly round the table and then helped herself again, to the last lemon puff.

Edward Glass looked at his defiant middle daughter with her mouth smeared orange, matching her clownish orange hat. Not one of the blithering draughtsmen at Glass & Co. would have had the nerve. He threw back his head then and laughed like a dog howling. He had not expected amusements to be laid on at this tea-party. He was rather glad that he'd stayed after all.

Their mother left the table abruptly and went straight downstairs to chastise Mrs Curzon for gossiping when the children could hear. 'I must ask you in future to curb your careless tongue!' Mrs Curzon thought the nasty child had sneaked on her – Milla, the middle one, the birthday-girl. Sarah retired to bed. Edward, who hated his wife to be ill when he was at home, took offence. He shut himself in the study and resolved to organize his affairs so that he need never visit York Street. An assistant could be sent regularly to see to whatever needed seeing to – that, after all, was what assistants were for: he would send the reliable Mr Eames.

Milla told her sisters. Stacia wondered why Milla had bothered to tell Mrs Glass about dear William – when he came home he'd be sharing his fortune with them, not with her. Helen never understood Milla's make-believe or the devotion to dear William, but she went along with it all the same.

'I thought you were showing her your scrap-book, not telling her about our dear William,' Stacia objected.

'I was . . .'

'So? Did she like it? Did she give you any scraps?'

45

'Well . . .' Milla hesitated.

'Well, then!' Stacia should have been jubilant but she was bored with her sisters, Mrs Glass, scrap-books, puff-adders, bored, bored, bored.

'Do you know what I know?' Milla asked: a governess was being interviewed that very afternoon. Mrs Curzon was to show her round the house and answer any questions.

'A governess?' Stacia and Helen repeated.

'A prospective!'

'A prospective?' Stacia was immediately suspicious.

'The child is wilful,' Mrs Curzon told Emily Housecroft. Milla looked quickly up at the visitor. So that is a prospective, she thought, still puzzled. Mrs Curzon did not see the need for this extra expense but who was she to question the decisions of a woman who could devise competent lists and divine your innermost thoughts? Emily Housecroft glanced across at Milla. Wilful?

Mrs Curzon could not feel she had sufficiently made her point, so she added suppressedly: 'The child hears and sees everything, she speaks up and tells tales. You want to watch out . . .'

'Indeed?' Miss Housecroft rejoined but without expression.

Milla, who presumed she was not meant to hear, went on reading her adventure book, set this time in Dahomey which sounded most Uncivilized and not very inviting. Once Milla had heard Dr Morgan, a friend of Poor Mamma's, saying: ' What a lovely, spirited child!' But she'd seen that he was looking at Stacia at the time. Stacia then was spirited, Milla on the other hand was wilful. And Helen?

'You'll have no trouble with Helen,' Mrs Curzon told Emily Housecroft.

'No, I won't,' the young woman said briskly, wondering whether she really wanted the job. She supposed with a sigh that she had little choice.

6

Stolen Handkerchiefs

'You'll be surprised what human beings can get used to when they must,' Stacia repeated the words to herself. She tried them out on Milla but Milla only blinked at her. Milla was too young – Milla had yet to learn. How grown up and abandoned Stacia felt.

The day after her mother's funeral Stacia had gone to the watercloset and discovered blood on her private clothes – and then more blood, thin, watery and red, seeping from the shameful privacy of her body. Nosebleeds and cut fingers you stopped up with handkerchiefs. Stacia could only try and stop this bleeding with the black mourning handkerchief she still had in her pocket from the funeral. Fortunately she had not used it for weeping. Hard as she'd tried and for all Mrs Curzon's prodding her in the ribs, no seemly tears had come. She folded the black muslin neatly. Her insides felt raw and tight.

'I am going to die,' Stacia thought, sitting in the watercloset, knowing not fear of death, but fear of this particular dying – the bleeding and the death being in a place you could not mention, or let be seen.

Stacia eventually entrusted herself to stand up. She left the watercloset a different creature from the carefree girl who only minutes before had entered it. Her days of giggling with Milla about nothing seemed to her to be over.

Stacia waited until she was sure Mrs Curzon was busy, Cora and Mary Ann not around, and her sisters absorbed in some stupid puzzle on the nursery floor. She went quickly to her dead mother's rooms and, in the room from which only yesterday her mother's coffin had been carried, she rummaged frantically through the drawers and discovered some handkerchiefs.

'I am reduced to stealing from the Dead,' she told herself and found comfort in the boldness of these words. Some of the handkerchiefs were lace, some embroidered (appropriately enough for Stacia too) 'S. G.', painstakingly hand-worked at the time of Sarah's accouchements which had been protracted and many. Stacia made no distinction: the plain calico, the embroidered and the lace, she hurriedly stuffed into the folds of her jacket. All were to become bloody rags which she would furtively burn in the nursery grate.

'You ought to go to school,' Mrs Curzon chided one day. The girls had taken advantage, she thought, for in the upheaval following Sarah's sudden death she had not realized it was Christmas and that even young ladies' seminaries shut over Christmas. Stacia had become dull and moody. Milla, disturbed by her sister's peculiar withdrawal, was louder, and to Mrs Curzon more insufferable than ever.

On Christmas morning Milla shook her sisters awake: 'It's Christmas!' she yelled. 'Christmas Day!'

'What?' said Helen. 'So?' mumbled Stacia and they both turned over and went back to sleep.

Milla sat on the edge of her bed. For once Stacia and Helen were right, it wasn't exciting after all and it was beyond Milla's powers to make it exciting. When Mary Ann came up to light the fires Milla said: 'Happy Christmas!'

'Is it?' The parlourmaid banged down the coal scuttle.

'I was thinking there might be an orange?' Milla said.

'Some chance!' Mary Ann laughed. 'Now if you'll just get out of my way, this really isn't my job . . .'

Mrs Curzon was insisting on large fires in every grate which made the house pleasantly warm, cost a fortune in coal and created plenty of extra work for the already overworked Mary Ann. But it was easier to get on than to argue.

On Christmas Day, Edward Glass paced the over-warm house. Fortunately the girls kept out of the way but Glass was bored and frustrated. How relieved he was when towards the end of the afternoon Philip Eames appeared with a bottle of something cheap (and wondered what could have prompted him the moment he rang the bell). Unable to bear sitting with his mother and her reproaches any longer, he'd bought the bottle on the way home from church that morning as an act of bravado. He'd pretended to his mother he'd been invited. He would walk the streets if necessary and improvise some story on his return. He knew, as soon as Mary Ann opened the door and her eyes popped out of her head, that his visit was inappropriate. But there he stood and say something he must:

48

'The Compliments of the Season!' He waved his bottle at her. Mary Ann noticed that the wine was a cheap one and naturally she assumed Mr Eames had brought it for *her*. But then Edward Glass emerged, seeking distraction. He stared at Philip Eames and remembered that Mr & Mrs Charles Preedy had invited him to dine.

Glass had had no intention of going; the man was a lumpish upstart, ambitious, dull-witted and workaday, his wife a sharp, watchful little woman. They pressed invitations on him, wanting it to be known that Edward Glass dined at their house and this was something he steadfastly had not done before. Sarah had been drawn into a friendship of sorts with Mrs Preedy, but Sarah had been a weak woman and easily persuadable. Ill-health had protected her from detecting the machinations of others. Other people and their affairs did not seem to rouse her proper interest. Mrs Preedy had been industrious with her calling-cards and on several occasions Sarah Glass had found herself sitting opposite the beady eyes of Mrs Preedy, discussing children's ailments and cures for rather vague women's conditions. She had never been certain what Mrs Preedy was talking about but she'd smiled and nodded weakly, proffering or being proffered heavily scented tea. 'Oh yes, yes indeed!' she'd repeated, feeling nauseous, though the woman, she could only suppose, meant well.

'She was such a dear friend to me, Mr Glass, really she was!' Mrs Preedy had sobbed in the graveyard. 'You must certainly dine with us on Christmas Day. In dear Sarah's memory, as it were . . .'

Edward Glass perked up at the sound of his assistant at the door, an emissary from a happier life. He welcomed Mr Eames, not with an orange, but with a little of the bonhomie that had been missing this Christmas Day. He invited Philip Eames to go with him and dine.

'Philip Eames, my assistant,' he introduced him. 'I believe you have met?'

Eames handed Charles Preedy the cheap bottle which he was still carrying for Mary Ann had been too confounded to relieve him of it. Eames could barely believe his luck at this turn in events. He threw himself into the role, shaking hands enthusiastically with his host and hostess, heartily wishing them, as earlier he had wished Mary Ann, the 'Compliments of the Season.'

Mrs Preedy was not amused. She concealed her considerable

annoyance beneath expressions of delight and commiseration – for had they not last met Mr Glass and the invitation to Christmas dinner not been pressed on him outside the church within ten minutes of his dear Sarah's burial? She introduced the other object of her charitable intentions that evening, a down-at-heel widow, Elizabeth Cathcart.

Mrs Preedy had been toying with the idea of asking Mrs Cathcart to be her lady's companion. With Charles's career taking off so – why in ten years' time he could well be as distinguished an architect as Edward Glass himself and it was common knowledge how little time Mr Glass was able to spend at home. Would not a lady's companion then be the thing? She was not altogether sure. Mrs Preedy was toying . . .

Edward Glass sat at the dinner table and ate the food they placed before him. A turkey was carved. Cranberry sauce produced. He worked his way morosely through a big meal and he drank well but without pleasure. He had never liked Charles Preedy.

Mr Eames asked deferential questions. Mr Eames talked of Christmassy things. Mr Eames turned from one to the other, affably commenting on the food, the wine, the china, anything! He raised his glass in frequent and eloquent toasts and was agreeably lavish with his praise and thanks. Even his mother could have found nothing to criticize in his behaviour here tonight.

Mrs Preedy sat smiling, furious that her charity had been thus abused. During Sarah's funeral she had wondered how, if she herself were to die, her own death might affect *her* husband. She wanted him to tell her that she was unique and altogether irreplaceable but she had concentrated instead on her scheme to bring the great Mr Glass to her house. With Christmas next week, what better excuse? It would please Preedy if she befriended the famous architect – she would flirt with the widower, cheering him up a bit. Already she liked to tell their acquaintances how Charles was Edward Glass's protégé, marked out by the great man for greater things. Certainly it was true that he had once won a Bronze Medal and Edward Glass had taken him by the hand. Mrs Preedy had never intended that Edward Glass should turn up tonight accompanied by this simpering monkey and proceed to eat his way glumly through a substantial Christmas dinner as though he were sitting down at home. She tried several times to ask him bright intelligent questions but he showed no interest. Next she endeavoured to advance Elizabeth Cathcart, but Edward Glass ignored that woman also.

All through dinner, out of the corner of his eye, Philip Eames was acutely aware of his bottle of cheap wine telling against him as it stood on top of the Preedys' festive sideboard where it had been placed when they first arrived. One by one the other bottles were gradually uncorked and drunk but his own bottle stayed, looking cheaper and more out of place as the evening wore on. At last it was the only bottle left but by now Mr Preedy had produced a decanter of port. The solitary bottle was still there when later they took their leave. He could not help wondering what had happened to it afterwards.

The Preedys' son and daughter, accompanied by their nurse, made a brief appearance. Bertram and Charlotte, tricked out like a pair of dolls, solemnly shook hands with the company and gave coyly awkward answers to adult questions, were patted on the head and sent away with their nurse to bed. Mrs Cathcart delved into her purse and handed each of them a coin.

'How sweet of you, Eliza!' Mrs Preedy sang, noting that it had been silver. Mr Glass could have given gold but it did not occur to him to give anything. Philip Eames felt it was not his place and besides, he had spent what money he'd not put in the collection-plate that morning on the cheap bottle of wine that stood across the room, uncorked, unwelcome and undrunk. Mrs Preedy wondered at the folly of it, Mrs Cathcart could have so little – she had even had to borrow that dress she was sitting in, and it didn't suit her one little bit . . .

Philip Eames met her eye, but only briefly. What he saw he did not rightly know, but it had been something unsettling enough to call her to mind later.

Mrs Cathcart caught Eames watching her and flashed a momentary glance of defiance. How could he be aware that these coins she had slipped into the Preedy children's sticky hands were among her last, carefully polished that morning for this very purpose? And yet, when she saw his piggy eyes fixed on her she thought perhaps he alone in the room suspected. He and she sat in this dining-room, this Christmas Day, on sufferance. She hated the wretchedness of her condition that levelled her with the obsequious Eames. She sat very straight and drank only moderately, encouraging Mrs Preedy to laugh and talk of happy Christmases gone by. The Preedys had brought a branch of a fir tree in from their garden and hung little bells on it.

'I do so like a decorated Christmas tree,' Elizabeth said bravely.

'If I'd been commissioned to design an Albert Memorial,' Charles Preedy remarked, for he knew of Glass's meeting with the Prince Consort and he wanted to give the man a chance to recount it, 'I'd have based the design on a Christmas tree. Rather appropriate, don't you think, Sir?'

'What was that?' Glass asked distractedly after a pause.

At the mention of Prince Albert, Philip Eames gulped and nearly choked in his tight collar. He quickly enquired what toys Bertram and Charlotte had been lucky enough to receive from Santa Claus.

'Toys? Santa Claus?' Mrs Preedy was shocked at the fellow's open impertinence.

'Didn't they get any gifts then?' Eames asked awkwardly. Even his mother had presented him with a knitted scarf. Mr Preedy hastily poured everyone except Mrs Cathcart, who declined the proffered bottle, another glass of dark wine. Mrs Preedy coughed. Surely it was understood that on Christmas Day dinner-guests were expected to bestow gifts on the children of the house? This assistant, or whatever he was, was sadly lacking.

Mrs Preedy proceeded to describe how she had taken Bertram and Charlotte to Madame Tussaud & Sons on the Marylebone Road to see the waxworks. 'They were bored, poor lambs, and I quite thought the entrance-fee wasted – but when we got to the Chamber of Horrors, they had the time of their lives. Have you ever been to the Chamber of Horrors, Mr Eames?'

'Why, no,' Philip Eames's mother had never taken him there.

'We encountered Burke and Hare, Mr Eames. Dr Black and the notorious Aberdeen poisoner Mrs Bertha Kilgarriff – such wonderful likenesses! I think you would enjoy yourself, Mr Eames, the children were utterly enthralled . . .'

Mrs Cathcart could bear no more. She scraped back her chair and stood up abruptly. Quietly she bade everyone an early farewell, touching hands, wishing them the best for the year to come, the same New Year she herself so dreaded. The Preedy carriage drove her home.

She shut the door of her rented room and turned the key in the lock and only then, still clinging to the doorknob on the inside, did she allow herself to break down: 'Henry! Henry! Look what you've done to me . . .' Elizabeth Cathcart wept. She could not know that in the unprepossessing person of Philip Eames she had met her saviour.

Mrs Preedy thought better of what had been a passing fancy. 'I like the woman well enough,' she told Mr Preedy so as not to seem mean-spirited. 'But I wouldn't want to have her here all the time – she makes me nervous.'

Charles Preedy considered that they had acquitted themselves well with the great man. It had often been on the tip of his tongue to suggest some joint project but he knew other men who had approached Glass in this way and feared more than anything that others should know he too had tried and been snubbed. Was it a good sign then that the fellow Eames had been brought along this evening? Mr Preedy considered a friendship with Philip Eames was probably in order. He would write the man a note and suggest an evening together.

By their own reckoning, Charlotte and Bertram had not done very well out of Christmas: one small coin each was scarcely sufficient reward for having to 'go downstairs'. What remained in Eames's mind was the flash of these silver coins as they passed from the young widow's dry hand into a child's grabbing fist, echoed by the hard flash in her angry eyes as she caught him watching her. He recalled Stacia Glass at her mother's funeral. By some strange transference which Eames could no more understand than he understood the other thoughts that had begun to trouble his sleep, it seemed to him that it was Stacia Glass whom Mrs Cathcart should have been handing coins to, Stacia Glass the little canary who should be fed handfuls of seed.

A few days later, mindful perhaps that he and this assistant had dined together on Christmas Day, Edward Glass expressed his irritation and despair. Eames respectfully reminded him of Mrs Cathcart. Her husband, they had been given to understand in hushed tones after she had taken her leave, had died only recently, leaving her in awkward circumstances.

'Poor creature!' trilled Mrs Charles Preedy. 'I'm sure she can't know which way to turn! Why, even the dress she was wearing was one that I lent her . . .'

Edward Glass had seen the way Mrs Preedy had treated Elizabeth Cathcart, he had clearly heard the simulated kindness and wheedling sympathy, the mock concern. It had been there in her voice also when she spoke to him after the funeral, harping on about how much he must miss 'her dear friend, dear Sarah', how empty the house would seem, how irreplaceable Sarah was – it was as though by carrying on in this way Mrs Preedy wanted him to know that she suspected the truth, whatever that truth might be.

Stacia bled, and hurt, and went to bed to die. Their mother had been ill, there had been bloody swabs which the children from time to time had accidentally seen, and then Sarah Glass had died. From beneath the coverlets of her bed, poor Stacia contemplated her own natural descent into a cold wet grave. Milla and Helen asked her what was wrong but Stacia imagined them giggling at *her* funeral and could not tell them. Milla stared helplessly down at her pale sister; she too feared that Stacia might die.

'What's the matter?' Milla kept asking. It wasn't possible that Stacia was missing their mother, and Stacia did not look ill exactly. Frantically Milla tried to cheer her sister up: 'You can have a look at my scrap-book if you like . . .'

'Oh, you and your silly old scrap-book . . .'

Later Milla tried again, this time attempting to interest her sister in an adventure book by Pasha. 'You can lose yourself,' she promised.

'Lose myself! Don't be ridiculous!' It was what Stacia feared most, losing herself. She groaned. 'I don't want to lose myself . . .'

'You'd better not let Mrs Curzon catch you in bed,' Mary Ann said, knowing immediately what was the matter with the girl but knowing also that it was not her place to speak.

Stacia heaved over and turned her back haughtily on the parlour-maid. Mary Ann was supposed to deal with downstairs. The housemaid's place was up here but there was no point saying so. Everything was topsy-turvy, but Stacia tried not to think about death, the slimy worms, the coffin. She concentrated on the horrible pain beneath her abdomen.

Five days later of course she was better. Then the second Mrs Glass arrived, advertising for and immediately installing Miss Emily

54

Housecroft, a young lady with impeccable references who saw to it then that they went to school. There was more bleeding but again it did not last.

One day Mrs Curzon called to check up on the new governess and found Stacia lying in bed. She glared at the girl's pale face peering from beneath the covers. 'Just like her mother!' she declared scornfully.

Miss Housecroft was genuinely surprised. 'I thought you were at school,' she told Stacia. She had assumed that after breakfast the three girls had departed together as usual. She enjoyed her days on her own. She had plenty of her own work to do. She was perplexed and also a little annoyed that Mrs Curzon should have caught her failing in her duties like this.

'I will speak to Stacia later,' Miss Housecroft said firmly, shutting the girls' bedroom door and leading Mrs Curzon into the school-room. The housekeeper had come to discuss the week's menus for the children, which was a pointless exercise as Miss Housecroft always agreed to everything anyway. On the few occasions when she had endeavoured to make suggestions, her ideas had been overruled immediately by some petty objection and it had never been worth arguing. Mrs Curzon only puffed her way up here to exercise her right to do so. There were a lot of books that were definitely not the Bible or any version of it, Mrs Curzon noticed as she looked along the shelves pretending to inspect for dust: *thou shalt have none other gods* . . .

'Sounds perfectly acceptable to me,' Emily Housecroft said airily. White fish, bread-pudding, mutton stew, dumplings of suet – what difference did it make?

When Mrs Curzon was safely back downstairs she returned to Stacia and sat down on the iron bed. Briefly, unembarrassedly, kindly even, she told Stacia what was 'wrong' with her. She held her hand as she did so in a dispassionate sorry way. She broke the news calmly to the girl.

'Every month?' Stacia asked, appalled.

'I'm afraid so!'

It was worse than Stacia could have imagined possible. Wildly she decided it was worse than dying.

'Even the Queen?'

'Yes, even the Queen!' Miss Housecroft smiled.

'I stole my mother's handkerchiefs,' Stacia confessed in a hoarse whisper.

'I'm sure she wouldn't have minded.'

'No, you don't understand – she'd only died the week before . . .' Stacia whimpered.

'Well then, she didn't need handkerchiefs any more, did she?'

In spite of herself – and the embroidered initials 'S. G.' had been her own – Stacia smiled. 'And the pain?'

'There's nothing you can do. Lots of women have their own remedies but you won't find any of them work. It's just something they enjoy talking about and swapping, rather like stamps or Milla's paper-scraps. I'm afraid, dear Stacia, it's a punishment, and you'll just have to learn to put up with it.'

'But,' Stacia protested with great earnestness, 'why should I be punished when I haven't done anything wrong – except take Mother's handkerchiefs, but that was afterwards.'

Miss Housecroft did not laugh. 'I dare say you're not the first to have asked that,' she said rather sharply. 'Fairness doesn't come into it – we all can expect to get punished in life for what we haven't done. I think you should get up now. I'll write a letter to the school.'

'You . . . won't tell the others, will you?' Stacia could not bear the idea of Milla and Helen finding out. She could not imagine how Milla would react to the indignity.

'They'll find out for themselves soon enough,' Miss Housecroft said. 'It's not so bad, you know. You'll be surprised what human beings can get used to when they must . . .'

'Even Milla . . .

'Especially Milla!' Miss Housecroft laughed.

Mrs Curzon, hoping that a Day of Judgement on earth at least might be close at hand for Emily Housecroft, reported the outrage she had discovered in the children's quarters: *Stacia Glass in bed at eleven-thirty that very morning!* Mrs Glass asked the governess for a 'private word' but luckily there was a straightforward explanation and nothing remiss. She suggested Miss Housecroft organize the growing girl some new dresses.

The second Mrs Glass then made it clear to Mrs Curzon that she was entirely satisfied with Miss Housecroft and wanted no more reports – it had led to awkwardness, unfortunate things had been discussed that needn't have been. Mrs Curzon went the colour of boiled beetroot and apologized for her false suspicions. It seemed there was no faulting Emily Housecroft. Best to leave these women to it: 'The Lord preserve thee now in thy domain, even as He preserves His fruits in the bottling of jam at the summer's end . . .'

7

The Despised & the Despicable

For six months now Edward Glass and his second wife had enjoyed the peaceful commerce and contentment of an ordered married life. Later, of course, Elizabeth would think the peace had been too good to be true, too good to last, like a long hot glorious summer, days of tea and honey held in suspension before the onslaught of some terrible interminable war. A peace whose glass-like fragility ensures, if not invites, its own destruction. When Philip Eames arrived as usual this apparently ordinary Friday afternoon and handed Elizabeth a generous purse Elizabeth blithely took the money and thanked her husband's assistant (as she had thanked him every Friday these last six months). Then she enquired with polite concern after her husband. Mr Glass had suffered a slight cold earlier that week but nothing serious, otherwise he was well and catching up admirably.

'I'm so glad!' Elizabeth smiled vaguely at Philip Eames.

Ever since the delays caused by Sarah Glass's unexpected death Glass & Co. had been working flat out, but the entries in the famous diary had been packed in so tightly that only now was Edward beginning to catch up slowly. So it was understood.

In fact, Edward Glass had no intention any more of catching up on his schedule. If Glass had suffered a slight cold that week only Mr Eames had noticed; Glass himself had had other more exciting concerns. The opportunity *Arcanum Arcanorum* had long been waiting for had actually arrived in his office *that Monday morning*, brought by a smartly tailored personage who introduced himself at once as a Mr Desmond Blaise. The schedule could not be abandoned altogether; jobs already started would have to be finished but, as most of the entries in the famous diary had already waited at least ten years, what harm could there be in making them wait a while longer? Glass intimated as much to a flabbergasted Philip Eames.

'Do you really think . . .' The assistant was nonplussed. 'Are you quite well, Sir? Do I not detect a slight cold in the head?'

'Don't be ridiculous, Eames!' It was the excessively diligent

Eames's fault that the diary was crammed quite so full in the first place. With dogged determination the man committed Glass & Co. to more and more work, relentlessly entering commissions in a frightful hand that sprawled with unremitting eagerness across the page.

'I trust you are not querying my decision, Eames?'

'No, but . . .'

'But what, Sir?'

'There'll be a lot of angry, disappointed men – Glass & Co. has made countless promises in *writing* and secured registered non-returnable deposits. Men will object to a newcomer jumping in at the front of the queue. I foresee unpleasantnesses and insurmountable difficulties . . .'

'That is the trouble with piffling little men like you, Eames! You see only unpleasantnesses and insurmountable difficulties! Besides, *you* made the promises. The writing was your unmistakable scrawl! You will be the one technically breaking the agreement, you are the one who will be held liable.'

'Anything I have written, any promises I have made, have been on your behalf, in your name and with your permission, Sir,' Philip Eames replied stiffly. 'It is what *you* employ me for. I do not believe that can make *me* liable for anything, technically.'

Edward Glass laughed. 'Come now, Eames. You take life far too *technically*, I fear. You should have a little fun once in a while!'

No wonder Eames did not see fit to mention any of this to the second Mrs Glass that Friday. Diplomatically he invented a slight cold instead.

'Let me introduce myself,' Mr Blaise had begun and though Glass had taken an immediate dislike to the fellow with his smooth smile, easy saunter and impeccable tailoring, when Desmond Blaise described his position of influence on the Board of Directors at the Paris Grand Hotel, Edward Glass forgot these first unpromising impressions.

'A shabby worn-out hotel today maybe, but sitting on a valuable and prominent site in the Strand, a site with infinite possibilities – if you catch my drift . . .'

Glass nodded, he thought he understood.

'An architect's dream of a project, I dare say – though *you* are the architect – unlimited reserves would be at your disposal, you may be as fantastic as you like, the more fantastical the better! This is to be the grandest of Grand Hotels and it is my conviction, Mr Glass, that *you* are the man!'

'Indeed?'

'I am given to believe you were on friendly terms with the late Prince Albert, Mr Glass?' Desmond Blaise asked chattily although he was a man in a hurry.

'We did converse on one occasion, yes.'

'That proves my point – *you* are the architect for the job! Once the Board has approved my recommendation to rebuild I could see to it that you are given a completely free hand and I could organize for you to start as soon as possible; I'd insist no expense be spared.'

'Indeed!'

'You are tempted, Sir?'

'An interesting proposition, certainly.'

'Good, good! There will be a few formalities, the usual . . .' Blaise spread his hands.

'Formalities?' This Blaise was very eager.

'Nothing that can't be taken care of, Mr Glass – Edward! You will need to meet my fellow directors, that's all.'

Edward Glass frowned – he had definitely *not* asked Desmond Blaise to call him 'Edward'. 'I make most of my arrangements by correspondence. I have an assistant who organizes my diary. A competent, fastidious man . . .'

'A mere formality, I assure you, Edward. No need for fastidious assistants and the inconvenience of correspondence! What an honour for us to have an architect, an Artist, of your Reputation . . . You must spend as much as you need, as much as you can! There must be no stinting with the New Paris Grand.'

Glass nodded his head. He knew the Paris Grand well for he had stayed there on a number of pleasurable occasions. What a challenge this would be for *Arcanum Arcanorum*; here was exactly what he had been waiting for. 'Well, I should certainly like to consider . . .'

'Ah yes – the consideration . . .' Mr Blaise hesitated firmly on the word and he looked Edward Glass steadily in the eye. 'I myself . . .'

Glass was puzzled. He was not sure what was meant although something most assuredly was being said. 'You, yourself, Mr Blaise?'

'Yes, naturally I, myself – we will need to settle on a reasonable

60

percentage of the gross expenditure. A modest consideration for my pains – the usual arrangement, payable discreetly when the Board has released the funds. I'll see your office manages the entire business directly, you will handle the whole account.'

Glass nodded his head non-committally. Desmond Blaise took his watch out and by pretending to look at the time he gave Glass time to decide. Glass however needed no time. He knew he had deferred long enough.

Edward Glass saw now why projects of this type had never been offered to him in the past. Had Blaise not spelt things out quite so clearly (Blaise regarded other men as stupid and took pains to explain himself) Glass might have mistaken or entirely missed his meaning. People liked to say that these sort of deals went on and that the lucky and the successful had the business sewn up between them – a comfortable theory that happily explained away the limitations and failings in one's life – but this was the first time Glass himself had been invited to partake in such a transaction. He had always known that to achieve his own artistic ends he'd need to disregard petty considerations. To build his Masterpiece, he need only conspire with human failing, with Desmond Blaise: 'I have work that must be finished off first and then I can make a start.'

'The sooner the better!' Blaise beamed. 'I will put it to the Board this afternoon. The men will go along with me – you can be sure I am owed many favours. You can start drawing some of those famous plans we hear so much about!'

'Oh?'

'You are talked of, Edward! Why do you think I have come to you? One word though – don't breath it around just yet.'

If Glass was capable of anything it was keeping a secret. *Arcanum Arcanorum* strode to the window and looked up into the grey overclouded skies. How exhilarated and expansive he felt. Here was his chance to soar! 'Mr Blaise, I will build you and your Board of Directors a hotel that will be the envy of the world: a building so magnificent it will stand for all time, the New Paris Grand will be a monument to the great achievements of our Great Nation in this Great Century! Something future generations will look to.'

'Sure, sure!' Blaise smiled impatiently; talking like this was all very well but he needed to get to the Board Meeting early, a quick word in each ear as the members arrived.

'The building will reflect the complex geometry of our lives, men will be lost in amazement as in a maze . . .'

'Yes, very good! I can see it all now!' What Blaise saw was how quickly the fellow had cottoned on. Complex geometry would not come cheap and the greater the expenditure the larger his own percentage share would be. Blaise took Glass by the hand. 'It's been a pleasure to do business. The Paris Grand is as good as rebuilt!'

On Monday afternoon Glass had said to his astounded assistant, 'There has been a change of plan – no one but you, Eames, need know at this stage . . .'

'Why didn't they write and make the usual enquiries?' Eames asked at once.

'Write?' It was hardly the kind of proposition that was ever set out in *writing*.

'It seems very odd!'

'Ah!'

'What am I to do with the diary on Friday afternoon?' Philip Eames did sound peeved! 'Is the schedule to be abandoned forthwith?'

'Don't be ridiculous, Eames! Carry on as before. There has to be a Board Meeting first – it may all come to nothing. Our other work will only be *delayed*, and then Glass & Co. will be more in demand than ever – just think of that, Eames!'

Philip Eames was relieved. His Friday afternoon visits to York Street were what he enjoyed most these days.

At first, Elizabeth had sat down assiduously each week at her escritoire to write Edward the letter which she would then give to Mr Eames when he arrived on Friday. In her neat rather childish hand she had painstakingly written out news about the girls and the running of the house, and then she had carefully recounted how his generous purses of money had been spent. It hadn't been easy thinking of enough suitable items – once Elizabeth had written: 'Milla was kind enough to bring her scrap-book to show me – what a sweet little girl she is . . .' It may not have told him much but at least it had helped to fill the page.

Gradually these letters had dwindled to short unhurried notes on nice paper and then it occurred to Elizabeth that her notes might look a little like acknowledgements for payment. After that she had not taken the trouble to write and Mr Eames, when he next came, had pointedly not remarked on this. She suspected now that her epistolary attempts had been entirely unnecessary. Possibly unwelcome, even. She wanted to show herself conscious of her husband's disrupted schedule and anxious to do nothing that might hinder his work further. For this reason, she told herself, a spoken message would do.

'Tell Mr Glass that we are all well,' Elizabeth said as she said each week now, and Eames obediently inclined his head. As soon as he could he disappeared into Mr Glass's study and shut the door. Elizabeth knew in a minute or two Mrs Curzon would send the parlourmaid up to the study with a tray of refreshments for Mr Eames.

'Will that be all, Sir?' Mary Ann asked.

'Yes – thank you,' Eames said without looking up.

'Are you sure there's nothing else?' she would like to have added, but the poor parlourmaid did not have the courage to speak to Mr Eames – to ask him about himself and to tell him about herself. Instead Mary Ann adjusted the curtains and straightened the chairs, then she found some books that had fallen over and carefully propped them up. When she could think of nothing else to detain her, she reluctantly departed leaving the door slightly ajar so that she would hear him from the hall-way if by some miracle he summoned her back.

Upstairs, at the back of the house, Stacia, Milla and Helen sprawled. Milla lay stretched out on her bed reading yet another book by the writer called 'Pasha', this time entitled *Journey into the Unknown*. Emily Housecroft had gone out and the school was on holiday for the summer so the girls were at a loose end. The tale had started off well enough but it soon became apparent that the 'Unknown' was not especially exciting and Milla had fallen asleep.

Helen was learning a poem to recite and Stacia had been set to sew hems on blouses.

'Oh, dear me, no!' Emily Housecroft had squashed any suggestion that they might go out too.

'I hate her!' Milla had said when she left.

Stacia yawned. 'Did you see her brown buttoned boots? In summer!'

63

'You shouldn't hate anyone,' Helen joined in, but neither Miss Housecroft nor her brown buttoned boots were worthy of further discussion.

The girls knew, but did not mind, that Miss Housecroft usually had better things to do than attend to their various needs. Mrs Glass did not know about these better things and would certainly have minded for she was paying the woman's salary. There had been nothing specific in the governess's contract that mentioned 'better things' and indeed the contract itself had been far from specific: 'All I ask is that you keep them occupied,' Mrs Glass had said at the interview. 'I ask only a quiet life.'

Emily Housecroft had assured Mrs Glass that she and her new charges would use their own staircase, with their own door on to the outside world. The girls would come and go under her direction and leave the second Mrs Glass in peace.

'What do you think Miss Housecroft is out doing?' Milla asked now, waking up to find that she had creased a few pages of Pasha's *Journey into the Unknown* by lying on the book. She couldn't have been asleep very long for Helen was still intoning her stupid poem and Stacia hadn't given up on the hems yet.

'Haven't a clue!' said Stacia.

'She was carrying a package; that ought to be a clue,' Milla said, for earlier in the afternoon they had watched from their landing window as she'd gone out. They had also watched Philip Eames arriving but unfortunately he had looked up and seen them. He'd taken off his hat rather self-consciously and they had collapsed in giggles of embarrassment. It had been the most exciting thing that had happened all week, they'd agreed extravagantly, although it did rather spoil the fun of spying once people knew you were there and they doffed their hats.

Philip Eames knew they were there all right. It was the school summer-holidays and Stacia Glass would be at home, upstairs. Eames had decided to marry Stacia Glass though he would have to wait a couple of years until the girl would be old enough and ready for him. He had decided this last winter standing behind her at Sarah Glass's funeral, impressed that Stacia and Milla had giggled and cheeped together despite the circumstances. Circumstances that included not only the solemn presence of their mother's coffin but also that of their awesome father, his employer, Mr Edward

Glass standing beside them in the pew while they behaved like little canaries in a cage.

Ever since Sarah's funeral it had pleased Mr Eames to think about Stacia Glass as he went around executing Mr Glass's orders. His mother, whom he rarely saw, had expressed the opinion that he was treated like nothing better than Edward Glass's 'glorified errand-boy' – a scathing comment in a scathing tone which had etched itself deep on the miserable plate of his mind. It strengthened his determination to secure the girl for his own.

While Edward Glass was at work in the offices of Glass & Co. vigorously scoring black lines across a draughtsman's work to indicate where weaknesses needed correcting, extra pillars put in and superfluous bolstering taking out, Philip Eames stood respectfully by and considered how one day he would likewise hack and trim the unruly Miss Stacia into shape.

Milla and Helen did not interest Mr Eames for it had been the ungovernable curls on Stacia's neck that had excited him, soft golden-yellow curls that seeped beneath her black mourning bonnet and bounced gently on her young white nape as she tittered in front of him with Milla. In his imagination he took a fold of her downy skin, pinching it hard between his ink-stained fingers and nipped and nibbled with his little pointed teeth until it darkened and bruised and Stacia Glass squealed in pain and was afraid. She'd be like the pretty canary he had kept as a boy, feeding it seed and defying his mother who said it was dirty and sullied his room. One day a neighbouring cat had got into the house, snapped open the cage and bitten its neck. He had wept – he remembered the little drops of blood caked on to the delicate bright yellow feathers and he recalled his mother saying she had it coming to her, singing so brightly, attracting attention to herself as if any creature had a right to be that happy . . .

If the canary was to blame for enticing the cat then Stacia Glass could be blamed for the viciousness of the desires she evoked in him. He had never before thought of himself as one of the despised and despicable who haunt the shadows and commit the crimes which fill the cheaper newspapers. You read about these things over someone's shoulder standing in a saloon or on a crowded omnibus and shuddered in broad daylight that such atrocities could ever take place, and not so far away. Later on though, alone with yourself in the cold small hours, shuffling shadows thrown against the walls from yellow street-lamps outside, alert to strange unidentifiable rustlings, these evil abominations returned unbidden to the mind and made you sweat. Philip sweated, and for this he blamed Stacia.

The men who worked for Edward Glass knew that Eames made regular Friday afternoon visits to Edward Glass's home. An irregular arrangement to be sure! They joked with each other and nudged him playfully about the possibilities for an indiscretion with the young and delectable second Mrs Glass.

'What's she like then, Philip?'

'We all know what you get up to on Friday afternoons, Philip!'

'Regular as clockwork, our Philip . . .'

He turned his back on them, but he felt humiliated. If the Master so despised him that such an indiscretion was considered unthinkable and no precautions needed to be taken he would show the man that even he, the quiet insignificant operative Eames, was not so inoffensive that he could be treated in this fashion.

Let them wait. Philip Eames informed a Batley cotton magnate that such an enterprise could not possibly be contemplated within twelve years, an interest-free down-payment of ten per cent of the estimated cost must be forthcoming even before any date in the famous diary could be entertained. Let them wait: his mother who mocked him for being Edward Glass's glorified errand-boy, the Master who entrusted him with his new young wife, and young Stacia herself. Let her wait, as she stood up there at a window chirping with her sisters and mocking him from the fragile safety of this tall dark house.

Charged by the current of his hidden intentions, Philip Eames worked with the intense and noiseless devotion of a man who is biding his time. His life revolved around three o'clock on Friday afternoons when he always arrived just as the clock was striking the hour (as it was such a short hour to strike this was punctuality indeed). To the outside world he appeared the indefatigably zealous servant so scorned by his mother. To Elizabeth Glass, he was simply useful, arriving promptly with her weekly payment, doing whatever he had to do in her husband's study and departing predictably and without fuss.

Item 103 on Mrs Curzon's weekly list was to oversee his refreshments before having her afternoon nap. Mrs Curzon did not trust

Mary Ann so she stayed awake long enough to check the girl did not linger upstairs. 'What kept you?' she enquired every time, for something kept Mary Ann every time. Mary Ann smiled secretively and speculated what it would be like to be kissed by Philip Eames with his little pointed front teeth.

Mrs Curzon despaired of Mary Ann: 'From prettiness, plague, sudden death and damnation, deliver this vainglorious parlour-maid!' It seemed to Mrs Curzon that the devil himself was tickling at Mary Ann's trim little ankles and she had only to look down at her own flat housekeeper's feet to rejoice in the solidity of her own salvation.

8

A Matter of Chance

Elizabeth counted out the purse Philip Eames had brought and found that this pleasantly amounted to fifty-seven pounds, seventeen shillings and sixpence. 'We are all winners and losers,' she thought, for by her own gambling she could hardly count herself better than Henry. Yet how she had despised Henry's fatuous dreams of solving their problems in the gaming-room at Monte Carlo; how she had despised poor Henry Cathcart at the last!

Elizabeth did not deceive herself that she had been clever. How lucky and in the nick of time she had been. The chance encounter with an elderly widower that had transformed her life might never have happened. She could hardly have gone on borrowing clothes that didn't quite fit, accepting charity people offered while they still chose to offer it. If only Henry could have seen her: with odds uncertain and stakes indeterminate, she had coolly borrowed clothes and won all this. Henry James Cathcart had fancied himself lucky at the tables and had frequently placed large bets with borrowed money on rather better odds – but Henry was never a winner and in the end he had lost even his life.

Elizabeth jotted down the date and £57 17s 6d and added up her new total in the little notebook she kept for the purpose.

The second Mrs Glass had begun her second married life industriously. The letters for Eames to bear back to Edward and her careful accounts were symptomatic of the way she had embraced her luck. How ably she had organized this large gloomy house to run itself; the servants kept in their place, worked through their lists and only referred to her as a last resort. The Housecroft woman was worth every guinea for there had been no more visits from a talkative Milla, telling her things she didn't want to hear, showing her untidy scraps she could do without seeing: 'It's not my concern,' Elizabeth told herself. She'd been right to employ a professional governess. Besides, she was tired out and everyone knew how endlessly tiring children could be.

Back in the days before Miss Housecroft took over, Elizabeth had gone upstairs on an impulse to help the children with their homework. Wasn't that what mothers did sometimes? Her own mother had deposited her in a smelly rooks' nest with a doddery old father who liked convivial drink and empty talk.

Stacia had been looking out of the window, the other two were working at their sums. 'Stacia, haven't you got any home exercises to do?'

'Not that I *have* to do . . .' Stacia said sullenly, resenting the interference. Look what Milla had done – Mrs Glass would be interfering all the time now. She scowled.

'Anything I can help with?' Elizabeth turned to the others. Without looking up, Helen said she was writing out her times-tables twenty times and she'd already done them fourteen.

'That's why they call it the "times-tables" – because of the number of times they make you write it!' Milla laughed. Elizabeth smiled. Milla, at least, was responsive.

'And what are you up to, Milla?'

'Well, it's very interesting,' Milla said in the earnest voice that signalled a discourse on her latest obsession. Stacia, who was used to Milla, folded her arms and let out a loud 'huumph!' but Milla, who was used to Stacia, took no notice.

' "If m plus n equals the whole number of cases," ' she read out, ' "and if m represents the number of cases which are favourable to a certain event and n the number of those that are unfavourable, then m over m plus n equals the probability of the event. If two events be independent of each other, and their respective probabilities be one over m and one over n, the probability that they will *both* happen is one over m times one over n equals one over mn." '

'That all sounds very clever, Milla!' Elizabeth said encouragingly. 'Far too clever for me, of course! Whatever can it all mean?'

Stacia and Helen were watching her critically, but Milla accepted her interest: 'It *is* clever – it's called "the doctrine of chance" . . .'

'Chance!' Elizabeth's ears pricked up. Chance was something Elizabeth knew a thing or two about.

'What the algebra adds up to, I think, is that chance simply doesn't exist . . .'

'But that's nonsense, Milla!' Elizabeth cried. 'Of course chance exists.'

'No,' Milla was adamant and jabbed her finger authoritatively at a page in her book. ' "Chance can hardly be said to have any existence . . ." '

'What?'

' " . . . many events commonly said to be 'mere chance' are in reality governed by rules. The Probability of an event is the ratio of favourable cases to possible cases similarly circumstanced with regard to the occurrence . . ." '

'Now, look here!' Elizabeth screamed, but Milla went on absorbedly: ' "Thus, from a receptacle containing 1 white and 2 black balls, the probability of drawing a white ball, by the abstraction of one is a third; in other words the odds are 2 to 1 against . . ." '

'QED – clever old me!' Stacia sang out disdainfully.

Elizabeth gripped the back of a chair. 'I don't care what it says in your algebra text-book, Milla! Chance is the only factor in the whole equation – how dare *you* sit there and tell *me* that "chance can hardly be said to have any existence"!'

Milla stared at her step-mother: *how could you, a spoilt little girl who has never been anywhere, possibly know . . .*

Elizabeth was no longer sure where her anger had come from. She was certainly not angry with poor little Milla. Helen resumed writing out her tables as though nothing had happened.

'Haven't you ever crossed your fingers for luck, Milla?' Elizabeth tried to sound calm.

'Luck?'

'You can't have luck without chance now, can you?' The second Mrs Glass laughed but the laugh came out harsh. 'The whole of life is a matter of chance – your good fortune isn't yours by rights, Milla!'

'I didn't mean to upset you . . .' Milla said falteringly. It was only algebra homework.

'You didn't upset me!' Elizabeth replied too quickly.

'I just thought it was interesting,' Milla said. 'I don't understand it myself – if chance doesn't exist why do people talk about it, why is the book so keen to prove it doesn't exist by having a special doctrine like in church?' And, Milla could have added, why does it bother *you* so much? Milla pushed the book away as though seeking to distance herself from the offending algebra. 'I didn't mean to upset you . . .'

'Well, no, I'm sure you didn't, Milla . . .' Elizabeth said.

Stacia had no idea what to make of what seemed in any case to be evaporating so she said nothing. What a trivial woman to get so worked up over algebra! She was as bad as Milla.

'I'm glad you're all busy,' Elizabeth said weakly as she retreated. So much for her attempts to be a mother! From below she had heard Stacia saying spitefully: 'Now, that'll teach you to show off!'

Elizabeth had gambled when she had married, on both occasions. The first time the risk had been unnecessary and the consequences disastrous. The second time, when she had only gambled because she'd had no choice, the outcome had proved most satisfactory but the excitement of the hazard had drained her. Or so it felt as she reclined this Friday afternoon on the *chaise longue* in her own drawing-room contemplating how this in itself was more than she could once have dreamed of, lying on a couch of her own, in a drawing-room of her own, with respectful servants downstairs to do everything, large sums of money at her disposal and no creditors making life awkward. Elizabeth had learnt the hard way how few problems in life cannot be solved by money, and few pleasures not be bought with it either.

Elizabeth spoke formally to ladies who called (Mrs Richard Styles, Mrs Charles Preedy, Mrs Pinder Simpson and Mrs Beresford Gurney, for instance) of her good fortune and of Edward's being the 'perfect husband'. But what she meant and what she allowed herself to be heard to mean were two entirely different things. Ease is not attained without considerable effort. How tired and weary Elizabeth Glass now felt. She resolved to buy Milla some nice paper-scraps.

'I tried to give the children a hand with their home exercises,' she had written to Edward Glass in one of those early letters. 'Dear little Milla is very keen on algebra.'

Mrs Curzon who approved above all things of economy, approved of the second Mrs Glass. She, who had saved her own wages so steadily, did not like to see money wasted. Elizabeth told her how much she could spend each week and what luxuries were to be allowed, when and for whom. Sarah Glass had not understood the importance of this and arrangements had always been vague; when Sarah was ill, which was nearly all the time, unsuitably costly dishes had had to be disposed of and were often eaten up by the children. The richness and the spoiling did them no good. Apart from the extravagance of a governess, there was no problem now on this score with Elizabeth. Mrs Curzon had once caught Mary Ann saying something to Cora about the new mistress being mean and she had rewarded the parlourmaid with a generous clout on the ear.

Elizabeth lay back thumbing idly through magazines, reading a paragraph here and another there and considering advertisements for things she could purchase if she chose. She would buy one of these stereoscopic viewers in a walnut box, and some sets of pictures to look at with the viewer – she had often thought it would be quite nice to own one.

Elizabeth turned quickly to the chat on summer fashions: 'For a day at the seaside: the Tzigane hat seems likely to be a great success, very pretty, wide-brimmed and coquettish, of unbleached straw and trimmed with a Madras scarf and scarlet feather.' Elizabeth yawned and wondered why anyone bothered; this dressing up to prance and please was such an effort, but hardly perhaps to be avoided. Elizabeth had been recommended a competent French dressmaker and had ordered a couple of costumes from fashion-plates. Presumably they would be ready soon. She must send a note to the Mademoiselle and enquire.

Elizabeth enjoyed herself most these days doing nothing. She cleared her mind of everything except the advertisements. Sleepily she turned the pages.

Downstairs, Mrs Curzon snored lightly over a well-earned glass of hot water and rum. Mary Ann could not settle to any task and hovered, waiting to clear away after Mr Eames. She primped her hair, holding up the little piece of mirror she kept hidden in a drawer. She was proud of the rich auburn curls set off so prettily by her parlourmaid's cap. For all Mrs Curzon complained, you couldn't straighten what the good Lord had made uncontrollable and curly.

The three girls cooped in their rooms at the top of the house squabbled irritably and intermittently.

' "Thou hast profaned the talents that Heaven in mercy gave, Living as man had never a God, and earth had never a grave . . ." ' Helen endeavoured to commit the heavy words to memory. Stacia had pricked her finger and splattered little drops of blood on a blouse that she had spent hours mending and had no intention of wearing. Meanwhile, Milla waged war on Pasha. She sat at Miss Housecroft's table, taking advantage of her absence, and wrote the author or authoress – who could someone who called themselves 'Pasha' be? – a letter, care-of the publisher.

'Dear Pasha,' Milla began. The ridiculous name made sure your letter sounded daft even before you got started, but Milla was not to be put off. She would tell them that they should be ashamed of themselves. The 'Unknown' could have been *anything* under the sun – the adventure need never have turned out so BORING! She would use the stamp she had discovered two weeks ago, after one of Philip Eames's visits, to post the letter. Stacia declared that he – or she – would never reply: this 'Pasha' brought out four or five new books every year; you obviously couldn't write that many books *and* answer angry letters from silly girls. Why, look how long it was taking Milla just to compose a little letter. 'You ought to grow up!' Stacia said.

Now Milla was furious, with Stacia as well as with Pasha and more determined than ever to send her letter and get a reply. 'Just you wait!' she said angrily and her writing took on an angrier tone: 'You have no business . . .' She went back and underlined the 'no'; 'You have *no* business to promise so much and deliver so little . . .'

'That sounds good,' Helen commented.

Stacia scoffed, her sisters were both children! 'It's a waste of time and I might go downstairs right now and tell Mr Eames you've stolen one of his stamps.'

'Go on, then,' Milla said. 'I dare you!'

Stacia smiled and stood up. But Stacia sat down again and stayed where she was. Milla continued with her letter; someone should tell this Pasha the meaning of the word *adventure*. Green parrots squawked in her ears, gold doubloons spilled from a seaman's old wooden chest and Milla's eyes sparkled as her pen sped blotchily over the page: 'In my opinion you ought to be *ashamed* . . .'

Philip Eames in the study below was also scratching away furiously but unlike Milla his mind was not absorbed by what he wrote. He signed a letter and sighed. There was work yet to be done. Thank goodness the woman no longer saw fit to write the letters he had been obliged not only to convey to her husband but also – though she clearly did not know it – to open, and read out loud to him. How red his face had been as he stuttered over references to Stacia. It was as well the Master had only listened impatiently for the end, hearing nothing, waiting for matter of import which had always been absent from Elizabeth's wordy missives. Why, since they said nothing, had Mrs Glass written them?

It had seemed to Eames sometimes that the woman knew of his discomfiture, and persisted with her pointless scribblings solely to mortify him. Perhaps she herself had been mortified by what he had done for her and this was her gentle feminine revenge. Eventually, however, she seemed to have relented, for the letters had become shorter and when at last they had stopped altogether Eames felt he and this new wife had reached an unspoken unspeakable truce.

From the start, Edward Glass and his assistant had each wondered silently why the second Mrs Glass could not simply accept the money as Sarah had done. Now that she no longer wrote them, Eames found himself unaccountably missing Elizabeth's letters. In a curious self-punishing way, he missed the ordeal of reading out loud about Stacia. Usually she had been included with her sisters in some throwaway phrase: 'the girls send you their filial regards'. Milla had got herself mentioned a lot for Milla was that kind of child. Once however the woman had written: *'Stacia at fourteen is blooming as young women do. I have seen fit to instruct Miss Housecroft to see about a pair of new dresses, with sufficient room in the seams to accommodate further growth.'*

The sentence housed more than it ought. Philip had glanced up confusedly from his reading but Edward Glass's eyes were on a plan young Withercott had completed that afternoon. Withercott was the perky new draughtsman who'd just replaced old Myers, found drunk and dithyrambling at his desk, claiming a rival architect had offered him a better paid job. Glass had sent him packing. He wanted men he could rely on – if he were to be free to concentrate on his masterpiece he'd need men who required no supervision.

By chance, a competent letter from a Harry Withercott had arrived in the post that same morning. It had not yet been answered so Glass had the man summoned for interview. The eager young Withercott was appointed even before the vacancy had been announced.

Harry Withercott arrived whistling a merry tune, climbed immediately into the vacated chair, spread out his rulers and pens and started joking with everyone. Edward Glass liked young Mr Withercott's bold self-assurance. He thought Harry reminded him of his own youth. Philip Eames was wary. Eames noticed the pencil behind Withercott's ear: a draughtsman who aspired to be an architect! He refused to laugh at the ambitious Withercott's inane jokes. The Master had brushed Eames's objections aside and now he felt his confidence in Withercott rewarded: these plans were excellent, entirely in keeping with his own calculations and yet imaginatively embellished in an acceptable fashion. Withercott was exactly the type of man Glass & Co. needed. Harry Withercott would go far. Meanwhile Edward Glass had been too distracted to hear the second Mrs Glass's description of Stacia's blooming or notice his sturdy assistant flush and burn.

Philip Eames sat in the study in York Street and did some calculations of his own. If the girls stood and watched him from a landing at the top of the stairs, could the rooms they retreated to be directly above him now? There were plenty of plans stored in cabinets in Edward Glass's offices to which Mr Eames had ready access. No plan of this house existed for Edward Glass had no interest in houses. And least of all it seemed in this house where he kept his wife (whichever wife) and family. This afternoon Withercott would be working in the offices of Glass & Co. in the City.

'It'll be Glass & Withercott before long,' someone had remarked yesterday, within Philip Eames's hearing. 'Glass & Withercott in bright gold letters above the door, you mark my words!'

All through a sleepless night Eames had done little else but mark them. How could a mere assistant hope to compete with a man whose name was already linked above the door: Glass & Withercott? Eames had lain awake tortured by the sight of Stacia Glass and Harry Withercott standing beneath the bright gold letters with their heads bent close together, convulsed in fits of unrestrained laughter. As the night wore on the jokes they found so funny had increasingly centred on him. They'd sniggered at his punctuality, his inky fingers, the way his mother chastised him and Elizabeth Glass embarrassed him with the delicacy of her correspondence; but what they had mocked most of all had been his burning passion for Stacia herself. Eames stabbed his pen viciously into the ink-well – let them wait, one day he would punish the defenceless little canary girl for cheep cheep cheeping at him all night and sharing her foolishness with the jaunty draughtsman Withercott.

The front doorbell rang. A package marked URGENT was delivered for Miss Emily Housecroft. Mary Ann took it in. 'I'll see she gets it,' she said to the carrier who winked at her and she winked back; he was only a boy so she banged the door in his face.

'I'll see Miss Housecroft gets it,' Mary Ann repeated so that Philip would know she was there should he desire her. She squeezed the package for clues: it felt like a couple of books but books could hardly be 'URGENT'. She glanced in through the crack – Philip Eames was too engrossed to look up. The room smelt rather of sweat. 'I am a little in love with him,' Mary Ann told herself, her eyes resting gently on the awkward crunched up features of his unhappily preoccupied face. She loved him as one loves the ugliest puppy in a litter – but Mary Ann kept herself going by being a little in love with just about every man she met. 'Man-mad!' Mrs Curzon had had occasion to call her – but Mrs Curzon did not know the half of poor Mary Ann's unrequited passions.

'Who was that?' Mrs Glass emerged swiftly from her sitting-room. 'I heard the door . . .' She saw the package in the parlourmaid's hands: 'Is that for me?'

'Miss Housecroft, Ma'am. It's marked "Urgent" but I rather think she's out for the afternoon. She goes out a lot, you know . . .'

Mrs Glass was amused. 'Mary Ann, what Emily Housecroft does in the afternoon is entirely up to her – the governess has my permission at all times, even if she does not have yours. So, no more tales!' Mrs Glass smiled firmly at Mary Ann. 'You'd better get back to work; we don't want you in trouble with Mrs Curzon now, do we?'

The mistress of the house returned to the comfort of her *chaise longue* and Mary Ann placed the mysterious package on the hall-table (beside what was left of dear William's faded photograph) and went back downstairs.

Late that Friday afternoon, as Mr Eames was preparing to depart, Emily Housecroft arrived home and having forgotten to take her key to the side door she came in by the front instead. She was delighted to find her URGENT package on the hall-table.

'It's arrived at last!' she exclaimed and only then noticed the presence of Philip Eames helping himself to his gloves and stick – he had preferred not to ring for the disconcerting parlourmaid this evening. He nodded respectfully to the governess.

'I've been waiting for these books,' Miss Housecroft told him.

So! This was the woman who had charge of his Stacia! In the quick glance Eames permitted himself he found that he approved of the brown buttoned boots and the creature's dull complexion. This was not someone who would encourage the girl in any lightheartedness or folly.

'Good evening!' Eames said, heading out of the door.

Miss Housecroft, intent still on her package, glanced up at the last minute. 'I'm so sorry, how rude of me! Good evening, Mr Eames.'

Emily Housecroft barely noticed Philip Eames but Mary Ann, emerging up the basement steps, heard this exchange of gentle farewells. The parlourmaid flounced rudely past the governess into the study to retrieve the tea things Mr Eames had used. Miss Housecroft had been chatting to her Philip, preventing him from ringing the bell so that she herself had not had a chance this week to hand him his gloves and stick and say her loving lingering 'Good-bye!' He'd preferred to converse with Miss Housecroft. Poor Mary Ann felt she could weep. Another unbearably long week must pass before she saw him again.

Vehemently sweeping biscuit crumbs from the desk, Mary Ann pictured her rival in a long white dress that looked frightful on her, clutching at Philip's arm, dragging him to the altar, dragging him down: 'Philip Eames, I thee take . . .' the governess cried out eagerly as she snatched him away from Mary Ann. Mary Ann banged the tea-cup so hard on its saucer a thin crack appeared in the china that would not be noticeable until later. How could Philip Eames have preferred the dreary Miss Housecroft? Presumably he thought a parlourmaid beneath him! 'I'll never forgive her,' Mary Ann vowed, hearing the brown buttoned boots stomping upstairs. 'Never!'

'The new Mrs Glass handles the servants remarkably well,' Eames would tell Edward Glass a few days later. 'I overheard her putting the parlourmaid in her place in no uncertain terms.' Eames felt somehow responsible: she had been his idea, although the Master would probably not remember this now.

'A competent woman! A most satisfactory solution,' Glass remarked complacently. 'Now, where were we, Eames? The next item on your list?'

For six months Edward Glass and his second wife had enjoyed the peaceful commerce and contentment of an ordered married life. Indeed, they had scarcely seen each other.

II

DISRUPTION

9

Stretching the Salmon

Saturday morning: a deceptively sunny summer's day. Edward Glass had finished in Manchester (a stroll in the sunshine, a pleasant lunch perhaps, a fond farewell and away). One job finished and on to the next – this had long been the pattern of his life but now Desmond Blaise, as good as his word, had sent word: the complete rebuilding of the Paris Grand was to go ahead at once, full-steam, no expense spared. *Arcanum Arcanorum*, here at long last is your chance! Exuberant designs buzzed about Edward Glass's head. The New Paris Grand would be the dizziest, most extraordinary building anyone had ever seen: Quintessential Glass, a jugglery of genius to make the great Professor Ruskin sit up and spit!

This sunny morning Glass feels he could do *anything*. He must return to London at once and confer with the useful Eames, Eames who even now is waking up in London with a stiff neck. It is a long time since Philip Eames slept well or enjoyed a walk in the sunshine. He has never felt that he could do anything, but there is work to be done – for Philip Eames, there is always work to be done.

'You ought to go out in the sunshine,' Miss Housecroft said. 'A walk in the park would do you all good . . .'

'So you need us out of the way!' Milla thought, not minding in the slightest as she wanted to post her letter to Pasha. Miss Housecroft wanted to open her 'URGENT' package in peace.

Downstairs meanwhile, in the quiet of a Saturday morning little different from the quiet she enjoyed any other morning, the second Mrs Glass reposed in anticipation only of the fresh salmon she had ordered for her lunch.

Unbeknown to Elizabeth, however, a certain Dr Lucius Morgan (Cantab.) was already hastening purposefully across London with the intention of dining at her table. He advanced towards her at great pace clutching an offering of colourful dahlias that he had picked just now in Lady Hildegard Blouvier's bountiful garden. He waved them affably at anyone who recognized him but he was too intent on arriving in good time for lunch to stop. He turned into York Street just as Stacia, Milla and Helen left the house – but they went in the opposite direction. He had missed Sarah Glass's daughters by three minutes.

Lady Blouvier encouraged Dr Morgan to avail himself freely of her magnificent Mayfair house and all her plenteous possessions (which included her daughter, Delia, and her dahlias). She and poor little Delia were abroad at present, traversing the Alps on foot, taking photographs with a full-plate camera and developing the prints as they went along. Lady Blouvier had invented that Indispensable Accoutrement of the Empire's Intrepid, the Infallible Blouvier – an indestructible darkroom tent you could erect on the most inhospitable glacier and purchase by mail-order for the reasonable sum of twelve guineas. Dr Morgan could never be certain of finding his energetic benefactress at home as she was given to disappearing on these edifying expeditions, but Blouvier hospitality was also infallible; it too should have been patented worldwide: instructions had always been left for Dr Morgan to be lavishly accommodated.

It was Cora who opened the front door.

'Ah, a pretty new maid, I see!' Dr Morgan exclaimed, entering before being bidden and divesting himself at once of his coat and stick.

Cora stared stupidly: she was neither 'new' – she'd been here over six months – nor by any means 'pretty'. Who was this man?

'Just tell Mrs Glass it's Dr Morgan, my dear.' The visitor beamed at the graceless Cora, making her feel as though she might be his favoured niece.

'Oh, yer . . . all right,' Cora knocked on Mrs Glass's door. The second Mrs Glass was surprised. Visitors had learnt to come, if at all, in the afternoons. Certainly not on Saturdays.

'Dr Morgan?' she asked. She knew no Dr Morgan. Was someone in the house ill? She would not have been told in any case – for those were her instructions. It was Mary Ann's job to open the door, so why this disruption?

Elizabeth planned to go shopping after lunch, to enjoy the sunshine and spend some of the ample purse Mr Eames had brought for her yesterday. To date she had bought very little, a few small ivory knick-knacks and the rosewood box she kept her funds in. The second Mrs Glass found it hard to part with the hard-earned cash. 'You had better show him in, Cora.'

Cora asked the gentleman to step in and Lucius Morgan immediately walked springily past her holding out his dahlias: 'Ah, Sarah! Sarah, my dear! What an age, truly what an age it has been!'

The hand holding Lady Blouvier's dahlias did not exactly drop. It hovered at a peculiar angle, mid-air. Dr Morgan looked round the room which he only partially recognized. Another woman stood in Sarah Glass's place. She did not come forward to embrace him as his cousin would have done. He was engulfed in hot confusion and stepped back abruptly, gripped by a curious fear. He stared at the woman before him as though transfixed. Mrs Glass was not Mrs Glass: a soul transported into strange new flesh. It was the sort of thing of which he wrote. The sort of thing of which people liked to read. And yet, you did not expect to encounter this sort of thing on a sunny Saturday morning in the drawing-room of an old friend from whom you sought only a light lunch and a good gossip.

'Sarah?'

This was exactly the kind of embarrassment Elizabeth had managed to avoid all these months since the hasty wedding. 'I . . . I think I had better explain.'

'Could I first prey upon your kindness . . .' Dr Morgan glanced meaningfully at the tray of decanters and bottles set out beside him on the sideboard.

'A drink? Of course . . .' Elizabeth Glass did not ring the bell. She wanted nobody there but herself. She took a tumbler and dusted it quickly with the edge of her shawl. She filled it full of Belgar Brandy, slopping a little as she did so. These bottles had not been opened since the former Mrs Glass's time.

Dr Lucius Morgan (Cantab.) sipped and struggled to piece together his splintered thoughts. His name may mean nothing to you, as it meant nothing to Elizabeth Glass before his appearance in her house that Saturday lunchtime. To thousands who clung to a snapped off branch of the theosophical movement, the man who perched on the edge of a chair and gulped down her predecessor's dusty brandy was a revered and important figure for whom they would do anything – die even, if need be! For Death was Dr Morgan's familiar terrain. He had left mainstream theosophy (even before he had joined it, such was his remarkable impatience) to track out his own separate course across that valuable uncharted territory, the After-life. Pickings were rich for the successful adventurer and Morgan's success could be measured by the enormous sales of his popular and stirring journal, *News from the Other Side*. Lady Blouvier was only one of many enthusiastic followers who flung open her doors to him, bequeathed her titled soul to his science and had high hopes that he would honour her by taking the anaemic, unmarriageable Delia off her hands.

Dr Morgan had just returned from a long and arduous Peregrination round Wales, walking and speaking and taking on eager new adherents who signed subscription forms and handed over cash up-front. Dr Morgan had a ready enjoyment of commerce and liked to see money changing hands. He would have returned to London much earlier but he'd met a distraught widow whose beloved and only son Huw had drowned the year before while boating carelessly on Lake Bala. Dr Morgan had felt obliged to comfort this unfortunate young woman in her distress. He balked at calling up the husband – jealous spirits can be dangerous, inconvenient things – but every evening he had summoned the careless Huw Back to tell his mother how happy he was, the bottom of the lake was as good a place as any, she must enjoy herself and was not to grieve. Every evening after Huw had departed Dr Morgan had devoured a delicious meal and then he and this stunningly beautiful widow had gorged themselves again on rapturous love.

Even the best things eventually pall. Dr Morgan was a restless man; Huw told his mother that Dr Morgan should leave at once to continue his great work. The meal that last night had been more abundant, more succulent than ever, their love-making held greater passion. In the morning Dr Morgan had kissed a fond farewell and set out on the best horse from her stable. The widow was wealthy and had been a good deal wealthier before encountering Dr Morgan, yet what need had she for paltry riches with her son and heir so carelessly drowned? 'Enjoy yourself while you can, Ma,' Huw advised and she had done so.

'I shall never forget you,' she wept.

'Hush now!' Dr Morgan whispered consolingly. No one ever forgot Dr Morgan. His was a large, shambling, ungainly presence, his bushy beard and piercing watery eyes made him seem older than he probably was. He looked now at the second Mrs Glass, and Elizabeth looked at him.

Cora said to Mary Ann: 'There's a Dr Morgan upstairs . . .'

'Dr Morgan!' Mary Ann paused; she'd been making a show of polishing candlesticks whilst listening to Mrs Curzon disputing the cost of a salmon. She had also been wondering about her chances of a holiday. All thoughts of a day at the sea-side, wearing a wide-brimmed Tzigane hat and pretending to be a young woman of independent means, receded instantly. She had sent Cora up so she could eavesdrop and now this. Mary Ann sighed. 'What did he want?'

'How should I know? He had a bunch of flowers . . .'

'Did he indeed?'

'Yer.'

Upstairs, Elizabeth Glass was wondering how to get rid of this intruder politely. Calmly she informed Dr Morgan of her marriage to Edward Glass and then he in his turn told her that Sarah Glass's maiden name had been Morgan; he was Sarah Glass's cousin. He was also the child Helen's godfather.

'Helen!' the second Mrs Glass exclaimed. From the fantastical Milla or the moody Stacia you could have expected a disturbance of this kind, but from Helen . . .

'I'll have the children sent down,' she said, rising to hasten upstairs. Dr Morgan swiftly reached out and seized Elizabeth's unwary hand. His own, wet from the dahlias he had been carrying which now sprawled on the floor at his feet, adhered tightly to hers.

Elizabeth was startled but before she could regain her composure the visitor spoke: 'He was called Henry!' Dr Morgan said firmly, looking Elizabeth in the eyes, feeling her body gently convulse as he uttered the name. He held the slight hand that bore the oversized wedding-ring in his own unflinching grasp. 'The Dead have a way of Returning!'

There was a long, slow-moving pause in which the Living seemed not to breathe. Then Dr Morgan spoke again. 'Even after all this time which really is no time at all, my dear, the memory of him haunts you and he Returns to haunt you.'

Elizabeth's body went limp and stiffened. Is Death like this, she wondered, for though the man held her against her will she had not the strength of mind nor body to struggle free. *Thou shalt not escape the Consequences*. Dark deeds, indeed! A blackness closing in, a blotting out; his words had vanquished her. When she recovered herself sufficiently to speak she turned to the visitor a defiantly proud and haughty face, but one from which all blood had drained: 'I don't know what you can mean, Sir! You have no business to talk to me in my house in this fashion.'

'The soul is my business, my dear! This Henry's soul is crying out, trying to tell you things but you will not listen. He is in agony . . .'

'I will not listen to this!' Elizabeth hissed, attempting to wrench herself free, but still Dr Lucius Morgan held on tightly. If there'd been a sharp knife in her other hand she would willingly have slashed through her own wrist at that moment just to escape Dr Morgan's grip, and all that it might mean. 'You have no right – I will not listen . . .'

Milla had said the same, here in this room: *if you clearly remember people, they're still there really as though they* were *still there.*

'No, I can see you will not listen! Neither to me nor to Poor Henry. But one day soon – sooner perhaps than you think – you will want to listen to me. And to Henry. Then you have only to summon me, my dear, and I will come. The Dead have a way of Returning, and I have a way of Returning them . . .' He released her hand. She took it from him, not quite snatching it away despite her haste.

Elizabeth paused and breathed deeply. The pay-out was no longer evens, her winning streak had ended, but she would not run. She could do with some of Sarah Glass's Belgar Brandy herself now but she fixed her steady practical eye on the repellent Dr Morgan and tried to sound as icy and unbelieving as a landlord's wife pursuing tardy rent. 'I find *that* hard to believe to be sure! Meanwhile, I will have the children sent down. I dare say they will be pleased to see their godfather.'

Elizabeth Glass escaped then and mounted the stairs two at a time. What a dream she had been living in: her perfect marriage, the large purse every Friday, her magazine subscriptions, the unobtrusive servants, her own *chaise longue*. How could she have expected to get away with it so easily? There had been no hitches. It had all been too free from embarrassment. Even the ladies who called who must have known of her position, even the mean Mrs Preedy who would never forget the lending of dresses tucked and tacked. And then that obsequiously respectful Eames. They had all made life easy for her. Far too easy. Between them, they had whittled her down.

Emily Housecroft glanced up and was startled to see the ghostlike face of her breathless employer appear in the doorway. She sighed quietly and hastily covered up her papers. 'The girls have gone for a walk in the park. I thought fresh air and sunshine would do them good – or, did you want to see me?'

The second Mrs Glass groaned and flung herself despairingly into a chair. The children were out and this man would have to be invited to luncheon (a politeness to hold whatever was looming and threatened to destroy in some sort of abeyance, if possible). But how could she sit at a dining-table and eat salmon with a man who spoke as he had spoken of Henry? In desperation Elizabeth took the governess into her confidence: 'There's a peculiar man downstairs, a Dr Morgan. A cousin of Sarah Glass, it would seem. He speaks of the souls of the dead or some such nonsense. It turns out he is Helen's godparent . . . I, I can't stand it . . .' She started to weep.

'Shall I deal with him?' Emily Housecroft was disconcerted to discover her employer given to hysterical over-reacting.

'Would you?' Mrs Glass pleaded. 'Oh, please . . .' Once she could have coped with *anything*; sending a man packing on a Saturday morning would have been nothing to Elizabeth Cathcart as she had been. Now, however, it was Emily Housecroft who hurried efficiently downstairs.

'Dr Morgan?' The governess entered Mrs Glass's sitting-room and found the visitor had settled in comfortably. He sat with his legs crossed, a drink beside him, apparently ensconced in a newspaper. Miss Housecroft coughed.

'Dr Morgan, Mrs Glass sent me. I'm afraid she is somewhat indisposed and Stacia, Milla and Helen are not at present at home. It is the school summer-holidays for another week; such a convenient school with only short holidays, so that the girls are kept occupied and out of harm's way even in July and August. Could I suggest you return and take tea with them on Wednesday afternoon at four o'clock? The side entrance leads directly up to the children's quarters – no need to disturb the rest of the house; Helen will be thrilled to see her godfather again!'

Emily Housecroft heard herself talking and continue talking as the visitor stopped reading and stood up. He retrieved his hat, inclined his head rather mockingly and briefly touched her hand. She saw him walk from the room and heard him putting on his coat and picking up his stick. It was only when the front door clicked behind him and she stood there alone that she found herself holding a bunch of unruly dahlias, full, wet, colourful blooms quite out of place in this room for they were freshly picked and brought from some brighter world. In her other hand Emily Housecroft discovered a curious edition: *News from the Other Side*, Volume XXIV, no. 56. Had she been in some sort of trance, mesmerized by the sound of her own voice? She could not explain how she came to be holding these things. More slowly now she mounted the stairs again and found Mrs Glass still very white and shaking, sitting exactly where she had left her.

'You brought the flowers with you,' Elizabeth eyed the over-bright dahlias with undisguised distaste.

'He gave them to me, at least he . . .'

'He . . .?' Mrs Glass started to formulate a question.

'He had an unnerving presence,' Emily Housecroft said firmly, glancing regretfully at the work she had left covered up. She was glad her private papers had not been touched, she wanted to get on.

'Hateful man!' Mrs Glass was angry now. 'You must ask Helen . . .'

'I hardly think Helen can be blamed . . .'

'I am not blaming her!' Mrs Glass snapped. 'If anyone, I blame Sarah Glass.'

There was an awkward pause.

'I invited Dr Morgan to visit the children on Wednesday afternoon for tea. It was the only way . . .' Miss Housecroft said.

'You got rid of him, that was the main thing. I will be out on Wednesday afternoon. I have no wish . . .' It was then, on an impulse, that Elizabeth Glass cried out: 'Have lunch downstairs with me!' She could not bear to return alone to the room where a man had walked towards her, his hands outstretched: 'Ah Sarah! Sarah, my dear!' The room where a man had spoken to her of Henry . . .

'How kind, but . . .' Miss Housecroft started to demur for she had her 'urgent' work to do.

'Fresh salmon,' Mrs Glass said sharply.

'Oh!' Emily Housecroft thought of the white fish, dumplings of suet, mutton stew and bread-pudding; there was never enough to go round, for the girls were growing and invariably hungry.

'A salmon can always be made to stretch,' Mrs Glass urged.

At that same moment, as chance would have it, Milla was excitedly stretching up to post her care-of letter to Pasha in a pillar-box outside the gates to the park.

'I wonder if Mr Eames will get into trouble for losing that stamp,' Helen queried.

'Let's hope so!' said Milla, for Philip Eames was creepy with a sly and creepy face.

'Don't be so silly!' Stacia exclaimed. 'I'm sure Glass & Co. can afford a penny stamp – it's not as though your precious Pasha is likely to reply and occasion the expense of correspondence! We'd better get back – we'll be late for lunch and you know the fuss they make.'

Stacia strode ahead so that people would see that she was the one taking the others for a walk.

'I'd like to live on my own and do whatever I pleased,' Milla said conversationally.

'Don't be ridiculous! You're far too young.' Stacia tossed her scorn back over her shoulder.

'We are lucky, though.' Helen recalled the sermons at school. 'Think of all those poor people less fortunate than ourselves. We get everything given us . . .'

'Everything?' Milla cried, angrily scuffing already scuffed shoes.

'We don't have to scrub doorsteps or sweep chimneys.' Helen could rarely see the point in Milla's anger.

'Or stand on street-corners plying our wares,' Stacia added, but so that her sisters behind could not hear. Women who stood on street-corners were something Stacia knew about privately.

'We are forced . . .' Milla began to explain, but what was the use? Milla wanted the greater, better life that Pasha pretended to purvey but somehow only managed to make small and cluttered with antimacassars, cut-glass cake-stands and lunches they fussed if you were late for. Milla wanted to travel the seas and meet tribal chiefs, lecture on her adventures to the Royal Geographical and visit dear William and bring him home. 'This is my brother who made a fortune in America,' she'd introduce the swashbuckler by her side, a green parrot on his shoulder; 'he was once bitten by a puff-adder with a bloated bladder and nearly died!' One day, she vowed to herself vaguely, as they rushed to keep up with Stacia, one day things would be different, somehow.

Stacia also knew what she wanted one day but any attempt to describe it in words was defeated by the colour and caprice of her desire. The three of them had once looked at a picture in the window of an art gallery; the others had had to coax Stacia away. When they went back later the wonderful picture had been replaced by a boring portrait of some woman with a dog. 'It's gone!' Stacia had moaned, but Milla and Helen refused to remember the picture Stacia would never forget.

Her sisters had been taken up with the new display: 'I'm going to have a dog like that!' Milla declared. 'Or maybe even two . . .'

'You'll need two dog licences then,' Helen said. 'Or the police will arrest one of the dogs and put it in jail.'

Stacia could not recall her picture properly now, but the feel of it remained. The rich oil, the flecks of light, the lavish dresses, the chandelier, the dazzle and the sparkle, the wide gold frame. In the rooms at the top of the house that smelt of soap-suds and custard, Stacia had only to shut her eyes and the texture of it wrapped her around as though an orchestra had struck up a waltz, *vivace e capriccioso*. Stacia Glass danced. She stood in front of a mirror and practised her curtsey. It had probably only been painted for sale, an overmantel piece sold by its size, but to Stacia the picture had been a vision of life's infinite possibilities.

At the moment that Elizabeth Glass said, 'Have lunch downstairs with me!' the new draughtsman at Glass & Co., Harry Withercott, was leaning over the back of a chair occupied by Lucy Winnup, a young lady of determined and independent character. Mr and Mrs Winnup encouraged their daughter, not minding, as many parents might, that young men visited her in her 'studio', the conservatory at the back of their house which she had been allowed to take over for her 'work'.

'I don't want an enigmatic conversation,' Lucy was saying to Harry as she pretended to concentrate on her drawing. 'I never want another enigmatic conversation in my life.'

'I thought enigmatic conversations were all the rage with independent young ladies these days.'

'Not this independent young lady,' Lucy dashed some black ink
into a shadow, overdoing it. Once she had prided herself on her
independence, now she would prefer people not to allude quite so
readily to it. She kept up the tone, however: 'They're far too
dangerous. I'd rather have diamonds!'

'Aren't diamonds dangerous?' Harry asked.

'Perhaps, but they have the virtue of being valuable a long time
afterwards.'

Harry liked Lucy Winnup in this mood. In fact, he liked her in
most of her moods. He fancied he might miss her.

'I'll come roller-skating with you – next week. That's a promise,'
Lucy said, though there was nothing she'd like more than to go
roller-skating that afternoon with Harry Withercott, but there were
these advertising-pictures to finish. Lucy Winnup had strong ideas
about earning her living which were quite ridiculous since she lived
with her easy-going parents in their comfortably appointed house in
Turnham Green. Harry looked at the stubborn set of her little chin.
Lucy was older than she should be.

'You can work tomorrow.' Harry, his hands in his pockets,
squinted at the wedge of black shadow that was surely a mistake. He
wanted her to come roller-skating *now*. It was his last chance.

'All right then,' she conceded grudgingly. Harry's face lit up as
she'd known it would. 'On condition you take that pencil out from
behind your ear. I don't want anyone thinking I'm with some
tradesman!'

Lucy Winnup's mother hopes Lucy will marry Harry Withercott;
Lucy secretly hopes so too. Harry has not told her how earlier that
week Edward Glass had invited him to run the Newcastle offices of
Arcanum Arcanorum – he, Harry Withercott who had borrowed
money from a doting aunt to attend night-classes!

In one of the pockets in which Harry's hands are casually thrust,
while he banters with the sweet and thirty-two-year-old Lucy
Winnup, there is a Great Northern timetable detailing times of trains
to Newcastle.

*

This same lunchtime, Eames is at work in the London offices of Glass & Co. 'Withercott not here?' He'd done his best to sound casual.

'Out celebrating,' one of the other draughtsmen said, not interested.

Philip Eames did not ask what Withercott could be out celebrating. Fellows like that always had something good on the go. He picked up a file and, sighing, started to draw up a list Elizabeth Glass herself would have been proud of, with its sections, sub-sections, divisions and sub-divisions. No salmon for Philip Eames! Mild steel in the shape of blooms, billets, slabs, flats and rounds. When he had finished his tabulation he would go to the wharfs to inspect the quality of the materials for himself. It was important to check suppliers hadn't slipped into the habit of overcharging or providing second-rate goods at top prices.

As Elizabeth Glass begged the governess to share her salmon, a Mr St John Tidy's hand reached out to turn the handle of Glass & Co.'s office door. The contractor had a proposal to put to Mr Eames. He had been told that Eames was the man: Eames was so well in with Edward Glass he had dined with the Master on Christmas Day and was trusted enough to visit the new young wife every week. St John Tidy would put his proposal to Mr Eames in rather a roundabout way, perhaps over a pint of beer at the Ring & Goose, next door. This sort of roundaboutness was not unknown to Philip Eames. He had once before been invited to a club by Mr Preedy. The invitation had come a week or so after the Christmas dinner.

Lulled by warm drink, soft music and flickering lights, unaccustomed to the close proximity of young and shameless female flesh, Mr Eames had been slow to catch Preedy's meaning. He'd been slow to understand that of course Charles Preedy had a meaning which was why he, Philip Eames, had been brought to this place. When the nature of what was being discussed had dawned on him, he'd banged down his glass, seized up his hat and departed from Preedy and from all the evil that was suggested round about them.

Philip Eames knew very well that although he could never be ensnared by the devil in the guise of Preedy or St John Tidy there was nothing in this world, or out of it, he would not do at Stacia Glass's bidding. Her seduction outraged and disgusted him. 'I am her slave, her vassal, her creature!' Eames repeated miserably and looked up in time to see St John Tidy entering the room.

'A word, sir? A beer perhaps, in the Ring & Goose below?'

'Get out! shouted Philip Eames to the startlement of everyone in the office. 'Before I call the police!'

'Steady on, old chap!'

'Not enough sleep, Philip?'

'Worried the husband'll find out, Philip?'

'Lunch downstairs with me!' the unsettled Mrs Glass urged Emily Housecroft, as a few streets away poor Dr Morgan hastened into an eating-house and ordered himself the one-and-sixpenny *table d'hôte* of which he was now in great need. He tucked a starched napkin impatiently beneath his chin. Over vigorous mouthfuls of roast beef and haricot beans he chewed over also the events of the previous hour.

It would be a shock for anyone to discover a dearest cousin dead, and another already installed in her place, but poor Dr Morgan had a professional interest in Death that should have forestalled the occurrence. 'If this should get out!' He trembled inwardly and thought of Lady Hildegard Blouvier exposing her full-plates to the elements half-way up the Matterhorn. Only this morning, not a few hours since, in untroubled innocence, he had helped himself to dahlias from her garden.

Although Dr Lucius Morgan was consulted by many of the highly placed and greatly born, he was not above offering his considerable services to ordinary folk as well. He was a truly modern man, happy to take money from anyone regardless of their station in life. He prided himself on his egality.

Dr Morgan had books to his name, some of which had caused consternation in ecclesiastical circles, not least because Dr Lucius Morgan had begun life in a strictly theological sphere on which he still drew most profitably for his credentials (hence the Cantab.). In his theological days he had been bluff and ambitious – marked out, many thought, for some bishopric no one else wanted, a cosy backwater where he could have been quietly and comfortably controversial – but Lucius Morgan had found another, brighter light to guide him. If penurious churchmen crabbily remarked that there was more money in what the man did now, their cynicism – if perhaps a trifle mean-minded – was nevertheless understandable. While they dined frugally in their rectories on home-grown spinach, Dr Morgan indulged himself in eating-houses on the best *table d'hôte*.

Sarah Glass had laughed out loud on more than one occasion, her mockery as egalitarian as her cousin had been in relieving other men of their money. It amused her to hear how the high and the low were taken in by her appalling cousin but, unlike the whispering church-men, she said what she thought to Lucius's face. Sarah had been a close cousin, she remembered the childhood incidents Dr Morgan might prefer to forget: Lucius chased by a goose who caught him and removed his trousers; Lucius wetting himself in church, leaving a stain on the wooden floor that had told against him for many years after; Lucius crying over a pet mouse that had broken its back. Of course she couldn't take Dr Lucius Morgan (Cantab.) seriously – why would she?

Dr Morgan took himself very seriously. 'The wall between the Living and the Dead has a door in it!' he would thunder to gatherings the size of congregations. 'I alone possess the key that opens this door' (he paused – there was deathly silence as the crowd held its breath and heard the click of the key in the lock). 'Whosoever bids it can send me through that door and I will return leading their Loved Ones by the hand. The Living and the Dead dwell not so far apart as you have been led to think!'

A woman slipped into the chair opposite Dr Morgan. He glanced up from helping himself to more gravy and looked into her eyes. 'You are troubled,' he observed matter-of-factly.

'Troubled! I am that!' the woman exclaimed, ordering a nine-penny lunch. 'My treat,' she told Dr Morgan when the waitress had written down the order. 'My son told me to treat myself.'

'Your son, Ma'am?' (A living son then.)

'Yes, my Philip – chief assistant to the great architect, Edward Glass, no less! Glorified errand-boy, poor lad, do this, do that and there's more work where that came from. Now if I had my way . . .'

Destiny is mine! thought Lucius Morgan, for a disgruntled mother was one thing, but an angle on Edward Glass! He recalled the dahlias that were growing rampant just then in Lady Blouvier's garden: 'I'd be honoured, dear Madam, if you would permit me to present you with a bunch of dahlias.'

'Dahlias!' Mrs Eames had not expected amusements this Saturday lunchtime. 'The name's Flora, in case you were wondering . . .'

At the moment in which the second Mrs Glass invited her governess to lunch with her, Edward Glass was still in Manchester, delayed by a Polish manufacturer of high-class chocolate who insisted on disputing his bill. Edward Glass rather liked this foreign gentleman who treated him without regard for his fame and standing. He was also rather partial to the Pole's dark daughter.

'I pay! I say what I want!' the chocolatier reiterated, jumping up and down in a fury and pointing at the offending invoice. 'You build something different – you spend my money, you build on my land! I say no windows – you, Mr Edward, put sixteen on every floor! The wind comes in, the surface, the delicate bloom on my chocolate is ruined! Destroyed! This is a chocolate manufactory, not a palace for an idle Prince . . .'

'My dear Sir! The job is done now.' Edward Glass half-listened, his head on one side, displaying the bemused English calm that had once so infuriated HRH of Saxe-Coburg-Gotha. Was the man not aware that Glass & Co. invoices were renowned for being both unequivocal and three times the sum expected?

'Over three times what I expect, what we agree,' Stanislav Szlabin hopped up and down. Glass was two feet taller than he and had the natural advantage.

Edward Glass raised his eyebrows. This could be settled here and now: a little give and take. Edward Glass had been quite taken with Szlabin's daughter. He held out a plan with signatures on the bottom and spoke with the studied clarity one learns to use with these excitable types: 'This, Sir, is what we agreed and what has been built, an agreed design at an agreed figure.'

'Seven years ago we agreed, yes! I write since! I want different – high winds, windows, bad weather, tall buildings, bad chocolate! . . .' Szlabin was clearly capable of continuing all day.

'Look, I frankly haven't time to argue.'

'I pay for your time . . .'

'My time is not for hire like some hansom-cab, Sir! You have had the full benefits of my talents . . .' And I have had the full benefit of your daughter – a fair trade-off, Glass felt.

Kkovah Works: the new Szlabin chocolate factory. Edward Glass knew, in truth, he had been a bit careless, left it rather too much to draughtsman Myers and the like. There must be no mistakes with the New Paris Grand. Why had he let the fellow Eames fill up his diary so? Couldn't they have turned all the humdrum work away? That was the trouble with humdrum operatives like Eames: calico, embroidered or lace, they made no distinction. Perhaps with the daughter in mind, Glass agreed eventually to halve the bill and go with Mr Szlabin to sample his chocolate.

'We reach agreement,' Szlabin said, satisfied now.

'You win, old chap!' Edward Glass replied, slapping the little man on the back.

Szlabin had a tall, dark-eyed daughter. A very proud, surprisingly refined and thoroughly English girl. Edward Glass lunched that day with father and daughter beneath the palms of the Midland Hotel, the quiet daughter wondering if her father had guessed, the soreness between her legs from last night, the famous architect's knee resting against hers beneath the table as he ordered rare wines and accepted compliments and business-cards pressed on him by fellow diners. 'I shall never be happy like this again,' Esther Szlabin thought wistfully. She had dreaded the day Kkovah Works would be finished and Edward Glass would leave. She did not know how to face tomorrow, next week, next month or next year. She looked anxiously at the clocks on the walls, unable to accept that their hands could go on moving and that her own life, that must also go on ticking away, would be finished. A Living Death, she thought with melancholy exaggeration. The delicate bloom, more subtle and sorrowful than any freshly picked dahlia, destroyed.

'We saw Edward Glass today – dining only a few feet from us! Such a pretty woman with him, of course!'

'What did she look like?' 'What was she wearing?' 'Do we know her?'

'I don't rightly remember, but she was very beautiful and her eyes . . .' What was there to say of Esther Szlabin's eyes, rich and dark but filmy like her father's damaged chocolate?

Mrs Curzon swallowed hard. *The lion shall sit down in the dining-room and stretch a small salmon with the lamb*: the Mistress and the children's governess lunching together! Had the Day of Judgement arrived, unexpectedly, just like that, this lunchtime? Was this new and untoward disruption the prelude then to everlasting damnation?

Elizabeth Glass watched her governess helping herself to vegetables. The woman was a 'governess', and yet the girls went to school for their learning: there was something decidedly ill-defined about Miss Housecroft. How could she hope to define a woman who had been living under her own roof for the last six months but to whom she had hardly spoken?

'We know so little of each other,' Mrs Glass said, noticing ink on the girl's sleeve which reminded her of Philip Eames's inky fingers. For all *she* knew, Emily Housecroft might be more suited to the company of Burke and Hare, Dr Black and the notorious Aberdeen poisoner Mrs Bertha Kilgarriff whom Mrs Preedy had visited in the Chamber of Horrors at Madame Tussaud's, than to sitting in her dining-room stretching a salmon. We might all be murdered in our beds, Elizabeth thought, eyeing the prim and pasty-faced governess whose complexion struck her now as distinctly waxy.

Ill at ease with a fish-knife, Emily Housecroft smiled uncertainly. She shared Mrs Curzon's discomfort at this new turn of events.

'Tell me!' Mrs Glass persisted. 'Tell me what I do not know about yourself.'

'There is *nothing* to tell,' Miss Housecroft said, adding quickly, 'I am happy in my work here. I like the girls, there are no problems.'

The two women fell silent. Elizabeth toyed with her food. Perhaps it was the sip of Belgar Brandy she had taken, or that disturbing reference to Henry not an hour before, or being mistaken for Sarah Glass and offered dahlias, there was no knowing. Anyhow, Elizabeth Glass looked at her harmless companion and heard herself saying: 'What utter nonsense, Emily! How can you be happy here? You no more want to run round after three spoilt little girls playing at being Jane Eyre than I do! It's just that you must because it's the only thing you could think of to do . . .'

There was a startled pause.

'It's quite obvious to me, as I'm sure it must be to you,' Mrs Glass continued, 'that you're not going to find a husband or even a blind Mr Rochester stuck up there with my step-daughters in the stuffy rooms at the top of this house.'

Miss Housecroft spluttered. Who had said anything about

husbands? 'I have my afternoons out,' she said with a nervous laugh. 'I have the time when the girls are at school. Who knows what may happen?'

'Well, yes.' Mrs Glass felt defiant on Emily Housecroft's behalf. She tried furiously not to think about Henry and the horrid hotel at Ventnor. Who knows what may happen, indeed! 'The first time I married, I was badly deceived. I don't think I shall ever recover . . .'

'Not even with all this?' Emily Housecroft gestured round the room, taking in the silver épergnes, the fussy Coalport china, the little bits of ivory, the antimacassars so despised by young Milla, the old oak furniture that Mrs Glass had already decided to replace.

'You think I married Edward Glass for this?' Elizabeth asked sharply.

'Well . . .' Miss Housecroft faltered, as well she might.

'You're not so far wrong!' Elizabeth cried. 'I couldn't take any more knocks – I was quite worn out. Look at me, I'm only twenty-five but you wouldn't know it. You saw how I didn't even have the strength to tell that man to get out of my own house.'

'Look,' Emily Housecroft said quickly, almost choking on a morsel of salmon, 'a lot of things are best left *unsaid*.'

'Maybe! But that is the sort of thing *you* are *paid* to say, Emily, just as *I* am *paid* to sit here and be the nice Mrs Glass. Mrs Glass, the second.' The women looked at each other in shocked astonishment. Elizabeth waved her hand: 'Don't worry, I'm not the petty sort. I won't turn against you in a few hours' time and work and scheme to find correct reasons to get rid of you just to hide my embarrassment. You ought to . . .'

'Ought to?' Emily Housecroft queried.

'Ought to, well . . .' Mrs Glass wondered what she did mean. 'Go outside, do things, see something – like men expect to. We're not short of money if it's money that's needed, which in my experience it generally is . . .'

A tap on the door and sweet was brought in, delicate pastries prettily decked with nuts and chopped *glacé* fruits. Mary Ann, who had been listening outside and heard the last exchange, assumed that the mistress and governess were acting out parts in a charade – the children were still off school and charades in the afternoon helped pass the time, she supposed. She lost interest and returned downstairs.

'About a holiday?' Mary Ann said to Mrs Curzon; she was planning her wide-brimmed hat.

'You can forget that right away! Get Cora to take the children up their lunch, and not too much butter on their bread, mind!'

In the dining-room Mrs Glass continued: 'Do you think *that man* is to blame?'

Miss Housecroft had not yet encountered Edward Glass. 'Er . . .'

'Dr Morgan,' Mrs Glass added.

'Oh – Dr Morgan!' Emily Housecroft knew what Mrs Glass meant in spite of herself she couldn't help feeling that these pastries were certainly more palatable than dumplings of suet, bread-pudding, jelly or shape), all this emotion must have come out of somewhere. Miss Housecroft was still a little shaken from finding flowers and pamphlets in her hands and having no way of knowing how they got there. Mrs Glass was clearly very disturbed.

'Perhaps you should lie down?' Miss Housecroft suggested.

'There you are – Jane Eyre again! I'm going shopping.' Elizabeth felt like a petulant child in a nursery. Perhaps Miss Housecroft had a vocation after all.

'He said something to upset you, didn't he?' the governess asked solicitously.

'The impertinence of the man, horrible creature!' Elizabeth Glass shuddered. 'Come shopping with me!' she pleaded, not wanting to be on her own. She did not want to think about what Dr Morgan had said to upset her.

'The sun has gone in,' the governess tried to protest, but at half past two the second Mrs Glass and a reluctant Emily Housecroft left the house to go to the shops. Milla watched them leaving arm in arm from her upper-landing window and then told the others what she had seen.

'Good riddance!' Stacia said rudely. 'They should go out more often together and leave us in peace.'

The second Mrs Glass and her step-children's governess roamed the shops all afternoon but purchased nothing. Elizabeth was too disturbed to concentrate and Emily was uncertain how to comfort her.

10

The Girls have Yet Another Piano Lesson, Mrs Preedy Organizes, Mrs Glass Asks Questions and Mrs Curzon Starts a New Campaign

'Godfather – I never knew we had godparents,' Milla said immediately.

'Oh?' Miss Housecroft was not altogether surprised. 'But Dr Morgan – Dr Lucius Morgan?'

'Oh, you mean Dr Morgan!' Milla laughed delightedly.

'My godfather? Is Dr Morgan my godfather?' Helen queried.

'Apparently. In any case, he is invited to tea at four on Wednesday. I dare say he won't stay long.' They do know the man, then . . .

'Dr Morgan not stay long – that'll be the day!' Milla mocked.

'Does Mrs Curzon know Dr Morgan's coming?' Stacia asked shrewdly.

Then Milla said: 'Mrs Curzon won't be pleased.'

'Oh?' In spite of herself, Miss Housecroft could not help being interested.

Milla needed no second invitation: 'Yes, Mrs Curzon liked Dr Morgan, at first, in fact she liked him a good deal, she was smiling all over him and you could tell she thought he was keen on her. She spent lots of her own money buying him this and that, cooking him delicacies . . .'

'Honey-roast ham . . .'

'Veal cutlets . . .'

'*And* she lent him money, telling him he could keep it. Then when most of her savings were gone, and she found he had no "intentions" . . .'

'Poor Mamma kept shouting "I did warn you!" and Mrs Curzon repeated a lot of things too, and after that they hardly ever spoke to each other and Mrs Curzon used to rush to the door whenever she thought it might be him visiting and not let him in, telling him Mother wasn't at home when she was, only she was in bed.'

'Poor Mamma was always in bed . . .'

'Sometimes when Mamma wasn't so poorly she'd get down in time . . .'

'We used to listen . . .'

'Mrs Curzon shouted about obligations and intentions; Mother said Mrs Curzon was a fool, she'd been warned, Lucius was her cousin so of course he could come in.'

'Mrs Curzon shouted that Father said Dr Morgan was a con-man and a charlatan and he'd forbidden him to enter the house and Poor Mamma said it was *her* house . . .'

'Dr Morgan stood with his arms folded, smiling. You could tell he knew he'd get his tea – and whatever else he'd come for – so he just stood there waiting for them to finish.'

'He liked having them quarrel over him,' Stacia said. 'I think *that*'s what he came for. Men like women quarrelling over them, there's nothing men like more!'

'And getting people's life's savings off them,' Helen added. 'He left Mrs Curzon without a bean.'

Emily Housecroft knew she should have put an end to this strangely unchildlike gossiping. 'Not a good habit to get into,' the governess told them now. 'No one likes a gossip.'

Stacia, Milla and Helen stared at her, their pleasure gone.

'There's not much else to do round here,' Stacia said sullenly. 'Anyway, we haven't seen Dr Morgan for ages.'

'We didn't know he still existed.'

'I didn't know he was my godfather.'

'I'm sure he isn't!'

'You're just jealous.'

'Like Mrs Curzon . . .'

'Well, don't forget – Wednesday at four!' Miss Housecroft was impatient. 'Now, Stacia, you had better practise that Chopin *nocturne* you've hardly touched – Mr Luscombe will be here for your lesson again. And, Helen, you learn another poem. School starts next week; you must all have things you need to do.' Miss Housecroft herself had no shortage of things to do but Mrs Glass had made her promise to go down and see her again. Mrs Glass had been agitated and unsettled since Dr Morgan's visit. Like Philip Eames she hardly slept.

'They are grown girls,' Elizabeth Glass said peevishly, when Emily Housecroft tried to say that she should be up with the children telling them what to do. 'They ought to be able to occupy their time.'

'They waste a lot of time,' Miss Housecroft said.

Mrs Glass looked sharply across at Emily Housecroft for no one 'wasted' time as deliciously as Elizabeth Glass had done these last six months (until Dr Morgan had called and put an end to her hard-won, new-found ease). Mrs Glass examined Emily Housecroft's bookish demeanour. There were quantities of books and papers on the woman's shelves and desk upstairs, the paraphernalia of a governess certainly. Mrs Glass knew that the woman went out regularly several hours at a stretch, for both Mary Ann and the suspicious Mrs Curzon had commented on it. Mrs Glass had not taken much notice at the time – it was curious also how Emily Housecroft had not particularly responded to the suggestion that she might take money and enjoy herself. If only someone had made such an offer to Eliza Cathcart! Unwillingly she recalled herself sitting in the hired deck-chair at the shabby end of Ventnor, Henry with his hands in his pockets sulking, telling her she asked too many questions. How different life might have been if they'd had money then for enjoyment. Cash to quibble over, instead.

Emily Housecroft hovered in the doorway. If Mrs Glass continued to press her, kindly though it may be meant, and despite the salmon lunch, she would have to leave. Reluctantly she resigned herself to wasting *yet another* afternoon walking round the shops with the second Mrs Glass. It was ridiculous how upset the woman still was about Dr Morgan's visit – if Mrs Glass were one of the girls she would tell her to pull herself together.

Stacia sat down at the piano and strummed a few reluctant bars of lifeless Chopin. She missed one note and then another. She sat and stared at her hands resting elegantly on the keys and imagined her fingers sparkling with rings. How she hated Mondays and Chopin, who seemed to tease her with all that she could not have.

Every Monday, in the early evening, Mr Luscombe presented himself by ringing at the side door of the Glass Residence in York Street. He arrived on a bicycle which was left rather precariously propped on its own fold-down stand. It blew round on itself noisily like a scarecrow flapping about a central pole and usually – even when there wasn't any wind – the rickety contraption unbalanced and teetered over half-way through the hour. They had learnt to wait for the clatter which they would hear from upstairs, even above the noise of the piano, and when at last it came Stacia, Milla and Helen would collapse also into fits of unstoppable giggles while Mr

Luscombe, unperturbed by the disturbance, continued with the lesson as though nothing had happened.

Mr Luscombe looked like a scarecrow himself, but one which a farmer proudly tended for there was something deliberate about Mr Luscombe's battered and shabby appearance. He had been coming to the house for years now to sit stiffly beside the giggling girls while they made their din at the piano.

'Mr Luscombe,' Milla would say – for who had the power to prevent the man coming? – 'Mr Luscombe is an institution!'

Stacia and Helen would giggle. Mr Luscombe was an embarrassment to them all and the reason for the useless piano lessons was lost, forgotten way back in history . . . But not forgotten by Mrs Curzon.

Mr Luscombe had been married to Mrs Curzon's sister-in-law, Ada, sister to the Dead, Departed and now somewhat vilified Mr Curzon. If Mrs Curzon still thought angrily about Ada Luscombe's brother, Mr Curzon, it was probably because Dr Morgan had encouraged her. Mr Luscombe had never met Dr Morgan so the memory of poor Ada Luscombe was allowed to rest in peace. Besides, Mr Luscombe had other more pressing concerns to occupy him, the concerns by which the Living truly bury the Dead. He still lived on his own in the dismal suburban villa he and the forgotten Ada had shared, a villa that managed to face so diffidently that its windows never caught a single ray of sun.

Way back when first Mr Luscombe and Mrs Curzon had both been widowed, Mrs Curzon had frequently suggested that she might leave service and spend her declining years with her brother-in-law. One dark house was as good as another and it seemed to her a sensible arrangement; the Luscombe villa could accommodate them both respectably and they would be company of sorts for one another. But Mrs Curzon had argued all this to no avail. Mr Luscombe refused to listen.

Eventually, in a moment of inspiration, Mrs Curzon had introduced the stubborn Mr Luscombe to Sarah Glass. The girls should have piano lessons, she'd said, pointing out that there was a redundant Conrad & Taylor Upright Piano occupying space in the 'school-room'.

'Oh, I suppose so . . .' The first Mrs Glass had been too ill to disagree. Mr Luscombe had been engaged for a good weekly fee and though this conflicted with Mrs Curzon's natural sense of economy, she regarded it as a potentially valuable investment now that the savings for her old age were gone. Did not all investment necessitate risk of one sort or another?

Piano-playing was probably an accomplishment required 'at Court' so occasionally between lessons Stacia would sit on the stool, if not to practise her *nocturnes* at least to fantasize. A Crown Prince might pause in the doorway during a soirée or a Royal Duke enquire of a footman the identity of the captivating creature at the piano-forte. 'That's Miss Stacia Glass, Your most Excellent Highness!' the footman would say, adding: 'Daughter of the famous Architect; I believe the family reside in York Street . . .' Stacia imagined Milla's jokes about glass slippers (Glass slippers, you see, as worn by Stacia and not Cinderella) when the pumpkin-coach turned up at the door. But it was Dr Morgan – Helen's godfather indeed – and not some fairy-godmother who was expected at four on Wednesday . . .

Milla refused point blank to take much interest in music, but by long-standing tradition she had her twenty minutes' worth of clumsily bashing out scales, arpeggios and finger-exercises. Helen worked her way steadily through the manuals and practised a little between lessons.

'I hate the piano!' Stacia said, waging war on Chopin by kicking at the Conrad & Taylor's ancient pedals so that one fell off and she had to get down on her hands and knees and fit it back on. How would the ever-attentive footman explain this away? 'Oh, Your Grace, I do believe the accomplished Miss Glass is a dab hand when it comes to repairs – she spends many an afternoon sewing hems . . .'

'I don't see why we have to have lessons,' Helen said.

'It gives Mr Luscombe something to do,' Milla replied. The others laughed but Milla had not been joking. The piano lessons were a waste of time and money, but now that they happened (twenty minutes each at the stool) there was no one to tell Mr Luscombe that he could be dispensed with. At the end of the hour he was handed a manila envelope which he immediately tucked away into the inner pocket of his dusty jacket. The contents of this envelope were of vital importance to Mr Luscombe, as gradually over the years the money he received from teaching the Glass girls had become his sole source of income. This was something you would never have suspected from the way he pocketed the envelope without opening or even looking at it.

It pleased Milla to think Mr Luscombe intriguing. It wasn't that there was anything necessarily intriguing about the piano-teacher, though he arrived from Nowhere and cycled back there again an hour later.

In fact, Mr Luscombe did have two ghastly secrets which were known, for the most part, only to himself: the hair on top of his head was not his own and the ears on the side of his head were now so deaf that the bewigged piano-teacher could hear practically nothing. These secrets he intended to keep to the grave. He bicycled everywhere so that his false hair and his clothes were always dishevelled and generally disguised in a forgiving layer of dust. He hid his awkward growing deafness by refraining whenever possible from all conversation. He adopted a perpetually preoccupied air. If spoken to he interrupted quickly, scowling as if a wrong note had been played and speaking of other things. He'd whistle a bar or two reminiscent of Chopin or he'd mention sheet-music that should be bought. Sometimes he answered a question that might reasonably have been asked. People assumed Mr Luscombe was batty. They thought him so musical that he did not listen; it occurred to no one that he could not hear. He had a watch he would pull from his pocket so no one detained him with trivial everyday chatter. No one ever recommended Mr Luscombe as a teacher now and this ensured that he encountered nobody new who would have spotted his obvious deafness at once.

Milla sat beside Mr Luscombe from 4.20 to 4.40 on Monday afternoons looking at the dry skin on his hands and the heavily marked indentations on his cracking finger-nails. At around the time when her session commenced Mr Luscombe was brought a cup of sweet tea with a biscuit in the saucer. As Milla bashed out her scales, Mr Luscombe noisily sucked at his tea, pausing to dip and nibble the biscuit, making hungry little animal noises of which he was patently unaware. Milla liked to perform the occasional experiment, turning her head away from him and saying preposterous things which he did not hear, just as he never heard his bicycle blowing over half-way through the hour. Half-way through the hour was also half-way through Milla, the middle one's allotted twenty minutes.

The three girls convulsed into giggles. Stacia smirked that a man who sold sumptuous Chopin for a living should ride around on a rickety old bicycle that could not even stand up of its own accord. Helen giggled because her sisters giggled. Milla had said nothing to anyone about Mr Luscombe's deafness as this would have ruined the private joke she shared with him. The poor piano-teacher didn't know it, of course, any more than he knew why his pupils would suddenly start giggling each week. The giggles pained Mary Ann who was obliged to sit through the hour keeping an eye on the girls although it was Mr Luscombe on whom her eyes were longingly, lovingly fixed.

This Monday afternoon, Mary Ann sat in the school-room gazing forlornly at Mr Luscombe. Mary Ann understood he was related somehow by marriage to Mrs Curzon who referred to him derisively, but proprietorially, as 'my Mr Luscombe'. This overwhelmed the parlourmaid with pity; no wonder the man looked so sad. How dearly Mary Ann wanted to take him in her arms, dust him down and kiss and comfort him until his sadness and loneliness dissolved and eventually he smiled. But this could never happen, for if the solemn Mr Luscombe glanced in Mary Ann's direction she would beam an encouraging smile and the poor piano-teacher *cut her dead* for fear the pretty girl said anything he could not hear. There could be no comfort in this world, or in Mary Ann's arms, for Mr Luscombe. He never smiled.

This hour between four and five o'clock on Monday afternoons was something the whole house had learned to endure. Mrs Curzon downstairs heard the faraway tinkling and fretted about the expenditure and speculated on her chances of getting a return on the long-term investment – the Lord was taking his time on this one. Mary Ann felt her passions rebuffed – Mr Luscombe refused to respond to her charms on Monday afternoons as resolutely as did Philip Eames on Fridays. What could be so wrong with her, she wondered, that neither man showed the remotest flicker of interest while she herself desperately craved kisses from them both? The second Mrs Glass found the overall soundproofing of the house defective. How could an architect who ought to know about these things live in a house where an Upright Piano sited somewhere away at the top could be heard in rooms on the ground floor? Then Elizabeth would remember that the architect in question did not live in the building, had told her he had no interest in houses, and for this she could scarcely feel sorry.

'Goodbye,' Mary Ann said this afternoon as Mr Luscombe picked up his battered bicycle and wheeled it away. He did nothing to acknowledge her existence. 'Goodbye, Mr Luscombe!' she called out again, ready to smile and wave.

'You come straight back inside, my girl!' Mrs Curzon loomed in the doorway behind the parlourmaid. 'Man-mad, that's what you are, Mary Ann – I won't have you pestering my Mr Luscombe . . .' But her eyes also travelled after the diminishing figure, balancing unsteadily now on the rickety old bike: 'The Lord might be made to answer that prayer, also,' she thought. With a little industrious praying, Mr Luscombe's days of living *on his own* in the sunless Ada-less villa could soon be numbered.

Mrs Charles Preedy decided it was time to organize a little entertainment, an Afternoon Tea, since this seemed to her the most economical and yet effective method of gathering people together. It also gave her a reason to go calling; there could then be polite general enquiries like 'Who else is coming?' which would lead on naturally to the mention of a name or two.

Tuesday found Mrs Preedy busy with her invitations. Mrs Pinder Simpson, first lady of the cement works Simpson, Holland & Co., must be invited, although she was only trade, of course – somehow one allowed oneself to forget this for the woman enjoyed a good gossip. One did one's best to forget the cement works, in deference to a good gossip. The Simpsons were obviously well-to-do; Pinder Simpson Junior had even been accepted into Harrow – though of course one rather wondered whether the cement works on Lime Kiln Wharf could be known about up there in Harrow-on-the-Hill and one rather pitied the little chap when his playmates made the discovery. 'Prize Medal 1851, Honourable Mention 1862' it said on Simpson, Holland & Co. cement bags – and you couldn't help remembering this Medal and the Honourable Mention when you spoke to Mrs Simpson sometimes, but these days, if you wanted a good gossip, it was not so easy always to persevere with the finer distinctions. Look at Mrs Edward Glass, for instance! Well, that was the point of the whole thing, to look at Mrs Glass. And to have a good gossip.

Mrs Richard Styles understood at once and said: 'Oh, Mrs Preedy, I shall be delighted! Wasn't it *you* after all who introduced the happy couple? And I hear she goes round with his children's governess. In my day a governess was employed to give geography lessons, and keep the husband amused, not to roam the shops purchasing knick-knacks!'

Mrs Styles clearly wanted to pursue the topic but Mrs Preedy (who could have informed her friend that nothing had actually been bought by the two women on Saturday afternoon, and that Edward Glass had never even met Miss Emily Housecroft) only smiled. 'I thought a Tea,' she said smilingly. 'One does so like a Tea – and a little entertainment!'

To the second Mrs Glass, Mrs Preedy said: 'You must bring dear Miss Housecroft, of course.'

Mrs Glass understood at once. 'I will find out if Emily is free,' Elizabeth said casually, yawning. 'Such a busy young lady, you know. Why, her appointment diary is quite something. Pages and pages bespattered . . .'

'She has friends, then?' Mrs Preedy pressed.

'Oh, I really think she must, not that *I* feel the need to check up on what she does all day . . .'

Mrs Preedy nodded. It had been on the tip of her tongue to enquire what Eliza Cathcart (of old) found to do all day now she was the new Mrs Glass and no longer needed to borrow dresses, but Mrs Preedy knew there would be fun enough at the 'little entertain-ment'. 'And the dear girls?' she asked instead. 'How you must enjoy being their step-mother! Why, when I think about it, Helen will be roughly the same age as my Charlotte . . .'

Elizabeth Glass had no idea how old Helen or Mrs Preedy's Charlotte were (she was not even aware that the girls attended the same school and were actually in the same class), so she smiled vaguely and Mrs Preedy knew to gather together her belongings which included the pile of invitation cards she had yet to deliver. 'I must go, my dear. So much to organize, but I can safely promise everyone a little entertainment . . .'

Mrs Glass rang the bell for Mary Ann to show the visitor out, and then rose herself to prop the invitation to Afternoon Tea *chez* the tiresome Preedys this coming Friday (*répondez s'il vous plaît* written out in full, but 'no need, my dear, since I know you'll come') on the mantelpiece.

'Eliza looked terrible,' Mrs Preedy gleefully told Charles. 'She looked as if she hadn't slept for days, so pale and drawn, poor thing – I wonder what can be wrong?'

'I dare say we'll find out . . .'

'Yes, I do hope so!'

When an exhausted Mrs Glass (after yet another long and sleepless night) informed Mrs Curzon on Wednesday morning that a Dr Morgan was coming to take tea with the girls that afternoon and could something suitable be provided for four o'clock, Mrs Curzon was unprepared for the shock: 'Did you say "Dr Morgan", Madam?'

'Indeed, Mrs Curzon. Dr Morgan.'

'Do you think it wise?' The housekeeper faltered.

'Wise or not, it is arranged,' Mrs Glass said coolly. 'A seed-cake should suffice, nothing elaborate . . .' Elizabeth had seen the colour drain from Mrs Curzon's cheeks and noted the icy hardening of her eyes, the tight drawing-in of breath, and above all the struggle above all to conceal this. Mrs Curzon is as perturbed by the man as I, she thought. Mrs Glass said: 'You must know Dr Morgan quite well? A celebrated person by all accounts . . .'

'By his own account! He used to call often enough in the *first* Mrs Glass's day. He and the former Mrs Glass were cousins.'

'A Spiritualist, I gather?' Elizabeth Glass persisted although she noted the censure: Mrs Curzon had made a point in the past of rarely referring to her predecessor.

'So I believe,' Mrs Curzon muttered tightly, adding dismissively: 'If you believe in that sort of thing, Ma'am.'

'And do you, Mrs Curzon?' the second Mrs Glass asked, trying to sound as sunny as it had been before Dr Morgan's arrival on Saturday morning. 'Do you believe in that sort of thing?'

'I don't think about it,' Mrs Curzon said glumly. So, this was what it led to, the Mistress stretching a salmon with the artful Miss Housecroft and then going shopping together. She noticed Elizabeth Glass's over-bright eyes and the unusual colour about her cheeks but she could not know that Mrs Glass had barely slept a wink since Lucius Morgan had grasped hold of her hand. *Oh Henry, Henry, look what you've done . . .*

Poor Elizabeth had gone to bed late each night and kept the light burning, whiling away long wakeful hours making lists of things advertised in her magazines that she could buy. Frenziedly she had concentrated on all kinds of pleasant acquirables with which to pack the house: painted mirrors, jardinières, pouffes, rugs from Turkey, blotting books, chair backs, tassled cushions, all manner of hangings and draperies. She read the advert for the Infallible Blouvier but the second Mrs Glass was not one of the Empire's Intrepid, mornings found her exhausted and anxious for company. She rang the bell and peevishly told Mary Ann to ask Miss Housecroft to come to her as soon as convenient, sooner if possible.

Mrs Curzon recalled the mauve taffeta again for the first time in months, bitterly recalling also how money put by for her old age had been used up. It was a puzzle to her that she had ever been susceptible to Dr Morgan's inconspicuous charms – the memory of the Dear Departed Mr Curzon had been tarnished irreparably by Morgan's uncalled for and expensive interference. Dr Morgan had made a point of speaking with her about Mr Curzon and on each occasion she found herself telling him things about the Dear Departed that would have better stayed Buried with the Buried.

Mrs Curzon had assumed Sarah Glass's death – despite the omission of a legacy – would have the advantage that Dr Morgan would now stay away. But no – here was the *second* Mrs Glass requesting seed-cake for him. If he didn't know already, Dr Morgan would soon discover how well provided for the second Mrs Glass was and then there would be no stopping him.

Mrs Curzon sighed heavily, thinking of her own spent savings. Hadn't the old mauve taffeta been a deliberate act of revenge? Did it not afford Mrs Curzon no small satisfaction that Dr Morgan's cousin, Sarah Glass, had gone so shabbily dressed to meet her Maker while a wardrobe full of expensive finery had been left behind, if not for Mrs Curzon's own use, then at least for the heedless moths to gnaw on? *The Lord gave only that we might take away.* Mrs Curzon descended to issue instructions regarding a seed-cake. If Dr Morgan was going to be around again, helping himself from the second Mrs Glass's substantial funds, she herself must lose no time in starting her new campaign. *The Lord will provide for His humble servant in her old age* even if it is with her dead husband's dead sister's widower, in a dark and sunless villa in a dark and sunless suburb the other side of town. With Dr Morgan eating seed-cake in this house again *anything* could happen . . .

Cora got out the caraway seeds. At least she'd be able to scrape fingerfuls of eggy mixture out of the bowl when the old fleabag wasn't looking – she'd never been so hungry as she was in this big house. She was a big girl herself and needed her food.

11

A Quarrel Patched & a Favour Asked

'I hear Edward Glass is back in London!' Mrs Preedy asked Charles if he had seen him.

'No – Glass moves in mysterious ways, he isn't often seen.'

'Eliza didn't know where her husband was – it can't be easy being the *second* Mrs Glass,' Mrs Preedy sighed. It couldn't have been easy being the *first* Mrs Glass, either. There had been no mention of Edward Glass when she'd called with her invitation and found Elizabeth looking as ill as Sarah had always done. 'I do feel for her, really I do!'

'Never mind, my dear, we have your Afternoon Tea and a little entertainment to look forward to on Friday,' Charles Preedy said soothingly. Secretly, he rather admired the way Edward Glass organized his life: a new young wife who was not too beady-eyed seemed to him an admirable asset. Still, Mrs Preedy was a good woman, and undeniably a good mother – Bertram, though young, was being carefully schooled. 'It'll be Preedy & Son one day, if you behave yourself!' Charles had overheard her telling the little boy. 'When you grow up you'll be a famous architect, like your father . . .'

Bertram Preedy's reply – the limitless wail of infant misery – was instantly checked by a maternal slap. Yes, Charles Preedy reflected, there was no reason why it should not be Preedy & Son, Famous Architects, given time . . .

For some reason, unclear even to himself, Edward Glass went to visit Elee – perhaps because she was an old friend, or the nearest he came to having an old friend. When he moved on he liked to move on altogether, taking as little as possible with him and certainly not the burden of old friends. Over the years Elee had been an exception and she suited his purposes this evening.

'Oh, it's you!' Elee was surprised. She had not expected to see Edward Glass again although she had heard that the man was back in London. His loneliness brought him back to her, she supposed.

'I was just cooking . . .' Elee heaved a mountainous sigh.

'I'm not hungry.'

'Well, you may not be, but I am.' Edward Glass sat himself down beside her stove. He was a man who could make himself at home anywhere, she thought, even in her kitchen.

'Alone?' he asked. Who knew what Elee got up to in his absence? The woman let out a shriek of laughter and told him to look in the cupboards and under the bed if he had any doubts. Edward realized that their quarrel of six months ago was over and he had been forgiven.

Elee turned her back on him and attended to her cooking. She'd been called Elsinora Lee on the stage, but 'Elee' by herself and those who knew her. She liked the safe officialness of E. Lee which made her feel less fantastical than 'Elsinora', the heroine she would tell people her dear parents had fondly envisaged. She had always looked more of an Elee than an Elsinora even in her days on the boards. Elee was past caring, she no longer needed a stage name.

Edward Glass watched the woman clattering ponderously about. She was a contentedly large, hideously featured woman for whom he'd long had a perverse liking; he'd last seen her when they had quarrelled about his second marriage. Elee told him he had been absurd.

'I've never heard anything so ridiculous,' she'd said, not laughing.

'It was Mr Eames's idea.' Glass felt weak. He'd been suffering unusual self-doubt which was why he had called. She was not sympathetic. He was wondering what he had done marrying a plain young woman, William's age, who liked nothing so much as a big pot of glue and a scrapbook. Suppose it turned out to be a complete and expensive disaster, an over-ambitious cupola?

'You follow advice on these matters from your assistant?' Elee mocked. 'I hope the whole thing topples about your ears!'

'I was at a loss. I wanted to get away from the house and memories of Sarah. Perhaps I felt guilty, Elee . . .'

'I should think you did!' Elee had always been irritated by the idea of Sarah Glass; she'd thought of her rather as one recalls a spoilt child. 'What can a woman like that know of life?' she'd demanded contemptuously, and not been surprised when eventually Sarah had died. The woman had tied Edward down, as wives do – Elee

113

had never been a wife, had little sympathy for wives – and then Edward had come back here and calmly told her how in the last few weeks, just as she was thinking he was now free of Sarah Glass, free to live as he ought, he had met and *married* Mrs Elizabeth Cathcart, widow of the notorious bankrupt. He sounded as though he expected her sympathy. She'd given him sympathy all right: 'I could tell you a thing or two about Henry James Cathcart!' she had said, for Elee had heard a thing or two.

'I'd rather you didn't.' Glass had been annoyed. He had come to her for comfort, not criticism.

'Why did you do it then?' Elee'd gone on. For a moment he had wondered if this woman, who was almost an old friend, could not perhaps be a little jealous. It hardly seemed possible, for this was Elee, and yet . . . He'd tried to mollify her then by explaining that he'd not have dreamt of inflicting Mrs Cathcart's job on anyone he was fond of.

'I could only marry a stranger, surely you see that – someone I did not care overmuch about.'

'But you know nothing of her,' Elee'd persisted. Edward Glass had never been fond of anyone but himself. 'The woman could be *anything* for all you know, and you've left her in charge of your house and children . . .'

'That is precisely why Elizabeth Cathcart was perfect for the task. I could never condemn anyone I *knew* to a life of such boredom as Sarah lived. You haven't met my three daughters – Milla, the middle one . . .'

'King Lear had three daughters and look what happened to him!'

Elee had once been an actress but not, Edward Glass reflected now, one who had played Shakespeare or she would have understood his dilemma rather better. Shakespeare's tragic heroes were unfettered by houses and papier mâché furniture. They were allowed to be elemental, to stand in the world with a minimum of props and get buffeted about by the raging winds. Now, it seemed, a man must have houses built of bricks and mortar and fill them with daughters and knick-knacks, dust on the ornaments, fires in the grate; they had temperamental, God-fearing housekeepers, taxes and operatives to pay, diaries to pack, offices to maintain, wives and accounts to be kept in a proper manner. Man is born free and everywhere you look he is hemmed in and pinned down.

'I have a competent operative, the fastidious Eames, who takes care of everything,' Edward Glass told Elsinora grandly, as if thereby shuffling off the responsibilities Hamlet at Elsinor had done without. Prince Hamlet who had deferred, and disastrously.

'I'm glad to hear it!' How dare the man come here whenever he pleased, whenever he had nowhere better to go? What did he expect by coming to see her and talking to her of Sarah Glass's daughters – Milla, the middle one, indeed!

'I haven't time to quarrel.'

'You and your busy schedule! I only hope the new young wife will be so understanding . . .' As understanding as I have always been, Elee thought but did not say, and Edward Glass departed in a temper. He would not have his busy schedule mocked, even if Elee was almost an old friend.

Next day Elee had wondered why she had been so cross. And now, this Tuesday evening, here he was back again. There'd be a reason of course; Elee glanced at Edward anew. He looked well pleased with himself. Life had treated him kindly in the half-year since their quarrel, you could see that. He would wilt and perish quickly if he ever gave up the work he thrived on. It probably accounted for – and what else could – the ill-advised marriage last winter; Sarah's death had disturbed his work rather than him, she decided. And that was how it should be. Sarah Glass had only been a wife.

Elee stirred her soup; her visitor sat absorbed with himself, saying nothing. Some said the man was a genius and he probably built fine buildings, ones that people admired well enough, but Elsinora Lee did not admire Edward Glass. Always having to prove himself, a little boy lost, determined not to cry. An orphan herself, Elee was hardened to the pain that knew no comfort.

Returning to London and about to embark on the most important project of his career (and also, perhaps, deprived of the adoring chocolate eyes of Esther Szlabin), Edward Glass forgot his resolution not to see Elee again. He had a favour he wanted to ask of her.

'I have been thinking about Sarah,' Edward said, for in thinking of the Paris Grand he couldn't help remembering how Sarah had died leaving nothing worthwhile behind her. Elee jerked the metal spoon she was stirring with but said nothing. Shouldn't Glass be anguishing now over his new wife? Mrs Henry Cathcart, as she had been?

She opened a bag of lentils and tipped too many into the mixture, which quickly coagulated and burnt.

'You ought to have servants,' Edward commented ironically, watching as Elee struggled with the window-catch to let out the smoke. Suddenly not minding whether he left or stayed, she said just to needle him: 'So what's she like, the new Mrs Glass? One hears so little.'

'A nice straightforward woman.'

'She doesn't mind the long absences?'

'That was our arrangement . . .'

'Ah!'

Edward coughed stiffly. 'Actually, Elee, I hardly see her.'

'I know.'

'I thought you said "One hears so little".'

'It is more that one hears so much! Rumour has it – the Great Edward Glass's business is everyone's business; you are talked of.' Elee paused and then added with malicious triumph glittering in her eyes: 'They also say there is soon to be a letter from Windsor Castle . . .'

'A bad habit to get into, listening to gossip . . .'

But Elee could tell Edward was pleased. She was not to know that he was thinking about the New Paris Grand; an extraordinary new edifice on the Strand could hardly go unnoticed at Windsor.

'And Charles Preedy?' she asked, to wipe the smile off his face. 'Perhaps the Fabbricotti Works he is building in Chelsea, with your Mr Myers – a sacked drunkard's – help, may also result in an invitation to Windsor. Everyone thought Glass & Co. would get the job but Preedy must have come in cheaper. Still, you and your new wife may meet him there, eating *petits fours* with Her Majesty – very companionable . . .'

'I did not want or need the Fabbricotti, Elee. With a diary so full – besides, Charles Preedy is a common copyist – there is nothing original in what he does . . .'

'He copies you?'

'I suppose I should be flattered . . .'

'And you are flattered, Edward?'

'Perhaps . . .'

'I mind less than you think,' he added after a pause – for how could he mind about anything when he had that prominent site in the Strand to think of? A site, as Mr Desmond Blaise had said, with infinite possibilities . . .

Elee was gratified to hear what she mistook for weariness now in Edward's voice. Edward was profoundly impatient but Elee detected only an echo of her own tiredness. She decided then that she was no friend of Edward Glass's – she did not wish the man well . . .

Many years ago after Edward had discarded her, Elee had got into the regular habit of paying men to visit the architect to ask for money. The men she had sent were other out-of-work actors, cast aside by life and glad of a bob or two. They'd had easy smiles and addressed him mockingly (if perhaps presciently) as 'Sir Edward'. On the last occasion, when the actor had insinuated that he might call on Sarah Glass at York Street, Edward had decided to teach Elee a lesson once and for all. He'd invited the fellow to talk with him in the privacy of his site office. The site office had been at the top of an eight-storey tower – privacy, indeed. The man had slipped backwards, the foreman, who'd turned round after it happened, said. Elee's foolish acquaintance had not heeded warnings about the wet wooden planks on the scaffolding and his back had been broken as surely as the young Lucius Morgan's mouse long ago, falling eight storeys with scarcely a squeak. Elee had learnt better than to repeat the exercise.

Edward Glass spent the night with Elee. It made a comfortable change from the intense yet repressed passion of the Polish chocolatier's over-sensitive daughter. The delicate Miss Szlabin had been delightful at first but after a while the whiteness of her porcelain skin had seemed too much in danger of bruising. The fragility of her brittle smile had unnerved rather than enthralled him. You did not need to be continually careful with Elee; her bloom had been so buffeted about by life's raging winds, that even without sixteen windows on every floor, nothing new could damage her.

In the morning, Edward Glass said, 'I want you to do something for me, Elee.'

'*Anything*, my dear!' Elee chirped. Now at last for the reason, Elee thought cheerfully, though quite why she owed Edward Glass any favours was beyond her. A man had fallen to his death, and she, who had underestimated Glass, had paid him to do so; a spot of light blackmailing that hadn't worked out. A Polonius behind the Arras ratted on, Elee might have said if she'd ever been in a theatre that did Shakespeare.

'What do you want me to do, Edward?' Elee asked, curious now with curiosity that had never been satisfied.

Once upon a time . . . Glass started to tell her a fairy-tale involving his middle daughter, Milla, the Middle one, the birthday-girl. 'But you see, Elee,' Edward Glass concluded, *'happy ever after* is an impossible injunction for all time.'

'You're telling me!' Elee laughed, the bright morning light showing up the thinness of her hair and casting ugly shadows in the creases of her face.

Milla had a way of making people laugh, Glass thought.

12

Strange Meetings

On Wednesday morning while Edward Glass was asking his favour of Elee, and Elizabeth Glass was ordering seed-cake, Lucy Winnup received a letter in a Glass & Co. envelope.

'Oh, dear!' Poor Mrs Winnup stood helplessly by. 'Where exactly is Newcastle-upon-Tyne, darling? I'm sure I've never been there.'

Mother and daughter got out Burkitt's School Atlas, blew off the dust and took a look. Neither said anything. Mrs Winnup did not ask if Harry Withercott had mentioned his new appointment at the rink last Saturday.

'You don't let your Lucy go *skating*, do you?' Mrs Winnup's acquaintances would cry in horror. It was well known what places of immorality these skating-rinks were.

'Oh, my Lucy can skate most proficiently,' Mrs Winnup would quickly reply, aware that her manner of parenting was regarded as 'progressive' and that there was a fairly undefined feeling in less enlightened quarters that skating in a common public rink was 'not quite the correct thing' for a young lady of Lucy Winnup's breeding.

Harry Withercott was an expert – he had skated on cement at the Prince's Club in Brighton, on marble at the Marble Rink in Clapham, on wood at the Imperial Rink in Hove. In Manchester, where he had gone for a day or two while Edward Glass checked on the final stages of a chocolate manufactory, Harry had fled to the attractions of the pleasure-gardens at Belle Vue. He'd wanted to invite the chocolatier's dark-eyed daughter, but Miss Szlabin had held back and in the end Harry had had to go, rather resentfully, on his own. He'd been wandering about the gardens on his way to the rink when he found himself at a crocodile-tank shaped like an Indian Temple. A mother was loudly instructing her crowd of inattentive offspring from a guidebook: 'They lie prone in the sun or motionless in the sluggish water. Animals and human beings are often seized and dragged down when coming for water. Remember Kipling's lines: "Wait, ah wait, the ripple saith – Maiden wait, for I am death . . ." '

Harry Withercott guffawed. The matron glanced at him with

annoyance and then hurried her children away so that Harry was left completely on his own with the unmoving crocodiles barely visible in the water. An eye blinked and for some reason Harry recalled the unctuous Eames – 'Wait, ah wait, the ripple saith – Maiden wait, for I am death . . .' He could not like the fellow.

Harry shivered and, turning to go, he bumped straight into a cheerful young lady who must have been silently standing close at hand. Like him she carried a pair of skates.

'I didn't see you!' he laughed. 'You were as still as that crocodile.'

'Would you rather 'av bin thrown to 'im or to me?' she responded easily.

'No need to answer that one!' Harry said with an eloquent smile. The girl had an open, blandly pretty face. 'Let's go and find the rink, shall we?'

'Yer; the name's Sylvie, case you was wondering.'

'There was a perfect maple floor at Belle Vue,' Harry told Lucy Winnup the Saturday afternoon he and she had skated their last together.

'He was a good skater,' Lucy sniffed. 'Edward Glass thought much of him.'

'There'll be others,' Mrs Winnup said.

'I wonder what Edward Glass would say if he knew his draughts-man uses Glass & Co. stationery for sending *billets-doux*.'

'He probably stole the stamp,' Mrs Winnup asserted, glad to see her daughter was drying her eyes.

After breakfast, Elizabeth had gone to her room and bolted the door. She took out her rosewood box and helped herself to a large sum of money. She did not suppose she would bother to keep accounts any longer. Shopping she had discovered was a good antidote to emotional upheaval, and shopping she intended to go all afternoon. It was a matter of regret to her that Miss Housecroft insisted on remaining behind with the girls. There could be no denying that they probably did need protecting from the unfortunate presence of the horrible Dr Morgan but Elizabeth would have appreciated company and an extra pair of hands to carry packages.

Henry in agony! Elizabeth stood by the window holding the money for which she had worked so hard. She thought again of

Milla's tatty homemade scrap-book, so different from the one she herself had once possessed.

I suppose I thought that if only I could overlay the past like in Milla's messy album, sticking one paper-scrap right over another, obliterating for ever what had been there before, blotting out Henry – but life doesn't yield itself to a sharp pair of scissors and a big pot of glue. Unfaded by sunlight, overlaid with new fears, feelings only become brighter by being hidden away underneath. The ancient rooks had been right after all, pedantically crawrring above her about the scraps they had bought, instructing her as she snipped and pasted, insisting on the importance of careful arranging and spacing. But for all the expense of her early education, the aunts had taught Elizabeth nothing; some things in life you could only learn for yourself. Ah Milla, poor Milla!

If you remember people and things, Milla had insisted here in this room, *they haven't gone away, have they?* Despite the messiness of her scrap-book, Milla had understood something perhaps that her own aunts had failed to grasp.

Why had Milla been so determined to show her that scrap-book in the first place, coming down here with it as though she had been sent, thrusting it at her so that its contents flew everywhere? It was as if the little girl with the bright-red ear had somehow known.

'I must be going *mad!*' Elizabeth smiled ruefully, feeling a pale image of herself. How tired she must be, standing here at the window; it was only a silly scrap-book. What a headache she had: this was what talking to the child Milla did for you. Her nonsense provoked all kinds of nonsensical thoughts. What was gone, was *gone* and could not be *returned* like some book from a lending-library. Pasted over and blotted out – she should save her energies for the long lists of shopping this afternoon.

As soon as luncheon was over, Elizabeth Glass put on her bonnet, took up her purse and instructed Mary Ann to hail her a cab. She had hardly been gone ten minutes before Mary Ann was summoned from the kitchens (where a seed-cake sat covered with a cloth in the pantry awaiting Dr Morgan's arrival) by a prolonged ring on the front doorbell. Strange!

'Mademoiselle Letellier to see Mrs Glass,' a voice from beneath a mound of fabric informed a dumbfounded Mary Ann. Mlle Letellier had called to deliver, and make final adjustments to, some costumes Elizabeth Glass had ordered several weeks previously. The dressmaker, who had been recommended by Mrs Pinder Simpson, generally kept up her French accent for about half an hour (when to her own relief and that of her customers also, she dropped it by mutual consent). For the rest of the fitting a suppressed cockney twang sufficed, punctuated exotically by a few French phrases of the most elementary school-book variety. The woman probably once had occasion to cross the English Channel and had been greatly affected by the experience. Still, you had to forgive these Continental affectations and absurdities, for a Parisian couturier would have been little different, cost ten times as much and, good heavens, how divinely the little creature could sew! When you consider what some of them are like . . .

Mrs Pinder Simpson had assured Elizabeth Glass that she could not recommend the woman highly enough, which was hardly surprising for Mlle Letellier had promised a generous discount when clients successfully introduced their friends. By offering up Elizabeth Glass, Mrs Pinder Simpson stood to gain a discount on her next hat.

'Mrs Glass has only this minute left.'

'*Mon Dieu!*' exclaimed Mlle Letellier, casting her eyes (since her hands were full) to the heavens. '*Les femmes! Les femmes – elles sont toutes les mêmes!*'

'Were you expected?' Mary Ann asked slightly insolently, for she was impatient with women and this woman was unmistakably trade.

'But, of course,' Mlle Letellier inflected huffily. '*Mais certainement!*'

Emily Housecroft had heard someone arriving at the front door and she hastened downstairs, feeling wrongly but nevertheless perceptively that Dr Morgan was capable of coming to the front door even after all she had said, and earlier than the appointed time if he so chose. As the governess descended into the hall Mlle Letellier's eyes lit up: 'Ah, but you are the same size, *chérie! Sans doute. Eh bien*, we will now do the fitting this afternoon, *certainement*.'

Miss Housecroft was caught off her guard and Mary Ann too was rather taken aback so Mlle Letellier gained her entrance and sailed determinedly past the two women and commenced setting up shop in Mrs Glass's private sitting-room.

'Oh dear!' said Mary Ann and Miss Housecroft together. It was an awkward alliance, on the parlourmaid's part at least. She could not forget how on Friday her Philip had preferred these brown buttoned boots.

Mrs Curzon meanwhile had been waiting as alert to activities upstairs as Miss Housecroft had been half-listening out for movements downstairs. This was meant to be her 'quiet hour' but how could she hope to have a *quiet* hour on a day when Dr Lucius Morgan was again to be expected? She thought of him as the thief who had come, if not in the night, then all the more stealthily for having been encouraged by her – 'Oh, no, I couldn't possibly,' he used to say and she'd hear *herself* urging him to help *himself*, telling him it was money put by that she didn't truly need. The Lord had given and Dr Lucius Morgan had taken away. It was as simple as that. 'You are a very special person,' he had whispered in her ear. 'How you, of all people, dear Lady, came to be a mere housekeeper!' How bitterly now she recalled the airs she had given herself following his syrupy words. How she had disdained the way Sarah Glass had been forced to compose her face so as not to betray amusement. How steadfastly she had ignored the woman's warnings so that later (amidst suspicions that Sarah had joked with her cousin adding Mrs Curzon to her catalogue of Lucius's misdemeanours, the gobbling goose, the wet patch on the floor in church) there had been the cries of 'I warned you but you would not listen!'

Mrs Curzon heard the dressmaker arrive and bustle her way busily in. *Mon Dieu* – Mlle Letellier had been accustomed to make clothes in the old days (were 'the old days' really only last year?) for Sarah Glass. Had Mrs Pinder Simpson, in her eagerness to acquire a cheap hat, mentioned this fact when she recommended the dressmaker to Elizabeth Glass? The shabby mauve taffeta had been an early Letellier creation. The apricot organdie that still hung in a cupboard upstairs was a later work. And now it seemed that just as Mrs Curzon had been Sarah Glass's size but had received none of her old clothes, here was Emily Housecroft having the *second* Mrs Glass's new clothes fitted on her.

Mrs Curzon's heart had leapt into her mouth the day Elizabeth Glass had informed her that Mlle Letellier was coming on Mrs Pinder Simpson's warm recommendation to see about some new outfits and could tea and wafer-biscuits be served at eleven, and thank you! Mrs Curzon had bitten her lip and trembled then, though that first consultation over fashion-plates had passed off without incident. Yet, how these things come back to haunt you.

Suppose Mlle Letellier should talk – gossiping on with her bogus French loquacity – and Mrs Glass become curious? Hadn't Mrs Glass taken it into her head just lately to start asking questions? And if Mrs Glass should be set to wonder about the wardrobes of clothes in Sarah Glass's bedroom? What then? The present Mrs Glass had left the room untouched, not out of superstition but out of laziness, although *someone* had been in (a drawerful of handkerchiefs was missing, and Mrs Curzon had said nothing to anyone, not wanting a discussion that might uncover her own guilt). And what if Mrs Glass should enquire, as many a trouble-making second wife might, after an old mauve taffeta of which Mlle Letellier might have spoken? *What exactly had Sarah Glass been buried in? And who had been responsible?* Mrs Curzon saw the hard earth that had covered Sarah Glass's coffin last December removed spade by spade, the lid prised open and the rotting mauve taffeta removed. This time there would be no lapse of human frailty. The corpse would have her apricot organdie with cuffs of broché silk, the diamond brooch that Edward Glass had given his wife on the birth of their first born, William, would be pinned to her sunken shrivelled bosom. That little round hat of gilt straw, trimmed with black velvet and tea-roses, perched rather foppishly upon what hair still clung to the decomposing skull. Then, only then, could Mrs Curzon have atoned for what she had done – Oh Lord, there appeared a great wonder in heaven; a woman clothed with the sun – well, with apricot organdie at any rate . . .

Mrs Curzon hastened up the steps to discover Emily Housecroft and Mary Ann in the hall, both of them uncertain what to do. Better that Mlle Letellier should chatter to the pasty-faced governess than to the second Mrs Glass herself. Miss Housecroft would never be so bold or indeed have cause to make awkward enquiries afterwards about Sarah Glass's things.

'It would be a service to Madam,' Mrs Curzon reasoned persuasively – Mrs Glass would be needing her new costumes for the Afternoon Tea at Mrs Preedy's on Friday afternoon, wouldn't she? *Répondez, s'il vous plaît!* And what if the dress should be found not to fit? There would be no time for alterations if the alterations were not set in motion this same afternoon.

'But I have an appointment upstairs at four,' protested Emily Housecroft. 'Dr Morgan . . .'

'We will be *finis* long before then.' Mlle Letellier had already spread her handiwork over the backs of chairs. Mrs Curzon took the thin little governess by the elbow and pushed her firmly through into Mrs Glass's sitting-room and pulled the door shut behind her.

Thus Emily Housecroft, who prided herself on her own simple attire, spent the early part of Wednesday afternoon trying on a visiting-dress of claret-coloured Indian cashmere, buttoned down one side with pearl-tinted buttons, fringed with droppers of the same shade and trimmed with loops of black satin ribbon. It was pronounced *parfait*!

Mlle Letellier swallowed her annoyance at Mrs Glass's absence, tucking with a pin here and a tack there as though she had completely forgotten that her mannequin was only the household governess. Once or twice Miss Housecroft felt she ought to remind the woman of this fact, but Mlle Letellier was taking such pains in the exactness of the fit and clearly enjoying the results of her own undoubted artistry – *oh là, là; c'est magnifique; quelle figure!* – it seemed a shame to disabuse her and spoil her fun.

'And now, *chère Mademoiselle*, for the *promenade toilet*,' the dress-maker proclaimed like a magician about to produce something extraordinary out of a box. And this she then did, for the 'promenade toilet' turned out to be not a white rabbit but – as Emily Housecroft had it described to her, for she herself lacked the vocabulary – a *Princess polonaise* draped in large folds and raised by wide hollow pleats trimmed round the lower edge.

'My, you have worked hard.' The embarrassed Miss Housecroft spoke in a tone she often used with Stacia, Milla or Helen. She dreaded to think what the girls must be doing upstairs.

Mlle Letellier, a tape-measure dangling from her mouth like a ridiculous piece of green spaghetti, cackled enthusiastically to herself. Now she produced from yet another bag a bonnet of pink *faille* trimmed with wild roses. Miss Housecroft would have liked to refuse to submit but Mlle Letellier had not sat up sewing all through the night to be deprived of seeing the hat properly exhibited. She nimbly climbed on to a chair and was soon twisting and turning and thrusting hat-pins and feathers into Miss Housecroft's hair. With Frenchish whoops of delight she at last completed her task and then, gripping Miss Housecroft firmly by the elbow, as Mrs Curzon had done, she drew her across the room to examine herself in the glass.

Emily Housecroft stared at the stranger in the mirror. 'That is myself in reverse,' she thought with unaccustomed interest.

It happened that Edward Glass needed a work of reference from his study which he could easily have told Philip Eames to bring back with him next Friday. He was impatient with his plans for the New Paris Grand and happening to pass near the end of York Street and as, after all, it was his own house and he had a moment or two to spare, he decided to call in quickly and fetch the volume.

Edward Glass used his keys and was thankful to find the house quiet. His study was exactly as he could wish and he retrieved the book without much searching. On his way out it occurred to him to put his head round his wife's sitting-room door and wish her 'Good day', for it might be considered more rude not to do so. When he opened the door he saw an attractive enough creature standing with her back to him examining her face and new hat in the mirror.

Mlle Letellier started. '*Monsieur!*' she declared roundly. '*En France, Monsieur*, a gentleman would never walk in on his wife's *assignation* with her *costumier!*'

'Er, no! My humble apologies, Ma'am, and my apologies to you, my dear Elizabeth! I will bid you farewell, I have an urgent *assignation* – an engagement, myself.' So saying, Edward Glass turned haughtily on his heel and retreated as hastily as one can ever leave one's own house.

Emily Housecroft turned and stared at the door which the man had banged behind him. Then she turned back, as if in need of reassurance, to the face that stared critically back at her from the mirror. Edward Glass had mistaken her for his wife, even if only in the mirror in reverse. There seemed no way round that fact, no other explanation.

Mlle Letellier meanwhile began busily packing away the dresses. She kept calm. She was satisfied with an excellent fitting: 'I will put the finishing touches on them this evening, *Madame*, and send round first thing in the morning.'

'Oh, thank you! Er, thank you,' Emily repeated distractedly. However you looked at it, Edward Glass had mistaken *her* for his *wife*!

'What an uncommon thing, to be sure,' Mlle Letellier thought as she left the house weighed down as she had come with all her boxes and bags. It was not the sort of thing you might expect, a woman pretending not to be at home and not to be herself, getting her servants to treat her as though she were someone else and then her husband refusing to play at make-believe and giving the game away. 'Why, if the husband had not walked in I might almost have believed the woman. Poor Madame Glass lost in a looking-glass, *n'est-ce pas!* But what of it – a little mad perhaps, but are we not all of us a little mad?'

Peering out from beneath her bags and boxes, Mlle Letellier saw Edward Glass in the distance talking to a considerably prettier and more colourful young lady than the one she had just left. 'Husbands,' she chuckled. *'Les maris – ils sont tous les mêmes!* But then, if the wife is a little mad, a poor mirror-image of herself, alas, who can blame him?'

Lucy Winnup meanwhile felt furious and thwarted. She felt a fool. She'd thought she had Harry Withercott eating right out of her hand – in the past there had been others completely captivated and under the spell of Lucy Winnup, but all these beaux had managed to slip away. Some had eluded her by marrying – on one occasion the man had actually married a dowdy friend of hers who would never have made such an excellent match had she not been for a while a moon to Lucy Winnup's planet. Some had been called abroad unavoidably, to family estates in Ceylon or Southern Africa. Mrs Winnup seemed to think it was only a matter of Lucy's waiting and choosing. 'Please yourself,' her progressive mother told her, proud that her daughter had not married the first fool who'd come along and that she endeavoured to 'earn her own living' and had taken lessons with all sorts of famous names which she, as a mother, could (and frequently did) mention: Alfred Stone, Maret, Sir Ernest Branagan, Harvey Milot. Herbert James himself had painted Lucy, some years back now. The portrait had been hung at the Academy and been much admired. Mr Winnup, a highly respected auditor with a highly respected City firm had refused to countenance the purchase price. 'Not a sound investment,' he'd said and paid no heed to his wife's and daughter's protestations.

'I'd like to have been an artist,' Mrs Winnup would say. 'It must be where Lucy gets it from.' Lucy would smile and cut her chunky hair to look artistic for her mother, and talk about deadlines and the perils and pitfalls of dealing with galleries and that projected trip to Italy.

The painting trip had been 'projected' for as long as the Winnups could remember but it remained in this fixed state of uncertainty because Lucy did not truly want to go and her mother would have been devastated if her daughter had packed up and departed. Once or twice the discussion about Mr Winnup taking six weeks away from his work and the whole family re-creating their Turnham Green existence in Florence, Rome and Naples had got down to the finer details, but they all knew that Mr Winnup's absence was out of the question. Winnup could not possibly be spared. Winnup's head for figures and his unrivalled skill at detecting errors was in great demand these days.

Lucy sat now amidst her plants and easels, tubes of oil and pans of watercolour and seethed with indignation. She plotted her revenge on the jaunty new draughtsman at Glass & Co.

'I wish you wouldn't go off without a bonnet,' Mrs Winnup protested helplessly as her beloved and only daughter swept past her out through the door and flounced away down the street.

Lucy Winnup knew where Edward Glass lived. Someone had once pointed out the house in York Street and for some unknown reason she had remembered it. It is amazing how useful seemingly useless information can become to a girl like Lucy. When she had first met Harry Withercott – she'd stumbled, he'd helped her up, he'd taken her arm, they'd skated a while, then he'd invited her to take lemonade – Harry told her about his new job with Edward Glass, the Architect.

'Really?' Lucy, like her mother, was impressed with the big names. 'I once saw the house where he lives.'

'I walked in off the street and the next thing I knew,' Harry Withercott said, 'there I was, perched at a drawing-board with the great man himself at my elbow.'

'That must have been quite an experience. I myself have had art classes with Alfred Stone. And once, Herbert James, the Academician himself, painted me – with my clothes on, of course!'

Over recent months, Lucy had asked the odd question about Mamma and Papa Withercott but had been met with a laugh and a deft change of subject. She knew almost nothing about Harry –

except that he'd visited her day after day, talked of everything that didn't pertain to himself, and quite got into her confidences and, she hardly liked to think it, into her affections. And now he had walked out on her. Well, here was Lucy Winnup jolly well going to walk back in on him!

A walk. An omnibus (for Lucy enjoyed to mix socially), another walk, another omnibus (for Lucy is a persistent girl) and she was there. Coming out of the very house that had once been pointed out to her was a man with a book under his arm. He was walking fast so she had had to run.

'Excuse me!' Lucy Winnup opened her eyes wide and appealingly. 'Excuse me for troubling you, but wouldn't you be Edward Glass the Architect, by any chance?'

'Why, my dear!' What man could resist being recognized in the street and gazed at with azure pools the depths of Lucy's? Edward Glass had no wish to linger just then in York Street, he needed distance between himself and the awkwardness of the last few minutes in his wife's sitting-room. 'I am indeed Edward Glass but I am also in a great hurry – you are most welcome, if you have a mind to it and can spare the time, to walk a little way with me.'

'Oh, certainly!' Lucy skipped eagerly alongside him.

'Do take my arm!'

Milla, absorbed just then in another book by her despised Pasha, missed this interesting little scene. Heaven only knows what she would have made of it if she'd been standing at the upper-landing window: arm in arm! Sharp as a sewing needle Mlle Letellier witnessed the spectacle though, from a distance maybe and half-obscured by her bundles of toile and velveteen roses, but seen quite clearly nevertheless. '*Oh, là, là* . . .'

13

Knick-Knacks, Seed-Cake & All the Horrors of the Universe Contained in One Chapter

Elizabeth Glass shopped. She bought so much she had to arrange for shops to deliver her purchases by carrier to the house. She walked along Oxford Street and down Regent Street and she worked systematically through her lists, handing over cash from her rosewood box as though she could not get rid of it fast enough. She was as a woman possessed.

'The Room that awaits us in the House of Death is as a Parlour packed with Knick-knacks . . .' Thus preached Dr Lucius Morgan (Cantab.) at advertised gatherings in Wales, in Lancashire, in North Yorkshire and in rainy villages on the Pennines. He liked a challenge. These were not easy pickings, not flushed susceptible London folk, the Lady Blouviers and Mrs Curzons of this world, but hardened sceptics who fully knew the value of money but who nevertheless had a fear of that Other Side of the wall with the door in it – Death.

Lucius Morgan, with the key in his pocket, stripped away that fear: 'We are all *equal* in death,' and if the Living but knew the secrets of the Dead they would know how to achieve Equality in *this* World also. Why were corpses all equal when, with breath in their lungs, they had not been? This was a notion that appealed to the downtrodden men and women who toiled on the land and sweated in the smoky manufactories. The breasts of the oppressed swelled with indignation as the pitch of Dr Morgan's voice rose: *Life* may not have been as good for some as it was for others, but in *Death* we could *all* be Kings, for whatever difference it might make . . .

Death in Dr Morgan's hands became somewhere you could imagine going with a valise like on an organized Cook's Tour. You'd know what to expect from a quick dip into the Baedeker. You could almost look forward to the agreeable Death purveyed by Dr Morgan (safe, and subject to description, no need for wordless fears). Everything amicably settled in advance by correspondence: you knew what you were getting for your money even before you set out.

People sometimes tried to abuse the good Dr Morgan, accusing him of all kinds of sharp practices, but for every detractor who carped, countless came forward of their own accord, vehemently affirming the strength and veracity of his powers. The Good Lord Himself had met with opposition *on earth*, but He had not had the benefit of Lady Blouvier's unfailing support. Lady Blouvier had taken photographs. Photographs were sold at Dr Morgan's meetings and printed in *News from the Other Side*. You could not argue with authorized photographs the way you could dispute both bills and the Bible.

Lady Blouvier's photographs pictorially demonstrated Dr Morgan's comforting assertion that the Dead are often better off than the Living; Death is nothing to be afraid of – quite the contrary, in fact: *The Room that awaits us in the House of Death is as a cosy Parlour packed with Knick-knacks we might never have been lucky enough to enjoy while we yet lived . . .*

Although this was not a dictum with which Edward Glass's *second* wife was familiar (Sarah had laughed her head off), nevertheless the lucky Elizabeth had devoted most of the afternoon to purchasing knick-knacks for the parlour back in York Street. Flower-pot stands, card cases, work-baskets to look pretty on the side-tables, scent-bottles in brilliantly cut and coloured glass, a pretty pocket-watch and a bead reticule to keep it in. Framed pictures of every shape and size; she bought a stuffed dog on a whim, paper-scraps for Milla, magazine racks for her magazines, bead pin-cushions, fire-guards, letter cases and a cheerful clutter of automaton canaries. With a hint of self-irony she wondered how she could have lived thus far without these things. There seemed no end to the whatnots you could buy if you set your mind to it.

Elizabeth, at the end of Regent Street now, decided to revisit the site of her momentous encounter with Edward Glass, amid the urns and statuary in the Grecian tea-room at the Café Royal. He and she had gone there in a hired cab the first time she had been invited to his house. The second time there had been Mrs Curzon's fish-paste sandwiches and a proposal of marriage. Her decision to return to the Café Royal now was not so much sentimental as due to the fact that her feet were tired and her ankles swollen slightly from the unaccustomed exercise. She needed to sit down.

To say that Elizabeth stopped in her tracks when she saw Edward

Glass entering the revolving doors of the Café Royal before her with Lucy Winnup on his arm, would be to exaggerate. Mrs Glass merely faltered, and without changing the pace of her walk, altered course and took herself back up Regent Street and hastily re-entered the new Liberty's store, resolving to take coffee there instead.

The second Mrs Glass felt dizzy at the nastiness that had been so narrowly averted. Her head span. She had only seen her husband at the last moment, it was impossible to believe that he had not seen her, and yet, and it scarcely seemed credible, she was also sure that there had been no jot of recognition when their eyes met. Edward Glass had not recognized her. She had been just another woman out shopping in Regent Street, another woman like any other.

Last Christmas, Mrs Preedy had said to Elizabeth Cathcart: 'The man is insufferably arrogant – his reputation far exceeds his worth, but there you are!'

Charles Preedy had also discussed Edward Glass. 'The man will overreach himself one day, you see if he doesn't!'

'I'm sure you're right, Charles,' his wife had eagerly agreed.

The man had not interested Elizabeth – she had been nothing if not practical – and during Christmas dinner at the Preedys and tea subsequently at the Café Royal she had paid Edward Glass very little attention. Far less attention apparently than had the prying Preedys. To Elizabeth he had simply been a 'dead cert', a shield she had found against poverty and against her awful memories of Henry.

Henry!

The second Mrs Glass looked at the dregs of coffee in her cup: *If love is said to be*, oh sweetest sugar! She knew now, with sudden and complete conviction, that what she desired above all things was not a parlourful of knick-knacks but another meeting with Dr Morgan. She needed to speak to him: about Henry James Cathcart. She had had no rest *and she would get no rest*, until she had done so. Elizabeth Glass drew from her new bead reticule the pocket-watch she had bought not an hour before. The jeweller had set it at the right time – the watch's hands stood at four o'clock precisely. Even now Dr Morgan was probably arriving at her house to eat seed-cake. As she could not possibly return home in time, she ordered another pot of coffee and sat in solitary splendour, content in her realization that Dr Morgan must have intended things to turn out this way. She had put up resistance and had held out as long as she could, but in the end she had been drawn back: *you will want to listen to me and to Henry. Then you have only to summon me and I will come!* Elizabeth would summon him; Dr Morgan *must* come.

'Well, I do declare!' someone across the room whispered. 'If that isn't the *second* Mrs Edward Glass . . .'

'We saw him just now, with someone rather dishy!'

'No wonder she looks so pinched, it must be such a headache . . .'

'Poor thing! If I ever caught *my* husband . . . '

'And look at all those bags of shopping. Whatever can the unhappy woman have been buying?'

Mlle Letellier's departure left Emily Housecroft peculiarly distraught and Mrs Curzon peculiarly exhausted.

'I will have my quiet hour now,' the housekeeper told Mary Ann. She poured herself a glass of something strengthening to help her snooze. It helped her snore.

With Miss Housecroft downstairs talking to Mrs Glass's dressmaker, the three girls squabbled. Summer holidays which were spoken of at school as something pleasurable to look forward to were utterly boring here, and yet school next week was nothing to look forward to either.

Pasha had not replied. Milla's anger with Pasha had increased. She was now reading about the Reverend Buckfast-Pinch, a halfhearted missionary who went among the natives of a mangrove swamp ineptly preaching and passing round a collection-plate, until an alligator got him. He was last seen as a large black shoe poking out of the reptile's jaw as it turned tail and disappeared down into the rippling depths of the swamp. This was the picture on the cover, and the cover was the best thing about the book.

'If Jesus didn't save the missionary from being eaten for breakfast why would He ever save anyone?' Milla argued. 'I'm sure if you didn't know about sin, you wouldn't miss it like chocolate or muffins.'

'Don't be so greedy!' Stacia said.

'Not to mention blasphemous!' chorused a disapproving Helen.

'If sin is so miserable that we say "miserable as sin" I'm sure it would be better to live in a mangrove swamp and never know it existed. Even if you might get eaten . . .'

Stacia flounced out of the room. She was fed up with Milla and Helen and all the sillinesses that went on and on. Milla argued for the sake of it and Helen encouraged her by taking her seriously. When Miss Housecroft came back upstairs useless tasks would be found to keep them busy. Stacia wandered idly down into the house and went into the room that had been their mother's and where she had once stolen handkerchiefs. She shut the door quickly behind her.

Towards four o'clock, Dr Morgan, preparing to leave Lady Blouvier's handsome Mayfair mansion, was startled to see a carriage draw up. Even before it had properly halted Lady Blouvier swept out in full Alpine dress. She was followed by a crumpled-looking Delia, clearly the worse for wear. Lady Blouvier immediately began shouting instructions for their numerous crates to be unloaded. Then she caught sight of Dr Morgan.

'Lucius!' Lady Blouvier pounced on him in delight. 'What a perfectly glorious homecoming! My house has been honoured in my absence by your presence.' She accepted the modest bunch of asters from her own garden which Dr Morgan, in his astonishment at seeing her, had quite forgotten he was holding.

'A pleasant change from edelweiss!' She kissed him enthusiastically on both cheeks.

'Oh dear!' said Dr Morgan, gasping for breath and mindful only of having left Mrs Eames (her of the ninepenny *table d'hôte*) inside the Blouvier residence and the lunch they had eaten off the Blouvier crested dinner-service with Blouvier crested silver cutlery not yet cleared away, for he and she had had better things to do once they had dined. Lady Blouvier would probably not feel her house to have been honoured by the lavender-scented presence of Mrs Eames. He had not anticipated his patroness back from the Alps until next month. 'I was just going to visit my nieces – actually my cousin's children, whatever relation that makes them . . .'

'Not the Glass family? Not poor Sarah Glass's miserable little orphan-girls?'

'Even they!' Dr Morgan replied grandly. 'But I am expected at four. Perhaps, dear Lady,' he said, thinking on his feet, an activity he was good at, 'perhaps dear Hildegard, you would care to accompany me?' It might be as well if Lady Blouvier did not enter her abode just at present and encounter a Flora Eames *déshabillée* and the left-overs from luncheon.

Lady Blouvier drew out the bulky timepiece which formed that bulky third lump in her already bulky bosom and which had been the subject of much ribald speculation in foreign parts, fortunately expressed in foreign tongues. The remarkable timepiece revealed now that it was precisely a quarter of an hour to the hour!

'Lucius, there is not a second to lose! Delia! Delia, have the footman separate out my apparati – we are going straight to York Street on a job. Dear Lucius is to help the Dear Departed Sarah Glass converse with her daughters and we must be there to Bear Witness. If Sarah Glass is to Return to York Street this afternoon, the least we can do is be there.'

Before Dr Morgan knew it, he had been thrust into the Blouvier carriage and the skinny Delia squeezed in precariously beside him. Luggage needed in Switzerland, but not for this enterprise, was hurriedly unloaded. The 'apparati' – sundry cameras, tripods, lenses, plates, etc. – were put back on board. Lady Blouvier seated herself opposite the Doctor and her daughter. Having remarked frankly what a handsome couple they made, she commanded her driver to 'Drive on!'

'What a homecoming, dear Lucius! I adore snow-covered mountains but there is *nothing* to beat a thick London fog. All that Alpine fresh air, so very un-British. And Wales, dear Lucius, how was that far-flung post of Empire? We quite thought you must have forgotten us and met with some new interest, didn't we, Delia?' Lady Blouvier leant forward and tapped Dr Morgan severely on the knee with her knitted steel bag. He yelped in pain as once years ago his little pet mouse, its back snapped neatly in two, had yelped before keeling over to die in his ministering hand.

The carriage delivering Dr Lucius Morgan to tea with Sarah Glass's daughters drew up in York Street at precisely four, against all the odds (traffic never moved smoothly when Lady Hildegard Blouvier was underway). This was punctuality of which Edward Glass himself would have approved. Lady Blouvier climbed down first.

'My word, what a poky house!' She'd forgotten how ugly York Street was. 'Fancy an *architect* living here!'

'Who has he got with him?' Milla and Helen stood together watching the visitors arrive. Miss Housecroft had not mentioned anyone apart from Dr Morgan.

'Where's Stacia? Where's Miss Housecroft?' Helen was anxious. 'They ought to be up here . . .'

'All the more cake for us!' Milla said. 'Come on, we'd better not stay in the window or they might see us.'

'Like Creepy Eames did . . .'

'You would never have made it for four, Lucius, had we not arrived home in time to lend you our conveyance,' Lady Blouvier observed smugly. 'What luck!'

'What a happy chance,' Dr Morgan agreed between closed teeth. He hoped Mrs Eames would have the good sense to betake herself back to her suburb by the time he and the Blouviers returned.

'We are to enter by the side door.' Dr Morgan beckoned them to the spot where Mr Luscombe was wont to prop his free-standing bicycle on Monday afternoons. Delia struggled with a crate of equipment, the intrepid Lady Blouvier threw everything with a strap attached over her broad shoulders and ordered Dr Morgan to follow on with what was left. The asters, which he had intended for Mrs Glass, and if she wasn't there for the other one who had come downstairs later and invited him to tea, were left behind crushed on a seat. The carriage was ordered to wait. The horses stomped their great hoofs impatiently.

Mary Ann showed the visitors up to the girls' quarters. Hopefully the old fleabag would snore her way through the whole of the afternoon. Mary Ann had seen to it that Mrs Curzon's glass of fortified wine had been rather more fortified than usual.

Milla and Helen were there on their own, picking at the seeds in the seed-cake. Lady Blouvier without further ado commenced setting up her various cameras around the room and adjusting the light-levels by vigorously opening and closing the curtains. 'What a shabby house!' she repeated. There was dust on everything and the children looked none too healthy. With any luck they would pass away shortly and Dr Morgan would have a further chance to practise his arts.

Emily Housecroft heard the visitors arrive and hastened upstairs. She had lingered in Mrs Glass's sitting-room following Mlle Letellier's departure. Although she had rearranged her straw-coloured hair which had been pulled this way and that by the hats, it had not been so easy to order her mind. What could she ever say to Mrs Glass? She would offer to hand in her notice, of course, and perhaps this was the excuse she had been looking for to leave, but where would she go if she left straight away? It was too soon – there was work still to be done. What would happen next time Edward Glass visited and realized his dreadful mistake? Surely a husband ought at least to know what his own wife looks like?

Downstairs Mrs Curzon was snoring. She dreamed she possessed a thousand earthenware jelly moulds. And what a headache they were, for Cora refused point-blank to dust them.

Emily Housecroft arrived upstairs to find Mary Ann handing round slices of picked-at seed-cake. There had not been time to clear away her work and she noticed that all kinds of brass instruments and lenses had been dumped on top of her precious papers.

Delia Blouvier, suffering from the effects of a blustery English Channel, reclined weakly and refused the dry cake with as much disgust as if she believed it to contain rat-poison. Lady Blouvier, however, stalked round the room munching heartily and blowing mouthfuls of crumbs as she erected the 'apparati'. Stacia was nowhere to be seen – where *was* the child? Dr Morgan endeavoured to remind Milla and Helen of things they could not remember and things they had never known.

Milla was simultaneously questioning the poor man uncomfortably: 'But were you Helen's godfather? Was there a Christening, then? There must be a certificate. Did you give her a silver cup? Do I have a godfather, too? And Stacia? What about dear William?'

'Girls, girls!' Miss Housecroft sought to intervene. 'Give your poor uncle a chance! Why don't we all sit down?' Miss Housecroft glanced round the familiar room at the unfamiliar faces and decided it was time to take charge. She observed rather pointedly that 'introductions were obviously called for'.

Lady Blouvier turned on Miss Housecroft dramatically. 'Well, for a kick-orff, young lady, who in the name of bally Belinda Belshaw are *you*?' Lady Blouvier prided herself on being able to deal with the lesser orders, and in Lady Blouvier's world only Her Majesty and a handful – but not many – of the Royal Family were not of a lesser order than she.

Helen said: 'Miss Housecroft is our governess.'

'But I thought you Glass girls went to school!'

'We do,' Milla said.

'How can you possibly need a governess if you go to school? What an unnecessary expense! No wonder Dear Sarah intends to Return this afternoon! The *second* Mrs Glass, whoever can she be? I certainly have never had call to meet the creature – and if this is the way she conducts her affairs I'm not sure that I'd care to. Entertaining her guests in the school-room!' She gestured disdainfully towards Miss Housecroft's books and papers. 'Making them use the side entrance. Serving up the most unappetizing cake – when I think what a Blouvier tea-trolley consists of! What kind of household have you brought me to, Lucius?'

Dr Morgan began to stammer apologies.

'This *second* Mrs Glass, what can she be like?'

'She's all right,' said Milla, but Lady Blouvier appeared not to hear.

'*Second* wives are little better than deceitful poachers and should all be transported to Botany Bay forthwith. There could be a gallery of them at Madame Tussaud's. I'll wager the creature is out at this very minute living it up on money that should rightly be spent on these poor deprived orphans. I shall have to have the woman investigated . . .'

'I think – ' Miss Housecroft tried to say. It was after all her school-room that they were now sitting in, her own employer who was being rudely castigated, and she herself who had been the one to invite Dr Morgan with no mention made – or allowed for in the size of the seed-cake – of any other visitors: 'I think, Ma'am, things have got out of hand . . .'

'How dare you *I think, Ma'am* at me, whoever you may be when you're at home!' Lady Blouvier retorted.

'She *is* at home!' Milla spoke out boldly.

'Yes, she's Miss Housecroft, our governess; I told you!' Helen added.

'Indeed? Well, I'll tell *you* something. In the days when my Delia had governesses not one of them would have dared to address me in such an insolent fashion or stand by while a child answered me back to my face. Besides, there are only two of you – *one of the creatures is missing . . .*'

'Stacia . . . '

'Where is she?' Lady Blouvier demanded. How could they get started unless *all* the subjects were in attendance?

'I really don't know,' Emily Housecroft said helplessly.

'You *don't know*?' Lady Hildegard Blouvier drew herself up and out. 'Do you mean to tell me you have lost one of your charges? I will see that you are sacked on the spot! I will see that you are run to ground and never allowed to practise your miserable profession again. This time next week you will be plying your wares, such as they are, on the street.'

Emily Housecroft had never experienced anyone like Lady Hildegard Blouvier before. She burst into tears.

Mary Ann stood grinning from ear to ear. This would serve Button-boots right for trying to get her claws into Philip Eames.

Dr Morgan turned and winked at the parlourmaid and she, with an uncanny feeling that Dr Morgan knew what she'd been thinking, blushed slightly and cut the man an extra large slice of what little was left of the cake.

'How kind!' he whispered and was about to say something else to her when . . .

It was then, as the tea-party floundered and the governess wept, that there came from below a scream that rose through the house like a corkscrew of smoke, piercing every atom of the air as it soared. It was a roar of animal terror. A long ear-splitting shriek, a wail that was absolute and contained all the horrors of the universe. It was the scream of a soul bared on the rack in naked torment, a guilty secret torn open, its innards ripped out, a guilty conscience routed. All the fear and anguish known and not known on Earth was contained in that one long penetrating Gothic scream. The occupants of Miss Housecroft's sitting-room froze as though sharp nails riveted them to the floor. They stood where they stood, petrified . . .

Mrs Curzon, rousing herself drowsily from her fortified slumber, had heard someone moving about above her. She'd hurried up the basement stairs sure now that something was not as it should be. The clock in the hall (item 196: she had wound the clock every evening for twenty years before anyone had seen fit to itemize the task on a list) stood at past four o'clock. Likely as not Dr Morgan would already be upstairs consuming the seed-cake Mrs Glass had requested and the pudding-like Cora had baked. As a befuddled

Mrs Curzon puffed her way up the stairs to the first floor, she sensed someone above her on the landing. She looked again and saw that the person standing there was none other than Sarah Glass. The Dear Departed Sarah Glass as Sarah Glass should have been, and but for Mrs Curzon would have been, arrayed to meet her Maker. Sarah Glass in the apricot organdie she herself had so vilely, undeservedly coveted, the diamond brooch that commemorated William's birth sparkling defiantly on her bosom. Sarah Glass looking expressionlessly, unspeakingly down at her, straight through her even. Sarah Glass, mounting the stairs, Brought Back from the Dead by Dr Lucius Morgan. Sarah Glass who had come to accuse.

Mrs Curzon covered her ears with her hands to block out the accusations. She did not need to hear them. She knew of what she stood accused and she shrieked as though demons were tearing the sound from her throat and then she fled, her heart thumping, to the safety of the kitchen where she threw herself on her knees on the cold stone floor and clasping her two hands so tightly together that they bruised she prayed for all she was worth: 'Look mercifully on my Dark Deeds, oh Lord, for I am horribly punished already – I have given my life to this horrible house, I have given my money to a horrible man, the Darkness was theirs but the Deeds were mine – I am but a housekeeper with itemized lists: I knew no better, I did no better . . .'

Stacia meanwhile was delighted by the effect she had had on Mrs Curzon. Swathed in garments that were pinned precariously and smelt of moth-ball, she continued primly up the staircase and opened the door on the seed-cake party. She practised her practised curtsey.

Lady Blouvier, camera ready as always for anything, pulled the trigger on the exposure cord. Lucius Morgan gasped as though a fierce farmyard goose were bearing down on him.

'Death,' hissed the well-schooled Stacia Glass, enjoying the gapes of her astonished audience, 'is as a Parlour packed with Knick-knacks. But who, I would like to know, Dr Morgan, is to do all the dusting? The second Mrs Glass will *not* have dust on the ornaments! It says so, item 73 on Mary Ann's list.'

'Dusting! In the House of Death!' Lady Blouvier exclaimed aghast. 'I never thought of that.'

Full of admiration for her sister's perfect performance, Milla started vigorously clapping. Helen gawped.

'Is this some kind of charade?' Miss Housecroft asked, dry-eyed now but weary. The girls had not told her they were planning theatricals for Helen's godfather.

Mary Ann pressed a hand over her mouth; she couldn't wait to tell Cora: Stacia, Milla and Helen had gone too far this time – there were bound to be repercussions and hopefully Old Button-boots would catch it for weeping in front of visitors and encouraging Stacia to terrify Mrs Curzon. With her free hand Mary Ann offered Stacia the measly last slice of measly seed-cake – Mrs Glass really was a mean old so-and-so! One miserable dry little cake to feed this lot and far from there being any over for Downstairs, there was barely enough to go once round up here. Mary Ann had seen the rosewood box and knew that it rattled a lot when shaken. The box had always been moved after Mrs Glass had locked herself in her room and presumably the little silver key Mrs Glass wore on a piece of ribbon round her neck fitted the rosewood box. What Mary Ann couldn't do with a rosewood box full of money! What Mary Ann wouldn't do *for* a rosewood box full of money!

Lady Hildegard Blouvier fixed another plate on to the back of her camera, and with the presence of mind that had made her famous worldwide she took her finest photograph of the afternoon: *The Spirit of Sarah Glass Greedily Cramming the Remains of a Seed-cake into her Mouth.* 'Dr Morgan,' she exclaimed with unbridled enthusiasm, 'you are a remarkable man!'

He knew now that, should his indiscretions in her house during her recent absence come to light, he was certain of the good Lady's forgiveness. Remarkable men were permitted indiscretions, indeed they were expected, if not demanded, of them. Dr Morgan smiled modestly and thanked Miss Housecroft for the tea. He thought perhaps they ought to be going, most pleasant to see her again and be sure to give his Sincere Regards to the *inestimable* Mrs Glass.

'Come on, Delia!' Lady Blouvier sang out. 'Pull yourself together, girl, help me pack the apparati away!' Folding up a tripod and picking a caraway seed from between her large front teeth, Lady Blouvier paused to examine young Stacia Glass through her eye-piece.

'I take it you are . . .'

'I am Stacia Glass!' Stacia said in as haughty a voice as Lady Blouvier herself could have managed.

Lady Blouvier beamed. This was the kind of orphan she might do something for. She'd need a fresh distraction after the thrills of the Continent; contretemps with the London traffic were hardly sufficient excitement for a woman of Hildegard Blouvier's energy and temperament. Like Philip Eames, Lady Blouvier saw nothing in Milla or Helen to interest her. She presented Stacia Glass with one of her majestic calling-cards.

Poor Stacia's eyes nearly popped out of her head: 'Lady Hildegard Blouvier,' she read with amazement. A fairy-godmother, after all! Stacia Glass glanced down at her slippers . . .

'You will be hearing from me, Stacia!' Lady Blouvier swept from the room, taking a chunk out of the doorpost with one of her boxes as she went. 'Lucius, my dear, we have done a good afternoon's work.'

When the visitors had departed Emily Housecroft turned to Stacia and said: 'You had better get those things off!' There had been altogether too much dressing up this afternoon, she decided. It did nobody any good.

'There won't half be trouble,' Mary Ann tittered as she collected up the plates. 'I'm glad I'm not in your shoes, any of you . . .' and her eyes, directed at Miss Housecroft's brown buttoned boots, silently said, 'And especially not in your horrid ones, Miss!'

Miss Housecroft quietly told Mary Ann that she could go: *the tea-party was over*. Milla and Helen still sat as though turned to stone, their mouths wide open. Stacia stared at the enormous gold-edged calling-card:

> Lady Hildegard Blouvier,
> Eulalia House,
> Eden Gardens,
> Mayfair.

It was a dream come true: You *shall* go to the ball! 'I wonder when I'll hear from her?' she mused.

'Oh, I wouldn't expect too much,' Miss Housecroft said immediately. She sounded, and felt, very tired.

'You're welcome to her,' Milla said, laughing now. 'Her bosom was like one of Mrs Curzon's jelly moulds.'

'Yes,' added Helen. 'She was horrible.'

'Don't be so silly!' Stacia said indignantly. 'How can she be horrible with a card like this? Look, it's printed *in gold* and there's an embossed crest . . .'

'Now do stop squabbling, girls,' Miss Housecroft begged. She did not feel well. 'What an afternoon!'

'Yes!' Stacia glowed. 'The most wonderful afternoon of my entire life . . .' She sat down at the Conrad & Taylor Upright and, deciding it was time to make her peace with Chopin, she started to play a *fantaisie-impromptu*. Milla, Helen and Miss Housecroft were rather startled. Stacia looked back over her shoulder at them and paused, her hands still on the keys.

'My!' said Miss Housecroft, who had been unaware that Stacia could play quite well when she chose. 'The piano lessons have not been entirely wasted.'

'But what a shame Mr Luscombe will never hear the results of his labours,' thought Milla sadly, for here was another private joke the poor piano-teacher would be unable to share.

Stacia narrowed her eyes scornfully, tossed her head high and finished the piece with a triumphant flourish. All that curtseying in front of the mirror – it was amazing what you can make believe to happen: who knew what magic might not take place one day soon at Eulalia House in Mayfair, *capriccioso e vivace?*

14

The Aftermath

'What do you imagine will happen now?' Milla asked, for surely something had to happen. There had to be an aftermath – didn't there?

'I dread to think!' said Helen excitedly, for *she* had done nothing wrong. Mrs Curzon had been very angry.

'I wonder when I'll hear from Lady Blouvier?' This was the only aftermath that interested Stacia. 'She said I'll be hearing from her but she didn't say *when*.'

Miss Housecroft felt irritated and went downstairs again to see if Mrs Glass had returned yet. She hadn't, but a letter had arrived. Miss Housecroft could not imagine who could be writing to Miss Milla Glass. 'Perhaps it is from *your* godfather!' she said, joking weakly, for like Milla she nervously contempleted the storm that must come.

'It'll be from Pasha,' Milla ripped open the envelope. She saw at once that the letter was rather short:

Dear Milla Glass,

What a happy surprise to receive a letter from such a devoted reader! Since you do not live far away and since I see so few young people these days, I would like to invite you to tea on Friday afternoon. You will of course come accompanied and we will talk of distant lands. Thank you once again for your happy words.
I remain, etc., etc.
Mrs Ruby Smith
(Pasha)

'Happy words! Devoted reader! Ruby Smith!' Milla was flabbergasted. An address in Acton was given, but yes, the envelope was certainly addressed to her: Miss Milla Glass . . . 'I don't think she – Pasha *is* a woman – could have read *my* letter at all!' Milla declared. 'It took me ages to write; I thought out every word and told Pasha what I really thought.'

'I wouldn't invite you to tea if you'd sent that letter to me.' Stacia gave a haughty sniff; she had been certain Pasha would not reply. She looked disdainfully at the scruffy note on cheap bluish paper that Milla was so excited about. She herself now awaited a letter inscribed on thick crinkly parchment and sent in a gold-edged envelope with a gold-embossed crest on the flap. 'Mrs Ruby Smith sounds very *common*.'

'Ruby Smith!' Milla's eyes opened wide and she saw now a sprinkling of rubies sparkling red amongst the gold doubloons that spilt from the old wooden chest. A parrot squawked angrily and Milla sighed; once again Stacia had been proved right: *Pasha* had *not* truly replied! In the first instance, a letter from Mrs Ruby Smith in Acton was not *exactly* a reply from Pasha care-of the Publishers and secondly, you could hardly call something a 'reply' to a letter when it took no account of what had been written *in* that letter.

Miss Housecroft was mystified. Why Milla, who was so con-temptuous of Pasha's books, had apparently written a letter, when it was difficult enough getting the child to do her school homework, and why she had wanted to get herself invited to Acton to discuss 'distant lands' was baffling. For the first time since she had been here, Miss Housecroft recalled Mrs Curzon's warning: 'The child is wilful.'

'You'd have thought Pasha'd be too busy,' Helen said.

'Either to write or invite you to tea,' Miss Housecroft agreed.

'I will go!' Milla said, as though someone had suggested she might not. 'I have to go *this* Friday because then we'll be back at school. Pasha and I have things to discuss.'

'Mmm,' Miss Housecroft took the letter. 'I had better come with you,' the governess decided, seeing this immediately as a way to avoid accompanying Mrs Glass to Mrs Preedy's (the Afternoon Tea and little entertainment was also to be held this Friday). They had only just had one disastrous tea-party. Surely she was not employed to attend tea-parties?

'And us?' Helen asked.

'Mrs Smith, Pasha, won't want an invasion.'

'No, I'm the one that wrote the letter. I'm the one invited. I don't want you two there joining in and telling me not to be silly. Pasha and I have business to discuss,' Milla said, and then added fiercely: 'On our own.'

'Business!' Stacia chortled. 'Business!'

'Yes, *business*. I think someone should tell her adventure books should be adventurous . . .'

'Yes, Milla, and that the Unknown should be unknowable – you *have* told us before,' Miss Housecroft remarked edgily.

'I'd like to meet Pasha,' Helen whined.

'Well, you can't!' Milla was adamant.

'Who'd want to go to Acton, anyway?' Stacia scoffed, for Stacia had dreams of Mayfair.

'You can stay here and keep creepy Eames company,' Milla observed with a twinkle. 'He can doff his hat again. You could even curtsey to him, Stacia, or play him a Chopin waltz!'

'I might go down and tell him about the stamp you stole,' Stacia whispered loudly, but fortunately Miss Housecroft did not hear.

'Perhaps Dr Morgan will come to tea again,' Helen suggested. The three girls giggled. Miss Housecroft said nothing. They had not yet had the Aftermath from today's visit.

Milla grinned. She looked forward to the fuss now, life was more exciting, things had hotted up. Stacia too was full of hope. As Milla's unlikely reply from Pasha had come, then why not the promised invitation to Eulalia House, Eden Gardens, Mayfair?

Miss Housecroft pretended to read her copy of the *Schoolmistress*. In fact she was scanning the advertisements looking for another job. She was not sure how much longer she could stand the tension. Eventually Mrs Glass would ask to see her. What would she say? How would she explain everything that had happened here this afternoon?

Cora put her head round the door. 'Mrs Glass wants yer!' she said. Miss Housecroft suppressed a sigh and laid her paper aside. Milla picked it up when she had gone.

'Yer've been having fun up here, I hear,' Cora said.

'You have done what you came to do, Cora!' Stacia replied in an imperious manner Lady Blouvier would approve of. 'As you can see, *we* are busy.'

'Yer, busy doing nuffing,' Cora smirked, and went back downstairs. Proper little madams; deserved all that was coming to them . . .

'Miss Housecroft takes her job seriously,' Milla remarked as she flipped through the *Schoolmistress*. 'I wonder why she doesn't teach in a proper school. She'd earn more with more pupils.'

'Perhaps she likes us?' Helen suggested doubtfully.

'Or Mrs Glass?' Stacia made a face. Was it possible to like Mrs Glass?

Milla thumbed the pages idly. She did not notice the job advertisements that filled the inside-front and inside-back pages. 'Listen to this.' She read from a column aptly entitled 'Chit-chat': ' "The Princess of Wales possesses a tea service consisting of sixty pieces, on each of which is a different photograph of herself . . ." '

'I wonder if Lady Blouvier will stick a photograph of *me* on a tea-cup,' Stacia said. Tea-time at Eulalia House in Eden Gardens, Mayfair, must surely be a sumptuous affair.

'You will be hearing from me, Stacia!' That was all very well, Stacia thought, but *when* exactly would she hear? *What* exactly would she hear?

Milla, full of herself now, continued reading aloud: ' "Sixty thousand elephants are slaughtered every year in Africa for the sake of their ivory. This seems terribly wholesale, for every complete set of billiard balls the tusks of three elephants are used and this is only one branch of the ivory trade." All those ivory things Mrs Glass has, it's disgusting – I shall tell her!'

'She wouldn't take any notice,' Stacia said.

'Sixty thousand elephants – every year! It's a wonder there are any left.'

'They don't shoot the ones in the zoo.'

'I wouldn't like to be an elephant in the zoo, even if you don't get shot. They can't like being cooped up in cages.'

'Any more than we do . . .'

'They cry for their mothers.'

'Without Mrs Curzon having to prod them in church . . .'

'I wish we could do *something* for the elephants.'

'Conrad & Taylor ought to be ashamed of themselves cutting up elephants for keys. It's horrible playing the piano anyway but when you think it's really a dead elephant.'

'Don't be so silly, Milla.'

'Mr Luscombe is as bad as the elephant hunters – he's only in it for the money.'

'In what?'

'Piano, stupid! Teaching Chopin . . .'

'Pretending to teach . . .'

147

'Like Miss Housecroft . . .'

'I wonder why she buys this newspaper.'

'Because she's a schoolmistress, sort of.'

'A schoolmistress?'

'If she isn't, what is she?'

The girls fell silent.

'She's an enigma,' Milla said at last. 'The dullest enigma in the Universe; unknowable and not worth knowing . . .'

Mrs Curzon, apprised by Mary Ann of the truth behind the vision of Sarah Glass, immediately declared that Milla the middle one was the one to blame.

'No, no,' said Mary Ann at once. 'It was Stacia all right, no doubt about it.'

'Well, Milla put her up to it, then,' Mrs Curzon decided. Milla, the middle one, the birthday sneak, must have known about the old mauve taffeta; the child was getting her own back.

'A photograph was taken so there'll be evidence,' Mary Ann told the housekeeper.

'Evidence!' Mrs Curzon gasped. 'A *photograph*, did you say?'

'Yes.' Mary Ann resented Mrs Curzon's 'down' on Milla, who was the only one of the three girls who ever talked to her. Stacia gave herself airs. Helen was quiet and proper, Milla the opposite.

'I shouldn't like to be a parlourmaid,' Milla had said, asking questions a daughter of the house has no right to ask. Mary Ann had told Milla how she'd been brought up in an orphanage where they were cruel. She told her this because she liked her: however dull and unpleasant it was in York Street with a step-mother and Mrs Curzon, life could be a lot worse. At least Milla had her sisters and went to school and didn't get beaten for silly things and then hired out for a pittance as soon as she was old enough to hold a broom. Last Christmas morning Mary Ann had passionately wished there was an orange to give little Milla, but if wishes were horses, beggars would ride, an orange for Milla, Philip Eames by my side . . .

'They're only children,' Mary Ann told Mrs Curzon.

'And you're only a parlourmaid so I'll thank you to curb your careless tongue!'

Mrs Glass returned home. Having glimpsed her husband outside the Café Royal with the slinky Lucy Winnup, she needed time to think about what she had seen. More than anything else she needed to summon Dr Morgan to talk with him urgently about the things that Henry was trying to tell her but to which she would not listen. What she certainly did not need as soon as she returned was an hysterical housekeeper recounting how her eldest step-daughter had dressed up as Sarah Glass and frightened the 'living daylights'.

'I blame Milla! I blame Dr Morgan!' The unhinged Mrs Curzon cast her accusations wildly. 'I blame Miss Housecroft for not keeping control, and Mary Ann let him and his women in.' Mrs Curzon did not go as far as actually to blame the second Mrs Glass for having invited the man to tea, arranging for him to eat seed-cake and then going out. Nor did she have the courage to blame the other culprit, the other Mrs Glass.

'Dr Morgan?' Elizabeth asked at once. She did not care to know what had gone on here in her absence – clearly Mrs Curzon resented Stacia's wearing the clothes the housekeeper herself wanted to dress up in. 'Tell me how I can get hold of Dr Morgan; I urgently need to speak to him.'

'How you can get hold of Dr Morgan?' Mrs Curzon stared at her mistress. 'You want to speak to him? Urgently?' She was aghast. There was no saving some people from themselves, she decided – as Sarah Glass had once decided before her. Stutteringly, painfully, she told the second Mrs Glass about her lost savings. At first Elizabeth could not make out a single word and then she understood that it was money that was being talked of.

'Money, Mrs Curzon, Money!' Elizabeth said laughingly. She heard the cruel edge to her voice but she did not regret it. Mrs Curzon was probably using this as a way of getting round to asking for a bonus or a raise. Compensation, anyhow. Presumably the girl she had seen on Edward's arm was only one of many, just as the girl she had once seen on Henry's had, it turned out, been of no particular consequence. Did Mrs Curzon, Mary Ann and Cora have to cope with impertinent enquiries? Had there been hints in the past which she, not understanding, had deliberately chosen to ignore? 'Why does everything always come back to money in the end?' she asked. 'It does make life very tedious.'

'He took every penny I'd saved for my old age, he had no intentions, he felt no obligation,' Mrs Curzon said, but Mrs Glass looked over at the door.

'Would you send Cora to fetch Miss Housecroft down?' Elizabeth had had enough of Mrs Curzon.

Mrs Curzon said nothing further. She bit her hairy upper lip and turned heavily on her heel. *I warned you but you would not listen!* When Sarah Glass had said this she had taken no notice and her pride had cost her dear. Had not the Resurrection of the apricot organdie this afternoon been some new warning from Sarah Glass? Mrs Curzon scowled and told Cora to tell the governess immediately that the Mistress wanted to see her.

Emily Housecroft admitted that the afternoon's events had got out of control. She apologized unreservedly. She did not trouble to think up any excuse. 'I can only say I am sorry,' she said, steeling herself now to mention Edward Glass's visit.

'No need to apologize,' Mrs Glass said at once. 'I have a dreadful headache, I don't want to hear another word about this afternoon. Tell me, Emily, how can we get hold of Dr Morgan?'

'Oh!' Emily Housecroft was surprised, and relieved. She tried to be helpful: 'He left a copy of his *News from the Other Side*, I've got it upstairs, published from an address in the City – Farringdon Road, I think – I imagine they would tell you where to find him.'

Miss Housecroft fetched Mrs Glass the paper she had found herself holding last week along with the dahlias which were now quite dead but which Cora had neglected to remove. 'I doubt if even Dr Morgan can bring dahlias Back from the Dead!' Miss Housecroft laughed to herself as she tossed them in the bin.

'I will visit the Farringdon Road tomorrow morning. Would you give these to Milla?' Mrs Glass handed Emily Housecroft a package. 'Some paper-scraps for her album. I promised them to her a while ago.'

'How kind – Milla will be pleased.'

Mrs Curzon sat in the kitchen, a desperate woman. She had had enough of the second Mrs Glass. She had invested heavily in her dead husband's dead sister's living husband. Mr Luscombe owed her and she was determined, however long it took her, but hopefully on Monday next, to collect. The time had come . . .

At the Café Royal meanwhile, Edward Glass found Miss Lucy Winnup charming. She liked him to find her charming and when he told her about his new project, the New Paris Grand, her beautiful eyes opened wide. She told him how she endeavoured to earn her own living, although she needn't. She was a designer, she said, and quite sought after in some quarters.

'I should think you are,' he gazed at her appreciatively.

'I was once painted by Herbert James . . .' she said.

'Never liked the man! Too full of themselves, these Academicians. Popularists, a faddish sort of art. No one will even have heard of him a hundred years from now, but you wouldn't think it the way he struts along the street.'

'Oh!'

'True Art does not lend itself to fashion; this new building of mine will defy easy description. Art Historians of the future will scratch their heads as if they have nits. There will be no category for Edward Glass in their simple-minded scheme of things. Why do you think John Ruskin has consistently ignored my work all these years? The man is an imbecile, he doesn't understand what I do any more than Marmaduke Blockhead in the street.'

Lucy giggled. Edward Glass took hold of her hand. Together they forgot the mundanity of the Grecian urns and the sense of propriety that prevents such intercourse in public places. After a while Glass spoke of the New Paris Grand again and Lucy listened. What an enthusiastic man Harry Withercott's employer was, how readily he talked of himself and abused the great Professor Ruskin.

'I love to hear you talk!' Lucy said. 'You are the most inspiring man I've ever met.'

'Why, Lucy, how kind of you to think it. Shall we order fresh coffee, a few more cakes?'

'I should like to stay here and drink coffee and hear you talk about Art for ever and ever,' Lucy sighed. She had messed up those illustrations of manufactured jams and then she had missed her deadline; it was unlikely the advertisers would use her again. Might as well see what else she could find.

Here was a quick little worker, quicker even than Desmond Blaise, Glass thought, pinning him down already with her piercingly blue eyes. 'How very kind of you, my dear, but I have work to do. The New Paris Grand to build . . .' He heard himself wriggling.

'Let me help you!' Lucy pleaded, fixing him very neatly (she would fix Harry Withercott neatly as well). 'Let me do what I can to save your valuable time.'

'You little sweetheart! You'd soon be bored, the New Paris Grand must occupy most of my time and attention.'

'Most, but not all. What little of your time and attention is not taken up with the Masterpiece, *Arcanum Arcanorum* can spare for me. I know a thing or two about Art myself. You will find no end to the things I can do for you.'

'Well.' Edward Glass wriggled no longer – the girl even knew his *nom de plume*.

Milla looked at the paper-scraps Mrs Glass had bought for her. 'I can't put them in my scrap-book,' she said at once for they were hideous and uninteresting. 'I shall have to lose them. Can I cut that piece about elephants out of your *Schoolmistress*, Miss Housecroft?'

'What?' Had the child been reading her newspaper? She herself only ever looked at the advertisements. Emily Housecroft felt spied on and furtive.

'About elephants – for my scrap-book.' Milla produced her pot of glue and scissors.

'I suppose so – why not?'

On Thursday morning Mrs Glass woke unrested and maniacally reckless. Her headache had worsened, she recked not whether Mrs Curzon stayed or left York Street. She had abandoned her neat little accounting systems. She tried on the *promenade toilet* which arrived, sent round by Mlle Letellier (who did not choose to bring it herself). Mrs Glass thought the costume had looked better in the fashion-plate. Miss Housecroft endeavoured to explain how Mlle Letellier had used her as a mannequin. She was trying to find a way of mentioning Mr Glass's unexpected visit but Mrs Glass misunderstood:

'My dear Emily! How selfish I have been! We will send for the Mademoiselle to bring her fashion-plates as soon as she's free. What fun we can have choosing – I see you in crimson velvet, or even . . .'

Miss Housecroft tried to convince Mrs Glass that she had no interest in clothes. She considered dressing up dangerous, she explained.

'Oh dear, yes, I know what you mean!' Mrs Glass said distractedly, not knowing at all what Miss Housecroft meant. She changed back into something more comfortable and set out alone for the offices of *News from the Other Side* in the Farringdon Road.

Elizabeth was met in a panelled outer office by the fixed smiles of a very helpful gentleman, a Mr Daniel Hake, and his crippled but cheerful assistant, Miss Adeline Cry: like something out of Dickens, the second Mrs Glass thought sarcastically.

'We are inconvenienced,' the kindly Miss Cry said when Mrs Glass asked for Dr Morgan. In their own way they were as preoccupied as she was. Advertisements for manufactured jams had failed to show up and were causing delays with the next edition.

'We thought you might be bringing the proofs.' Mr Hake sounded mildly reproachful.

'Me!' exclaimed Mrs Glass. As though *she* could possibly have anything to do with advertisements for manufactured jam.

'In any case,' Miss Cry added excitedly, 'we are to double the print-run this week. We have a sensational sensation.' Lady Blouvier again – the most sensational yet apparently. One had to hand it to Dr Morgan. 'If you want to be sure of your copy you could order it from us now.'

'You could take out a subscription.'

'Far more economical in the long run . . .'

Elizabeth stood where she was and looked from one to the other. Neither offered her a chair or asked her her business. She was not to know that women frequently called at the offices of *News from the Other Side*, all of them tired, distraite and trying to hide it, all of them asking where they could find Dr Morgan without delay. Many a woman before Elizabeth had discovered the ponderous curtain of smiling goodwill to be quite immovable.

'Leave your card, Madam, we will see that he gets it . . .'

Mrs Glass meekly left her calling-card – a considerably humbler piece of art-work than that which Lady Blouvier had yesterday bestowed on her step-daughter Stacia. As she went reluctantly away determined to steady herself by doing some more shopping, little Miss Cry and Mr Daniel Hake stared curiously after her: *Mrs Edward Glass*!

When Lucy Winnup told her mother that she was off to Newcastle, and tomorrow, Mrs Winnup went into a motherly panic.

'It's not what you think,' Lucy Winnup said. 'Edward Glass has invited me to be his Artistic Secretary. I will be back in London before you can miss me, Mamma. Edward Glass has work up there that needs checking and I will be able to put Mr Withercott straight on a matter or two.'

'But I thought . . .' Mrs Winnup thought vaguely and in vain about her daughter's artistic ambitions, her exhibitions, her painting, the trip to Italy. All now abandoned. 'A secretary?' she queried feebly.

'Yes, he already has a permanent steady man, Philip Eames, to do the humdrum work. I shall be advising on the artistic side.'

In spite of everything, Mrs Winnup was relieved to see her daughter looking happy again. 'Don't tell your father,' she conceded. 'Not too much, anyway.'

'I could say I'm off to Italy.'

'Oh, Lucy, darling, perhaps you will be – on a honeymoon.' Fond mothers do not give up easily.

Lady Blouvier knew she had excelled herself, too much so, alas! The problem was that the pictures, wonderful in themselves, were so clearly an out-and-out con. She and Dr Morgan went into urgent conference in Eden Gardens. In the Farringdon Road work was suspended.

'Proud though I am of these pictures, dear Lucius, and carried away as I was at the time, I do not see how we can possibly use them. The girl was the girl, very much alive alas, and not her poor mother after all.'

'Nonsense!' said Dr Morgan. He held before him Lady Blouvier's photographs of his Dear Dead cousin. 'Sarah was always partial to a slice of seed-cake.'

'But Lucius,' protested his patroness, gratified to have her work so openly admired but conscious nevertheless of the absurdity of the situation. 'We can't forget that the subject is only dear little Stacia dressed up. People will accuse us of chicanery. Edward Glass himself may have something to say on the matter . . .'

'I'm sure he will!' Dr Morgan laughed. He was not a con-man, whatever Edward Glass and other detractors liked to say. Dr Morgan was perfectly aware of the extent of his powers and he was careless of the truth as only honest men can be. Liars and charlatans, sensitive about their dubious honesty, feel the need to guard their beleaguered reputations. They are the ones who must be concerned about the ease with which their activities can be proved mere trickery. Lucius Morgan was above such workaday worries. What did it profit a man to go about worrying all the time? Morgan was a man rather fond of a profit. He'd been very fond of Sarah also . . .

It had upset Dr Morgan to find his cousin had Departed without ever a word to himself. She might have said something, come Back from the Dead if only to mock, for Sarah Glass had known him all his life. She'd been the only one to treasure him in the days when he'd been a studious, pale-faced lad, useless about the Morgan farm high in the scrubby Welsh hills. The other boys had despised him as a weakling but he'd been good at his learning and the local school-master had filled his head with ideas of Cambridge. No wonder he had peeed in church after they locked him in the ecclesiastical watercloset for six hours so that he dared not go in again. They had mercilessly teased his little pet mouse until it jumped backwards, breaking its back and dying in his hand in great pain. They had taunted a fierce goose and let it loose on Lucius, so that it chased the terrified boy who tripped and fell head-first into a dung heap. Then the furious creature had borne down on him, deftly removing his trousers, while the whole village turned out to watch. It had been Sarah who shooed the nasty bird away and lent Lucius her shawl to cover his naked legs. The oafish Morgans had called her a 'spoil-sport', teasing Lucius was a favourite sport, but then he had gone to Cambridge and she to Llandudno where she had met that stuck-up architect. Poor Sarah – she only married Edward Glass to get away. And poor Edward too when he hears that her photograph has been splashed all over the front of this week's *News*. Serve him right, he never looked after the dear old girl. And serve the *second* Mrs Glass right too; when she summoned him, he would go to her eventually, but not in a hurry: let the woman sweat!

'I was rather taken with young Stacia,' Lady Blouvier said.

'Were you?' Dr Morgan was not surprised. Lady Blouvier was constantly on the look-out for new interests. 'Why not invite her here to live with you? I dare say Stacia could benefit from a little of your kindness, Hildegard.'

'If it would please *you*, dear Lucius, and I am sure I need a new hobby.'

A theft had been discovered at the house in Mayfair. Pieces of Blouvier silver had gone missing. 'Let it wait!' Lady Blouvier had declared, for silver was only silver, purchasable any day of the week in Chancery Lane. She was more concerned about these doubtful pictures. Dr Morgan had enemies who might swoop on such an obvious fraud. There were too many witnesses to what had actually taken place, but if Stacia Glass were kept safely in Mayfair until the whole thing had blown over, who would dare to say anything? 'I will summon young Stacia at once!'

'There's no hurry,' Dr Morgan said, hurrying now to the Farringdon Road with the photographs of his dead cousin's Spirit. 'What an attractive diamond brooch she is wearing,' he thought. He had not known Sarah possessed such a thing.

'Mrs Glass was asking for you,' Daniel Hake told Dr Morgan.

'Mrs Glass was asking for you,' Adeline Cry repeated shrilly. Anxiously she handed him Elizabeth Glass's visiting-card, along with four or five others from ladies who had called that morning. Dr Morgan smiled.

'She won't make trouble will she?' the ever-cautious Mr Hake enquired, for naturally he assumed Mrs Glass had come in connection with the Sensational Spirit photographs.

'A wife cannot like a former wife to Return from the Dead,' observed Miss Cry, who was not a wife herself and could only imagine that this would be so.

'Elizabeth Glass will not make trouble,' Dr Morgan promised.

Miss Housecroft accepted a pen-wiper and said it was a thoughtful present. Milla too was delighted with her paper-scraps but over-excited at the moment about her letter from Pasha. Miss Housecroft would accompany Milla to visit the writer on Friday afternoon. Milla had asked if they might please take a cake.

'Oh, but Mrs Preedy's Afternoon Tea,' Elizabeth protested in dismay. 'I wanted you to come with me!'

'I'm sorry.'

'Ah well,' Mrs Glass sighed. She had a splitting headache and felt mildly delirious. 'Tell me about Milla's Pasha – a venerable novelist? A handsome gentleman with whiskered moustachios who will be swept off his feet the moment he sets eyes on the pale young governess?'

'No, a woman called Ruby Smith,' Miss Housecroft said shortly – Mrs Glass read too many empty-headed weeklies.

'Oh! Mrs or Miss?'

'The letter did say, I'm afraid I don't recall.'

Emily Housecroft and Mrs Glass hesitated. The governess said: 'I had better go upstairs; the girls will be wondering.'

Mrs Glass looked forward to having Emily Housecroft to herself when the children returned to school. Poor Elizabeth no longer enjoyed her own company or reading magazines on her comfortable *chaise longue*. She wondered irritably when Dr Morgan would come.

On her way upstairs, carrying the elaborate pen-wiper, Emily Housecroft treacherously considered which of the jobs in this week's *Schoolmistress* to apply for. She'd regret leaving York Street, which was eminently convenient to her purposes at present, but it couldn't be helped. Mrs Glass had become too demanding.

15

Pasha, I Presume

Mrs Preedy had gone to a lot of trouble and expense. Her Afternoon Tea had been disappointing. She knew herself to be snubbed. Elizabeth Glass had not even seen fit to send word of apology for her absence.

Mrs Pinder Simpson smiled and chattered idly with Mrs Beresford Gurney. This was not quite what they had come for but they obliged Mrs Preedy by smiling and chatting together nevertheless. Charles Preedy felt insulted on his wife's behalf. The dear lady had gone to a lot of trouble and expense, she deserved better.

Charlotte and Bertram Preedy benefited from the general mood of disappointment. They only picked up a sixpence or two from the disgruntled guests but there were plenty of sweetmeats and bon-bons left over: no one stayed long, no one had been very pressing with the plates of food.

'A little entertainment, indeed!' declared Mrs Richard Styles gleefully when she returned home early. 'So little entertainment we were barely detained at all.'

Some speculated that perhaps Mrs Glass found company difficult. One or two went so far as to say that Mrs Glass had no business to find company, whether she found it difficult or not. They had all done their best to be kind to the second Mrs Glass, Eliza Cathcart, widow of the bankrupt drunkard, but who did she think she was snubbing their dear friend, Mrs Preedy?

'A lot of men lost money,' Mr Pinder Simpson of the cement works on Lime Kiln Wharf remarked, not that he had lost any himself, but he knew men whose money and wives H. J. Cathcart had tampered with who, even after the fellow's untimely death, could feel no forgiveness.

'One of his bankers thought of doing something for the widow until he discovered her to be quite half-witted.'

'Simple-minded, I heard.'

'Do you know what I heard?' Mrs Pinder Simpson had had it from

Mlle Letellier when she'd gone to claim her cheap hat: Elizabeth Glass was so mixed up she'd pretended to be the household governess. She fancied herself as Jane Eyre! 'A novel way of trying to catch your husband's eye, to be sure!'

'Jane Eyre? Half-witted? Simple-minded? Mrs Cathcart, the second Mrs Glass? Oh, surely not. I've always thought the woman rather cunning. Look how cleverly she extricated herself from her difficulties.'

'A regular Houdini.'

Elizabeth Glass had spent the wet afternoon of the Tea shopping, on her own this time, though nobody knew where Emily Housecroft had gone, but definite sightings had been reported of Mrs Glass ambling and idly shopping. How dare she deprive them of their little entertainment?

Meanwhile, across London, Milla was almost sick with excitement. She clutched a box containing the cake that she had begged to be allowed to bring. She had hardly slept the night before, tossing and turning, imagining the plot she would discuss with Pasha, a suggestion for the next book Pasha would write. A vast improvement on previous Pasha books, a *real* adventure story: *A young man who once upon a time set out to seek his fortune and supposedly that of his family too, for it was somehow assumed that he would return one day and share the fortune with his three lovely sisters.* Pasha would not groan like Stacia, or simply join in to show willing like Helen. She would not listen disbelievingly like Mrs Glass or impatiently because she was paid to like Miss Housecroft. Pasha would be grateful for the good suggestion. Pasha might know about America and what dear William was doing over there. She might even say: 'Why, Milla Glass, you understand adventure. You and I could work together; you must help me write the book.' All night Milla had tossed and turned. All morning she had scrubbed and dressed herself. Milla had never looked so scrubbed and dressed.

Milla and Miss Housecroft alighted from the cab to find themselves in a road full of tall terraced houses. The house, when Miss Housecroft found it, was unremarkable, but Milla had never given any thought to the place where Pasha would be living. 'Care-of' the publishers had seemed an altogether more appropriate address. Miss Housecroft reached up and rang the bell. She was bemused by the whole event. She took the box containing the cake from Milla so that the girl could concentrate on the meeting that meant so much to her.

'It's like Stanley and Livingstone,' Milla whispered with an impish grin. Parrots squawked excitedly in the trees overhead. Any minute now . . .

The door was opened after a long wait by an elderly woman who, though she pretended not to expect visitors, knew immediately who Milla and Miss Housecroft were.

'I never thought you would come,' Mrs Smith welcomed them. Milla peered impatiently into the house beyond the woman but it was cold and dark with hardly a book in sight, no ostrich eggs, tribal spears or painted masks covering the walls and mantelpieces. 'I suppose now you're here you had better come in. My Mary has her afternoon off,' Mrs Smith added to show just how inconvenient the visit was.

Milla turned now to the woman at the door. 'I'm Milla Glass, and this is my governess Miss Housecroft. We've come to see Mrs Ruby Smith.'

'I dare say you have,' Mrs Smith curled her lip.

'We were invited,' Milla assured her.

'Of course you are. But why would a little girl from a prosperous family in the City of Westminster travel all this way with her governess to Acton just to visit me?' Mrs Smith knew how to be nasty.

'*You* are Pasha?' Milla could not disguise her dismay.

'That is the ridiculous name my publishers insist on, and since they pay the bills, who am I to argue? Don't say it too loudly though, I wouldn't want any of the neighbours knowing the depths to which I have sunk.'

'Depths!' exclaimed an astonished Milla.

The disappointing Mrs Smith led the way into the depths of her sitting-room and indicated where her unwelcome visitors could sit. She looked uninterestedly at Milla. Milla lowered herself regretfully into a great fusty armchair that shrank her into a small, over-dressed child whose feet did not quite reach the floor. The antimacassar over the back of the chair was stained a patchy yellow.

'Well? What questions do you have for me, Camilla?'

Milla almost squirmed round to see who this Camilla could be.

Reluctantly accepting what she already knew, that there were only the three of them in the miserable room, she repeated, 'Camilla?'

'Isn't that your name?' Mrs Smith was practically jeering now.

'I'm always Milla.'

'But isn't that short for something? A baby's name that has stayed with you, perhaps?'

Milla winced. 'Millicent, I think,' she said hesitantly.

'How very common for Westminster! Why, even I have a cousin called Millicent.' Ruby Smith laughed outright. 'And I'm afraid my cousins don't live in Westminster. Or anywhere near it.'

Milla, with little choice now, bravely persevered: 'Is York Street in Westminster, then?'

'You should know, you're the one that lives there!'

'I don't know,' Milla admitted.

'Not much point coming half-way across London to talk about distant lands if you don't even know where you live yourself, is there?' Mrs Smith laughed again. Miss Housecroft smiled compliantly.

'No,' Milla agreed miserably. There was an awkward pause and then she asked: 'Didn't you ever travel?'

'Me? Travel?' Mrs Smith was getting into full stride. Opportunities like this were rare.

'Didn't you? Or . . .' Milla felt weak. She had hardly slept last night.

'It's not what you expected, is it? A well-dressed, well-scrubbed child from a prosperous family. I take it your father is *the* Edward Glass, the architect one hears so much about?'

'Do you? Well, yes, I suppose . . .'

'How were you, Milla Glass, daughter of a famous architect, to guess that the Pasha who provides excitement beside your cosy nursery fire every evening is a miserable old lady who has had to write rubbish all her life to earn her crust? You've probably never even been in a poky house like this before.'

'No . . .'

'There you are then!' Pasha was triumphant. 'And you can take this back to Westminster: I've never been anywhere or done anything. I married a man a long time ago who talked of doing things, but he never got round to any of them, except dying of course, the miserable old bugger . . .'

' "Miserable old bugger"?' Milla queried.

Miss Housecroft scowled at the interruption but Mrs Smith maliciously continued apace: 'That's right. Died off, didn't he, the miserable bugger, leaving me penniless and at the mercy of the market. Mr High-and-Mighty at the publishers tells me what stupid adventure they want next and if I don't want to starve I have to sit down and write it: a headless dog and a Dayak in Borneo, pirates seizing the mail at Singapore, frying the sun in a pot in darkest Bamangwato – wherever that is – an escapade in Dahomey. You name it, Milla Glass, and I have to get on with it.' Mrs Smith sighed wearily; Pasha had been a burden she'd carried so long the intolerable weight had crippled her.

'Oh, I see,' Milla said quietly.

'You see, Milla Glass, do you? A spoilt little girl who has never been anywhere, who doesn't know where she lives, and who isn't even certain of her own name?'

'Well . . .'

'I'll tell you something else, Milla Glass, while I'm at it. Sometimes, nasty interfering children write letters care-of the publisher suggesting preposterous plots: "Dear Pasha, Write us a story set in a Colorado gold-mine . . ." and next thing I know, I'm obliged to oblige the spoilt blighter.' Mrs Smith looked suspiciously across at Milla. 'I hope *you* haven't come here with some ridiculous plot you were hoping to discuss?'

'Nnnnno.'

'Thank goodness for small mercies!' Ruby Smith paused. 'Colorado is in the United States of America. I discovered that this morning.'

Milla went very quiet. So did Mrs Smith. Having satiated herself now, she did not offer any refreshment and Miss Housecroft did not like to say they had brought a cake, as the unpleasant Mrs Smith might misconstrue the gesture. Miss Housecroft said they must be going and told Milla – as if she were indeed the child of three both the armchair and Pasha's treatment had rendered her – to thank Mrs Smith for her kindness in sparing the time.

Milla, in the thin voice of a three-year-old waiting for her tea, mentioned the cake. Miss Housecroft handed it across. Ruby Smith opened the box and critically inspected its contents. She wrinkled her nose. 'Very tasty,' she said derisively. 'I can't afford cake myself.'

She shoved the box into a drawer as if she feared a headless dog or a Dayak from Borneo or even Milla Glass herself might try and snatch the cake back from her. She did not thank them or offer them any.

Milla did not speak on the way home. Miss Housecroft tried to engage the girl in conversation but Milla stared expressionlessly out of the window at the rain. If the afternoon had been unpleasant, the governess would tell Mrs Glass, it was regrettable of course, but the child had only herself to blame.

That Friday afternoon the house was quiet. Milla was enjoying her adventure in Acton with Miss Housecroft. Mrs Glass was out shopping. Mary Ann brought Philip Eames his tray of refreshments. 'Will that be all?' she asked softly.

'Yes, thank you.' Eames tapped impatiently on the desk but Mary Ann lingered as usual. She knew her beautiful hair was at its best this afternoon for she had concealed her jagged piece of mirror in her pocket and checked her appearance on the way up the stairs. This complicated manoeuvre (balancing the tray on one knee) had taken as much practice as Stacia's curtseying and, like Stacia, Mary Ann had had a lot of practice.

'Everyone is out,' Mary Ann plucked up courage to remark.

'Everyone?' Philip Eames felt as if he had been stabbed. Even the girls? Even his Beloved? This afternoon he had not dared to glance up to see if She was watching from an upper window, but he assumed nevertheless that She would be there. He felt angry now that She had not cared to wait. It had been a long week of waiting for him.

'Miss Housecroft is not here.' Mary Ann was reassured not to notice any particular disappointment at her words. Philip Eames seemed to be waiting now for her to go on. Mary Ann knew she had already exceeded her position, but she continued: 'Miss Milla went out with Miss Housecroft and a cake. Miss Helen and Miss Stacia are upstairs, though.'

'Then Everyone is not out,' Philip Eames thought. He barked at the maid in a voice strangled with fury: 'Young woman, you are not – correct me if I am wrong – paid to come in here and waste my time with idle chatter!'

Mr Eames and Mary Ann glared at each other in mutual astonishment. To hear the name of his Beloved uttered so casually by this pert servant-girl, when he himself could barely find it in him even to think the sacred name, cut him to the quick. Mary Ann felt the rebuke deeply. Humbled now, not by a pudding but by Philip Eames himself, she knew she was more hopelessly in love than she had ever been. She hurried downstairs to where Mrs Curzon sat scratching herself in her sleep.

'What's the matter?' Cora whispered.

'Nothing!' Mary Ann sobbed silently into her pinafore.

'It's that Mr Eames, n't it?'

Mary Ann nodded.

'He touched you, didn't he? He touched you where 'e shouldn't 'ave, Mary Ann.'

'I wish he had,' Mary Ann gulped.

'Ugh!' Cora shrugged her shoulders. They all deserved each other, the lot of them. Even Mary Ann must be funny in the head; 'Creepy Eames' the children called him, and you could see why. She'd not stop in York Street any longer than she had to. Wasn't healthy, apart from being hungry.

Stacia and Helen had enjoyed their afternoon.

'We won't ask Milla about Pasha,' they decided, Stacia saying it, Helen nodding her head. 'You know how she'll go on and on.'

'She'll probably go on anyway.'

'We won't encourage her.'

Miss Housecroft and a far from ebullient Milla eventually returned. 'Now then, Stacia, Helen, what have you been up to?' the governess asked.

The girls shrugged and looked blank. 'Nothing much.'

'Mmmmm.' As Miss Housecroft had thought! She was sensitized now to this wasting of time.

'When do you think I'll hear from Lady Blouvier?' Stacia asked.

'Well, I've told you, I wouldn't expect . . .'

'Has Creepy Eames gone yet?' Milla asked.

'Don't know,' Helen said. 'We haven't been watching.' It wasn't so much fun watching from the window when Milla wasn't there. 'A lot of parcels were delivered for Mrs Glass but that was earlier on.'

'She likes buying things,' Stacia said.

'You must stop talking about your step-mother,' Miss Housecroft said.

'She hasn't been looking well lately,' Milla said.

'Not looking well?' Miss Housecroft was surprised.

'Is she all right?' Milla asked.

'I expect so.'

Stacia, noticing how Milla had avoided any reference to Pasha, now raised the subject herself: 'So, what was she like?'

'Who?'

'Pasha, of course.'

'Oh, well . . .'

Miss Housecroft, Stacia and Helen all looked at Milla. Milla paused for a moment and then she said: 'She was wonderful. Exactly what you might expect from a writer, really. She said dear William is probably making his fortune in a Colorado gold-mine. She's going to write her next book about him. I gave her some advice and she said she was very grateful. Didn't she, Miss Housecroft?'

'Err . . . yes.' Miss Housecroft was surprised into complying with the fiction.

'Did she like the cake?' Helen asked.

'Oh yes, she said she can't afford cake herself . . .'

'Can't afford cake!' Stacia repeated. 'If Pasha can't even afford cake there isn't much point in writing all those silly books, isthere?'

'Well,' Milla thought for a second. 'I meant she can't afford the *time* for cake. She's so busy writing she's too busy to advertise and take on a cook and then spend time issuing instructions for silly things like cakes . . .'

'Oh!' Stacia and Helen looked sharply at Milla. Miss Housecroft looked sharply away.

Milla went over and sat down by the window. She bunched her knees up to her chest and put her arms round them tightly and stared silently outside, hugging herself.

Stacia picked up Lady Hildegard Blouvier's much handled calling-card again and ran her finger longingly over the gold-printed contours of the embossed crest. She sat down at the piano with the card in her lap and swayed dreamily to some Chopin in her head.

Miss Housecroft sighed at the waste of yet another afternoon. 'I shall go mad,' she thought.

*

Downstairs Mrs Glass had returned to the house. Mary Ann was tidying up after Mr Eames. He had left without ringing for her and although this was disappointing she was glad he had not chatted again with her rival Old Button-boots.

Mrs Glass put her head round the study door. 'Mary Ann, come with me, will you?' Elizabeth handed the parlourmaid the packages she had been carrying.

'Has anyone called?' she asked over-brightly. 'Has Dr Morgan been to see me?'

'No, I'm afraid not, Ma'am.'

'Oh.' Elizabeth was disappointed. She watched Mary Ann untie the parcels and arrange their contents on a table. She had summoned the man to her and he had not come. Why was he taking his time?

Mary Ann unwrapped a silver-backed mirror. Involuntarily she held it up to look at herself.

'You must have it!' Elizabeth laughed curtly. How her head throbbed! Let Mary Ann prance and please.

'Oh, but I couldn't.' Mary Ann went on admiring herself.

'Yes, you could.' There was amusement in this.

'You don't understand. Mrs Curzon forbids mirrors downstairs. She claims they are the work of the devil.'

'If I looked like Mrs Curzon I dare say I would forbid mirrors too,' Elizabeth said. 'It is my house and *I* have never forbidden my maids to use mirrors. How else are you to see what you look like?'

'I generally use this.' Mary Ann produced the jagged piece of mirror she had been using. Elizabeth was reminded of Milla proudly producing her tattered scrap-book.

'Mary Ann, keep the hand-mirror, you have surely *earned* it!'

'Oh, Mrs Glass, I never dreamt of owning such a thing,' Mary Ann cried out in delight.

'Well, now you do. Take it downstairs or wherever you keep your things. A pretty girl like you should have a nice mirror to look at herself in.'

Mary Ann flicked her curls. 'It's very kind of you,' she said, almost in tears. 'No one ever said anything so kind to me before.' She thought of Philip Eames, who had only that afternoon reviled her.

'Kind? Oh Mary Ann, never use that word with me,' Elizabeth said wearily, losing interest.

'But you are kind. There's no doubt about it.'

'Take it if you want it, but leave it at that.' Mrs Glass lay down on her *chaise longue* and closed her painful eyes.

Mary Ann looked at the exhausted woman she had once called 'mean' with a new tenderness. 'Can I get you . . .'

'No, nothing. Make sure I am not disturbed.'

'Very good, Madam.' Mary Ann went on her way rejoicing.

'You thieving magpie!' Mrs Curzon darted at Mary Ann who almost dropped her prize in the scuffle.

'Mrs Glass gave it me!' she cried, hitting out at Mrs Curzon.

'Yer lucky thing!' Cora said.

'Did she indeed?' Mrs Curzon drew back and said nothing further. Stretching a salmon with Miss Housecroft, encouraging vainglory in the parlourmaid, what next? Why not an indulgence for a downtrodden housekeeper? It was time to mention Sarah Glass's things again.

'Did yer see the jealous fleabag's face?' Cora laughed later, when she and Mary Ann were undressing for bed. 'Yer'd better watch yer step, Mary Ann, yer'd better look out!'

But Mary Ann, who now had both permission to use a mirror and also a beautiful silver-backed mirror to use, did not heed the housemaid's sensible warning. That night Mary Ann dreamt an impossible dream: both Mr Luscombe and Philip Eames came towards her smiling, their teeth bared for kisses, their arms outstretched, their passions eager . . .

16

Truth (Not Tooth) Extraction

A week or so later, Milla knocked on Mrs Glass's door.

'What is it?' Elizabeth Glass called.

'Me!' Milla called back.

There was a pause. 'Oh, Milla. Come in then.'

Milla looked round the room and noticed all the new things the ill-looking Mrs Glass had been buying. 'I wanted to say something about ivory,' she said.

'Ivory?' Elizabeth's worsening headache quickened.

'I don't think you should buy any more ivory,' Milla opened her tattered scrap-book and riffled through until she found the cutting about elephants. 'You must listen to this: "for every complete set of billiard balls the tusks of three elephants are used and this is only one branch of the ivory trade." So you see . . .'

'Milla, I haven't bought any billiard balls.'

'No, but elephants are threatened with extinction.'

Milla and Mrs Glass looked at each other. Milla saw that her hollow-eyed step-mother had lost the wedding-ring; it had been an ugly ring and hardly a loss. Elizabeth did not notice the less obvious change in Milla.

'Have you stuck in the scraps I bought you?' she asked. She certainly wasn't going to buy the child a billiard-table!

'Well, it was kind of you, but they are far too, er – far too *good* for my scrap-book,' Milla said tentatively.

'I know they are.' Elizabeth sighed. This was the problem with giving children presents: it only encouraged them to want more. 'I'll buy you a proper scrap-book next time I go shopping,' she promised wearily.

'But I don't want – I think I'm a bit old for scrap-books,' Milla said. 'I'm thirteen and . . .'

What was it Milla wanted then?

'About the *ivory*,' Milla went on, but Elizabeth was already asking: 'Did you enjoy your visit to the nice writer?' Miss Housecroft had said something about it not being all Milla had hoped, but Mrs Glass had been too preoccupied to listen.

'Yes, thank you,' Milla said flatly.

Elizabeth's head was throbbing. 'Could you close the curtains for me, Milla dear?'

Milla did as she was asked. Elizabeth shut her eyes but when she opened them a few minutes later the child was still standing there, looking down at her quizzically.

'Was there something else?' Elizabeth snapped and then quickly attempted to assuage her bad temper with a smile. If it wasn't a brand new scrap-book what was it that this awkward child of another woman wanted?

'Are you all right, Mrs Glass?' Milla asked anxiously.

'All right?'

'You don't look very well.' In the light from the half-closed curtains, Milla was horribly reminded of her mother, and the blue-stoppered bottles of pain-killer, and the shiny steel syringe with the drop of blood on the end that she had once found by peering beneath the flannel on a kidney-bowl. But there were no covered kidney-bowls in this room, only rows of new ornaments for Mary Ann to dust.

'Of course I'm all right,' Elizabeth replied impatiently. 'I'm *tired*, Milla. Very tired.'

'I just thought . . . I've seen you go out a lot lately, perhaps you've overdone . . .'

'You've seen me *what*?' Elizabeth was practically shouting now. 'You little Preedy you! I reprimanded you once before for spying on me. I've only been shopping. Isn't that what women spend their afternoons doing? Isn't that what your mother used to do?'

There was a pause. Milla thought hard. 'She must have done once, unless she bought everything by mail-order.' Milla wondered desperately what could be wrong with Mrs Glass. 'I think it's nice the way you buy things, though I do wish you wouldn't get any more ivory.' There were a lot of new things in this room. With a shock Milla noticed the stuffed dog.

'Take it,' Mrs Glass said tersely.

'What?' Milla cringed; the poor little dog was a wire-haired terrier like in the window of the art gallery. It was sitting up with its little

169

front paws outstretched, looking at her soulfully and begging for a titbit, only it wasn't because it was dead.

'You take it!' Mrs Glass ordered.

'No, I couldn't,' Milla demurred as Mary Ann had done. She looked at the tail that had once wagged and the black button nose that had once twitched and she wanted to sob.

'Take it, Milla,' Mrs Glass said insistently, thinking she was being generous.

'I'm glad you're not ill!' Milla cried out as she ran blindly, clutching her battered scrap-book, from the room. Of course dogs were not threatened with extinction like elephants, but there were limits to humouring a step-mother. Even Mrs Glass.

'Emily, I must insist. The girls must stay upstairs.'

'I think the child was worried about you,' Miss Housecroft said.

'You must impress on her that my health and my shopping are none of her business. She was trying to tell me what I should and should not buy,' Elizabeth continued, her head thumping.

'Oh, surely not,' Miss Housecroft tried to introduce a measure of reason. 'I know she is concerned at present about elephants. I heard her telling the piano-teacher that ivory piano-keys are scandalous things.'

'And what did the poor man say to that?'

'Mr Luscombe pretended not to hear.'

'Well, I suppose it's his livelihood. He can hardly afford the luxury of Milla's girlish scruples.'

'That was what I told her. As for coming down here, Milla hasn't been the same since her visit to Pasha. She probably wanted to thank you for the scraps . . .'

'She demanded an expensive album to put them in! She wanted a billiard-table. Make sure she doesn't come down, Emily. I am quite worn out as it is. Why hasn't Dr Morgan come? What can be keeping the man?'

'Do you really . . .' Miss Housecroft did not understand Mrs Glass's determination to see Dr Morgan whom earlier she had been so determined to get rid of, but it was not her place to argue. Miss Housecroft had written several letters enquiring about other posts; with any luck this would not be her place to do anything shortly.

Mrs Glass lay back. It occurred to Emily Housecroft that if Dr

Morgan did not come soon another sort of doctor would have to be summoned. No wonder Milla was concerned: Mrs Glass looked very ill. 'Is that all now? May I go?'

Elizabeth nodded weakly and Miss Housecroft, like Milla before her, fled back upstairs.

Philip Eames cleared his throat. He looked at the pallid Mrs Glass, who received him this week lying down, and asked her why she had bought the automaton canaries.

'A whim, I think,' Mrs Glass said, rather taken aback.

'I had a canary once,' Eames said. Both Mrs Glass and Philip Eames himself wondered what he could be leading up to. 'A cat got it. I was very upset . . .' Eames had it in mind, he supposed, to warn her. About the feline Lucy Winnup, about looking so ill, about Stacia waiting for him upstairs. He wanted to warn the world about Philip Eames.

Elizabeth Glass regarded her husband's assistant who arrived like clockwork every Friday afternoon on the stroke of three as something of an automaton himself. She assumed he coveted the canaries. 'Take them!' she spat. Of course the man must know how much money her husband sent her each week: for all she knew, it was Eames who counted it into the purse. No wonder the fellow expected a present. 'You take them if you want them so much,' she conceded nastily.

'Oh, I couldn't,' Philip Eames demurred, exactly as Milla and Mary Ann had done. 'I'm afraid I find them . . .' He sniffed disapprovingly. 'I find them most distasteful.' He might have said that the mindless happiness of the mechanical canaries set off fears inside he did not understand and could not control.

Elizabeth Glass raised her eyebrows. Her purchases were no more Mr Eames's business than they were Milla's. How ill she felt, too ill to see clearly. She accepted this week's generous purse and dismissed the man abruptly to the study. She heard Mary Ann take him his refreshments. Was any amount of money worth all this?

Time passed and Dr Morgan came to her at last, just when she had begun to despair of his ever coming. Mary Ann had instructions to tell the man to step straight in if and as soon as he arrived. This he now did. Even Dr Morgan registered the dramatic difference

171

between the second Mrs Glass he had last seen proudly holding him off as he grasped hold of her, and this gaunt and fretful woman who lay exhausted on her *chaise longue*, unable to rise and greet him, when by contrast she was now grateful for his coming and much relieved to see him.

'Oh, my dear!' he said solicitously, bending towards her and taking hold of Mrs Glass's feeble hand. Dr Morgan noticed at once, as Milla had done, that the over-large wedding-ring had gone. 'You have not been well!'

Elizabeth smiled wanly up at him. She was to remember the encounter later only in the way that one recalls the feel of an intense dream, the dream forgotten, its details blurred, its colours heightened and casting shadows of their own. They stayed for a while without speaking, he bending over her, she feverishly clinging to the hand he proffered. She felt too weak to chastise him for his tardiness as a landlord's wife might have done. He did not owe her any rent, though the time he had taken to answer her summons had cost her dear.

Dr Morgan spoke: Henry, he told her again, had been trying to get in touch. Elizabeth had no strength to resist. She broke down and wept.

'I hated him,' Elizabeth gasped painfully. Dr Morgan held her in his arms, gently as a father might. 'He was a rogue and a gambler. He said he was a gentleman and my foolish father took him for what he said he was.'

'Your father should have known better.'

'I discovered that at Ventnor,' Elizabeth whispered.

The stormy turbulence of recent weeks quickly died away; in the gentle undertow of Dr Morgan's quiet concern Elizabeth grew steady and becalmed. So complete and sudden was the sea-change in her, she might have been injected with something powerful from a blue glass bottle (such as had been used on the first Mrs Glass to kill *her* pain). Dr Morgan could smoothly draw out festering septic truth that caused great agony in much the same way that a skilful dentist can easefully extract a painful blackened tooth. He needed no steel syringe with a drop of blood left on its tip which poor little Milla might find later by lifting the flannel on a kidney-bowl. Milla had always been too inquisitive for her own good.

Rotten teeth are harmful but Dr Morgan could put extracted truth to good use; he bowed his head and let Elizabeth talk.

Henry James Cathcart had become as insufferable to his wife in life as his memory had become intolerable to her after his death. He'd taken the eighteen-year-old Elizabeth for an heiress, her father unwittingly encouraging him by telling Henry that his daughter would inherit *everything*. He assumed from all Henry said that Henry was much too wealthy to be interested in knowing how the splendid house Elizabeth and her father lived in was only rented and the parklands surrounding it were part of someone else's estate. Nor did he mention that the rent on this house was paid by collecting in turn the rents from other properties in the area. These were then paid over to the owner, the son of someone who had befriended one of the aged rookery of aunts and taken pity on their pitiful annuities. The landlord lived abroad. Elizabeth's gentle ways had been tended on charity and paper-scraps, not income. There had been no income.

No income? Henry felt himself bitterly deceived. He told his young bride so as they sat together out of season at the cheap end of Ventnor and watched the chilly sea from hired deck-chairs. He'd gambled heavily on his great expectations, he said. How did she propose they could repay the debts she had foolishly encouraged him to incur by agreeing to marry him?

'That is your problem, Sir,' she had said as icily as the icy wind that blew contemptuously in their confused young faces.

'It's your problem too, now,' Henry said glibly.

'Only because you have made it mine,' Elizabeth replied.

'We all have problems of one sort or another!' Not one to let things get him down for long, Henry laughed charmingly to show he forgave his bride her lack of income. 'Problems only require solutions.' He leant over and gave the new Mrs Cathcart a consolatory kiss. 'Answers are generally printed upside-down at the back of the book,' he assured her.

Elizabeth turned her face coldly away. 'I had no problems until I met you. I am not accustomed to solving them or to cheating by sneaking a look at the back of the book . . .

'We quibbled and bickered from that day on. All the time we were married, neither of us could say anything without the other tidying away some clever reply. I have even found myself quibbling with poor Henry since his death . . .'

'Ah yes, my dear, it does happen,' Dr Morgan assured the second Mrs Glass. 'A relationship with a Loved One will continue much the same as before. *The Living and the Dead dwell not so far apart as you have been led to think!* In many ways Death is a fallacy that makes little difference.'

'A Loved One! Makes little difference!' Elizabeth heard herself quibbling. 'Oh, I suppose I did *love* him, that was what made the difference. That was why Henry's problems *did* become my problems too. If I hadn't loved him I'd have risen from the damp salty canvas, taken my things and quitted Henry and Ventnor there and then. Never mind the waste of the hire-fee for our chairs. But no, I stayed where I was with Henry beside me complaining that this wasn't much of a married life and that any minute now it was going to rain.'

Staring stubbornly at the chilly sea from her hired deck-chair, Elizabeth had not wept. She had read something uncomfortably similar in *Our Mutual Friend*, where the undeceiving had been described with great gusto, a disillusionment that had also taken place on the Isle of Wight. What could be funny in Dickens was horrid in life; the comic precedent only served to increase the mockery, the humiliation.

'We have deceived each other,' she told Henry frostily, although she had deceived no one except perhaps herself. She had thought he loved her, he had told her so many times but that had been before he found out how little she was worth, in terms of the hard cash he now needed.

'Ventnor is not as I expected,' she wrote restrainedly to her father. There had been a small casino in Ventnor. Henry struck up a friendship over the tables which was likely, he assured her, to help them out: 'Nothing ventured, Nothing gained!' he said glibly. Elizabeth was not sure what had been ventured. Henry had been convinced he was 'on to a good number' and as a result they had even had to leave the cheap end of Ventnor, and what was left of their honeymoon, in an undignified hurry.

'He came to me at night,' Elizabeth told Dr Morgan, half-aghast at the recollection, half-relieved to be able to speak about the horror of it all at last. 'I could not forgive him for deceiving me. I thought he loved me but it was only my non-existent income he was after, and even if income had existed it would quickly have been gambled away. I used something I'd seen in the stables, some tartar emetic, I added it to his water-bottle to make him sick at nights, to put him off. Pleasurable as intimacy with Henry was, of course, Henry did not deserve any pleasure, he had been so deceitful. The tartar emetic worked very well.'

'Women are driven to these things sometimes. It is not uncommon, my dear; you must not distress yourself.'

'Yes, but you see,' Mrs Glass gulped and spoke into Dr Morgan's sympathetic ear what no one else had known. She told him of Henry's womanizing, how when she lay wasting and desperately sick from her miscarriage (tartar emetic had not always been effective) Henry had taken a girl called Jane Fox to Amsterdam for a week. Jane Fox had been an art student, a promising pupil of Herbert James (the Academician who had painted the celebrated portrait of Lucy Winnup with her clothes on). Jane Fox had taken an idle fancy to Henry Cathcart, a married man she could play with for a while and then return to the toy-cupboard when she got bored. She fancied a week with Henry at the roulette tables in Amsterdam. Jane Fox had money of her own, which was just as well for Henry's pockets were, as always, empty.

Elizabeth, glad of the respite and nothing if not practical, had looked on Miss Fox as a solution to the problems of Henry. Soon, however, Miss Fox had looked to this wife as a solution also: she had discovered Henry's weaknesses for drinking and for other women. The clever, painterly Miss Fox refused to put up with loutish behaviour. Besides, Henry was naturally unlucky; what she had won at the wheel Henry Cathcart had immediately lost. Jane Fox did not like losers.

Henry Cathcart slunk home then, his tail between his legs, meekly begging Elizabeth not for biscuits but for forgiveness: 'I'm so sorry,' he'd said, sounding almost as if he might mean it. 'Ours has not been a fortunate marriage, I will try for your sake to do better.'

'Perhaps we can get some medical advice,' Elizabeth had suggested, for she had been more miserable without him than she would ever have thought – being nothing but practical for *a whole week* without Henry had not been pleasant.

'Nothing ventured, Nothing gained!' Henry had said. The old

Henry, how dearly she loved him! Although they had sought medical advice on his drinking, there had been no money to pay for the costly cures that were suggested. Once, during one of his more serious bouts, she had with great difficulty borrowed a sum to send him to Matlock in Derbyshire where, she had been told, the waters did wonders for weaknesses of this kind. Henry, however, got wind of her intentions; he helped himself to the money and spent it more enjoyably. His drinking was bad enough, his clever words became slurred, his speech abusive, he lost the ability to quibble effectively. If it had been the only problem Elizabeth could have endured it.

'We quarrelled horribly. He humiliated me in front of everyone and in private, when he came to me reeking of drink and other women's kisses, unable to quibble even when I quibbled, it was more than I could bear. Every day then I added the poison to his brandy. I put it in his water too, a crystal at a time. I thought it might prevent him seeking out other women the way at first I had kept him from me. Everyone knew about his drinking, no one suspected me of exacerbating his weak and erratic condition. Nobody suspected me of killing him slowly, surely, grain by grain.

'Then he went to stay with people he knew, some house-party where he wanted to do business, I understood, although I did not understand: no one could have wanted to do business with Henry, the condition he was in. I was frantic, I had to make something happen. I put several big crystals in his brandy-flask before he left . . .'

There was a pause. Dr Morgan waited. Elizabeth's voice was hoarse now and faint: 'When they told me my husband had fallen from his horse, I was not sorry – except for the horse. They said Henry'd been ghastly and sick but had stubbornly insisted on taking the poor beast out . . .'

'Now I have told you! Of course, there was so much to clear up. So many grim-faced bankers and creditors with claims and nothing to claim on. His books were examined, his financial affairs were upside-down and inside-out – such a mess . . . I killed him, you see, no wonder he was in agony. I thought if I couldn't have him to myself, I didn't want anyone to have him. I was a jealous wife. I killed my beloved handsome Henry! I didn't see why I should share him . . .'

Dr Morgan patted Mrs Glass's arm. 'You'd be surprised how many women have done such things,' he comforted her tears.

'Death is not so bad as you have been led to believe. Henry was probably better off in many ways.'

'I know I was!' Elizabeth said, some of her old spirit returning.

'Well, then . . .'

'You said he was in *agony*, Dr Morgan, I could not bear to think of Henry suffering . . .'

'Perhaps I was mistaken: it was *you* who were in agony, keeping your silence.'

'I know,' Elizabeth admitted the truth of what he said. 'It has been a relief to me to be able to speak at last. And, Dr Morgan, I must beg you to keep my silence too – always!'

'Of course, my dear. You are not the first to ask this of me. Eternal silence, Mrs Glass, I swear!' She looked into the deep glaze of Lucius Morgan's eyes and saw only what she could trust.

'And Henry?' she began.

'Henry is comfortable. He is well-housed. Death, I tell people, is as a Parlour packed with Knick-knacks, a cosy parlour full of occasional furniture . . .'

'It is I who have all the furniture and knick-knacks!' Elizabeth Glass glanced round her room and saw it as Henry might see it. Perhaps she had tried too hard to pin him down. 'I think Henry would prefer a gaming-room. He talked so much of the tables at Monte Carlo. I almost believe him to be playing there now . . .'

'That is a good way to think of him, certainly,' Dr Morgan said, adding: 'How is Stacia?'

'Stacia?'

'Yes indeed. My friend Lady Blouvier particularly requested that I ask for Stacia.'

'A friend of yours, a Lady Blouvier, wishes to befriend Stacia?'

Dr Morgan was pleased to note how quickly Mrs Glass understood what was said to her. This would be useful later. 'Indeed, she was most impressed with the girl and would like you to take the child to her house in Eden Gardens. I have the invitation here . . .'

Dr Morgan showed Mrs Glass a large parchment envelope addressed in a large flamboyant hand to 'Miss Stacia Glass'. It looked like a royal summons.

'Not *the* Blouvier, of the Infallible Blouvier, some new-fangled darkroom tent I saw a big advertisement for in one of my magazines? It can be erected on glaciers, money back if dissatisfied – and if you

can prove it – the essential prerequisite for every serious Alpin
photographer?'

'The very same! The formidable Blouvier herself! I believe sh
could do much for young Stacia,' Dr Morgan said.

Why not the others too? Elizabeth Glass wanted to ask. Hadn'
Milla said her mother bought everything by mail-order? Why no
take Milla also to this house in Eden Gardens? The child could sho
Lady Blouvier her scrap-book and read to her about elephants an
talk about puff-adders and dear William. Lady Blouvier would kno
how to deal infallibly with the child. She calmed herself: 'How ver
kind of your friend. I shall see that Stacia answers at once. Woul
you like to take that stuffed dog away with you?'

'Stuffed dog?' Dr Morgan looked at the pitiful creature and made
face. 'Oh, my dear lady . . .' Funny idea of a present, he thought

'Yes, take it. I insist!' Why did everyone pretend they didn't war
the things she offered them? Elizabeth, overcome with an over
whelming tiredness, lay back and almost at once fell into a deep
heavy sleep, enjoying at last the much needed rest she had bee
cruelly deprived of for many weeks.

Dr Morgan summoned Mary Ann to cover her mistress with
shawl. 'She is exhausted,' he commented dispassionately. Peopl
never ceased to amaze Dr Morgan, and glancing at the sleepin
woman he almost felt sorry for her. Yet this wicked woman was hi
own cousin Sarah's usurper, no less! A soul transported into ev
new flesh. He wondered at the foolishness of her disclosures.

'She has been poorly of late,' Mary Ann told him, sensing som
explanation might be called for: people did not usually fall aslee
when they had visitors.

Dr Morgan patted the parlourmaid's hand. 'You are a good girl,
can see that,' he said. 'I know your mistress values you greatly.'

'She must do,' Mary Ann said cheerfully. 'She gave me the mos
beautiful hand-mirror with a silver back. I feel like a true princes
when I look in it.'

'Well, well!' Dr Morgan glanced again at the sleeping second Mr
Glass; no shortage of spending-money, then. 'She gave me thi
stuffed dog!' he laughed. It would do to be getting on with, a
earnest of a greater prize as 'twere: *More is thy due*.

Dr Lucius Morgan hurried from the house, the stuffed wire-haire
terrier poking its stuffed little nose out from under his arm.

'She managed to get rid of it,' Milla said as they watched from upstairs.

'Do you think he brought me a letter from Lady Blouvier?' Stacia asked.

'He might have done.'

'You come away from that window,' Miss Housecroft called out. 'I've told you already, there's to be no more spying . . .'

On Dr Morgan's departure, Mary Ann found herself holding a sixpence and a large parchment envelope with an enormous crest embossed in gold on the flap. It was addressed unmistakably to 'Miss Stacia Glass'.

'Why not Milla?' Mary Ann thought. It was Milla what wanted adventure, Milla what deserved. She left the letter on the hall-table for Miss Housecroft to deliver.

'What kept you?' Mrs Curzon was waiting downstairs in a fury. Mary Ann showed her the silver sixpence Dr Morgan had given her. She would now be able to buy that wide-brimmed hat for the seaside.

'By rights that is mine,' Mrs Curzon said, gazing at the coin in disbelief. He must think he's on to a winner upstairs, she thought bitterly. No wonder Sarah Glass had Returned to warn them. The Lord watch over the second Mrs Glass, for only Divine Vigilance, and probably not even that, could save the woman now.

Mary Ann slipped the coin safely into her pocket. If she had a new hat perhaps Philip Eames would go with her. Surely a day out in Margate was just what the man needed? A day with Philip Eames in Margate, wearing a sixpenny wide-brimmed hat, was certainly what Mary Ann, herself, felt she most needed.

'Are yer going to bring the pooch Back from the Dead for us, Mister?' a knowledgeable street-urchin shouted after Lucius Morgan half an hour later in one of London's less salubrious streets. Mrs Glass's stuffed dog seemed to wag its stiff tail. The little black varnished nose, peeping out from under Dr Morgan's arm, twitched. The urchin ran off in fright.

III

DESTRUCTION

17

Item Thirty-five: A Sealed Envelope

There were two factories, a vast warehouse and a lunatic asylum scheduled to be built simultaneously in Newcastle. Edward Glass took one look at what Harry Withercott had achieved in only a few days and was delighted. Here was a draughtsman who could be left to his own devices, a draughtsman with flair, capable of becoming an architect in his own right one day. This would leave Glass free to concentrate on the Paris Grand Hotel; the prestigious project was no longer confidential. The Architect had been officially appointed: Edward Glass of Glass & Co.

'No wonder he was so pleased with himself,' Elee thought. She remembered the favour she had promised to do the man and she wondered again at his asking such a thing of her.

Elizabeth read in a newspaper about Edward Glass's success. The following Friday when Eames handed her another generous purse she told him to convey her congratulations to her husband. Eames nodded and was about to make for the study when Elizabeth added: 'I also want you to take a letter to Mr Glass. You must be sure to put it directly into his hands: it is for his eyes *alone*.'

Philip Eames looked suspiciously at the second Mrs Glass and then at the sealed envelope she handed him. Never before had she specifically instructed him not to read a letter. He hoped to be spared whatever embarrassment it contained.

Edward Glass! The New Paris Grand! But the man was meant to be in Burnley. In Plymouth. In Birmingham. In Bournemouth. There was another building scheduled in Manchester. There were rumours that in Newcastle Glass had put an *unschooled draughtsman* in sole charge of two factories, a vast warehouse and a lunatic asylum. There was widespread confusion, and then letters were received in all these places written in the untidy hand of Philip Eames (an assistant!) apologizing for unavoidable, unquantifiable delays. The arrogance of the man! But when you read the small print in agreements unwittingly signed ten years ago, it seemed Glass & Co. were entitled to do as they pleased. You might as well whistle for your deposit back; Glass had covered himself against all eventualities. Having waited this long already, there was nothing to do but resign yourself and wait a while longer.

Elizabeth snipped the announcement out of the paper and gave it to Miss Housecroft to give to the girls. Stacia, Milla and Helen looked blank.

'I think the Paris Grand must be a very important hotel,' Miss Housecroft explained.

'Not exactly a mansion, or a palace, is it?' Stacia remarked disdainfully. 'I think Mrs Glass means you to stick this in your scrapbook.' She poked Milla sharply in the arm. Milla made a face. Now that Stacia had been summoned to Mayfair at last, she had become insufferable; it was Lady Blouvier this and Lady Blouvier that the whole time now. Stacia was sure her ordeal of going to school with Milla and Helen was nearly over; already she scorned the starchy pinafores they wore and the school-books they carried.

The original hotel had been spectacular when new, but expectations had risen, people wanted something altogether grander of a Grand Hotel nowadays. A few years back the Board of Directors had held a competition for an imaginative rebuilding scheme. When the entries flooded in the Board had been unable to agree on a winner. One director contemptuously suggested it might have been better to commission a top-notch architect outright than rely on second-rate chaps who had time to waste entering competitions. Then the directors had wondered again whether the Paris Grand needed rebuilding at all: they had a natural affection for the old familiar shabbiness and a natural reluctance at parting with good money to replace it. But that was back in the days before Mr Desmond Blaise had married above himself and thereby acquired the means to acquire a seat on the Board. Mr Blaise was a man who liked to see things happen and things were certainly happening now: an Extraordinary Board Meeting had been called. Edward Glass was invited to attend. He described the Masterpiece he intended to build in flamboyant detail that sailed high over most of their heads.

'It will cost,' Edward Glass concluded.

'How much?' the Directors asked in chorus.

'Of course,' the Directors said, not quite a chorus.

'Sounds a bit too clever to me,' someone piped up. He was quickly hushed: Glass was their man. They were lucky to have him, Blaise

184

had told them so. Everyone knew Great Art does not come cheap. This briefing was only a formality but a necessary one. Blaise would not want it said later that he had stampeded his fellow directors into anything against their own will. Blaise, like Glass & Co., was careful to cover himself.

The fellow directors looked at Lucy Winnup as she sat artistically with pencil poised. Women weren't as a rule allowed into the Board Room but this was an Extraordinary Meeting, and Lucy Winnup's extraordinary figure was something to look at while the architect descanted at tedious length on his plans to spend their money.

'There'll be a knighthood for you, I dare say,' someone (with both ready wit and a knighthood already) remarked to Edward Glass when he had finished speaking.

Everyone laughed good-heartedly (including those, like Blaise, who had yet to get their own knighthoods). Glass blushed. Lucy Winnup liked banter about knighthoods: this was the sort of company a girl who had been painted in her prime by Herbert James, the Academician, should be keeping. Too bad if her auditor father ranted and her fond mother wept back home in Turnham Green.

'I envisage the project taking a fair while,' Glass said. He would not rush his Masterpiece. He had deferred so long he must certainly take his time. Were not posterity and taking one's time somehow inextricably linked?

'How long exactly?' asked Vizetelly.

Glass shrugged.

'How long is a piece of string?' Blaise laughed. Most of the Board of Directors laughed with him. 'Great Art, Sir, cannot be trotted along like some great cart-horse.'

Lucy Winnup nodded vigorously. The elderly directors who had been gazing at her nodded vigorously also.

'We will need estimates, surely,' Mr Vizetelly said. Vizetelly was the one man in the room who owed Blaise nothing, a distinction of which he himself was blissfully unaware. He could feel though that the tide was strong and inexorably against him. He made one valiant last stand: 'Gentlemen, this is nothing short of madness! The Board cannot possibly enter into so open-ended a commitment where we know neither how long the rebuilding will take, nor what it will eventually cost. Nor indeed what we are getting for – with respect,

Sir – though you described your projected edifice at great length, the details went clean over my head. Your plans, Mr Glass, are decidedly obscure. It seems to me that the Board has taken leave of its senses!'

There was an uncomfortable shuffling of feet, some venerable coughing of ticklish throats and the heavy creaking of Chippendale chairs.

Edward Glass rose to his feet. 'Sir, I can only presume you do not know whom you are addressing! I must have a free hand or none at all; I thought that was understood.' The architect frowned. Lucy Winnup was frowning too, and very prettily. 'I was given to understand that this Meeting was just a formality; I have been misled. Gentlemen, if you have anything further to communicate . . .'

'No, no,' Mr Blaise intercepted quickly, scowling down the carved mahogany table. Everybody looked at Vizetelly. Mr Vizetelly turned the colour of best claret and, waving his gloved left hand, he signalled his own defeat: he had no choice. He kept any reservations he had to himself after that. He did not want to be known as the director who had scuppered the modernization programme. Mrs Vizetelly was finding it hard enough already to get herself the invitations.

'We are honoured,' Blaise told Edward Glass, shaking hands with the architect on behalf of his fellow directors. Lucy Winnup smiled at the dignified faces round the table and was gratified when most of them smiled back at her.

Edward Glass and Lucy Winnup took up residence in a small building that had been part of the old Paris Grand but was to serve as a residence and office during the demolition of the old and the planning and building of the new hotel. The skeleton Paris Grand staff who had been kept on could use the building also. A limited dining-room was to be maintained for everyone's convenience. Blaise had arranged things most satisfactorily.

Mrs Winnup – despite her 'progressive' parenting and her love for prestigious connections – felt flustered whenever Edward Glass was mentioned. She did not know what Mr Winnup would say. Fathers can be so difficult when they find out about their grown-up daughters, but Mrs Winnup was a brave woman. She came from Turnham Green to see Lucy. It took her ages to locate her daughter even after she had found her way in through the unmanned entrance of the now derelict hotel. She wandered amid the scenes of systematic demolition and noticed how materials from the old building were being carefully sold off. As an auditor's wife, Mrs Winnup wondered if these multifarious transactions would be entered properly in the books. She banished such thoughts from her mind, for Lucy would call them 'bourgeois' and she had not come all this way to argue with Lucy.

'What are you doing here?' the horrified daughter asked. 'It's my life,' Lucy spoke in a hard voice her mother had not heard before. 'You always said I should do as I pleased and this is what I am doing. You can go home and tell Papa.'

Mrs Winnup sniffed and dried her eyes. There was little she could do with her Lucy now. Tea was rung for and brought. The maid called Lucy 'Ma'am' without a hint of the salacious sarcasm Mrs Winnup had detected among the labouring types outside. The tea was served on Paris Grand silver.

'Old-fashioned stuff,' Mrs Winnup glanced at the markings stamped on the side of the milk jug. The hotel was certainly in need of modernization.

'I am designing, or rather, having a say in the designs for the new hotel's silver,' Lucy told her mother brightly and Mrs Winnup was able to return to Turnham Green with a small crumb of comfort for her motherly ambitions: Lucy works for Edward Glass. Whatever anybody might maliciously imply, Lucy is in fact design consultant on the metalware.

'Design consultant on the metalware! I've never heard such utter bunkum. You get straight back there, woman, and tell the girl to come home immediately!' Winnup raved at his wife across their comfortable drawing-room, bereft now of the picturesque presence of their daughter Lucy. Outside, the conservatory was a conservatory again, for Mr Winnup had ordered a servant to sling out the redundant easels, abandoned paintings, hardened tubes of oil and dried out pans of watercolour. 'I blame you for this, you and your *progressive*, so called, ideas. Design consultant! Artistic secretary! Do you expect me to swallow such nonsense?' He choked angrily.

Mrs Winnup gulped. 'Mrs Beresford Gurney's brother is Second *Secretary* at Our Embassy in Paris.'

'Don't fog the issue, Madam! Even if Mrs Beresford Gurney's

pantry-boy is related to the Man in the Moon, *you* are a foolish woman. You have encouraged my daughter to go astray.'

'I encouraged her to go to Italy.'

'There you are then.'

'The girl is thirty-two,' Mrs Winnup pointed out.

'Then she should have more sense. And so should you all these years, filling the girl's head with piffle when she should have been hunting down husbands. Whatever happened to that nice . . .' Winnup tried to remember a man who had fled to Kimberley some five years ago but since been mauled by a hungry lioness and buried on a lonely hillside thousands of miles away. 'And then there was . . .' he had forgotten that man also, who had escaped by marrying a dumpy and deservedly erstwhile friend of Lucy's. The distinguished auditor's head for adding and substracting columns of numbers was considerably better than his recollection of Lucy's long line of vanishing beaux.

Mrs Winnup wept. How ill she had been when she'd had the baby. How unsympathetically her husband had computed the bills, double entries to be used in evidence against her every time she proposed an endeavour that might make her ill and occasion him fresh expense. And now here she was, suffering again on account of Lucy, his daughter. What it was to be a mother. Mrs Winnup buried her sore nose in a handkerchief and wept.

A room in what remained of the old Paris Grand was established (by a notice on the door in Lucy's finest calligraphy) as the SITE OFFICE. Here Eames sat with papers on the table beside him trying to report on the week's activities. Edward Glass was distracted by his grand design for the Grand Salle, a dining-room that would be constructed on many levels using the latest in electrical tricks, a vast moving machinery of deceptive perspectives and landscapes. Diners would sit down to look about them wonderingly: food for thought and a feast for the eyes!

Lucy had shrewdly pointed out what hard work all the climbing and descending would be for the waiters; people went to dining-rooms to talk to each other and to eat nice food, not to contemplate the unnerving and look at the unforgettable. Edward immediately dismissed her flirtatious objections as bourgeois housewifery. Teasingly he'd accused her of being in Preedy's pay, seeking to undermine his Great Art, his lasting monument, his knighthood. They had laughed together then but inwardly Lucy had registered the need to be careful.

Philip Eames, who knew only too well the need to be careful, got to the next item in his notes: *Item 35 – York Street*: 'I went on Friday at 3 p.m. as usual,' he recounted.

'Yes, yes – get on with it.' There were electrical devices to be had from America that could make the walls themselves appear to shift slowly.

'I have a letter Mrs Glass told me to put directly into your hands,' Eames said tentatively. Supposing he be asked to read the hateful thing out loud and Stacia was mentioned in terms he'd understand but not be able to pronounce? Supposing his hot confusion betray him and his vile craving be revealed at last? Fearfully he wondered if he didn't wish it . . .

'Tell me the gist.'

'I haven't read it, Sir. I thought – I mean your wife . . .' With surgical precision Eames slit the envelope open in one smooth stroke of his sharp paper-knife.

Edward Glass turned towards him irritably. 'Then read it *now*, Eames. What do you think I pay you for?' How insufferable Eames was becoming. Why not sack the man and use Lucy Winnup instead? Even she would make a better assistant than this Eames. What a shame, he could hardly send *her* to York Street. Special compatible light-fittings needed to be designed of course. 'Get Blake from Blake's Ironware in. I could breakfast with Mr Blake tomorrow,' Glass said.

Eames added a hasty note: 'Blake's: Breakfast' to his list as he drew Elizabeth's letter from its envelope. He read. He spluttered. He coughed. 'Maybe you should read this for yourself, Sir!'

Edward Glass glared at Eames. Was the man being deliberately obstreperous? He'd been only too helpful at dinner that Christmas Day! It seemed to Glass now that Mrs Elizabeth Cathcart was connected with Mr Eames in a way he no longer recalled. Could it have been coincidence, the man's turning up with a bottle of wine like a timely reminder of the Preedys' unwarranted invitation? Both Eames and the widow had been present at the indifferent meal, both for no apparent reason. And wasn't it the fastidious, competent Eames who a day or two later had suggested this complete stranger as a solution to the structural problems at York Street? Glass smiled;

Eames was nothing better than a dogsbody and incapable of colluding with anyone, let alone the second Mrs Glass. He was simply a means by which things happened. An agent of chance. One of life's operatives and a thoroughly unlikeable man.

'I asked you to give me the gist, Eames,' Edward Glass said, with barely restrained anger. How plainly Eames resented Lucy Winnup who would insist on doing jobs that might otherwise have been his. Eames had pinned a scrap of paper to the door with 'Glass & Co. SITE OFFICE' scrawled illegibly across it. Lucy had taken it down and nailed up a carefully designed sign in measured stylish uncials.

'What happened to my sign?' Eames asked.

'Sign?' Lucy repeated with a provocative laugh. 'You don't mean that scrap of paper.'

'Yes, my sign. What did you do with it?' Eames shook with immoderate rage.

'It went in the wastepaper basket. I designed something a little more *artistic*.'

'Yer, and equally unreadable. All them fancy letters!' someone across the room remarked.

Lucy darted a spiteful glance. 'You'll regret that,' she said, but when she reported the man to Edward Glass he only laughed. Eames smiled the sly smile of a waiting crocodile then, although Lucy won the day, for it was her illegible sign that remained on the door. Now Glass repeated himself angrily: 'Tell me the gist, Sir!'

'Mrs Glass asks for more money,' Eames summarized bluntly. He had of course been shocked by the tone of the letter. Lucy Winnup had not been referred to by name, nor the encounter outside the Café Royal described in detail. The word 'blackmail' crossed Eames's mind as not inappropriate. (Even after the good Dr Morgan's ministrations Elizabeth could not return to the quiet life she had happily led during the first six months of her second married life. Elizabeth found shopping expensive; her rosewood box needed replenishing. The girls had grown demanding, she'd written. She had had to buy paper-scraps and a stuffed dog for Milla. Now the girl wanted a proper scrap-album and who knew what else? The letter had rambled on incoherently but its import had been – like Glass & Co. invoices – wholly unequivocal. Elizabeth Glass demanded more money in her purse on Fridays.)

'Let her have it then, *three times* whatever we've been giving her!'

Edward Glass did not add 'to keep her quiet', nor did Eames protest that fifty pounds plus a week was already an inordinate sum. He thought no sum of money big enough when you considered the slight Mrs Glass was suffering at the hands of that interloper, that neighbourhood cat Lucy Winnup.

Edward Glass, in so far as he gave it any thought, supposed that people like the Preedys had been making unpleasant comments. He remembered the young woman looking at herself in the mirror. If she hadn't been his wife he might have advanced and spoken, or – bearing in mind the anxious solicitations of the dressmaker – he might have returned to the house later to dally and discover more. Wives were tricky creatures; so much simpler and lighter an ambitious little kitten like Lucy!

'Item thirty-six,' Eames continued. How curious that husband and wife who scarcely knew each other could have so much in common. Their mutual propensity for endless ordered lists, for instance, this futile attempt to control the chaos around them by itemizing everything.

When the recalcitrant Eames with all his folders of finicky paperwork had taken himself off at last, Edward Glass lay back on the couch and closed his eyes. 'The Paris Grand will be my monument,' he thought, by which he meant (having regard possibly to the delightful tension down the dark mahogany table between directors Blaise and Vizetelly): No expense must be spared.

Lucy put her head round the door. She was glad to see the fellow Eames had gone. There was something altogether repellent about that man. She had tried to tell Edward Glass this but he had only laughed. 'Eames? Been with me for years. You cannot expect to have me entirely to yourself, my dear!' Lucy had known better than to pursue the subject.

'My mother came,' she said chattily, 'all the way from Turnham Green!' Glass pretended to be asleep: families and chatter did not interest him.

18

Enter Valentine Birtles

'He is to rebuild the Paris Grand!' Mrs Preedy said.

'That was a well-kept secret!' Charles Preedy frowned.

Mr Pinder Simpson sent the selected architect an invitation he knew would be refused, but would at least serve to remind Edward Glass of the cement works on Lime Kiln Wharf. Simpson, Holland & Co. made a point of marking down their prices and selling cement at a slight loss to themselves when a prestigious connection would be good for business.

Glass did indeed opt for Pinder Simpson's cut-price cement. Simpson, Holland & Co. offset the losses by taking out large advertisements in newspapers announcing the fact: theirs was the cement that had been chosen to hold together the bricks of the New Paris Grand. The public were respectfully reminded once again of the Prize Medal of 1851 and the Honourable Mention of 1862, proudly displayed on the side of every Simpson, Holland & Co. cement-bag. These advertisements soon brought in so many fresh orders that the gamble of allowing such a ridiculously good bargain to Edward Glass paid off many times over. Mrs Pinder Simpson congratulated Mr Pinder Simpson as they dined together to celebrate the boom in business. Inwardly she congratulated herself also on having married such an astute man. How well they did out of Mr and Mrs Glass between them! She turned her head in the mirror to admire the hat Mlle Letellier had made very reasonably but for which she had been able to charge her husband full price. A wife likes a little money put by for private contingencies.

One person, however, did not do so well out of these transactions. Publicity in the newspapers ensured that at Harrow-on-the-Hill young Pinder Simpson Junior was mercilessly ragged. Inevitably he became known as the Honourable Mention, a name that would stay with him for the rest of his life. Whispers of '1862' could be heard round bends down corridors and he'd find 'H. M. 1862' plastered large and anonymously on blackboards and defacing the covers of his exercise books. Even schoolmasters could not resist the odd clever quip, sometimes in Greek, sometimes in Latin, but always involving Medals, Mentions, mortar and bags of cement.

Many years later Pinder Simpson Junior was to stand to attention on the bridge of his ship while it sank slowly, slowly down into the cold grey waters off Jutland. The last conscious thought that rushed with the wind and swirled with the water, buffeting him about, knocking him sideways and senseless as once gangs of rough schoolfellows had done, was of the Honourable Mention that Lieutenant Simpson was even then earning himself. Dispatches sent out from the Admiralty in Whitehall told how gloriously the brave heir to the Simpson, Holland & Co. cement works on Lime Kiln Wharf had drowned for King & Country, an ironic smile frozen forever on his heroic, but taunted, cement-coloured face. *Dulce et decorum est.*

'What contractor are they using?' a lot of people were asking but no one as yet knew the answer.

St John Tidy tried to find out. He hung around buying pints in the Ring & Goose. If a contractor hadn't yet been appointed Tidy could drop what he was currently engaged on (repairs to a workhouse in Hackney; the sums allowed were so tight that the work was only worth doing to keep his men occupied and so available). He waylaid Philip Eames one morning and told him so. This time Eames did not shout, he merely shrugged his hunched up shoulders. It turned out later that the Paris Grand contractor was a distant relative of Blaise's, a Mr Fine. The work had never been open to tender.

'They have things sewn up,' Charles Preedy said; you could be sure Mr Fine would be knocking something back to Mr Blaise.

Who was this Lucy Winnup? Not much of a mystery as it turned out. Mrs Beresford Gurney informed Mrs Preedy that Mr Winnup was a highly respected auditor in the City.

Richard Styles however was a disappointed man. He had sent in a carefully worked design for the original Paris Grand competition and before the result was known – the result that had been an *impasse* – he had approached Vizetelly. Mr and Mrs Vizetelly had accepted all his invitations but it hadn't done Styles any good. 'It's a Board decision,' Vizetelly had insisted. Later when Blaise joined the Board, Styles had wined and dined Mr Blaise also.

It had been Richard Styles who had set Desmond Blaise thinking. Styles told Blaise that before he acquired the means to acquire his seat on the Board, there had been an architectural competition with no very clear result. Why not resuscitate the project? There'd be a lot of money floating around. Styles then hinted, speaking low and close in Blaise's ear, that if *he* got the job Mr Blaise might find a percentage of the overall expenditure useful . . .

Desmond Blaise had smiled inscrutably and promised to give the matter discreet consideration. Having done so, he had called upon Edward Glass. Nothing but the best for Blaise, he had told Glass so himself.

'They say Glass & Co. will soon be Glass & Withercott,' Mrs Styles said.

'We know nothing of Harry Withercott,' Richard Styles remarked.

'Someone said he's learnt what he's learnt by attending Evening Instruction at an Institute, paid for by some doting aunt.'

Richard Styles smarted. An institute! A doting aunt!

Charles Preedy did not like Richard Styles any more than he liked Edward Glass but Richard Styles had the virtue of not being inordinately successful. When Glass got to work on the Paris Grand the other two architects conferred together, but it had been exactly the same stumbling block as before: should it be *Preedy & Styles, Architects* or *Styles & Preedy, Architects* in florid gold letters over the door? Neither of them would budge. Why should they?

The scene that had taken place back in Newcastle between Lucy Winnup and Harry Withercott could barely be described as a scene. Harry's astonishment at seeing Lucy Winnup on Edward Glass's arm was considerably greater in many ways than Mrs Glass's astonishment at precisely the same sight outside the Café Royal. Poor Harry confessed himself baffled.

'I confess myself baffled . . .' he'd begun, catching her alone and hoping his honesty would elicit some explanation.

'I'm delighted to hear it, Harry!' Lucy picked up what she had pretended to come back into the room for and smiled delightedly at the man who'd had no family estates in Kimberley or Colombo to pretend to flee to. She tossed her nose prettily into the air and, with the air of a woman biding her time, she walked directly from the room. And from Harry.

York Street meanwhile was in a state of upheaval. *Tell Mrs Glass to bring you!* Lady Blouvier had written.

'Tell Lady Blouvier that I will take you!' Mrs Glass said. She thought the woman's invitation decidedly high-handed, but Dr Morgan had described her as his friend and Stacia seemed altogether set on going. She added: 'Tell her that Milla will come too.'

Stacia stared at Elizabeth. 'Milla!' she said. 'There's no mention of Milla in the invitation.'

'I'm sure Lady Blouvier would like to see Milla . . .'

'Milla is not invited!'

'Yes, but I'm sure . . .'

'I am the one!' Stacia screamed at her step-mother. 'I am the one . . .'

Elizabeth was unprepared for this fury. 'I am Alice!' Aunt Alice had raged, as though there were really much difference betweeen Alice, Maud and the other rooks. They had all joined in then, shrieking and swooping down at her, their beaks looming large in her face, their black clothes stinking like in Sarah Glass's room. Elizabeth Glass looked calmly at Stacia: 'If you want to be selfish, I cannot stop you.'

'I am the one,' Stacia repeated again, rubbing her eyes and sniffing a little. No one, and certainly not Milla or Mrs Glass, was going to be allowed to spoil her chance, *vivace e capriccioso*. She had waited long enough; long unbearable weeks of waiting and dreaming and practising Chopin. Now Lady Hildegard Blouvier had summoned her to Eulalia House, and to Eulalia House, Eden Gardens, Mayfair, Stacia Glass intended to go.

Elizabeth told Mary Ann that she wanted to do something about Sarah Glass's room. She by-passed Mrs Curzon these days: the woman had become impossible. It was only a matter of time and careful timing before the demented housekeeper could be pensioned off. 'Clear the room completely. Give any jewellery to Stacia,' she instructed. 'Take whatever else you like for yourself, Mary Ann, and burn the rest.'

'Very kind of you, Madam, but I can't see there being anything in *that* room I would want! Have you smelt the smell up there? I don't know what it reminds me of or how anyone could possibly have *lived* in it. No wonder the poor woman was always ill, and then she died.'

Mrs Glass smiled. She had a loyal parlourmaid.

Emily Housecroft with the girls back at school was at her wits' end. There was always something Mrs Glass wanted. She went to an interview for another position. Mary Ann told Mrs Glass that she thought Old Button-boots was applying for a new post.

'Surely not,' Elizabeth said at once. 'Why would Emily do a thing like that?'

Mary Ann shrugged. 'Because of Philip Eames, I think,' she said.

'What?' Mrs Glass was astonished. Mary Ann smiled and said it was a joke. Philip Eames wasn't exactly a ladykiller, now was he?

Miss Housecroft was asked to a house about a mile away, which was close enough to York Street for her purposes. A governess was being sought for a boy and a girl. Miss Housecroft was unprepared for the rigorousness with which the father, a Mr Josar, questioned her. Sternly he worked through geography, history, religious knowledge, and made no secret of the fact that he had interviewed at least a dozen other prospectives in this way and so far no one good enough had been found. He prided himself on his high standards.

'We are marking you each out of ten. A figure for knowledge, attitude and bearing.' Mrs Josar was huddled fearfully over the scores, while the two pupils, Proserpina and Jeremiah, sat beside their parents on the other side of the table and stared at Emily Housecroft with sickly scrutiny.

'*Et maintenant*,' Mr Josar said finally, '*nous parlerons français*. We have eight more candidates to see this afternoon, Miss Housecroft, we must get a move on, pray hurry yourself. *Quelle heure est-il?*'

At last the question-and-answer session was over. Mr Josar said he would be writing to the successful candidate, if one was found, by the end of the week. He told his wife to add up her scores and told the children to write some notes so that they would be able to remember something about Miss Housecroft later: prospectives all looked alike, he remarked to Miss Housecroft as he showed her out of the house.

Emily followed the solemn Mr Josar downstairs and, as she was taking her leave in the porch between the inner and the outer door, he hotly took hold of her hand and moved close to her so that her way was momentarily obstructed. She fled down the steps in disarray, conscious that if Mr Josar was giving marks for compliancy she had surely failed, but if he fancied a governess who would put up a struggle, perhaps she would indeed be offered the post. Another prospective coming up the garden path turned in surprise and stared after her as she ran. Emily Housecroft felt trembly and chastened when she arrived safely back in York Street, thankful to be home.

An enormous fire was blazing in the back garden. Mary Ann was burning Sarah Glass's things. As an act of contrition, Emily House-croft joined Elizabeth Glass at the window in her sitting-room. While they stood together watching the domestic inferno, Milla walked out into the garden and threw something on to the fire. Little bits of paper flew about everywhere.

'That's never the child's scrap-book, is it?' Mrs Glass asked.

'Milla has not been the same since her visit to Pasha.'

'She will have to grow up sometime,' Mrs Glass said sadly and then quickly changed the subject. 'Mrs Curzon has been in here ranting at me for my wickedness in burning Sarah Glass's things. The woman is dead, she cried, as if I didn't know it. Then she doesn't need her things any more, does she? I said . . .'

Miss Housecroft smiled brightly at her employer. Elizabeth decided Mary Ann must be mistaken: Emily could not possibly be applying for another post. Why, she and the governess were almost as good as friends.

Mrs Curzon endeavoured to speak to the deaf Mr Luscombe. She had tried on numerous occasions now to remind him of all that he owed her. She tried to explain how intolerable life in York Street had become. Mr Luscombe appeared to listen to the turbulent house-keeper but all he heard were the inner beatings of his own bewildered heart. It was disconcerting enough being buttonholed outside the door by Mrs Curzon, the Dear Departed Mrs Luscombe's Dear Departed brother's wife, but when at last he got upstairs he found that there were two instead of three pupils waiting to sit down at the piano. He was sure there had been another one, or had he imagined it? The friendly maid seemed friendlier than ever, pressing biscuits and smiles on him so that Mr Luscombe sensed, rather than heard, the upheaval in York Street and he was terrified. He tried to calculate whether he could possibly manage without his weekly envelope from the Glass girls' lessons safe in his inner pocket and he decided what he knew already, that he definitely could not. Without that manila envelope and the parlourmaid's biscuits he would starve. He would end his days in the Hackney workhouse that St John Tidy's men were even then repairing, at scarcely any profit to

Mr Tidy himself for an honest contractor's lot is little easier than a stone-deaf piano-teacher's.

Mrs Curzon seethed. Tight-lipped, grim-faced, the housekeeper endured this new nightmare. Time after time throughout the day, the door bell rang with carriers delivering Mrs Glass's latest purchases. A seemingly endless stream of paid-for knick-knacks arrived, an unstoppable tide flowing inexorably into the hateful house.

'So,' she thought in her bitter melancholy, 'this is how it is! This is how one must prepare for the Land of Darkness and the Shadow of Death.'

'You're not yourself,' Mrs Glass remarked, meaning to be kind, meaning to look as if she cared.

'No, indeed!' Mrs Curzon spat venomously. 'I'd retire if I could. If I had anywhere to go, I'd go without hesitation.'

'Oh!' Mrs Glass was taken aback. She said nothing further. Mrs Glass not unnaturally concluded that people had talked. That her husband's women (as once Henry James Cathcart's women also) had been known about by all but herself and that her servants found the remarks among other servants and about town intolerable. They must assume she condoned her husband's behaviour, and yet until that moment outside the Café Royal she had known and suspected nothing.

Mrs Glass watched Mary Ann removing the wrappings from some purchases that had just been delivered. She looked at a pair of cranberry glass vases. She was 'on to a good number', she told herself, with no small satisfaction in being able to apply one of Henry James Cathcart's glib phrases to a situation all her very own. What Edward Glass did or did not do was of no more concern to her now than it had ever been. She had written as much to him, mentioning at the same time in fairly strong terms that she needed a lot more money. Shopping was, after all, an expensive pursuit. Mrs Edward Glass, wife of the prestigious architect of the New Paris Grand, had a position to maintain, and maintaining a position did not come cheap.

'Mrs Curzon is a bit put out,' Mrs Glass observed.

'Yer, well . . .' Mary Ann was caught unawares.

'She said she would leave if she could,' Mrs Glass continued, hoping to learn something from the girl. 'It seems she has no one . . .'

'She has her Mr Luscombe,' Mary Ann volunteered. Mrs Glass had heard the name but could not remember in what context.

'They're related, by marriage somehow, poor man.'

'Indeed? But who exactly is this Mr Luscombe?'

'The piano-teacher, Ma'am. He comes on Monday afternoons to teach the girls.'

'Ah, but of course! I pay him a few pence each week to have my house pervaded for an hour by that dreadful noise the children probably think of as music.'

Mary Ann grinned. 'Perhaps Mrs Curzon could go and live with Mr Luscombe,' she suggested. She wanted to add 'then I could be housekeeper here', but Mrs Glass said it for her.

'Perhaps if that were to happen you could be housekeeper in her stead, Mary Ann. I am certain you would make an excellent housekeeper.'

Mary Ann flushed with excitement. Until this moment she had had no ambition in life. Most of her plans had involved men who took no notice of her and thinking about anything which helped to banish memories of a loveless infancy spent in an orphanage with a deloused shaven head. She flicked back her beautiful auburn curls and smiled. If she were housekeeper she needn't wear a parlour-maid's cap. She too would be able to afford cranberry glass vases, some better clothes and any number of wide-brimmed hats for the sea-side. And then, couldn't the seemingly impossible happen? Couldn't Philip Eames look up one Friday afternoon and actually see her?

'I was wondering,' she began, shivering with excitement.

'Yes, Mary Ann?'

'Well, I was wondering if I could have your permission to go to Margate. I have never seen the sea and I . . .'

'Never seen the sea! Why, Mary Ann!' Elizabeth wished that she too had never seen the sea as she had done, sitting miserably beside Henry at Ventnor. But Margate was not Ventnor; why not one scrap pasted over another, blotting out what was underneath? 'Look, I'd like to make it up to Milla and Helen – Stacia being taken in hand by Lady Blouvier – why don't we *all* of us go for a day at the sea? What a happy household we would be. I'll ask Mr Eames.'

'Oh, Ma'am!' Poor Mary Ann assumed her mistress meant to ask if Philip Eames would care to join them. Elizabeth Glass had been thinking that she might mention Margate to Eames as something to say, to show Edward Glass she was carrying on as normal. Mary Ann flushed as red as the cranberry glass: 'I can think of nothing I would like more. You are so kind, Ma'am, even if I'm not allowed to say the word. Kind, that's what you are. Kind, kind, kind!' Mary Ann fled downstairs to hide her emotions.

'Margate!' she told Cora. 'We're all of us to have a day out at the sea.' Philip Eames would have to come if Mrs Glass herself invited him.

'Don't s'pose that includes me,' Cora said sullenly, for Mary Ann was the lucky one and it seemed to the pudding-like Cora that luckiness and prettiness were somehow inextricably linked.

Elizabeth resolved to speak to the piano-teacher about Mrs Curzon. A generous pension should solve the problem – few problems in life cannot be solved with money and few pleasures not be bought with it either. She'd not be sorry to see the last of Mrs Curzon, and Mary Ann would do the job just as well. Next Monday she would ask Mr Luscombe to step downstairs for a word. Next week. Once, in this house, long past, unknown to Elizabeth Glass, the other Mrs Glass had laughed: 'Next week, dear Edward, if you have a *weak*ness, it is for next week!'

Edward had found Sarah Glass's gently expressed mockery irritating but he barely took any notice, of her or of his own irritation. At the time he'd been passionate about the actress Elsinora Lee. Before Elee there had been another girl, a girl Sarah had known about although she had never known about Elee. The girl Sarah had known about had been nameless and what she had done could not be named.

Mrs Curzon had had a name for her. Mrs Curzon had told Sarah that harlots and Jezebels could expect no better in this world, or the next. Mrs Curzon had been angry on Sarah's behalf. And Sarah had been angry with Mrs Curzon; by speaking of these things it gave them form. What you do not speak of has no substance. What you do not see does not exist.

The girl had been William's friend, but William's father's friend first. The girl had had a child; both she and Edward had blamed William. Sarah assumed Edward's anger was rooted in jealousy. She had once suggested to Edward that William could become an architect. Glass & Co. could be Glass & Son given time, but Edward had dismissed the idea. He'd not wanted a son for a rival. Leave that to Preedy and Styles, he had said. For her husband's sake, because she was a good wife and all that a wife should be, she had told her son he had behaved disgracefully and that he was not any more a son of hers. William had not told her his father's part in the misery. He had made the girl his wife and took his wife and the baby he took for his son (although he knew the child to be his part-brother) and departed for the New World. At first he had written intermittent correct letters home. He despised his father and pitied his mother. Separately, through their pride and denial of the truth, they had ganged up on him with a fiction to preserve themselves. The fact that the child and then the girl had died in a cheap tavern near the docks in Liverpool even before the boat sailed in to sail out to the other side of the globe made no difference. He had been only too happy then to leave these shores and this distorting of the truth.

'I hate you,' William had said, first to his father and then in a different way to his ineffectual mother. Mrs Curzon he had silently hugged and she had hugged him back and commended him to her God: Enter not into judgement, O Lord; for who is there who can see as the Lord see-eth?

He'd been unable to kiss his sisters. The impish Milla had been his favourite, he had liked to read her stories about heroes and adventure as she leaned on his shoulder like a pretty little parrot, her naughty eyes round and shiny like sparkling gold doubloons in a pirate's pocket. He could not bear to say 'goodbye', so dear William had slipped away like a coward, leaving Milla to grieve for ever for what she could not know.

'What shall I tell the girls?' Sarah Glass had asked.

'That is your problem, Madam,' Edward told his wife. They were her girls, her problem, it could be her story.

'Tell them William has gone to seek his fortune,' Dr Morgan suggested, making light, for he could not bear to see his dear cousin Sarah so upset. One day he would avenge her. 'Little girls like Once upon a time,' he said comfortingly.

Elizabeth Glass and Stacia went to visit Lady Blouvier in Mayfair. Lady Blouvier looked Stacia up and down approvingly and decided that the girl should leave school at once and come to live with her and Delia. As Mrs Glass and Stacia were about to take their leave, two men arrived in full evening attire.

'A little soirée,' Lady Blouvier explained, inviting Mrs Glass to dine some other evening and having her shown at once to the door. 'Delia and I do so enjoy a little soirée. Why, next time Stacia will have to play us some of her Chopin.'

'Who was that quaint little specimen?' Valentine Birtles enquired. 'Such perfectly darling little shoes!'

'Why, Mr Birtles,' bellowed Lady Blouvier, 'I do declare our Mrs Glass has caught your fancy!'

Valentine Birtles bowed but refrained from replying.

Mr Vizetelly however enquired: 'Mrs Glass, Ma'am? Not Edward Glass's wife?'

'The same,' boomed Lady Blouvier. 'His *second* wife!'

Vizetelly recalled the other young lady who danced attendance on the architect. Vizetelly's estimation of the man rose considerably, confirming in fact Mr Blaise's assertion that they had hired Great Art. Which was just as well: for Blaise and the others certainly seemed bent on spending whatever the fellow should require.

Delia Blouvier explained to Mr Birtles in her bored, whispery voice, so very difficult to hear, that the orphaned Stacia Glass was coming to be her companion. Or her mother's companion, she was not sure which. 'Mamma feels flat after the excitements of the Continent, Mr Birtles,' Delia said. 'She needs a new *divertissement*.'

Mr Birtles, now positioned strategically by the window, turned his head and raised his monocle to observe how, while new faces were eagerly arriving to join this evening's Blouvier soirée, Mrs Glass and her plump step-daughter were seating themselves in the Blouvier carriage, a vast imperial contraption, which was to drive them home. Valentine Birtles lowered his monocle to attend to this evening's proceedings but resolved very shortly to encounter the woman again. He could do with a new *divertissement* himself!

19

Desperate Dancing

Weeks ago the edition of *News from the Other Side* that contained Sensational pictures of Stacia Glass eating seed-cake had been dispatched across the country, causing a mild stir in some quarters. Grocers quickly sold out of caraway seeds when a superstition arose that the Dead could be lured Back to tea-parties cheaply, using seed-cake. You can't please everyone and there were those who complained that a Sensation ought to be sensational or relegated from the front page: who had Sarah Glass been when *Alive* that her Return to scoff cake was deemed so remarkable?

One of the photographs was stereoscopic, two images almost alike which readers could cut out and stick side by side on a piece of card: the left eye and the right eye. Seen through a stereoscopic viewer the apricot organdie would look three-dimensional. Elizabeth Glass had purchased just such a viewer which folded neatly away in a walnut box. They were quite a craze, every household had one. A standard knick-knack so to speak.

Mrs Curzon showed Mrs Glass the *News*; she had been given it by another housekeeper further down the street. She said nothing to Mrs Glass, she did not need to: the photographic evidence was there on the front page which she thrust under her employer's nose.

Mrs Glass was mildly amused, though at the time she'd been tired out with waiting for Dr Morgan to come in answer to her summons. Stacia Glass, her very own step-daughter – it really was rather funny. Mrs Curzon heard Elizabeth giggle. 'Men go to prison for upwards of twenty years for any one of the offences Dr Morgan has committed in this house,' Mrs Curzon muttered as she heard Elizabeth laugh.

'They were playing charades,' Miss Housecroft had said, describing the party she had missed. It had been a childish party prank: Stacia dressed up as her mother. Lady Blouvier entered into the fun and took some photographs. Mrs Glass did not bother to cut out the stereoscopic prints; why go to the trouble of snipping and pasting and folding the viewer out of its walnut box just to look at her eldest step-daughter in three dimensions?

A show-down of some sort had been long overdue. Mrs Glass mounted the stairs to speak to Miss Housecroft. She knocked on the governess's door and as there was no reply she entered the room. Papers and books were scattered all over the desk. The papers did not look like letters of application exactly. When Miss Housecroft returned to her room she was disconcerted to find Mrs Glass waiting for her.

'We must talk,' Emily Housecroft said, seizing back the initiative. She thought another luncheon of idle chatter or another leisurely shopping expedition would send her round the twist. 'I fear there has been a misunderstanding.'

'Mary Ann told me you were applying for another position.'

'I did, but it didn't work out.'

Elizabeth Glass stared at the young woman. She had more or less offered all her own hard-won resources to allow Miss Housecroft to do whatever she pleased and the governess had responded by hiding herself mysteriously away, working at whatever those papers on the table meant she was working at, and at the same time applying for posts elsewhere. 'What can you expect of a friendship forged over a stretched salmon?' Elizabeth asked herself ruefully.

There was in truth little mystery about Emily Housecroft. Her father was something lowly in the High Church and Emily had been sent to a boarding-school for Daughters of Impoverished Clergy. Mrs Glass's light-hearted allusions to *Jane Eyre* had been more apt than either she knew (having learnt nothing of Emily's past), or that Emily herself knew, for she had never read anything so low-brow as a romance by Charlotte Brontë. The governess's reading did not extend beyond the Classics, dead languages which she sought to bring back to life by valiantly struggling with the original.

Emily Housecroft had grown into a pale and earnest young lady and had acquitted herself well, but not outstandingly, at school, an establishment run by the philanthropic Mr and Mrs Dean. At the end of their education girls stayed on a couple of years to teach the younger ones. There was no remuneration for this privilege as it was accounted valuable experience. When Emily Housecroft had completed this apprenticeship, Mrs Dean suggested she might study the

Schoolmistress for a post somewhere near the North London Institute where she had heard interesting scholarly work was being done.

'A Professor Arthur Fahey is always on the look-out for students; just mention my name. Meanwhile you could find some light governessing duties nearby.' Mrs Dean sighed and promised an excellent reference (she wrote excellent references for all her pupils, having seen nothing of their work, or in their behaviour, not to).

Initially, Emily Housecroft returned home to her father's rectory, a crowded house attached to St Asaph's. Her sisters called her 'stuck up', her brothers were jealous of the attention her parents paid her. She felt a stranger there. Dr Housecroft smiled fondly at his daughter's pointless ambitions. The girl had been at home some months now sitting around with Caesar and Plutarch which did nothing to contribute towards her keep. He mentioned that Mr Simms, the churchwarden, was prepared to take on a wife. Mr Simms was nearly fifty. Emily had just passed her seventeenth birthday. Emily Housecroft recalled Mrs Dean's advice and purchased that week's *Schoolmistress*.

'There is nothing of which Miss Housecroft is not capable,' Mrs Dean wrote amongst other things. This was the phrase that had attracted Mrs Glass.

'I ask only a quiet life,' Elizabeth had told her, a remark Emily Housecroft now recalled with some bitterness. It was all that she herself asked but it was Mrs Glass who kept interrupting her work with silly demands.

'The child is wilful,' the housekeeper had said, but Emily had soon discovered that 'wilful' did not altogether sum Milla up. Now as she looked at Mrs Glass she tried in vain to think what one word could accurately describe this woman either: none in any of the languages she had in stock.

After her interview with Mrs Glass when she had agreed to commence work immediately, Miss Housecroft had walked to the Institute. 'Mrs Dean sent me,' she told Professor Arthur Fahey, who offered her a cup of tea from the pot they had just brought him in his rooms.

'Mrs Dean?' He looked mystified. 'Can't say I've ever had the pleasure.'

'Oh!' Emily Housecroft then proceeded to sip the weak tea and explain her position.

Arthur Fahey had accepted an enormous commission to edit, adapt and annotate most of the major Classical texts for Schools Editions. He could not possibly have coped with this task without the help of willing female students who freely undertook most of the burden. Within days of being installed in York Street Emily Housecroft too was making detailed footnotes to Virgil's *Aeneid, Book X*. Fortune helps those who help themselves: *audentis Fortuna iuvat*, and Emily Housecroft felt she had indeed helped herself very nicely.

'I am not the woman you think I am,' Miss Housecroft told her employer. 'I can do without any desperate dancing, I want only to sit with my texts and my dictionaries. I am a slow worker, I have no special gifts. I like my Professor, I need my time.'

'Emily, why didn't you tell me all this before? Of course you must do your work. How clever you are! But it will be easier for you when Stacia has gone. You must have a proper study to yourself downstairs where you will not be disturbed; I know how disturbing Milla can be.'

'How kind you are!'

Mrs Glass winced. 'No more job applications, then?'

'No, indeed.' Miss Housecroft smiled. She did not want to engage with the eager hands and hungry lips of another Mr Josar.

Milla and Helen stood watching while Stacia packed her belongings into the smart valise Mrs Glass had bought specially for her to take to Lady Blouvier's.

'How long are you going for?'

'I don't know,' Stacia said, although as far as she was concerned she was going for ever.

'Will you come and see us sometimes?' Milla asked.

'Oh, I don't know.' Stacia pinned her mother's diamond brooch carefully on to her blouse.

'That looks nice,' Helen said.

'It belonged to Poor Mamma,' Milla said. 'It was ever so kind of Mrs Glass to give it to you.'

'Since, as you pointed out, it belonged to Mamma, it was more mine to have than Mrs Glass's to give me, wasn't it?'

'Well, yes.'

'So that doesn't make her *kind*!'

'Will we come and see you?' Milla asked. 'In Mayfair?'

Stacia glanced across at Milla. The last thing she'd want would be visitors, from here. 'Well, perhaps. I'll see what it's like. You must wait for an invitation, it may be difficult.'

Milla was sure it would be difficult. She still could not imagine how Stacia could bear to go and live with Lady Blouvier. 'Aren't you at all sorry to be going?' she asked.

'Oh, do stop going on and on,' Stacia said. 'Just because you're not the one invited.'

'Won't you miss us?' Helen asked and started to cry.

'You'll be surprised what human beings can get used to when they must,' Stacia handed Helen the last of the handkerchiefs embroidered 'S. G.' that she had once stolen from their mother's room. 'Blow your nose on that,' she said roughly.

'Even Lady Blouvier?' Milla asked, but Stacia did not hear. Stacia was swapping the Conrad & Taylor Upright whose pedals fell off and whose ivory keys occasionally needed Milla's pot of glue for the ebony Grand Piano she had seen in the drawing-room at Eulalia House. Her only regret was that she had not taken her piano lessons more seriously all these years.

'Say "goodbye" to dusty old Luscombe for me,' she laughed, stuffing her Chopin scores in her valise.

'We'll miss you, Stacia,' Milla said quietly as her sister picked up her things ready to go. They could hear Mrs Glass calling from downstairs.

Stacia looked awkwardly across the room at Milla and the sobbing Helen. 'I'm only going to Mayfair,' she said. 'It's not the other side of the Globe, or the Uncivilized World. It's not exactly the Argentine or Dahomey!'

Stacia hesitated then. She and Milla looked unblinkingly at each other. Neither knew whether to laugh or cry. Helen flung herself howling passionately on Stacia's neck. Stacia and Milla shrugged their shoulders and grinned bravely. Mrs Glass called again from below, urgently now.

'I'd better go.' Stacia pushed Helen firmly away and hurried downstairs as fast as she could.

Milla and Helen went to their upper-landing window. Miss Housecroft had told Milla to stop spying on Mrs Glass but Stacia was the one they were watching. Their sister ran eagerly down the front path and climbed up into the cab without so much as a quick backward glance to see if they were up there. Even Philip Eames had paused to doff his hat.

'Eulalia House, Eden Gardens,' Mrs Glass told the driver.

'The Garden of Eden!' Stacia whispered excitedly.

'Hardly!' Elizabeth and Stacia exchanged frosty glances and settled back into their own separate silences.

'She's gone,' Helen said when the cab was out of sight.

'Yes,' said Milla. It felt final like the last page of a book, the end of a disappointing adventure.

With Edward Glass spending most of his time in London at the site of the Paris Grand, Philip Eames could think of fewer excuses for not visiting his mother. Her perpetual state of waiting for his visits meant that he spent his life perpetually avoiding her and letting her down.

Philip Eames entered his mother's house and was surprised to find the woman and the house unaccountably changed. Flora Eames did not tell her son about Dr Morgan. She considered Spiritualism a 'load of mumbo-jumbo' and like Sarah Glass before her, she had told the doctor so: 'The Dead are dead and gone, thank goodness!' she'd said, the late Mr Eames being a case in point. Mrs Eames respected Dr Morgan's brain for business, however, and she had been wondering whether Philip couldn't team up with the man. Looking at her son now as he entered her house she saw the hopelessness of her plan: Philip would always be the clerk he preferred to remain. She curtly offered him a bite to eat.

'Oh no! No, thank you, I've already eaten,' Philip said quickly although he was hungry. His mother could not have known he was coming and yet here was the table elaborately laid with only herself apparently dining. This added to his sense of guilt. Presumably his mother went to all this trouble on the off-chance that he might turn up. To test her, he said: 'You weren't, um, expecting anyone?'

'Who would I be expecting?' the lavender-scented Flora Eames countered ingenuously. 'Except you, of course, dear Philip.'

She had given up expecting the police. The last time she had seen Dr Morgan he'd brought her a stuffed wire-haired terrier, and then he had asked her about a theft that had taken place at Eulalia House.

'It could have been very awkward for me, Flora! Her Ladyship might have thought I deliberately set out to create a diversion. How ever did you manage to carry away so much silver and porcelain in one go?'

'Lucius, any woman married to a man like Mr Eames and then widowed with a son like my Philip, would have mastered the delicate art of survival.'

'How Darwinian, dear Lady!' A woman too much after his own heart, he feared. He could see no use for her. (By now he had found a far better angle on Edward Glass than Mrs Eames's living son could possibly provide. If the second Mrs Glass was not sweating, then she ought to be. Dr Morgan had not finished with Elizabeth yet.)

Flora Eames smiled at her disappointing son. 'You're welcome, any time, you know that,' she lied.

Philip flinched. Visiting his mother was an act of self-abasement: he came to discover how far from grace he had fallen. He chose to live at an unclean inn near a railway station on the excuse that the offices of Glass & Co. all over the country were served by the railway and Philip often caught very early and very late trains. In the anonymous room that heaved as trains shook past through the night, suffused with the glare of yellow lamplight that the flimsy curtains could not block out, Philip Eames trembled at the violence of his thoughts. His very presence corrupted the air he breathed and he burned with shame at bringing to his mother's house all that was detestable and sickening in his unhappy soul. He refused the food she offered for he would not compound his sins by sullying her table.

When the garrulous parlourmaid had told Eames that they were alone in the house – only a younger sister and a few servants scattered below – Philip had shaken with fear. The girl might have come down to him on some pretext that afternoon as She often came down to him in his fancy. A timid knock like a gentle caress and She'd have entered: he'd barely been able to breathe, hearing Her walking towards him. He thought of the little white hand he'd have seized, the untried flesh he'd have crushed to him, stifling Her startled cries as his inky fingers closed over Her delicate mouth. Only he would hear as Stacia Glass fluttered her wings and cried out in pain.

Philip Eames flinched again. He cursed the creature that had so bewitched him that even before his own mother he thought of Her and what She would make him do to Her. He had loved the little canary he had kept as a boy. The yellow canary that had sung so happily until a cat got into the house and destroyed it in its cage.

Mrs Glass had told him that they might all go to Margate for a day. 'Just let me know when,' he'd said at once and considered himself invited. He looked forward to hiring deck-chairs for them both. While the others strolled and sunned themselves he would sit Stacia down, to begin the process of taking the little canary girl in hand and shaping her song to his needs . . .

Edward Glass had acquired a secretary, a young lady who had thrown herself at the Master rather as Harry Withercott had thrown himself into the empty draughtsman's chair. Lucy Winnup was always present at the Paris Grand site, making life intolerable with her interfering. The men in the offices smirked, and dug Philip Eames in the ribs:

'All these women, Philip, it's a wonder you get any sleep!'

'It's a wonder you're not exhausted, Philip!'

'You're a wonder, Philip!'

No *wonder* Mrs Glass had written as she had written. Philip hoped he'd have done the same in her shoes. Lucy Winnup knew what she wanted and she reached out her paw like a cat tipping over a silver creamer. Only Eames had read what Mrs Glass had written in her letter, her husband had merely asked for the gist.

'I think he'll get the gist, all right,' Philip thought.

'Fifteen years you've been working for Edward Glass,' Flora Eames was saying. Philip eyed her wearily. Mrs Eames had a new recitation. She had heard through someone who vaguely knew someone who knew Mrs Winnup of Turnham Green: Lucy Winnup had usurped her son. She berated Philip now for putting up with this outrage. 'A mother needs something to be proud of,' she told him.

As Eames leaned back wretchedly in his chair, an old copy of *News from the Other side* that had begun to yellow chanced to catch his attention. Philip Eames started. Picking the paper off the sideboard, he held it accusingly before him, unable to believe what he was seeing. Mrs Eames started also. The subscription had been a small luxury to remind herself of her little *rencontre*. Mrs Eames was a realistic woman and did not suppose Dr Morgan would seek her out again. She had taken the stuffed wire-haired terrier for the parting-present it had been.

Mrs Eames did not like animals in the house but she made an exception of the stuffed dog for it was a kind thought from a kind man and in any case the pooch was dead and wouldn't make a nuisance of itself. When he'd been a little boy, Philip had insisted on keeping a noisy canary. His father had bought him a cage. Annoyed by its ceaseless singing, Flora Eames had left the back door open one day for a neighbourhood cat to get in and help himself to the bird.

Philip Eames stared accusingly at the picture of his Stacia; a canary should be fed seed, not seed-cake. 'I must have this,' he eventually managed to splutter.

Mrs Eames raised her eyebrows and said that as he was obviously so keen to take it away with him he could have the back copy as a parting-present. In fact she was grateful that the *News* had drawn her son's attention away from her dining-table, for what would she have said if he'd noticed the Blouvier crest on her plates and started asking awkward questions?

When Philip had gone she lifted the cloth from the apricot and vermicelli tart she'd been concealing. She had not made enough for two and did not see that her son could expect to share her meal with her, arriving unexpectedly as he had. She wished that he wouldn't get it into his head quite so often to come disrupting her life – the boy reminded her of Mr Eames who had also disrupted her life and whom she would also prefer, despite his having paid for her pew in the church, to forget.

At Eulalia House, Valentine Birtles took Elizabeth Glass's ringless hand. Lady Blouvier winked at him and instructed Delia to conduct Stacia up to the beautiful room that was to be hers while she lived with them.

'For me?' Stacia gasped, making certain before she got too excited. 'All for me?'

'Of course,' Delia smiled wanly. Her mother did nothing in half-measures.

Stacia walked round the room touching the beautiful curtains, the lace pillow-cases, the soft blankets, luxury in line with her wildest dreams. 'I have always had to share everything with my sisters,' she said.

'Your sisters could come if you like,' Delia said.

'Oh no, that would ruin everything,' Stacia answered at once. 'You don't know what they're like. I couldn't bear . . .'

'I had a sister once,' Delia said in a bored voice. 'I can't remember her at all. I don't remember being sorry when she died.'

'I would be sorry if Milla or Helen *died*, it's just that I don't want them *here*,' Stacia said. 'I had a brother too, dear William, but he went away. I can't remember him.'

Delia wasn't listening. She languished on the bed while Stacia ran round the room picking up and putting down everything she could find, opening and shutting drawers. In the wardrobe she discovered hundreds of lavish party frocks.

'Put one on, why don't you?' Delia said, without interest. Stacia held dress after dress against herself as she gazed in the mirror. This was better than dressing up in moth-eaten old stuffs from her mother's smelly wardrobe. She patted the silks, the satins, the beautiful brocades. This was living at last! Living *vivace e capriccioso* as she'd always intended.

'Found you!' Lady Blouvier sailed into the room. 'Hiding away up here, you naughty young things!' She eyed Stacia exploring the wardrobe.

'I never had a choice before . . .' Stacia said.

'A tedious business,' Delia remarked.

'Oh, no!' Stacia cried. 'It's wonderful.'

'You'll get used to it, I dare say.'

'I could never get used to all this,' Stacia declared, gesturing happily round the room. 'It's perfect!' she breathed.

Lady Blouvier and her daughter exchanged a look of amusement as Stacia slipped a diaphanous blue sash over her shoulders and practised her curtsey in front of the mirror. She tried on a couple of pairs of shoes. They were all a bit tight and pinched her toes, but they were beautiful and they were all for her.

'What a mess you are making!' Lady Blouvier remarked delightedly.

'Oh, I'm sorry,' Stacia started to pick things up.

'It's common to pick things up,' Delia told her. 'You don't want to insult the maids or they'll never forgive you.'

'My, you *do* have a lot to learn!' Lady Blouvier said.

'Yes, yes, I know.'

'We'll have to see what we can do with our little Cinderella, eh

Delia?' Mother and daughter exchanged another look of sardonic amusement. 'But what of the ugly sisters back home?'

'Milla and Helen aren't *ugly* exactly – they're only children and boring,' Stacia said and then added, 'Has Mrs Glass gone?'

'Why, ages ago, child!'

'She never said "Goodbye".'

'Hardly the motherly sort,' Lady Blouvier observed with some satisfaction. Her Delia lacked for nothing.

'She's not my mother,' Stacia declared, pushing Mrs Glass away like Milla dissociating herself from her algebra book.

'A silly woman,' Lady Blouvier said. She had seen Mrs Glass smiling at Valentine Birtles. Lady Blouvier had an oft-expressed theory that a properly run drawing-room was like Noah's Ark in reverse: crowd enough silly creatures in together and they soon pair off and depart, two by two.

'She likes nothing better than sharp scissors and a big pot of glue. She told us so herself,' Stacia said. 'You should have heard her carrying on when Milla told her there's no such thing as chance.'

'As I thought, a silly woman,' Lady Blouvier remarked. 'It was only by chance we arrived home from Switzerland just in time to accompany dear Dr Morgan to York Street in our conveyance. Another three minutes and we'd have missed him. What a happy chance it was for us all!'

'Yes it was!' agreed Stacia emphatically.

'She gets on better with your younger sisters then, Mrs Glass?'

'She and Milla talk about puff-adders, algebra, paper-scraps.'

'Paper-scraps!' Lady Blouvier was aghast. 'You were wasted there, child! Your star is destined to shine in a greater, loftier sky.'

A Mayfair sky, Stacia thought. Lady Blouvier was the first person in her life who agreed with her own assessment of herself.

'She's a little young for your father, don't you think?' Lady Blouvier asked.

It was a peculiar question, but most of the high-minded conversation at Eulalia House was a little peculiar. Stacia regretted how lacking her education had been. 'I'm not sure how old she is,' Stacia said. 'Or my father for that matter.'

'Do they . . . ? Is there . . .?' Lady Blouvier began. She and Delia exchanged a look Stacia saw but could not begin to interpret. Like a vast sailing vessel mid-ocean, Lady Blouvier changed tack: 'It will be such a pleasure for us to have you here. Delia will enjoy showing you how things are done.'

Delia smiled dimly. Lady Blouvier continued: 'Now first we must teach you to curtsey.'

'Er . . .' Stacia looked at her benefactress. 'Curtsey?' she asked. Curtseying was just about the only accomplishment she had already mastered.

'I hardly like to tell you this, Stacia dear, but when you curtsey at the moment you look like a top-heavy fairy dangling from one of dear Albert's decorated Christmas trees!'

Delia smiled in faintly amused agreement.

'Oh!' Stacia felt not a little crestfallen.

'Don't worry yourself, child!' Lady Blouvier laughed loudly. 'You are here to learn. Now, you mustn't detain me any longer; I need to prepare this evening's soirée. You've brought your Chopin, I see,' she tugged at the bundle of battered scores poking out from Stacia's valise and tossed them carelessly down on the table so that the *nocturnes, études* and *polonaises* flew everywhere and had to be retrieved. 'What fun we will have!' Lady Blouvier swept from the room singing an aria in a staccato, rather English, Italian at the top of her voice as she went.

Stacia sighed happily. How lucky she felt! She looked at herself critically in the mirror and then, frowning a little, she rather hesitantly curtsied. 'What *is it* that I do wrong?' she asked Delia. She really had no idea.

'Don't worry about it,' Delia smiled. 'These things take years of practice. You can't expect to become one of us just like that, you know!'

Stacia looked in the mirror again, but now she saw how dumpy and unrefined her splendid new surroundings only served to make her. For the first time since she'd left York Street she wondered what Milla and Helen were up to. She was glad they weren't here but it was a shame nevertheless that they could not see her wonderful room and all her lovely clothes and giggle with her over her new-found luck, the pumpkin-coach and the glass slippers.

20

An Everlasting Kiss

'About our trip to Margate.'

'Margate?' Mrs Glass had had other things than Margate on her mind. Mary Ann, meanwhile, had thought of nothing else. 'Oh look, some time . . .'

Mary Ann smiled bravely.

Valentine Birtles had been seen about town with Mrs Glass.

Elizabeth wrote again requiring more money from her husband. Again Edward Glass was too busy to read the letter. Having asked for the gist, he instructed Eames to increase the woman's already increased allowance. Vaguely he presumed *assignations* with her dressmaker could not come cheap.

Desmond Blaise called at the site office.

'He'll be with you in a moment,' Lucy Winnup smiled her radiant smile and offered the Director a chair that was covered with manufacturers' and merchants' catalogues and compendiums which she quickly heaved out of the way.

'Why, look at this!' Blaise retrieved a catalogue from the floor. 'Well, I never! The very latest in cyanide tanks. You are a dangerous lady, Miss Winnup.'

Lucy smiled indistinctly. Somehow she doubted her powers against those of a cyanide tank.

Blaise was not a man to be kept waiting even when a pleasant young lady was available for light banter. He asked how long Edward Glass was likely to be. Lucy Winnup respectfully reminded him how he himself had said: 'Great Art cannot be trotted along like some great cart-horse . . .'

In the adjoining room Edward Glass was staring at a vast sheet of blank paper. All things are possible, he thought. I could do anything.

Lucy put her pretty little head round the door. 'I'm sorry to disturb you, Edward, but Mr Blaise is here insisting . . .'

Confound the man! What it was to be in the pay of petty men like

215

Desmond Blaise. Even with this, his Masterpiece, it seemed there was no escape. Nothing, and certainly not Desmond Blaise, must be allowed to trip him mid-air.

Blaise strode in. Hands in pockets. He glanced round the room and laughed. 'Where are all the plans, then?' he asked. 'I've been looking forward to my own special preview.'

Glass nodded curtly in the direction of the vast blank sheet.

Blaise followed with his eyes, and laughed again. 'No, where?'

'Up here,' Glass said, tapping the side of his head. 'Ring courses, spring courses, voussoirs – the lot.' The man wants circus-tricks *and* a ringside seat: a triumph of trickery, architectural acrobatics balanced dextrously on a per cent!

Mildly disconcerted, Blaise glanced at Lucy, but she did not smile back this time. 'Ah ha, keeping it confidential, I see!'

'Do you see, Mr Blaise?' Glass asked. 'Oh, I very much doubt it. What is this jugglery of genius, you will ask.'

'We can't all be Great Artists,' Blaise said easily. Blaise who was content to be Blaise. The two men looked at each other with the hostility of mutual convenience.

'I'll leave you to get on,' Desmond Blaise said then, hoping the man *would* get a move on. You couldn't collect a percentage of money that had yet to be spent.

What a haphazard thing it all was, Glass thought. There had been a moment in time before he'd met Desmond Blaise. No wonder an individual felt helpless in the face of this chaos that must be wrestled into shape like space on an empty sheet of white paper.

How proud they had been of William, he and Sarah. He could hardly remember her now, but he remembered the fateful day when for some reason known only to herself she had said: 'It'll be *Glass & Son* one day. William can be an architect too and take over from you.'

Sarah had assumed it was jealousy that made him react as he had. He supposed that in the moment before she spoke, he had still felt something for her. Afterwards he could not bear her or William near him: the idea that it could be William Glass or Edward Glass, interchangeable, indistinguishable, totally replaceable and neither entirely themselves, upset him. There must be more to life than merely replicating life, wishing one's own limitations on the children of one's own flesh. What hope or happiness could there be in that?

And then there had been Kitty. The lovely, beautiful, destructive Kitty who cared nothing for hope or happiness but knew how to get her own back. It wasn't a straightforward transaction of money she was after. No meek percentage would satisfy Kitty; when she found even a baby would not pin Edward Glass down she had turned her deadly talents on William. The foolish boy had fallen for her tricks and then stood by her, understanding her destruction even as she destroyed.

Ah, secret of secrets, but perhaps not so secret. In the end we find out for ourselves that there is *nothing*, the void inside is outside also. The space on the blank page is the space in our heads and our hearts bounded for ever by ourselves.

Arcanum Arcanorum started to draw, two pencils in each hand, four lines moving across the large sheet of blank paper, symmetric on a rotational axis. At least he had never nurtured false hopes in the children he had not wanted, Stacia, Milla and Helen, the daughters he had refused to have anything to do with. He had raised, so he thought, no expectations. He remembered Milla's jelly-stained mouth. The birthday-girl, going on and on about William as though she could possibly know, or care. The other side of the globe indeed: the girl had never even been the other side of London! He did not know about the visit to Pasha.

Emily Housecroft was invited to dinner by her beloved Professor Fahey. Mrs Fahey had a sarcastic tongue which was reputed to need regular and vigorous exercise. It amused Mrs Fahey to provide dinners for the thin young women who slaved over Classical texts for her husband. She assumed, not incorrectly, that the pale girls were all in love with him. Mrs Fahey cast critical eyes over the earnest creatures who sat down to dine on cold meats in her cold dining-room.

'If I should die,' she asked the Professor after Emily Housecroft had taken up her papers and returned to her warm study in York Street, 'would you marry that one?'

Professor Fahey, not averse to waging pitched battles of hypothesis, admitted to finding Miss Housecroft's work thorough, accurate but fairly mundane, and concluded truthfully that he most likely would not. The good thing about that particular girl was the way she translated her devotion into industry.

'I hope you don't stay up half the night,' he remarked enthusiastically, noticing how tight the skin had become about her eyes. Emily Housecroft flushed red as School Board ink and Arthur Fahey decided to reward her with a mention in one of his acknowledgements. It was always useful having someone to blame for inaccuracies when fuddy-duddy scholars wrote in.

If Milla and Helen had been bored before, they were more so than ever now that Stacia had gone and Miss Housecroft had been given a study of her own downstairs, fully equipped and furnished, no expense spared. Mrs Glass had enjoyed herself: 'If this is what you want, Emily, it is what you shall have!' She personally affixed a 'Do not Disturb' sign on the door.

Elizabeth, wondering if she hadn't been a little neglectful, decided to visit Milla and Helen in the school-room. 'What, no algebra?' she asked, laughing.

'Stacia hasn't written,' Milla said.

'I expect she's busy,' Mrs Glass said.

'She could have sent a postcard,' Helen suggested.

'Stacia's not one for sitting down at a desk when there's something better to do, is she?'

'No,' Milla admitted. 'I can't think why she wanted to go and stay with that horrid Lady Blouvier.'

'Horrid?'

'Yes,' Milla did not like what she remembered. 'She was loud and bossy and very rude about you. I cannot imagine her being kind to Stacia for no reason.'

'She probably has her reasons,' Mrs Glass said. 'She's extravagant, that's all.'

'She spends a lot of money?' Milla asked.

'I'm sure she does, but I meant that she is loud and enormous with herself because she can afford to be. A lot of money makes people bold and careless.' Elizabeth felt herself becoming bold and careless. She did it in defiance of Henry. Why shouldn't she be a little neglectful, rather than the one left neglected? 'She was probably poor and penniless before she married Lord Blouvier but now she doesn't care to be reminded.'

'She was lucky then?'

'I don't think luck had much to do with it.' Mrs Glass paused and looked playfully at Milla. 'Perhaps you were right all along, there's no such thing as chance: good luck is something people work hard to earn.'

'She was in a funny mood,' Helen said when Mrs Glass was gone.

'It's probably just as well Stacia isn't here,' Milla agreed, for you could imagine how rude Stacia would have been.

'I think you should look at this, Sir.' Philip Eames handed Edward Glass the back copy of the *News* and watched with quiet satisfaction as his Master's eyes narrowed. With Sarah's demise Edward had thought he'd heard the last of her cousin, the charlatan. Evidently the trickster was back in business!

'I'll pay the fellow for trying to make a laughing-stock out of me,' he thought, coldly returning the paper to his assistant whom he despised for showing it to him. Eames admired the restraint with which Mr Glass responded, but he was disappointed. He'd hoped for fireworks. He did not like the way Stacia had cunningly eluded his grasp. When Mrs Glass had informed him that Stacia had gone to stay with Lady Blouvier he connected the event immediately with his own passions. The little yellow canary had hopped out of its cage, fluttered its wings and *flown*. Philip Eames had covered his confusion by telling the second Mrs Glass again how much he disliked her automaton canaries. 'I do not like ornaments sitting around, gathering dust,' he said.

'Ah, a natural bachelor!' Elizabeth lightly remarked, as though detecting and seeking at once to allay his matrimonial designs on her step-daughter.

Stacia meanwhile was enjoying the finery of Eulalia House. It never occurred to her to write a letter or even a postcard to her sisters. It did occur to her once (and only briefly) that this life was merely a new sort of boredom, another type of sitting around, but she dismissed the irreverent thought as rapidly as she had allowed herself to entertain it. Delia Blouvier was teaching her some useful airs and graces.

Emily Housecroft wrote to her father, and Dr Housecroft journeyed to town to visit. He looked round the pretty furnishings Mrs Glass had chosen and had to admit that his daughter had done very well for herself. He did not tell Emily that Mr Simms, the church-warden, had married her younger sister Clara who was with child.

He flicked through the leather-bound Greek and Latin dictionaries and smiled sadly to himself, for the plush books contained worlds no longer open to him. Dr Housecroft could not admit himself even mildly jealous. His Bishop had told him lately that his lack of worldly ambition, his willingness to dine on home-grown spinach from the rectory garden, had been his own undoing. He would stay at St Asaph's until he was too old to stand at his lectern and then presumably room would be found for him and Mrs Housecroft in a Home for Retired and Impoverished Clergy. Such was this life . . .

Leaving his eldest daughter's room, mindful that he might never see her again, for he could not afford the train-fare and even if he could there were always a thousand and one more pressing uses for money back at St Asaph's, he chanced to notice something lying on top of the davenport that made what few hairs he still had on his head stand on end. 'Emily!' he shrieked. It was more than the poor man could bear.

As far as the Church was concerned, Dr Lucius Morgan (who gorged himself now on the best *table d'hôte*) had, like Lucifer himself, begun life on the side of the Angels. Morgan's *News from the Other Side* was bad news. Dr Housecroft may have forgotten his Greek and Latin vocabularies but he recognized Evil whatever the language. Like a brass lectern eagle spotting an errant field-mouse at harvest-time, the Reverend Housecroft swooped down on the paper and raised the wickedness aloft: 'The printed outpourings of Lucifer in my own daughter's room! Emily, child of my own (and Mrs Housecroft's) flesh, tell your poor Papa that this sheaf of diabolic wheat is none of your nibbling! This foul profit-making publication has nothing to do with you!'

Thankful that all of the family were away from home (for Mrs Glass was attending a matinée performance with Mr Birtles, Milla and Helen were at school and Stacia was in Mayfair), Emily was able to reassure her distressed parent: 'Someone called at the house and left it, Papa; it is only in here out of harm's way waiting to be burned!'

Dr Housecroft let the matter drop, in the wastepaper basket. 'Bless you!' he said, as if his daughter had sneezed.

It was unlikely Edward Glass would let the matter drop quite so easily, but at present he was preoccupied with the New Paris Grand. Philip Eames felt indignant too. His Stacia had been more or less adopted by the same Lady Hildegard Blouvier who was credited with having taken the offending photographs.

'An influential woman,' Glass observed. He knew that Vizetelly knew her, everybody probably knew her, even Sarah had once known her and Sarah had known no one. Whatever action he took he would have to take it carefully.

It was at about this time that Mary Ann went missing. Cora was certain the girl had gone to Margate and met a feller. Dr Morgan had given her sixpence and she had probably bought that wide-brimmed hat.

Valentine Birtles knew how to enjoy life. He was endeavouring to teach Elizabeth Glass to enjoy life also. You don't want to stay cooped up in that miserable dark house, he urged, and invited her to accompany him on a trip to Italy. When Mrs Glass capriciously and idly mentioned to Mrs Curzon that she might be going on holiday, the housekeeper reacted strongly.

'If you do that ma'am, then *I go!*' Mrs Curzon was adamant. What was the world coming to?

'I will give you a generous pension,' the second Mrs Glass pledged at once. She looked forward to the day when the loyal, pretty Mary Ann would take over from Old Sourpuss Curzon (as Valentine had hilariously dubbed the woman one evening). 'I'll see you have money enough.'

Mrs Curzon was surly; enough was never enough, she knew that much. 'Wine maketh merry: but money buyeth all things. I require a *generous* pension. I know my rights.'

'Indeed?' Mrs Glass raised an eyebrow.

'I have been here twenty-six years and more, obligations and intentions are soon forgotten, promises breached . . .'

'We will sort something out,' Mrs Glass said, full of distaste. She had been intending to speak to Mr Luscombe but somehow life had been frantic of late. At the first opportunity she sent Mary Ann to visit Mr Luscombe. 'Explain the situation to him,' Mrs Glass said. 'Explain that he will be amply rewarded for his pains. For goodness' sake, don't whatever you do come back without a firm arrangement. It's in both our interests, Mary Ann, for I wish you to become my housekeeper.'

Mary Ann needed no second bidding. Philip Eames would respect her once she was a housekeeper with more than Dr Morgan's silver sixpence to her name. Mary Ann skipped off at once to visit Mr Luscombe. She would *make* him listen, whatever it took.

'What *can* be keeping her?' Mrs Glass asked.

'Something always keeps Mary Ann,' Mrs Curzon grumbled. 'The girl was never reliable.'

'That is a lie, Mrs Curzon!' Mrs Glass said.

'She will have found herself a new place,' Mrs Curzon went on glumly. 'She probably couldn't stand it here a moment longer.'

'That is quite untrue! If you really want to know, Mrs Curzon, I promised her your place when you leave. Mary Ann is healthily ambitious, she will make an excellent housekeeper. I sent her to enquire of Mr Luscombe what recompense he would consider for taking you to live with him. I understand that you are related by marriage and that the arrangement would suit you. I can tell you this, Mrs Curzon, the arrangement would certainly suit me and I am prepared to pay Mr Luscombe whatever it takes.'

'He is *my* Mr Luscombe, you had no right.' Mrs Curzon had not been prepared for Mrs Glass's outburst. She was the one who had invested heavily, she was the one due to collect with interest. There could be no going back now. Although it was dark she resolved to visit the piano-teacher and settle things once and for all. Even before this direct confrontation the atmosphere in York Street had become too awful to live with. The second Mrs Glass was a godless creature; the Lord, Mrs Curzon supposed, could not be expected to get it right all the time. And as for Valentine Birtles, she would not sully her lips with speaking so absurd a name.

Mrs Curzon arrived at last at the dark sunless villa in which she was determined to end her days. Breathlessly, the housekeeper pounded Mr Luscombe's doorbell. She could hear it ringing inside the house but she got no response. Mr Luscombe's curtains were closed but there was a light lit somewhere at the back, so after a couple more rings she made her way along the side passage, snagging her skirts on his bicycle which she didn't see in the dark. It clattered noisily to the ground and though the noise might have brought the man out, no one appeared. When she got to the back of the house she rapped loudly on the kitchen window.

Mrs Curzon was on the point of giving up, when she noticed the curtains across the kitchen windows were not quite closed and there was some movement in the room, detectable through the tiny gap. She applied her eyes and as she peered she saw an entirely bald and wigless Mr Luscombe busily engaged in digging an enormous hole right down the middle of his kitchen floor. She watched a while longer and then she tapped again on the window. Noticing it was slightly ajar she prized the window open and called 'Mr Luscombe!' loudly. She was certain now that it was not his concentration nor the noise of his undertaking that prevented him from hearing her: the man who had been teaching music in York Street all these years on her own recommendation was totally deaf, and none of them had known. The girls must have known and for some reason said nothing. It was Milla, up to her strange tricks again!

As Mrs Curzon stood watching and puzzling how the girls could have learnt what little they had, she saw Mr Luscombe bend down and tenderly pick up the parlourmaid, Mary Ann, and lower her limp, lifeless body, still warm, down into the dank earthy hole. Mrs Curzon felt her heart racing. Mary Ann who had meddled, who had sought to usurp her – the man-mad parlourmaid had got what was coming to her and no mistake!

The housekeeper raised her hands piously in prayer and cried out loud for the murderer could not hear her: 'Lord, the tea-party is well and truly over! Now lettest thou thy vainglorious servant Mary Ann who, it seems, has ended *her* days in this sunless villa, depart in peace.'

Mrs Curzon departed also as quickly as she could, returning purposefully to York Street. She informed Mrs Glass that Mary Ann had told Mr Luscombe she had been offered a better position in a respectable house – she stressed the word 'respectable' and Mrs Glass at once understood her meaning. She added that Mr Luscombe did not see fit to continue coming to the house to give piano lessons to the Glass girls. Mrs Glass accepted this. She had little choice.

Mrs Curzon then wrote a letter to the piano-teacher. She delivered it herself and returned home to await a reply.

Dear Mr Luscombe,

Once before I suggested I keep house for you and I now beg you to reconsider your rejection of my proposal. I am to be given a generous pension. You on the other hand will feel a shortage of wherewithal for there is no longer a need for piano lessons in this house. These were arranged, at my instigation I may say although I have never been shown any gratitude for my pains, but let it rest. Let me stress, Mr Luscombe, that you and I can lead separate lives in your house. There need be no talking or other intercourse if you so wish it for I have observed that you are a constrained man in this respect and I must confess that I have become very deaf and would find it well-nigh impossible to maintain a conversation. We would need to communicate the household needs in writing, and I trust this would not inconvenience you greatly. Let me finally remind you of this generous pension I am promised and look forward to hearing from you with some speed.

Yours, etc., etc.,

Grace Curzon

Mr Luscombe wondered briefly at this. Chiefly he mourned the loss of the manila envelope. In view of Mrs Curzon's 'generous pension', he abandoned his bicycle and assented to the late Ada Luscombe's brother's widow's wishes. He had little choice.

Mrs Curzon gratefully departed from York Street. 'Get your bank to send the pension to my bank,' she told Mrs Glass, as though she could only countenance an indirect contact. Cora left at about the same time, for Cora's respectable mother had made her large daughter give in her notice. The unsavoury connection with the scandalous Mrs Glass would not necessarily hinder a large house-maid in getting a new place. Future employers might enjoy having a celebrity below stairs, polishing their candlesticks, making iced crêmes and recounting shocking goings-on witnessed first-hand in York Street.

Mrs Curzon organized Mr Luscombe. Not wanting to be mur-dered in her bed at night, she locked her door. Not wanting him to go out, she hid his wig. Like the young Elizabeth Cathcart before her, Mrs Curzon purchased a bottle of tartar emetic such as is used in stables. If Mr Luscombe had had a tendency to enjoy the odd tipple previously, now he drank heavily and took on a dishevelled appearance that surpassed anything the dust from his bicycling days had effected. The neighbours nodded sadly when Mrs Curzon informed them that she was nursing her brother-in-law through his final illness: 'How kind you are,' they said. 'How lucky he is!'

Eventually a coffin was brought to the house. Before it could be carried away again Mrs Curzon had had heavy work to do. When the woman came to lay out Sarah Glass she had said, 'We keeps ourselves to ourselves.' She knew what to do. Atoning perhaps for the shabby mauve taffeta, Mrs Curzon took pity on Mr Luscombe in death in a way she had not while he was yet alive: she dusted the piano-teacher down and sent him to meet his Maker wearing his wig and lying in the tender embrace of the re-interred parlourmaid.

'The Lord lift up his countenance and give thee both peace everlasting,' Mrs Curzon whispered, forgetful of the absolute silence Mr Luscombe had already enjoyed for many years. The flighty girl was only a parlourmaid so the housekeeper made sure she wore her parlourmaid's cap. In any case there was no wide-brimmed hat to bestow on Mary Ann who would never go to Margate now to sit in a hired deck-chair on the beach and sun herself beside Philip Eames and the sea. But in death Mary Ann did get to lie beneath Mr Luscombe, her eyes shut, her mouth wide open to receive the everlasting kiss she would never have been lucky enough to enjoy while she yet lived . . .

Mary Ann had not screamed. There had only been a whimper at the last for Mary Ann had misunderstood the nature of Mr Luscombe's embrace. He had not wanted to kill the girl but she refused to go away, chasing after him to his house, forcing her way in with her smiles, talking at him words she would soon realize he could not hear. And what then? They would not go on employing him to teach the piano once it was known he had become stone-deaf. His terror of the workhouse caused him to smile back at Mary Ann and put nimble hands whose fingers had once played Chopin *vivace* on the ivory keys of a piano round the parlourmaid's slender ivory neck. What pretty hair she had, he thought, as her slight body slumped gratefully in his arms. He stroked the beautiful curls the colour of burnished copper and he wept – weeping for himself who had always been gentle, for Mary Ann who had only ever smiled and for the silent unkind world that had allowed this horror to happen.

After the funeral, a bargain affair, for Mrs Curzon approved above all things of economy, two bodies buried for the price and time it took to bury one, Mrs Curzon re-entered Mr Luscombe's tomb-like house happy that there was now no need to share the generous pension bestowed on her by Mrs Glass. Paid by one bank into another. Frenziedly she rearranged everything. The tell-tale slabs on the floor in the kitchen, where if you looked carefully you would notice that they had recently been taken up and put back down again twice, she covered with rugs and furniture. She kept the neighbours at bay as Mr Luscombe before her had done. She dare not risk having visitors though luckily there were few people likely to come. You never knew what prying eyes might notice, what prating tongues might say. These things had a way of coming back and back to haunt you . . .

Milla wrote once. Milla dutifully said she hoped Mrs Curzon was happily settled, to give their love and best wishes to dear Mr Lucombe, and then she suggested that perhaps she and Helen might call. It had in truth only been a half-hearted friendly suggestion but Mrs Curzon, remembering uneasily how the wilful child had once foisted herself on a writer with a funny name in Acton, and insisted on taking that writer a cake, sat down and wrote Milla an unpleasant note. *The child hears and sees everything. She speaks up and tells tales*. If she had a thousand earthenware jelly moulds she would not want Milla Glass anywhere near them. 'May the Lord forgive you, it is more than I will ever do,' she wrote.

'How rude!' Helen said; she knew Mrs Curzon had been accorded a generous pension.

'Forgive me for what?' Milla asked. 'Why should I be forgiven, or not forgiven, when I haven't done anything wrong? Mrs Curzon obviously holds some sort of grudge. She knew dear William . . .'

'She knew everything . . .'

'But she still didn't want to know!' Milla would not trouble Mrs Curzon again. It never had been any use with Mrs Curzon whose mind had always been quite made up.

Sniffing and muttering in the late Mr Luscombe's sunless villa, Mrs Curzon looked forward with gleeful misery to a long and lonely old age. Even after Pinder Simpson Junior had perished with his ship for an Honourable Mention and Milla's own son William had died heaving his bayonet out of a muddy trench at the Somme, Grace Curzon would still be there in the same half-light, still swigging unmeasured measures of unwatered rum while cursing, complaining and blaming.

21

An Entrance & an Exit

Time passes as time will. A new housekeeper wound up the clocks in York Street and was untroubled by their ceaseless ticking. She said to Mrs Glass: 'This photograph is faded beyond belief; oughtn't it to be in a drawer?'

'That would be sensible,' Elizabeth replied and what was left of William Glass's likeness was put away out of the light. Already faded, it ceased to fade. Stacia Glass, under Lady Blouvier's direction, blossomed into a disdainful young lady worthy of a Mayfair drawing-room. Milla and Helen were as bored as ever, but more used to it too. If Milla noticed that dear William's photograph had gone from the hall-table she said nothing.

In the Strand, the New Paris Grand was proceeding apace: the old hotel demolished, its parts sold off at extravagant prices, sums of money that entered sundry back pockets, the perks of the job. Things were starting to happen behind the hoardings which had been erected round the site (to excite curiosity, some said) and Mrs Preedy asked Charles if he had looked through the gap yet.

'I wouldn't descend!' Charles Preedy replied although, chancing to pass that way the week before, he'd been unable to resist a quick squint through the fence. What he had seen had been as incomprehensible as he'd feared it would be, for Edward Glass had always been incomprehensible to Charles Preedy.

Ever alert, the loyal Mrs Preedy detected the furrow in her husband's brow. 'Don't fret,' she whispered encouragingly, 'men will also frown over your buildings before long.'

Desmond Blaise meanwhile was collecting his share of the costs. Eames did not like Blaise. Blaise, who did not notice Eames, had decided to re-invest his 'earnings' by acquiring seats on other Boards. If he could repeat this same exercise often enough, his rapidly multiplying pyramid of percentages would stack up enormously and fast. If it worked out as smoothly in practice as it did on paper, Blaise could soon end up owning half of all England! Blaise was busy dining useful men and enquiring after other Directorships which were likely to become available in the near future, at what cost and for what return? These useful men were promised substantial introductory fees when they had proved their usefulness.

Dr Lucius Morgan (Cantab.) had been away again on another very successful Peregrination, this time up in the heavily populated North. A whole succession of Sensational Sensations in the *News from the Other Side* had eclipsed one another so effectively that the pictures of Stacia Glass eating seed-cake were largely forgotten, double the print-run given away free at meetings as inducements to new subscribers.

Time passes as time will.

'To Italy?' Dr Morgan looked mildly surprised. He was not even mildly surprised. He had already heard that the second Mrs Glass might be going to Italy with Valentine Birtles. Because of this he had decided to capitalize on his assets and collect up his eggs before the bird flew the nest and the eggs were yet warm and viable. He wanted Elizabeth to see that he was mildly surprised she should contemplate such a venture, so he repeated himself clearly, 'To Italy?'

'I may as well,' Mrs Glass said lightly, wondering why Dr Morgan should have come unexpectedly to visit, uninvited. Why should he be interested in her movements? What was it to him if she went to Italy? What was it to anyone?

There was a pause. Dr Morgan sat back tapping his fingers on the wing of the armchair, marking time. 'Your nice parlourmaid has been replaced, I notice,' he said.

Elizabeth was irritated. What business were her activities and her household to this man with his peculiar watery eyes? 'Yes, you were always one for noticing things, Dr Morgan! We have an entirely new staff – very efficient, far less trouble. I can only wish I had seen to it before.'

'And Mrs Curzon?'

'She left a while ago. They have all left. Servants can be so unreliable when they've been around too long. They think it gives them the upper hand.'

'Indeed?' Dr Morgan shifted emphatically in his seat. 'Lady Blouvier tells me . . .'

'Oh, I wouldn't listen to gossip,' Mrs Glass snapped. Where was this leading? Why had such a busy man bothered to come?

'I have known Valentine Birtles a long time,' Dr Morgan said, fixing his fathomless eyes on Elizabeth.

'Oh, yes.' Mrs Glass did wonder now what was being said to her. She had not known that Valentine Birtles numbered Dr Morgan among his friends, but Valentine Birtles knew everyone, he had scores of friends, none of them meant anything.

'I am very fond of the young man. His Dear Departed father once had occasion to speak severely to his son – through me, of course.'

'Of course!' Elizabeth interrupted.

'Of course,' Dr Morgan went on. 'Sir Benjamin Birtles was anxious about his son's "good" living. I talked to Valentine, but I'm afraid it made little difference. However, I still take a friendly interest in the man for his Dear Dead father's sake.'

'He is a pleasant sort of fellow,' Mrs Glass replied quickly. She did not want to discuss Valentine Birtles of all people with Dr Morgan of all people. Dr Morgan with whom, for some forgotten reason, she had once spoken about poor erstwhile Henry.

'As I say,' Dr Morgan continued, speaking with a disconcerting deliberation, 'I am fond of the man. I should not want anything you might call *untoward* to happen to dear Mr *Birtles*.'

Mrs Glass's cheeks reddened. And then whitened. Can he be meaning what I suspect he might be meaning? She scarcely dared ask herself, but she said briskly: 'No indeed. There can't be anyone in the world who wouldn't wish the man well.'

'I sincerely hope there is no one in the world who would wish the man *harm*,' Dr Morgan replied steadily. 'I think you get my import, Mrs Glass – Elizabeth!'

'Well . . .' Mrs Glass glanced irritably at her visitor and saw his unkempt beard and his impenetrable, unpleasant eyes. How could she ever have trusted this horrible man, of all men, with her innermost dreadful secret? The damage was done. She was probably nothing if not practical. She felt a strong physical distaste for the old words. She was scared. 'Shall I ring for coffee? A glass of Belgar Brandy, perhaps – I know you like that – or are you busy? Such a busy man; you'll have duties that call you . . .' her voice faded away. They looked at each other then, a spider and his fly.

Her guest did not move. He sat watching her and after a pause he began again, moving forward as deliberately as before: 'Mrs Glass,

Elizabeth, my dear, I have a duty to watch over our dear Mr Birtles. I wouldn't want anything untoward . . .'

Elizabeth felt an impatient surge of rage. Why did he have to keep repeating himself? Did he think she was stupid because she had once behaved stupidly? How dare he? She feared his insinuations, she feared the worst. Her voice was icy and scarcely controlled: 'You drew a confidence from me once, Dr Morgan. I trust you are not referring to that.'

'The truth is not easily forgotten or concealed, Ma'am. I think you have discovered this also.'

'I see!' Elizabeth stared with hatred at her persecutor. The spider advanced slowly, there was no rush.

Lucius Morgan continued: 'If my dear cousin Sarah's husband – the celebrated architect, Edward Glass, no less – chooses to remarry in my absence, and chooses moreover a murderess for his bride and as mother to his young children . . .'

'I thought that matter was finished!' Elizabeth cried. 'I took you for an honourable man. For a friend. I can see I was mistaken! You promised me your silence. Eternal silence was what you said.'

There was a pause. A pause in which an invisible layer of dust settled on the knick-knacks, on the cranberry glass vases so admired by the dear departed Mary Ann, the automaton canaries so reviled by poor Philip Eames, the walnut box containing the stereoscopic viewer through which Elizabeth had not cared to view her eldest step-daughter, Stacia, in three dimensions, the unused work-baskets, the fire-guards, the flower-pot stands, the web.

'Eternal silence does not come cheap, Ma'am,' Dr Morgan replied simply. 'You should know that by now.'

'I dare say!' Elizabeth swallowed hard. 'And can you put a price on it, Dr Morgan? A price-tag on your eternal silence?'

'Oh yes, I believe so, Ma'am.'

'How much do you want?' Elizabeth spat. Henry James Cathcart had slipped away from her as surely as he had slipped from his bolting horse, incapacitated by the tartar emetic she had fed him in his drink. Dr Morgan was right! Elizabeth Cathcart, the second Mrs Glass, the woman Edward Glass the Architect had positioned as a mainstay to take care of his house and his children, was a cold and cunning murderess. She was as calculating as Glass was with his buildings: 'I leave everything in your very competent hands,

Elizabeth!' he had said. She looked at her hands anew, the hands of a vile murderess fit only to be cast in wax. Her rightful place was not here in this pretty parlour but exhibited as a waxwork in the Chamber of Horrors at Madame Tussaud's, alongside Burke and Hare, Dr Black and the notorious poisoner, Mrs Bertha Kilgarriff:

'It will have blood; they say; blood will have blood;
Stones have been known to move, and trees to speak;
Augurs and understood relations have
By magot-pies and choughs, and rooks, brought forth
The secret'st man of blood.'

Oh yes, the secrets, augurs, understood relations, that ancient rookery of aunts all had been there, but few problems in life cannot be solved by money. Elizabeth's own blood rushed: 'How much exactly do you want, Dr Morgan?' she demanded.

'Three thousand pounds,' Dr Morgan stated his price.

'Eternal silence can be purchased for three thousand pounds?' Elizabeth repeated.

'Even so.' The spider blinked.

Nothing if not practical, Elizabeth asked: 'How do I know you won't be back for more? How do I know you won't keep coming back? Like Milla wanting first expensive printed scraps and then a proper leather-bound album to put them in so that eternal silence must be bought and re-bought for the rest of time.'

'No need to get hysterical, Madam! I am a man of my word.'

'A man of your word! You swore once before to keep eternal silence. You did not say anything about *money* then. How do I know what you will be asking for next?' She recalled the stuffed wire-haired terrier; what had happened to that?

Dr Morgan ignored the woman's tone and restated his terms: 'Eternal silence at three thousand pounds seems very reasonable to me but if you prefer – as a special favour to yourself, for bankrupts and their dependents are not usually allowed credit and it will mean waiving the rules, I think I can trust *you*, Mrs Glass, you will not be going to Italy or anywhere – I can arrange for *you* to pay by easy instalments . . .'

'In which case, no doubt, I incur interest charges at two per cent above bank rate!' Elizabeth was being sarcastic, but Dr Morgan calmly nodded his head.

'Compounded, of course!' Elizabeth went on.

'Naturally, Ma'am. These things are generally compounded. That is why I wish to watch over Mr Birtles. For his father, Sir Benjamin's sake.'

'I see!' Mrs Glass looked at Dr Morgan in a controlled frenzy of disgust and despair. Dr Morgan calmly returned her gaze since, as you can be sure, he was not entirely unaccustomed or averse to being looked at in this way.

'You took advantage,' Elizabeth said, 'of the unwary . . .'

'Of the unwise,' Dr Morgan promptly corrected her. He continued in a matter-of-fact voice: 'Purging a guilty conscience was always an expensive exercise, Madam. In Italy you would have seen extravagant churches raised by the purging of innumerable Papist consciences.'

'I never thought of it like that,' Elizabeth said in a spent and passionless voice. The glue had stuck to the opposite page making a proper mess of her expensive album, ruining all the finely printed, carefully arranged paper-scraps the ancient aunts had bought her. She might just as well have had a tatty scrap-book like Milla's and then committed the whole thing to the flames as Milla had done. 'And now I must ask you to leave. If you call again on Saturday afternoon I will somehow endeavour to have three thousand pounds ready for you to collect. I will instruct the maid, for I do not wish to see you again myself.'

Maybe there is a fable about the clever fly who bought herself time from a spider. In any case, when Dr Morgan had left the house Elizabeth locked herself in her bedroom and counted out the contents of her rosewood box. Even with all her shopping she had managed to save a fair amount, for Edward had been very generous to her. But this amount which seemed fair when thought of in the abstract amounted now, she found, to a mere eight hundred and twenty-seven pounds. Less than a third of the price Dr Morgan had put on his eternal silence.

Elizabeth straightened herself and drew a mantle about her shoulders, picked up her gloves and an umbrella in case it should rain and set out resolutely for the Paris Grand. 'I am nothing,' she told herself again, 'if not practical.'

Only part of the old building in the Strand was still standing, though even that was scaffolded and its façade had been stripped away. The shell of the New Paris Grand was in place, a vast complicated structure on which Edward Glass was to suspend his masterpiece. Elizabeth did not pause to peer surreptitiously through a gap in the hoardings as Charles Preedy had done but hurried to the gate and joined the throng of workmen and delivery-men pouring inside.

Here was a great ants' nest of industry: men carrying bricks, wheeling wheelbarrows, hoisting planks and scaffolding poles, moving bags of Simpson, Holland & Co. cement and shifting large blocks of rough-hewn stone. Others stood huddled in earnest groups arguing with engineers and surveyors over details on the waterproofed plans that billowed about in the wind. A Mr Fine loudly disputed the price of some blue lias-lime but wondered why he bothered, for while margins weren't tight on this job, time was. No one paid the diminutive intruder any attention. How slight she felt, how brittle. How nothing.

Elizabeth stumbled across the site damaging her shoes as she went, the dainty shoes that Valentine Birtles had once admired. She entered the doors of the one extant building and was surprised to find that inside a degree of normal hotel life was being maintained. 'Not another one!' the doorman exclaimed with a doorman's privilege of insolence – under his breath, and so that only she heard – directing her up a staircase to a large office in an old smallish ballroom on the first floor. The door was ajar. Mrs Glass could see Lucy Winnup lounging fretfully on a sofa. Edward sat at a desk surrounded by obsequious tradesmen who had brought samples of their wares for his inspection. Lucy was bored. This was the contractor's job but for some reason Glass had demanded the final say. He had tried to mollify her by getting her to express an opinion on the designs, but the girl was annoyed. Her mother had been right: she was wasted here. The man might be a big name but he was also pernickety and pompous, too full of himself and too old for her. She sprawled in his office in an elegant huff.

Elizabeth Glass swallowed hard. Dr Morgan must have his money; traces of tartar emetic could be found in a corpse long after and she did not want Henry James Cathcart – who had been hidden away underneath, one paper-scrap stuck over another – exhumed. Wherefore all that snipping and pasting if he were only to be brought back snipped and pasted by some forensic pathologist to confront her again and quibble at the Assizes about the nature of his death? *They're still there really as though they* were *still there* (although what could Milla Glass know of anything?). You could not deny the love buried away underneath; you could only learn to live with it, for you would be nothing, your neck in the noose, if not practical.

Elizabeth shuddered and boldly threw back her head. A head that, if she hesitated now, might in time be judiciously severed from her body, and her body brought back from the dead not by Dr Morgan but in wax at Madame Tussaud's Chamber of Horrors for Mrs Preedy to take Charlotte and Bertram to visit as a special Christmas treat: 'Dear Eliza, such a wonderful likeness, I'd never have thought it of her!' Mrs Preedy would trill to whoever would listen. 'To think how I lent this waxwork murderess my own dresses tucked and tacked, and fed her on turkey and cranberry sauce . . .'

Elizabeth Glass entered the temporary office of Glass & Co., labelled on the door in measured stylish uncials that were not the sprawling hand of Philip Eames. 'I have come to speak to my husband,' she announced.

The tradesmen shuffled and took up their samples. Lucy Winnup cocked her pretty head to one side and, in spite of herself, almost glad of the diversion, she flounced straight out of the room. A dangerous lady, a cyanide tank indeed: at the first sign of trouble Lucy Winnup was off! A letter had come three days before from Harry Withercott. For three days she had resolved not to read it. Now she retreated to her room to wonder again what it might contain.

'Gentlemen, if you would be so kind and call back later . . .' Edward Glass thought angrily about Philip Eames. Why hadn't the man forestalled this? Or warned him? Or sorted out whatever it was that needed sorting out himself? What did he pay the relentlessly obstinate fellow for? He sighed, fearing some sort of scene. His whole life seemed to have consisted of difficult encounters with difficult females being deliberately difficult.

'Edward . . .' Mrs Glass stood composedly on the other side of the desk.

'I have nothing to say to you, Madam! I'd have thought you'd have known that by now!'

'Edward, you must understand, this isn't easy for me. I wouldn't have come except . . .'

Edward Glass kept his eyes on the papers in front of him. He spoke quietly: 'Our marriage has been a mistake, I admit that. It has cost me dear . . .'

'It has cost me dear, also,' Mrs Glass murmured but without accusation. She had ruined the shoes she had come in. Ours has not been a fortunate marriage, Henry James Cathcart had said, promising immediately 'to do better'. At least Edward Glass made no empty promises.

Husband and wife looked at each other now. It had only ever been a practical arrangement, devised by two people in desperate circumstances. Glass noticed that his wife had lost the cheap wedding-ring he had given her.

'I have always been absorbed in my work,' Edward Glass broke the thoughtful silence. It wasn't an apology or an explanation; he owed her neither. He owed this practical woman nothing.

'I like that in a man,' Mrs Glass said and then, recalling Emily Housecroft, she added, 'In a woman too. It makes sense of living, having something you passionately want to do, even if it's only translating dead languages nobody speaks any more. I wish I were the same but my early education was severely lacking. I learned nothing of any use . . .' She talked because she was nervous.

'This will be my most important commission,' Edward Glass said by way of reply.

'I can see that. I am glad for you, Edward. It all looked most impressive as I came in. I am glad to think there will be such an important monument to your talents.'

Glass was surprised. Gratified even – although he could not have said why he should have cared what Elizabeth thought. Perhaps to alleviate the awkwardness, he suggested: 'Come and have a look round, why don't you?'

Mr and Mrs Glass walked arm in arm down the stairs and out past the uniformed doorman who surveyed them as they went to survey the building work on the surrounding site. It was as incomprehensible to Mrs Glass as it had been to Charles Preedy but Elizabeth saw her husband's happy enthusiasm and was happy to see it.

'The fun part comes later, I suppose,' Elizabeth observed.

'The fun part, Madam?'

'The rugs, curtains, lights, chandeliers, paintings, mirrors, mantelpieces, things that go on the walls.'

'The "fun part" – why, yes, I see what you mean. As a matter of fact, I have commissioned revolving painted panels for the dining-room so there will not be walls in the ordinary sense.'

'Revolving walls!' Now here was something that Mrs Glass had not contemplated in all the hours spent reading the magazines that came every week on subscription.

Edward Glass, pleased by this woman's open interest and obvious delight (long ago Lucy Winnup had tired of hearing about nothing but the project, had tired of hearing nothing about Lucy Winnup), continued enthusiastically: 'Indeed! The electrics will be housed in a false floor. I have ordered £70,000 worth of furnishings from Fisher's alone . . .'

'Seventy thousand pounds!' Mrs Glass repeated.

'Indeed. I have chosen or supervised the choice of just about everything myself . . .'

'But of course you have, you couldn't possibly leave it to anyone else! Why, it wouldn't be the same at all. I dread to think what would happen if I sent someone else to do my shopping,' Mrs Glass remarked, although her husband's shopping was evidently on a scale that in every way superseded her own. 'Oh, I can see why all this should excite you, Edward.'

'Can you?' Edward Glass asked, delighted by the glow in her face, an enthusiasm that responded to his own. He invited his wife to stay and lunch with him for he relished her unguardedly open appreciation of all he was doing. None of Lucy Winnup's artistic posturings or bourgeois carping – what a pleasant surprise to discover how congenial one's own wedded wife could be!

The Paris Grand had retained a limited dining-room during the rebuilding. The Board of Directors (and Blaise in particular who needed a useful place to bring his useful associates) had considered it essential not to risk losing the Parisian *chef de cuisine* who would surely be snapped up by a rival concern at the first opportunity. This celebrated chef was concentrating his artistry for the benefit of a small room of diners and the food was exceptionally good. Elizabeth Glass was impressed. No stretched salmon today making life awkward later.

Over a delectable *selle d'agneau de lait poêlée*, Edward Glass said: 'I shan't let him get away with it, you know.'

'Him? Away with . . .' Mrs Glass gulped and almost choked. For one horrible moment she thought her husband was referring to the fact that she had been seen around town with Valentine Birtles, a man who assumed he could get away with anything for he had got away with everything (despite the late Sir Benjamin's disapproval), so far.

'Dr Lucius Morgan, making a laughing-stock of us all. I'll pay him . . .'

'Ah, good.' Mrs Glass was relieved. That was why she had come, to beg for the money to pay Dr Morgan off. 'He's an evil man.'

'I'm glad you see it my way!' Edward Glass had previously assumed that the spirit-photographs of Sarah Glass had been done with Elizabeth's consent, or worse still, at her spiteful instigation: a curiously novel revenge on an errant husband. An eccentric new way of pinning him down.

'Oh, I most certainly do!' Mrs Glass assured him.

'The problem is that the charlatan is well-connected,' Glass said.

'Charlatans generally are,' Elizabeth warmly remarked. Edward smiled. She went on: 'Lady Blouvier, who by way of apology for her part in the outrage has taken dear Stacia in hand . . .' She hesitated, for she was uncertain about her husband's attitude to this development – Eames had been most unstraightforward when she had told him – and she was relieved now to see that Stacia's father did not seem put out by the arrangement.

Glass nodded his head vigorously. 'And so on! Not only the Infallible Hildegard Blouvier – darkroom tents, indeed – it seems to me that the whole of London Society subscribes to Morgan's dubious activities. I suppose they are all so idle they have nothing better to do, but it might make life difficult.'

'The man seems bent on destroying . . .' Elizabeth began tentatively.

'It was Sarah's fault, of course. She would keep teasing him about a farmyard goose removing his trousers. It was years ago. He is most unforgiving.'

'Yes, I know.' Unforgiving was an understatement. 'I wondered . . .' Mrs Glass thought of the £70,000 worth of furnishings that had been paid out to Fisher's alone. With sums of money like that, her own impossible needs appeared paltry, derisory even. She looked across the table at Edward Glass whose concerns were altogether of a different scale and on a greater plane. 'It occurred to me, Edward . . .'

'Ma'am?' Edward Glass wondered if this woman sitting opposite him to whom he was actually married might after all have some sensible solution.

Elizabeth, with the £3000 she so desperately needed uppermost in her mind, said: 'I think money would solve it. I have often thought how few pleasures are not purchasable and few problems not solvable with money. I believe this to be the case here.'

'Money?' Edward Glass remembered how before he had respected Elizabeth's practical view of the world.

'I think he could be paid to go away.'

'Yes, but how much would that cost? And would he stay away?' Edward recalled Kitty's refusing to be bought off with money and later the man Elee had sent to him for money who had fallen from the wet scaffolding and broken his back as surely as Morgan's pet mouse. None of Shakespeare's tragic heroes had had to account for themselves in this way or been obliged to keep accounts.

Elizabeth knew she must gamble again. *Faites vos jeux*: 'I think so. I think that for a sum like three thousand pounds he could be made to see sense.'

'It would be certainly be worth it, Elizabeth! But do you really think it would work?'

'Yes! Yes, I do!' Elizabeth Glass looked the man who was her husband steadily in the eye and put all her chips on the table: '*Money* is the only thing petty-minded men like Morgan understand. I think you should invite him here and give him three thousand pounds. In fact I will send him to you on Saturday afternoon. You must say you have discussed everything with me and that if he so much as opens his mouth and breathes a word to anyone – and don't even give him the opportunity to say anything while he is here for it can only aggravate the matter, Edward, and it is aggravated enough as it is – threaten him! Say you will have him fined and imprisoned and pronounced a phoney. Tell him that Society, Lady Blouvier included, for he seems to think much of that preposterous woman, will turn its back on him once and for all. Remind him how we have all the evidence and witnesses too; Stacia dressed up as her mother, it was only a childish prank at a tea-party, a charade in the summer

238

holidays of which he took unfair advantage. For another thing, on the day when he first visited me in York Street Sarah Glass, his own cousin, had been dead six months and Dr Lucius Morgan, who professes to be able to speak to the Dead, *did not know*! He thought I was she; it was just the sort of embarrassment I had sought to avoid. If his own dear dead cousin could not return from the Dead to tease him about a fierce goose removing his trousers, why would anyone else bother to come back at his say-so? He cannot want this generally known: it would do his professional career no good at all. Tell him that we will *not only* expose him like a photographic plate but, as surely as the wretched goose removed his trousers, we will run him hissing through the courts for blackmail, necromancy, misrepresentation, false pretences, libel, slander – and anything else you can think of . . .'

'Elizabeth!' Edward Glass gasped. What a woman she was! And no fussing couturier to send him away from an infernally pricey *assignation* this time! A choice of *pêches petit duc, comtesse marie, friandises* and pastries were offered for dessert.

'Some of each!' cried Mr Glass, for he was partial to delicacies, and otherwise he was speechless.

Lucy Winnup watched the couple dining. The uniformed doorman watched her watching. It was extraordinary and uncomfortable to observe how much younger Edward Glass's wife was than she. 'Well, Lucy,' the girl who was neither a Shakespearean actress nor a cyanide tank told herself, 'we have our exits and our entrances. You've had your fling!' She went upstairs past the insolent doorman to pack her valise. She had succumbed to temptation and read Harry Withercott's letter: she was weeping; she was leaving.

'Do you remember the day I proposed to you?' Glass asked over the after-dinner wine, sweet as sweetest sugar.

'A cold afternoon! Mrs Curzon – whom you will be delighted to hear I have at last pensioned off – made us some disgusting fish-paste sandwiches!'

'And you sat clutching your coffee-cup and I couldn't think what to say!'

'You used a speech out of a book.'

'I never!'

'You did.'

'Did I? Another glass, Elizabeth – a glass for a Glass!'

'Did you learn the speech specially for the occasion, Edward? I was intrigued at the time.'

'Were you, my dear?'

'I was so intrigued I hardly listened to a word you said. I could have been agreeing to *anything*, Edward!'

'If you didn't listen to a word I said, how did you know it was a speech from a book? Really, Elizabeth, you were ever the sweetest little chancer!'

Edward and Elizabeth laughed. Elizabeth was delighted to discover Edward not above a little light quibbling.

'The girls are all right? The one in Mayfair, the other two?'

'Oh yes, perfectly all right, no problems. How earnest and keen the three of them are. You know, Edward, I really think one becomes less "responsible" as one gets older.'

'I know what you mean.'

'The longer you live the more you realize how little you can do to properly alter anything.' Elizabeth knew the sweet wine had gone to her head. 'That sounds awful, doesn't it, but the girls take everything so seriously – as though *they* could possibly make any difference to the world.'

Edward Glass said: 'To tell you the truth, I could never tell the difference between the three of them, except once on Milla's birthday when she wore a silly paper hat and took advantage of it being her birthday to eat jelly and show off.'

'Oh, I know what you mean.' Elizabeth laughed the laughter of mutuality. 'I had some ancient aunts who were just the same, and so offended when I muddled them up. They liked everything very orderly.'

'How can Life be ordered when the Universe is in chaos?'

'Milla would tell you that the world is subject to the principles and equations in her school algebra book.'

'Milla is an equation of her very own!'

'The sort of child you give presents to, to make up for I don't know what . . .'

Mr and Mrs Glass chattered happily for a while. She told him Valentine Birtles had invited her to Italy.

'Go to Italy, Elizabeth, why don't you? I only wish I had the time to come with you. The air and the sights would do you good. Some of us have never been privileged to pass beyond Britannia's windswept shores! I told Milla that once. She was terribly offended.'

'People will talk!'

'Let them! You only live once – you must live.'

'No, I probably won't go. I won't go because I can go, if that doesn't sound ridiculous. I like it at home with all my nice things. I once told the governess she could do as she pleased and *she* just stayed upstairs in her room . . .'

'I must come and visit.'

'Yes, Edward, do that. You are such a friend.'

'We seem to understand each other, certainly.' He blinked at his wife. 'I am surprised how well we know each other.'

'Yes,' she smiled. 'How *lucky* we are! I must go. You have work to do; it has been a lovely lunch. Thank you so much, Edward.'

'Send Dr Morgan to me on Saturday. I will sort him out exactly as you say.'

'Good!' She rose to leave.

'It has started raining outside.' Edward Glass was concerned. Building-sites like scaffolding boards were dangerous places in the wet.

'I brought an umbrella.' Elizabeth touched him on the arm. 'I am a practical woman, I came prepared for anything.'

Husband and wife kissed each other then, with a great and new affection, gently on the lips.

22

Her Majesty's Ear

'Her husband! But, my dear . . .' Mrs Preedy was shocked of course when Mrs Styles told her. It seemed unthinkable, Elizabeth and Edward seen lunching together. Several times. What did these *augurs and understood relations* portend?

Milla had been writing letters to Stacia at Eulalia House almost as regularly as Elizabeth Glass had written to her husband when first she was married the second time. Milla's letters were never more than short friendly notes which said nothing because it was difficult to think what to say to Stacia. Milla frequently asked whether she and Helen might not visit. When occasionally Stacia replied her brief careless lines made it clear that she was rather too busy: one waltzed and whirled *vivace e capriccioso* in Mayfair, there was simply no time.

Now, however, Lady Blouvier instructed Stacia to invite her sisters at once. 'Let them come!' Lady Blouvier said as though Milla and Helen were some invading army.

'They will expect to gobble cake,' Stacia objected. 'They are both greedy children.'

'We will store up provisions against the day,' Lady Blouvier promised, for emissaries arriving in Eden Gardens from other parts of the globe deserved a little unextravagant *pourboire*. 'Tell them to arrive on Thursday prompt.'

Milla and Helen were excited to see Stacia again, but when they arrived at the imposing residence, Stacia did not run out to greet them. An over-underparlourmaid opened the small door within the greater front door, an under-overparlourmaid showed them into an enormous room and announced their names: 'Miss Milla and Miss Helen Glass!' At the far end beyond a grand piano of blackest ebony, Milla could clearly see Stacia, Lady and Delia Blouvier lounging like statues on *chaises longues*, ignoring the commotion and seeming not to hear or notice anything. They did not move as Milla and Helen walked down the length of the room, their shoes squeaking mercilessly on the floor which was as polished as a glassy ice-rink on which you could dangerously skid.

'Hallo!' said Milla and her voice echoed round the cavernous room. 'You look as if you've been turned to stone!'

Stacia turned her head slowly (as slowly and steadily as Pinder Simpson Junior's sinking battleship) in studied surprise. Milla gasped. Stacia but not Stacia. Stacia utterly transformed. She looked like a duplicate of Delia who also reclined there languidly, occupied rather sarcastically in doing nothing. Three-dimensional but without the stereoscopic viewer in its walnut box. Milla looked from the snipped and pasted Stacia to Delia and back again: Stacia yes, but not the Stacia she knew.

'We were wondering where you'd got to,' Stacia said.

Milla had to admit that she and Helen were five minutes late. They lacked the advantage of Lady Blouvier's bulky timepiece. Besides, it was raining heavily outside.

'You have come for tea, then?' Lady Blouvier boomed.

Milla had been invited to tea once before with Pasha, when she had taken her own cake. There had been no tea but a lot of unpleasantness. Today she came empty-handed, you never knew what to expect.

Lady Blouvier arched her eyebrows and leaned over wearily to ring the bell. 'These visitors have come for tea!' she barked at the maid who had entered the room as nervously as if it were full of headless dogs and Dayaks from Borneo. 'See what you can rustle up!'

Lady Blouvier gestured towards some vacant chairs. Milla and Helen tiptoed over and perched uncomfortably on them. Semi-recumbent, Delia and Stacia regarded the guests languidly through half-closed eyelids. No one spoke.

'That's a lovely dress!' Milla said. She thought Stacia looked like a princess.

'Is it?' Stacia glanced down at herself. 'Not one of my favourites, actually.'

'You're not like sisters at all,' Lady Blouvier declared. If Edward Glass had once had trouble distinguishing between his three daughters, he would have no difficulty now. A magic wand had been waved and Stacia had acquired unmistakable Mayfair polish, a sheen as flawless as the squeaky floor, and all the airs and graces of a lady. She had grown tall and haughty. She had a bearing that was pleasurably burdened by fashionable *ennui*. Milla sat uncomfortably hunched on her uncomfortable chair, her soaking wet stockings bunched at the ankles.

'So, what's this we hear?' Lady Blouvier enquired.

Milla was not sure who was being addressed. Just then an enormous trolley piled high with a whole cascade of splendiferous tea things was wheeled into the room and carefully parked beside Lady Blouvier. Stacia, Delia and Lady Blouvier ignored the event. Milla and Helen gawped at the silver and crested china and at the plates and stands loaded with mouth-watering delights of every description. Milla could not believe her luck.

'I asked you a question!' Lady Blouvier howled at the distracted Milla. She was unaccustomed to having to repeat herself.

Milla did not understand. All three of them had appeared not to hear when she and Helen had arrived and as their shoes had squeaked noisily across the floor. She wondered if, like Mr Luscombe, they had something wrong with their ears? Too much loud Chopin in the evenings perhaps – the elephants getting their own back . . .

'Come along, Milla! Tell us everything!' Stacia cajoled her infuriating sister.

'Everything? I – I don't understand,' Milla said blindly. She looked from Stacia to Lady Blouvier, to Delia, and back again to Stacia. She looked then at Helen sitting beside her. Helen only shrugged.

'Milla is usually quite quick,' Stacia apologized. 'I think the child is distracted by all the bonbons.'

Milla indeed could not stop herself glancing at the mountains of confection, sandwiches, cream pastries, sugar-plums, filled brandy snaps, tartlets and fondant fancies. It was the sort of thing you glimpsed through windows in tea-shops or tantalizingly illustrated in picture-books, not the sort of thing you might expect to find but a few feet away from you in somebody's drawing-room on a wet Thursday afternoon.

'The girl clearly has a healthy appetite!' Delia observed in a voice of amused boredom.

'Like her father, I dare say,' Lady Blouvier remarked acerbically, adding: 'We understand your father and Mrs Glass have had some sort of remarkable reconciliation. Or was it, in truth, a show-down? You can – and you must – tell us all about it, in strictest confidence, of course!'

'We quite thought you would bring us the details.'

'People ask us. They assume we must know.'

'Because Stacia is here.'

'Oh!' Milla felt slow. Her father had come to the house and taken tea a couple of times, certainly, but that was hardly a row or a reconciliation. Mr Birtles had called once or twice and voices had been raised. But more in laughter than in anger.

Delia told an attendant maid in the sharpest voice the confounded Milla had ever heard to pass some sandwiches *at once*; it sounded more like smelling-salts the way Delia spoke: 'Can't you see the child is in urgent need?'

Milla attempted to help herself from a plate of sandwiches held too close to her eyes. She could not see properly and her fingers fumbled and groped about clumsily. There was no pleasure after that in eating the sandwiches even though they were cut from delicate white bread, lightly buttered and filled with the thinnest slivers of succulent cucumber. The minute ladylike portions disappeared down in less than a gulp and only served to make Milla hungrier.

'I'm afraid our Milla's mind is more with the *pâtisserie* and *confiserie* than on recounting Mrs Glass's various exploits for *our* delectation,' Delia remarked. Stacia laughed a cruel grating laugh. Neither Delia, her mother nor Stacia took any interest in any of the fantastic tempting food. It seemed to Milla now that the trolley piled with cakes and sweets had been placed before them across the room merely to taunt and to torture.

'Oh, I . . .' Milla felt ten years old again and jelly-stained. She had opened her mouth but had nothing to say. She knew nothing of Mrs Glass's 'various exploits'.

'Yes?' The three interrogators leaned eagerly forward.

Milla looked over at the cakes and then back again and saw the accusation and disappointment in the three pairs of harsh, furious, waiting eyes. She felt sick.

'Go on then!' Lady Blouvier rose angrily and swung into action. She mounted the tea-trolley like Boadicea at her chariot and manoeuvred it fiercely across the room towards Milla. The piles of sweet things advanced violently clattering and rocking furiously this way and that. 'What have you come for, you greedy little girl?' Lady Blouvier's war-cry rang out as she bore down on Milla brandishing her bread-knife and wielding the cake-slice. 'What will loosen your prim little tongue, Milla Glass? State your demands and name your price!'

Milla heard the battery of abuse and saw beyond the tea-trolley, over the mountains of delicious cakes and fondant fancies, Delia's hard quizzical stare and Stacia's perfect imitation of the same.

'They are enjoying themselves at my expense,' she thought simply. It was some sort of tea-party prank, a charade in which they had given her a part: information was required of her in payment for her tea. Lady Blouvier, Delia and Stacia wanted her to tell them what Mrs Glass and her father were up to. She had only been invited here because she liked standing at the upper-landing window. They wanted her to be their spy, their nasty little sneak.

'Milla was always being told off for spying on Mrs Glass,' she heard Stacia saying. 'Milla was always piping up, telling people things when she had no business, when I was the one . . .'

Helen reached out to help herself to something that could have been a lemon puff but was probably known by another grander name here in Mayfair. Milla reached out also and seized Helen's unwary hand as it hovered over the trolley.

'Come on, Hel,' she said, jumping up and sending her own plate with the Blouvier crest crashing and smashing to the floor. 'This is no place for us – we don't belong in Mayfair!'

'Oh, but . . .' Helen started to protest.

'Come on!' Milla had found her tongue. She gripped Helen securely by the wrist and tugged her reluctant sister with her. At the other end of the enormous drawing-room Milla swung round abruptly and shouted back from the doorway: 'This might just as well be the other side of the globe, Stacia. The manners and customs of the savages of Dahomey are more Civilized than this!'

Cool as a chip of ice from a glacier, Stacia stared stonily at her sister, for she had been taught that in Mayfair one does not look at anything one does not wish to see, nor does one listen to anything one does not want to hear. One simply freezes.

Lady Blouvier, however, called out to her retreating guests like Boadicea jeering at a routed army: 'Do come and see us again, any time you are passing!' Delia and Lady Blouvier had enjoyed the scene well enough: it had provided a little entertainment on a rainy Thursday when nothing much seemed to be happening.

*

Elsewhere though, something terrible had happened. Poor Mrs Glass! She had only just left him that afternoon (Lady Blouvier's intelligence had been sound, husband and wife had taken to lunching together) when Edward, hearing shrieks from below, had hurried out in alarm and then attempted himself to carry the injured Elizabeth in. It had been impossible to move her for she had stirred in his arms and cried out in pain at every jolt. He crouched down beside her, shielding her, holding her hand and whispering encouragement until a doctor arrived and injected her with something that helped to ease the agony.

'I was admiring the mosaics,' she managed to tell him. Such an ordering of fragmented scraps: 'So beautiful – you are so clever, Edward . . .' She had tripped. Edward wanted to go with his wife when she was taken to the hospital but she whispered to get on with his Masterpiece. Later, when she was taken home to York Street, he came to see her and she told him off for wasting time that could be better spent on his revolving walls.

'What impractical shoes to wear on a building-site – you'd have thought an architect's wife would know better!' someone said censoriously and was quickly hushed, for it was unlikely that Elizabeth would ever have need of shoes again.

Blaise said: 'Our commiserations, Sir. I trust this will not sound callous, but we do hope there won't be excessive delays. With the old Paris Grand gone and its replacement not yet built, every day that passes costs the Company in unearned revenue.'

'There will be no delay, no changes in plan.' Glass turned his back. If anything Elizabeth's accident helped speed the building work up.

'I want you to get on and finish it,' Elizabeth urged. Although a doctor had once said a wheel-chair might one day be possible, it was now considered unlikely that she would ever leave her bed.

Milla found she had inadvertently left school at some point during the ensuing chaos. Someone needed to take charge of the house in York Street and sit with Mrs Glass when the pain was unbearable.

'I never liked her,' Stacia told Lady Blouvier when they heard the news. 'She and Milla get on quite well; it will give the child something to do.'

'Perhaps you are needed at home?' Delia suggested.

'Perhaps you should go and take charge?' Lady Blouvier added.

'We don't want to be selfish and keep you if you are needed elsewhere, Stacia!'

Stacia had no intention of returning to York Street. She was relieved when Lady Blouvier smiled and said they would have been sorry to lose her. She couldn't help feeling a little aggrieved that the Blouviers could have contemplated such a thing.

Mrs Preedy went to York Street in person with a large basket of fruit. Milla reluctantly received the fruit but she did not invite the unavoidable woman in. Mrs Preedy was obliged to stand on the doorstep to ask her questions but Milla misunderstood (or deliberately misunderstood, Mrs Preedy was not sure), what information was being requested.

'Rather a horrid girl, I thought, Sarah Glass's middle daughter. She as good as shut the door in my face!'

'The child has her father's manners. You remember how abominably he behaved here that Christmas?' Charles Preedy consoled his wife.

'You used to read so much, Milla!' Elizabeth asked Milla to read to her. Milla tried, for it would indeed help to pass the time, but after a few sentences she always gave up. There are some kinds of pain nothing out of a stoppered blue glass bottle could ever benumb. 'You used to remind me of when I was young, Milla, for I too was always reading. *Our Mutual Friend*, *Great Expectations*, *Jane Eyre*, I always had my head in a book . . .'

'So, why did you stop?' Milla asked. She was dusting Elizabeth's favourite knick-knacks, which she had rearranged so that they could be seen from the bed.

'I got married, I suppose,' Elizabeth said. Living with Henry James Cathcart had been fiction sufficient but it was easier to blame money than anything else: 'After that I used to skim books on booksellers' stalls.'

'I don't want to read any more,' Milla said firmly; what was the point when your days must be spent doing the cleaning and nursing which the servants could not find time for or be trusted with? She rubbed a little too vigorously and a glass drop on an arrangement of crystals clanked against the next. Elizabeth yelped for she had turned sharply to see what Milla was doing. Milla stepped over and smoothed her step-mother's hair on the pillow. 'Is there anything I can get you?' she asked. Elizabeth shut her eyes, blocking out the light, blocking out Milla. How she loved her beautiful things; she could not bear to see Milla mistreating them.

A very nice and very young man, the son of a substantial landowner in Ireland, took it into his head to call on Stacia. It was rather amusing at first for he would run the gauntlet of Lady Blouvier's boisterous wit and Delia's cutting disdain in order to sit and look at Stacia for hours at a time. He himself rarely said anything for he was too much in awe of the girl who looked like a fairy-tale princess. He brought Stacia foolishly extravagant presents that must have taken up a large portion of his young man's allowance. On one occasion he presented her with a handsome Siamese kitten.

'You really must learn to discourage him,' Lady Blouvier told Stacia playfully. Later she said the same thing in a different way, for the young man's youngish mother had called on Lady Blouvier. The boy's father was displeased, he had ideas other than Stacia Glass for his son and heir. The estates in Ireland needed a substantial injection of cash, something an architect's daughter was hardly likely to provide.

'But I haven't encouraged him!' Stacia protested – the handsome Siamese had been swiftly disposed of, trampled underhoof by the Blouvier horses as they were being harnessed up to the Blouvier carriage. 'No one can think I have encouraged him.'

'We must find you a Crown Prince,' Lady Blouvier said.

Stacia wrote now to Milla. 'I have an admirer, but not a Crown Prince, as yet . . .'

Milla wrote back: 'I should think you have lots of admirers, Stacia.'

Milla also told Stacia how their father often returned home these days to York Street. 'It's rather strange,' she said.

Emily Housecroft found it strange too; Edward Glass did not appear to recollect their previous meeting in front of a mirror and in front of Mlle Letellier, so all the embarrassment was entirely on her side. Her image in reverse probably did not resemble her unreflected self, she decided. She worked harder than ever to please Professor Fahey, poring over her books long hours at a stretch. She was grateful that Milla had wilfully accepted all responsibility for Mrs Glass and the running of the household. She hoped everyone might forget she was even in the house so she could devote herself entirely and for ever to her work for Arthur Fahey.

'I'm glad you got rid of Mrs Curzon,' Edward told his wife, coming one evening to sit beside Elizabeth. It seemed to him now that Mrs Curzon had been the only reason he had not liked being in this house with Elizabeth before.

'She was rather a sourpuss!' Elizabeth admitted with a nervous laugh. Valentine Birtles had had the nerve to send a postcard from Italy where he had gone with someone else. Elizabeth, who had lost another baby, wondered how many other women in London that morning had received such a postcard.

If she had not fallen on the wet mosaics, if the baby had not died, this regular Houdini would have juggled a bit with dates – but even if she had not fallen it had been unlikely a child of hers could have survived. They had told her once before she could never keep a baby the full term. She tried to tell herself that she did not mind much either way. Dr Morgan had been paid. She had fallen as Henry had once fallen; she lay in agony and knew herself duly punished. Purging a guilty conscience had never been easy or cheap.

Eventually The New Paris Grand was completed. The hoardings were taken down and everyone gasped at this exuberant stretching of a vast and daring imagination. Blaise spoke to someone who spoke to someone and soon His Royal Highness, the Prince of Wales mounted the temporary podium erected in the Strand to cut the inaugural ribbon. Edward Glass put on his best suit and spoke with the Prince briefly. He mentioned his now famous encounter with Albert, the Prince's own Dear Departed father (Glass did not give Dr Morgan's services in this connection a plug any more than he mentioned how Glass & Co. had greatly benefited from unbuilt Albert Memorials). 'Your father was still learning English at the time,' Edward Glass said. 'He was overheard to remark: "I do not comprehend what is this *Arcanum Arcanorum*?" '

The Prince of Wales smiled politely. 'How interesting!' he replied, though of course he had not heard a word above the din of the assembled multitude. Unruly louts were throwing orange peel, lumpish hands pointed up at this and that, everyone in the mêlée was craning for a better view, jabbering all at once. The building was too fantastic, it was impossible to see how the New Paris Grand could possibly stand up and yet here it was, undeniably standing: quintessential Edward Glass. Questions were asked and answers vociferously debated. How, what, which, where? Mounted police were ready on standby in case the excited mob got out of hand. His Royal Highness was glad to get down off the temporary podium. If like his father he said anything memorable to his equerry nobody could possibly have heard.

Word came at last: Edward Glass was to be knighted.

Mrs Preedy raised an eyebrow. 'Well, well!' she said. 'Goings on in York Street have evidently not reached Her Majesty's Ear.' You'd have thought the Palace might have been more searching in its investigations, more thorough certainly than Elizabeth's father had once been into Henry James Cathcart's affairs.

Mademoiselle Letellier was somewhat *vexée* to think that one of her creations might actually have been worn in the Royal Presence but for Elizabeth's unfortunate accident. She was of the private opinion that the *désastre* was in truth a discreet device to remove a madwoman from public view. There would be no more commissions from that quarter; she had quite unnecessarily given Mrs Pinder Simpson the reduction on her hat for a worthless introduction. *Oh là là, mais c'est la vie!*

Stacia was also disappointed: why weren't eldest daughters invited as well as – or instead of – crippled second wives? All her life she had dreamt of being at Court, and compared now to Windsor even Lady Blouvier's drawing-room must pale into insignificance. Now when she looked at the Blouvier crest she noticed the absence of a crown.

'Sir Edward Glass!' Elsinora Lee cackled for she had bought fish and chips wrapped in newspaper and noticed the name through the grease. She talked to herself, having no one else to talk to: 'When you think how long he's been expecting – and his wife was expecting . . .' Elee, like Lady Blouvier, had accurate sources of information: 'Her fall was a happy "accident" for him – there never was such a man for happy accidents.' The time had not yet come to do Edward his favour and it seemed to Elee that it never could for Edward Glass would go on and on; there would be many more triumphs before him and it seemed impossible that she could ever outlive the man to do as he had asked. 'I hate Edward Glass. I dare say a lot of women hate Sir Edward Glass,' Elee laughed. 'It don't never affect *him* though.'

*

Vizetelly roared like a caged lion. The men had been fools. They should have listened to him at the time. But he too had been a fool. He should have insisted on being heard. Blaise had been blinded by the favours he wanted to do, for his cousin Mr Fine the contractor, for example, and he'd been blinded by Edward Glass's Reputation. Look what comes of employing Great Art! 'I don't know how we ever expected to support that scale of expenditure,' Vizetelly shouted down the mahogany table at the dismayed and dismal faces gathered around. Edward Glass had got himself a knighthood while they had been left deep in debt.

'It's too late whingeing . . .'

'You should have said something at the time . . .'

'No use crying over spilt milk, old chap!'

The accounts spoke for themselves. The New Paris Grand had only been open a year or so and, although the hotel had never had an empty bed and was booked up completely for several years in advance, the Company was threatened any day with receivership. It would have been wound up a long time back but creditors already owed large sums of money hesitated to act for fear of losing those sums altogether and then going bankrupt themselves. The Board of Directors sat round the mahogany table unable to understand what could have gone wrong. Some £500,000 was lost without trace. Writs poured in. The situation became irretrievable and unconcealable. There was still at least another £100,000 outstanding to the builders. The uniformed doormen could not hold back the tide of frantic tradesmen repossessing furniture and fittings so they accepted the inevitable, and they accepted and pocketed tips for their help. There were scenes of chaos and hysteria. Majestic potted palms were knocked over on the staircase in the rush. Chambermaids who were to forgo their wages sat on unmade beds and wept. The *chef de cuisine* was quickly whisked away to a rival Ritz. When he paraded out of the New Paris Grand with his team of under-chefs like a cricket captain leaving the pavilion, the spectacular dining-room with revolving walls, which Elizabeth had never been well enough to see, could no longer even serve toast and jam.

It was as serious a case of mismanagement as Winnup had ever witnessed. He sat stony-faced and implacable. The auditors had sent along their senior partner who took an inflexible approach.

Winnup would not budge. 'The figures do not stack up,' was all he said. The rapidly multiplying pyramid of disasters stacked up though, enormously and fast. The rating authorities had taken the Paris Grand to Court over the new assessment. The Board cried out that the demands were iniquitous but the Court looked at the expansion that had taken place and found in favour of the rating authorities. They even commended them on their vigilance. The architect had taken no account of the greatly increased charges his grandiose design would necessarily incur. The Board were horrified now to find that, apart from their own vast debts already mounting as fast as Winnup could calculate them, the grossly inflated rates were to be backdated and hefty fines imposed for culpable negligence. It was the end of the book for the Paris Grand.

The waiters could not admit to being sorry. They had demanded from the outset, and had had to be paid, double the wages payable elsewhere and even this was scarcely sufficient inducement or recompense for the mountaineering involved in serving at table.

Mrs Fahey died. The resilient Professor proposed to Ellen Riddout who turned him down. He proposed to Miriam Hicks who found an excuse. After two or three more attempts Arthur Fahey asked Miss Housecroft if she had 'other plans'. 'No,' she replied and within three weeks she had cleared out of her pretty study in York Street and moved round the corner to become the *second* Mrs Fahey. She it was who now invited fresh-faced students to a cold collation in the cold professorial dining-room. In York Street her departure made little difference to anyone.

Philip Eames was (in his own eyes, at least) restored to favour, Lucy Winnup having married Harry Withercott. Mrs Winnup was delighted to see her Lucy also restored to happiness once more.

'To think of it, my son-in-law an architect!'

'Well, he will be one day.'

'It may soon be Glass & Withercott . . .'

'Not if I have anything to do with it!' Lucy said in the tone of one who intended to have plenty to do with it. 'I always get my own way in the end.'

Harry, had he heard his bride, would have said she had stolen his line, so they were probably well-suited. It was a quiet wedding with only the tight-lipped Mr Winnup, his weeping wife and the doting aunt who had funded Harry's night-school in attendance. Philip

Eames heard about the marriage with relief: he no longer had a rival for Stacia's hand. He had only to go on biding his time and the girl would be brought back from Mayfair to be *his* bride. Philip congratulated himself, almost believing it now.

Eames cleared his throat and said to Edward Glass: 'About your daughter . . .' But Edward Glass did not hear him any more than once Mr Luscombe might have done. Sir Edward Glass was bewildered by the turn taken in events: 'I confess myself baffled,' he said to Elizabeth.

Lady Blouvier decided to go touring again, this time in the Himalayas. She made the decision during a soirée when the young man whose father owned large chunks of Ireland sat gazing across at poor Stacia who was obliged to sit and play irksome Chopin (*capriccioso* yes, but only *vivace moderato* this evening) and pretend not to see him although he did look rather nice. What a shame he was not a Crown Prince . . . Mr Vizetelly strode down the room towards Lady Blouvier, his shoes squeaking furiously on the dangerous floor. He informed her about the fiasco at the Paris Grand.

'My poor Vizetelly, have you lost all your money?' Lady Blouvier raised her eyeglass mockingly high.

'By no means all, Ma'am! But to lose *any* money, even twopence-farthing, is totally unacceptable, I'm sure you will agree! A lot of men will soon be very angry with Sir Edward Glass. An extravagant reckless man . . .'

'Mrs Elizabeth Cathcart as was, Mrs Glass as is, has a way of picking men who lose other men money. If the woman should marry again we must remember to give the fellow a wide berth!'

'From what I hear it's unlikely she'll ever stand up again, let alone marry.'

Stacia returned to York Street and waited with less and less hope for a letter, from Delia, from the nice young man, from Lady Blouvier herself – posted in an office at the foothills of Mount Everest perhaps and conveyed across the world by the Imperial Mail Service.

'Take a few things with you,' Lady Blouvier had said. 'The rest can wait for when you return.'

'Only enough for while we are out in the East,' Delia advised. 'How we will miss you, Stacia!'

'But what fun we will have together again on our return!' Stacia had decided not to let the wonderful dresses that she wore in the drawing-room at Eulalia House get sullied by having been taken to York Street. She returned home with only the small valise she had taken. Now she wondered why she had not asked Lady Blouvier and her daughter outright exactly how long they were going for and when they would be back. Answers to unasked pertinent questions had always been avoided in Mayfair.

Besides, rumour had it . . .

Orders were cancelled. No one wanted the services of Glass & Co. any more. It was said that the man bankrupted you. Furthermore – allegations had not been entirely proved yet, but Winnup's thorough, unimpeachable investigations made sure that a lot of mud was flying about of which plenty was starting to stick – *large sums of money were said to have gone missing.* Clear accounts had not been kept for any of the many separate enterprises Glass had had on the go simultaneously. In Newcastle contractors, surveyors, engineers and even brick-layers only got jobs with Glass if sizeable sums of money changed hands *sideways* first. Glass's working practices had been careless; Edward Glass had been careless with his money and too trusting with his men. He had been ridiculously trusting with Harry Withercott, but then Winnup himself had entrusted his only daughter to the man. Winnup received helpful information from his new son-in-law and yet secretly he despised him for blabbing so eagerly. Winnup publicly suggested that Edward Glass might have deliberately kept his diary so busy to cloud subsequent investigations into his activities. Diversification as a means of fogging the issue was a ploy well known to any experienced auditor, he said. Everything Glass had had a hand in was now considered to have been unnecessarily expensive. Commissions were cancelled, or wriggled out of, deposits gladly forfeited when they could not be retrieved. Countless legal suits were being lodged.

Harry Withercott set up in practice on his own. It was an opportune moment: a lot of men had been waiting a long time for Glass to get round to their particular entry in the famous diary so Withercott stepped into the breach.

'We don't need Edward Glass,' Lucy urged her husband. 'We never needed him.'

Harry liked having an ambitious wife; it was what a man who had started out with a pencil behind his ear needed.

Stacia noticed an announcement in the paper. Her young admirer had married an American heiress.

'Whatever's the matter, Stacia?' Milla asked, noticing Stacia's face crumple like the sheet of newspaper she had been reading. Stacia told her.

'Oh I am sorry!' Milla said. 'Did you love him very much?'

'Love him!' Stacia scoffed. 'Why Milla, I thought you'd grown up a bit. You always did read far too many books.'

'I'm sorry anyhow.'

'I don't see why! I was forbidden to give him any encouragement. I barely spoke one word to him,' Stacia said but there was a regretful edge now to her cruel Mayfair laughter. Those stomping horses hadn't given her whiskery little kitten a chance. It had been horrible riding along in the carriage afterwards thinking of his blood on the great clopping hoofs.

York Street became increasingly dusty and shabby. Sir Edward spent more and more of his time at home doing nothing. He and Stacia sat about moping. Only Milla did any of the things that the hard-pressed servants had no time for. It was Milla's task to attend to Mrs Glass's knick-knacks.

'What a good job I did all that shopping when I did,' Elizabeth said, for it was unlikely now that she would see the inside of a shop again. 'I cannot help thinking though of all the little purchases that got away, all the items I never saw, all the . . .'

'Hush now!' Milla had said. 'You mustn't upset yourself.'

'It is nice to have you home, Sir Edward!' Elizabeth said on several occasions and her husband smiled down at her. He liked being 'at home'; he had several places he thought of as 'home' and this cluttered one with an undemanding invalid wife would do.

Elizabeth's mind started to wander. She imagined that the baby she had briefly been carrying had in fact been born and that it had died. In her muffled half-awakeness she told Milla to bring her the rosewood box which she opened with the key she still wore round her neck. She took a large sum of money from the box that no one else knew about (for only Mary Ann had observed it and Mary Ann was long gone) and in her delusion she rose from her bed and went again to the shops in Regent Street. She bought the baby the most expensive coffin that money could buy. She bought little things for the child to take with it, silver trinkets and lace, a porcelain doll and even a clever wind-up monkey from France that walked along playing a little tin-drum. It pleased her in her sleep to think that in death her child would have its own pretty nursery full of nick-knacks, without the need for Dr Morgan's nightmarish ministrations, but when she awoke again to her pain and her bed she was startled to think that even Dr Morgan could do nothing for a little soul that had never been alive enough to die. You could not bring back what had never been there to go away. You could not paste over what had never been stuck down . . .

A child of her and Henry's flesh had died also but it had been buried without anything for there had been no money for even the most modest of satin-lined coffins or the smallest of boots for its little naked feet. It had had no toys, it had had no chance. How she had hated Henry then. People often went to the tables with nothing in their pockets, Henry had said glibly. With a clever system at a place like Monte Carlo you could come away with gold coins spilling from your purse. Then there'd be no end to the whatnots you could buy.

Milla tried to ask her step-mother for advice on domestic matters, but between bouts of pain she told Milla only to do as she pleased. Now, just when Milla could have done with some of Elizabeth's hard-won talents at economy and list-making, Elizabeth withdrew further into herself and down into the covers of her bed. Let Edward's daughters keep house for him; they were old enough now and otherwise idle.

'Dear Pasha,' Milla wrote on impulse one day to the house in Acton where something in her had died that could never be brought back, like losing yourself irretrievably in a book: 'We are no longer prosperous. I thought you would like to know this.' But the letter was not worth wasting a stamp on and eventually she consigned it to the wastepaper basket.

The Company owning the New Paris Grand was declared bankrupt. Winnup turned his inexorable attentions on Glass & Co. There were questions, he said, that needed answers.

'Oh dear!' said Mrs Winnup in Turnham Green. 'I do so hope you're not being a little vindictive.'

'I don't know what you mean, woman!' Winnup said coldly. He

sat steadily over long sheets of figures. Extraordinary calculations to make buildings stand up were one thing but jugglery with the accounts and with the accountant's daughter were another and Winnup was Master here. He added and subtracted. He may not be a genius who could draw straight lines without a ruler or draw to scale without ever needing to measure, but Winnup could reckon up sheets of figures and bring a man, any man, to his reckoning.

A sensational package arrived in the Farringdon Road, brought from the Himalayas by courtesy of the Imperial Mail Service. Lady Blouvier had invented yet another form of darkroom tent on which patents were even then pending: the New Indestructible Blouvier could be erected at high altitude and was built to withstand wind-speeds of over an hundred miles per hour. 'Put a full-page advertisement in *every* issue of the *News*,' she wrote, enclosing a blank cheque and some remarkable photographs of the yetis she and Delia had encountered high above the Khyber Pass. She urged Dr Morgan to join them at once: 'Dear Lucius, You would be more than welcome!' she said, attaching a card embossed with her uncrowned crest which would act as a guarantee of safe passage without let or hindrance among the local tribesmen. 'They are in my pay; remarkable the affection Hildegard Blouvier can command with only a few gold doubloons! I have had a species of rhododendron named after me and will see to it shortly that clippings from the *Rhododendronos blouviensis* are shipped back to Eulalia House for the Royal Botanic Gardens at Kew.'

Milla asked Stacia if she had heard from Lady Blouvier. Stacia shook her head.

'Perhaps it's hard to send letters from where they are,' Milla suggested.

'Perhaps!' Stacia now knew for certain that the Blouviers had lied to her. She blamed Milla and Helen: it was Milla's fault not telling them what they had wanted to hear; it had been a small price for such a magnificent tea. If Milla had chattered away about puff-adders and scrap-books Lady Blouvier might not have been so keen to go to the Himalayas. The clock had struck midnight; the carriage had changed back into a pumpkin and the horses become mice that a Siamese cat could have chased. Stacia said nothing, but when she saw Milla running round like a parlourmaid taking the burden of the house on herself she decided that it served her wilful sister right.

She was blowed if she was going to lift a finger to help her. She needed all her energies to hunt down a husband. He had been such a nice-looking young man, the one she had not been allowed to encourage . . .

23

Milla Reflects

Milla had left off there, unable to think beyond that. Thinking back Milla could not think forward. She had needed help then, but there was none to be had: no pot of glue, sharp pair of scissors or algebraic equation to help repair, re-shape, restore. Milla had been perplexed and unforgiving.

Stubborn, Stacia said.

Upset, thought Helen.

Help! screamed Milla wordlessly, like a wild animal caught and stuffed.

At twenty-five, alone in the big house up for sale, Milla considered the possibility of walking away; she wandered idly from room to room, her footsteps loud on the bare floorboards. Surely here at last she, like the echoing empty house, had some sort of chance – to forget, to start afresh? But Milla doubted herself. Unlike Dr Morgan she saw no use for unpleasant knowledge, she saw little use for anything at all.

She'd tried to say as much to Stacia and Helen, but they were both busy and refused to listen to Milla's nonsense. Stacia had a household of her own now, a dull but adequately connected husband, umpteen children, servants, invitations. Helen had her East End Mission for Overseas Works, her earnest array of goodly godly causes. A stout little figure who knew how to organize the world, Helen had become very active and devout.

But neither Stacia nor Helen knew what Milla knew. Milla who meanwhile had stayed at home. They crushed the fantastical out of me, she thought, pausing at the upper-landing window to trace her finger in the dust on a pane of glass. She had colluded in her own destruction, nursing her father and the second Mrs Glass as they each had turned slowly, wittingly, towards death. Milla's had been a humourless task.

'A Land where the Light is as Darkness' – Milla found the printed text down the back of a kitchen drawer. Mrs Curzon's, no doubt.

Milla had liked Mary Ann, had thought of the parlourmaid as a friend but evidently it had not been so: when Mary Ann left she left nothing of herself behind. There was nothing in this kitchen to show she had ever existed. Mrs Curzon, who left the scrap, had never liked any of them and especially not Milla. Milla lit another bonfire in the back garden and burnt everything burnable that could not be sold. She burnt what remained of the photograph of dear William, the fairy-tale brother who had died from syphilis in New York. He moved just as the picture was taken: it had never been in focus and had always been too faded to show what William looked like.

Years ago Milla tried to tell Mrs Glass about the photograph. 'I can't remember him,' she imagined herself confessing the awful truth. 'Even this photograph doesn't help me to picture dear William.'

'Photographs only record a chance moment frozen in time,' Elizabeth replied. 'You either remember him or you don't.' *She* had no photograph of Henry Cathcart, and did not need one.

'There's no such thing as chance,' Milla told her step-mother, finding the place in her algebra book.

'That's as maybe!' The second Mrs Glass turned unaccountably angry. Perhaps she'd thought there was no such thing as dear William.

'In the first instant when you look at the photograph,' Milla explained, 'it's as though he's standing there, frozen in time, as you said, so that the light over your shoulder might thaw him out. He'd unfreeze and focus and come alive. Then dear William would be here again . . .'

'Alive!' Mrs Glass shrieked as though Milla the middle one had accused her of something. 'You won't find an equation in your grubby algebra book to stop your precious picture fading. Or to help you remember your brother. Or to bring the Dead back to give evidence against the Living! Chance is not as haphazard or higgledy-piggledy as your horrid scrap-book might suggest. Sometimes you just have to cross your fingers, Milla, and *make something happen*: snip, snip and then slap on the glue . . .'

'QED. Well, slap-happy me!' Stacia jeered in a loud whisper. 'That'll teach you!'

Mrs Glass overheard. 'Be careful with the glue, Milla dear,' she said gently. 'It's so easy to come unstuck.'

261

A valuer had been to the house, an efficient stocky man called Mr Frewitt. He took one look and was frankly disappointed, sucking in his breath and apologizing: the house was dark and shabby, the furnishings were worth 'precious little'. Having 'had their day', they had 'seen better times'. He toured the rooms quickly after that, shaking his head in continual agreement with himself. The Conrad & Taylor Upright needed re-stringing, which would cost more than the piano was worth even if it still had all its own ivory keys, which it had not. The papier mâché was scuffed and tatty, most of the knick-knacks chipped. 'Fashionable items that have gone out of fashion.' He advised Milla not to expect too much.

'We'll be glad to take whatever, Mr Frewitt.' She felt guilty at wasting the valuer's valuable time.

Elee came a few days before the sale. 'I'd have come before but my legs have been bad,' she told Milla.

Milla glanced down at the old lady's lumpy legs, unaware that the hideous woman who now stood on their doorstep trying to push her way in had once been an actress in the smaller music-halls, much admired for fleeting glimpses she would allow of her slender calves and pretty ankles.

'I'm afraid you have the *wrong* day,' Milla said.

Elee threw back her ugly head and gave a loud ugly cackle. 'Bless me! There never was a *right* day for what I have to do!' she exclaimed.

'But the sale isn't till Friday; viewing starts tomorrow, from twelve o'clock onwards. The valuer will be here to answer any questions,' Milla said patiently. Frewitt had warned her how people would come early pretending they had misread the sale notices, hoping to sneak a preview of what was on offer.

'I'd like to meet a valuer – or anyone else – who could answer the questions *I'd* like to ask!' Elee laughed. 'You don't think *I* want to buy anything from *here* do you? From Sarah Glass's house! No, I promised your father to come and see you, that's all.'

'Promised my father?' Milla stuttered. 'I don't understand.'

'Course you don't, deary! He was a friend of mine, see?'

'A friend? Of yours?'

'That surprised you, didn't it? Not a man for friendship wasn't your father!' Elee looked at Milla curiously. 'Which one of them are you then, Stacia, Milla or Helen?'

'Milla.'

'Ah ha, the middle one! Well, aren't you going to invite me in, Milla? Don't you want to hear what old Elee has to tell you?'

'So you haven't come for the sale,' Milla murmured confusedly, leading Elee down into the kitchen where everything had already been laid out by Frewitt's men in numbered boxes. Edward had not mentioned the girl was slow, Elee thought; too quick by half was what he had implied. Out loud Elee said Sir Edward had once asked her to do him a favour.

'A favour? My father?'

Elee it was who told Milla then about William Glass, telling her to pass the information on to her sisters.

Milla drew out a chair but did not sit down. 'Why didn't my father tell us himself?' she asked, not really asking this ugly stranger this question.

'For some stupid reason Sarah Glass convinced you William was some sort of story-book hero. Edward asked me to tell you the truth, but only after he'd died.' Elee had an official document, sent across the Atlantic from some mortuary in Brooklyn, to show Milla. It had come, she said, accompanied by two letters marked 'Return to Sender' (Edward's letters detailing the death of Sarah Glass and his marriage to Elizabeth Cathcart), which William had apparently never received.

Milla did not want to see the document. She did not ask who Elee was. She stood holding on to the chair, waiting for the peevish old woman to go, but Elee, like Mrs Preedy, decided the girl had inherited her father's arrogant manners. She was only doing what she'd been asked to; it had not been *her* idea to come. It riled Elee that Edward should have left behind this proud and bloodless daughter who reminded her of Sarah Glass, a woman she had never met: 'I could tell you a thing or two about your respectable father – Sir Edward Glass – that I dare say you wouldn't want to know!' Elee sneered.

'No. Thank you!' Milla cried, determined not to hear: other people found it easy to hear or not to hear, to pick and to choose.

'He used to visit me, Milla the middle one, when he had nowhere else. He was a lonely man, your father . . .' Milla stared blankly until Elsinora Lee (a name once posted in small type among the Added Attractions at the bottom of many a cheap theatre bill) took up her scrap of paper from the Brooklyn mortuary and shuffled away at last. *Once upon a time* – the exact time and date written out officially, recorded in full. Elee had done what she had to do, now she could forget all about Edward Glass: 'Enough fanciful fiction, your father thought it best you know the facts.'

Milla wept, she knew the facts all right. It was official: there never would be a bright green parrot. Or heaps of treasure spilling from a seaman's chest like in those expensive heavily printed scraps fretted with gold that Mrs Glass had forced her to stick in her scrap-book. Yet what had been destroyed was not immune from further damage: someone had torn the burnt scrap-book open, snipping malevolently at its charred remembered pages, leaving great ugly gaps. Elephants' tusks ripped out for ivory; gaping black holes you could fall through and keep on falling . . .

'What are you going to do?' Mrs Fahey asked. She had invited Milla to visit and Milla, not wanting to see prospective purchasers viewing in advance of the auction, agreed to go to Professor Fahey's cold house to see the former governess.

Milla shook her head uncertainly. The second Mrs Fahey, like the Reverend Housecroft before her, had by now forgotten her own Latin and Greek. Nor did she know what to say to Milla; she had not expected her to come. She tried to engage the ill-looking girl in conversation but was uncomfortably reminded of a far from ebullient Milla on their way home from Pasha's house. *Wilful* Mrs Curzon had said, it was a shame probably that the child had not been more so. Milla should have told Pasha that they had been *invited* to tea. She herself should have stood up for Milla and remonstrated with Mrs Smith for taking her bitterness out on a child whose own feet could not quite reach the floor.

Milla told her sisters that she had written to dear William telling him of their father's demise and then of Elizabeth's mending sufficiently to go to France for the cure that could have no success. She said there had been no reply, dear William was probably making his fortune in a Colorado gold-mine, he'd be too busy to spend time writing back; they'd both shrugged their shoulders and marvelled that Milla had bothered: Milla always had been one for sitting down and writing unnecessary letters.

'Why the South of France?' Mrs Preedy wondered. It had been

said that Mrs Glass could not get out of bed so why, after ten years, had she taken it into her head to get up like Lazarus, and walk?

'The woman had a remarkable capacity for self-renewal,' Charles Preedy observed, somewhat inappropriately since Elizabeth had died nastily and among strangers.

'I always thought it odd the way Edward Glass picked Eliza out, as though he chose her to spite me,' Mrs Preedy expressed what had rankled in her mind for many years.

'Surely not?'

'I got the feeling he knew I was toying with taking her on so he hastily married her and installed her in York Street like some ill-conceived cupola on top of a building. Goodness knows what we ever did to upset him: I went out of my way to be kind to poor Sarah, and we put up with that monkey, Mr Eames, at Christmas . . .'

'Edward Glass was perverse – you can see that in his buildings.' There had been a new surge of interest in Sir Edward Glass following his death. It often seemed to happen when someone died, Preedy said. Great Art . . .

'Don't go dying off just to get some critical attention!' The dependable Mrs Preedy clutched her husband's arm almost playfully. 'Think of the expense – you know how undertakers charge! Besides, Charles dear, the children and I might miss you.'

The Preedys smiled together. 'Why the South of France?' Mrs Preedy wondered again. 'Poor Eliza. I don't suppose we shall ever find out now.'

For Milla there had been that last conversation with Mrs Glass. Not the last probably, but the last that Milla would remember (there had also been a last conversation with her father, a conversation Milla was determined to forget): 'What will happen to all my nice things?' It was the middle of the night; Milla had been called to Mrs Glass's bedside by an irrepressible shriek of pain. Elizabeth hated Milla to see her sweating and shivering like this. She resolved to take herself off somewhere private and far away. She had once read in a magazine about hospitals in the South of France where you could die in peace in the sun. She heaved in her bed and spoke as a way of not succumbing again to the pain that was racking her insides. 'What will be done with all my nice things?' she demanded tetchily, for Edward had died and there was only Milla in the house and Milla was a dangerous, haphazard creature.

'I will keep them and look after them,' Milla said softly. She poured her step-mother a glass of water and attempted to bathe the invalid's feverish forehead.

'You will sell them, Milla. You were always careless with glue oozing . . .' Mrs Glass gasped accusingly but accepted the water, gulping painfully. This was a cruel variation on the party-game, dying-off, when the one left behind in the rookery not only had to find for your funeral expenses but did so by selling off your precious things for whatever they could fetch.

'No,' Milla lied. 'I will keep them carefully dusted, for your sake, dear Mrs Glass.' It was late at night, Milla had had little sleep, she was no actress posturing on a stage, part of some performance even then unfolding; she did not sound convincing.

Elizabeth turned away and fell into a fitful sleep. She did not want to die off like the old battered rooks or to be part of someone else's variation on the game. 'I will arrange my own death as I have arranged my own life,' she decided, thinking of all the snipping and pasting. 'I will arrange my own death as I arranged dear old Henry's.'

'Thank you for all the kindnesses,' she had said limply, kissing Milla goodbye and refusing the girl's offer to travel with her. Milla's lies had dealt the mortal blow: Milla would not keep her knick-knacks carefully dusted or even keep them at all. Of this the second Mrs Glass was certain. *Things took on the value your thoughts put on them. A value that lasted as long as your thoughts.* She did not need Mr Frewitt to waste his valuable time telling her that all her things were worthless . . .

'You can't go like this,' Milla tried to protest. Her step-mother could barely stand but Mrs Glass's mind was made up as firmly as if she had been Mrs Curzon. On the train south, Elizabeth had thankfully kicked off her shoes. Fellow-passengers had mostly been kind, mainly ignoring her.

'Nothing ventured, Nothing gained!' Elizabeth spent the journey dozing, content to be rattling through the night towards the sunlit Riviera of which Henry James Cathcart had so often spoken. 'If only . . .' he used to say, standing with his hands in his empty pockets, a frown on that handsome brow: *if only* he could implement the 'dead cert' system he himself had devised for the gaming-room at Monte Carlo, their problems would be solved as surely as if the solutions were printed upside-down at the back of the book. What an eternal optimist dear dubious Henry had been! What agony the equation of her own life without him to quibble with on this, the *other side* of his dubious death. But *she* was the one who had cheated, by looking in the back of the book: she was the one who had known the ending so that dear old Henry had had some luck – the art of winning being to die off first. Oh Henry, *rien ne va plus*, Now or Never, the chips are down, the wheel is spinning and we shall soon see each other not through a glass darkly or even through a stereoscopic viewer in a walnut box but three-dimensional, face to face, once and for all . . .

A large woman came to the sale with a large basket, plonking herself right in the middle of the front row and bidding enthusiastically for all the lots no one else wanted. When her basket was full and her purse was empty she pushed her way out. 'I always had an eye for a bargain,' Cora boasted to Milla who was sitting on the front doorstep. My, how thin and tired Miss Milla had grown! What an eager cheerful child she had been, you'd never have thought it! Cora herself was more pudding-shaped than ever now that she got plenty to eat. 'I'm surprised Mary Ann didn't make it from Margate – she was always one for the Mistress's doodahs.' Cora dug into her basket and pulled out the cranberry glass vase she had bought. There was a crack across its base; as she tugged the vase broke up in her hand.

'Look at that!' she cried, flinging the pieces angrily down on the path. 'Don't s'pose I can get my money back, Miss Milla? There weren't no crack in it yesterday at the viewin'.'

'Oh, I'm sure . . .' Milla started to say.

'The items are Sold-as-Seen, Madam!' Mr Frewitt bobbed up beside Milla. 'What you didn't see for yourself was your own look-out – it always is.' Having shown himself adept with awkward customers the valuer turned affably to Milla. The sale had been a lot quicker than expected, he said. He had another to attend and he would let her have his account, and the balance of the monies, as soon as possible.

'You want to watch it, Miss Milla,' Cora said loudly so that the beady-eyed, beady-headed Mr Frewitt could hear. 'You'll end up owin' 'im more for sellin' this stuff than the sale of it fetched altogether.' Cora wondered what could become of a girl like Milla Glass out there in the tangled jungle, but she said nothing further. It was not her place now, and never had been her place to speak.

'You are looking very well,' Milla observed.

'Married the coalman, didn't I? We makes enough in winter to spend the whole summer at Margate so 'e can sit in a deck-chair and gawp at the girls!' She laughed heartily. They'd been lean times she'd spent in this tall dark house. 'We don't never see Mary Ann though . . .'

'Look, I'd better . . .' Milla smiled.

'You're busy, I can see that – and not doing nuffing an' all. I'll be getting on, 'e'll want 'is tea. Coal don't arv give a man appetite!'

Cora swung the vast bulging basket on to her broad shoulders and staggered off home to her coalman: proper little madams these Glass girls, and look what had 'appened to them.

Milla swept up the fragments of cranberry glass. What a world this was where a downtrodden housemaid could return well-shod and make off with her pick of the Mistress's knick-knacks. It was surprising though not to have seen Mrs Preedy standing in the side-aisle watching the proceedings. Perhaps she had come to the viewing and seen nothing to take her fancy.

Charles and Mrs Preedy were not yet Sir Charles and Lady Preedy. A year later, when the Fabbricotti factory in Chelsea collapsed with the loss of nine lives (within an hour over a hundred hands would have been in the path of the girders and rubble), any hope of that invitation to Windsor crumbled also. Myers, the draughtsman Preedy had poached, may have understood the rudiments, but he lacked the magic touch Glass had brought to the buildings he designed. Lucy Winnup, who had known the Master's touch, thought Harry Withercott a man she could make something of though not a man probably to be summoned to Windsor. And indeed, Mr and Mrs Withercott were quite content except for the doting and now dotty old aunt who on Harry's insistence had come to live with them. Once or twice poor Lucy had been driven to contemplate adding a solution of weedkiller to the dotty old lady's drink but Lucy Winnup knew herself no match for a cyanide tank; Lucy Withercott would never be cast in wax.

Milla, however, inhabited a vacant Chamber of Horrors lodged in her own head. A crisis of emptiness no one else knew about.

Standing now in the sold up house she wondered vaguely about the new Century not so far away. Milla had seen the damage, had observed lives lived carelessly of each other pursuing engrossedly their own selfish ends and it had done Milla no good to see as she had seen. Couldn't things be different in the future? It was hard to imagine 1900 but she supposed that the year would eventually come and go. Life would go on; it always seemed to, in spite of everything.

In spite of everything, in one last desperate attempt, Philip Eames had called at the house and begged Stacia not to marry the dull husband she was set on. This dull husband, though not a Crown Prince, was decidedly better connected than Mr Eames. With Mayfair manners, Stacia told him so. 'He isn't even worthy to lick your boots,' their father's glorified errand-boy said.

Haughtily Stacia held up one of her boots and told Eames to 'go on then, if you're so keen. You lick it!' Eames bent down, his tongue out like a dog and did as he was told. He'd stood up unabashed and Stacia had laughed in his face.

'There, I told you so – you *are* only worthy to lick my boots!' Stacia said, sweeping imperiously from the room, pausing at the door to add: 'You can't expect to become one of us just like that, you know!'

There had been a savage series of violent killings that started at exactly the time Stacia had married. Young women walking late in the thick London fog had been subjected to indescribable abuse and the most ghastly of deaths. A sharp paper-knife had been used with surgical precision, though even the cheap newspapers balked at retailing the details. The last of these killings occurred a week before Philip Eames killed himself.

The Coroner to the South-East Division of the County of London adjourned the inquest on the body of the last of his victims for several months and thanked the jury for their attendance, adding: 'I trust that in the meantime there will not be a case of a similar nature. People having the character of these sorry women have it entirely in their hands to prevent this sort of thing. If we could only induce the creatures not to assist the man who does this work it would be stopped, but unfortunately I think it is hoping against hope, because they lend themselves to it.'

Philip Eames read the Coroner's words reported on the inside page of the *Standard*. Knowing that a cat never receives assistance from the canary it kills but rather from the self-righteous men who can pronounce on the innocent and the driven in this way, and that *they are the ones* who have it entirely in their hands to leave the back door wide open, he flung his abominable self purposefully into the rippling muddy waters of the Thames.

Milla alone made the connection; Let them wait! Philip Eames had said, but 'Wait, ah wait, the ripple saith – Maiden wait, for I am death . . .' The knowledge of what her father's operative, the automaton Philip Eames, had done, incapacitated her. In her dreams, Milla visited Eames in prison while he waited to be hanged.

He doffed his hat to her, one eye blinked: 'I did warn you!' Eames said, thanking her for the apricot and vermicelli tart, mistaking her for Stacia. Confusing the sisters as though they were interchangeable, indistinguishable and not somehow themselves. 'I'll be watching over you.'

'I don't want you watching me,' Milla said.

'I waited and waited like the cat in the yard,' the man recounted sadly, the violence quite gone out of him. 'All the time you were chirping Chopin at soirées in Mayfair I waited, but by the time the back door was left open you had flown away . . .'

His lawyers argued half-heartedly that the defendant was insane; anyone who worked as Eames had worked for Edward Glass *must* have been insane. 'Year after year, my Lord, rain or shine, the man arrived at York Street each and every Friday on the stroke of three.' The lawyers pointed out that as three o'clock was such a short hour to strike this was insane punctuality indeed. Keen as a sharpened paper-knife, Eames had even turned up at the house with a bottle of something cheap one Christmas Day. There was a clarity now about Philip Eames that made pleas of insanity untenable. His punctuality inextricably linked his name for posterity to the anonymous perpetrator of one of London's most disgusting series of crimes. It was a suitably haphazard link.

Stacia said gently (only it was Milla dreaming herself as her elder sister saying it): 'Philip, my star may have been destined to shine in a greater, loftier Mayfair sky but even *I* wasn't worth *this*.'

Milla perceived the horror of Eames's life, yet throughout all those years none of them had given him any thought except perhaps to laugh at his dogged loyalty. At the creepy way he arrived, rain or shine, exactly on time, trotting up the garden path, a dogsbody with ears alert and tail wagging. She thought of the wire-haired terrier Mrs Glass had tried to press on her, which she refused to touch and had last seen carried away under Dr Morgan's arm. She was not to know that he had hurried across London to give the dog to Eames's lavender-scented mother as a parting-present: the woman who had deliberately let a cat into the house to kill a defenceless canary. Its singing had annoyed her and Philip had taken too obvious a pleasure and delight.

Philip Eames rose now from his stone seat in the cold prison cell, inky-fingered, impassioned and unrepentant: 'Oh yes, Miss Stacia, my fluffy little canary girl, even though you never thought about me and flittered and chittered with your sisters in my face, you gave me something to live for, someone to dream and care about. *You should have a little fun once in a while, Eames!* I always obeyed your father, I was employed to slit letters open and give him the gist, I do not believe that can make me liable for anything, technically . . .'

Milla wept. The lurid murders had ceased with the operative's untimely death. Milla alone connected the end of the gruesome killings with Eames's suicide, sticking the pieces together as if accidentally spilling glue.

'Milla should go on holiday,' Helen told Stacia. It wasn't good for her mooching about that empty house, brooding on the past. The strain of being the one who stayed at home with the ill and the dying and clearing up afterwards had taken an obvious toll. Milla should get up, get out and get on with things, the sisters agreed. Stacia generously offered to take Milla along with her and her nice dull husband, their children and the children's nurse to Margate. 'She can give a hand with the little ones,' Stacia said. 'She can share the expenses. The sea-air will do her good.'

Milla declined the invitation.

Dr Morgan sent a businesslike note expressing condolences. He did not offer to Bring any of the Dead Back from the Dead for he had given up Spiritualism: the market was saturated, he said. Instead he conducted courses and wrote manuals on *memory*. He had just completed the Seventh (Enlarged, Improved and Illustrated) edition of his practical treatise: *Morgan's Ideal System of Memory*, modestly priced at only 1/-. He also sold curious devices by mail-order which might interest them: a pictorial multiplication table, a historical chronometer and a mnemonical globe were on special offer this month.

What had happened to Lady Blouvier and her daughter Delia was a shame. It was a shame, even though Dr Morgan had no shortage of other patrons in London only too happy to open their doors and offer their unmarriageable daughters to him. An avalanche in the Himalayas would hardly have made the column inches of *The Times* but for the fact that two of the Empire's most intrepid explorers, Lady Hildegard Fredericka Blouvier and her daughter Delia Blanchetta Angelica Victorina had been swept into a deep crevasse in a glacier while pitching their patented darkroom tent during a stormforce gale. An argument between two factions of local tribesmen over who should have the bulky timepiece from her bosom caused a local war to break out that was still raging twenty years later when the bodies were washed from the glacier and the famous timepiece retrieved. Still working! Neither tribe wanted it then: it was demonic. Time was meant to stand still in the ice but the vast timepiece had, in the manner of the rest of Lady Blouvier's awesome bosom, defied all the known laws of nature. Reverentially the tribesmen laid down their arms and, for fear that the two frozen English ladies might thaw out and come alive again they joined forces to rebury them hastily, this time beneath a fine specimen of *Rhododendronos blouviensis*. The one Lady Blouvier had intended sending cuttings from back to Kew.

Milla asked Stacia if she had seen the account of the tragedy. Stacia smiled. Time never stood still, midnight always eventually struck and bodies wash from the ice as surely as coaches revert to being pumpkins and conservatories are conservatories again. If they hadn't wanted her out of the way they might never have gone to the Himalayas. They had lied to her and played with her, dressing her up like some porcelain doll from France. She owed them nothing, for Stacia had discovered that Mayfair airs and graces were of little use outside of Mayfair.

Milla paused at a bookseller's stall before an impressive display of *Morgan's Ideal System*. 'Some things are better forgotten,' she decided, flipping open the cover and looking at a photograph of Dr Lucius Morgan (Cantab.) taken by the Dear Departed Lady Hildegard Blouvier. Next thing she knew she had bought the book, although she did not want it and could ill spare the shilling. All that was wrong with *her* memory was that it already retained far too much.

Contemplating Dr Morgan's photograph and considering the effect it had had on her, Milla concluded that the man did possess extraordinary powers after all. He had not been a con-man or a charlatan as her father had said. Just by looking at people when they looked into his eyes he induced them to do what he wanted. Her mother's cousin could hardly be blamed for the hypnotic strength of his eyes even though it had cost her a valuable shilling. If we could all effect our intentions by our eyes alone! Given the strength of his own natural talent, Dr Morgan had been quite harmless, and had probably given a lot of pleasure or unease to whoever deserved it.

The sale of the house and furnishings over, the money divided – what little there was, it transpired there had been various mortgages and charges on the house – Milla was free at last to travel the world in search of heroics and adventure. The furniture, the antimacassars, the cut-glass cake-stands had all been swept away.

She sat on the kitchen table and swung her legs. Once she had triumphed over the sewer-rats, eating left-over fish-paste sandwiches and promising herself buttered tea-cakes every afternoon when dear William came home. What an ambitious, greedy child she had been! The table had been sold by Mr Frewitt: Lot Number 213. Whoever had bought it had not come to collect it. Perhaps they got carried away at the auction and did not really want a table. Milla smiled to think that in the end it was Mrs Curzon's scrubbed kitchen-table that shared the uncertainty with her.

Milla smiled. Here at last, she told herself indulgently, was her chance to start afresh and be somebody else. To climb out of the old picture with its untold layers – for there are always untold layers – of heavy varnish and dust, the ugly great gilded frame and cluttered corners and all the unseeing, uncaring faces that filled every inch and looked only to themselves. Mrs Glass had barely been able to stand and had grieved bitterly at leaving her precious knick-knacks behind, but in the end she had hazarded all on a one-way ticket taking only a small valise for a very short stay. Now she was no longer there Milla could appreciate what her father had liked about Elizabeth Cathcart. The woman had been a mainstay, while I, Milla thought, I fall apart and do not like what I find. I prefer unsound fabrications to facts – I blame my father for both. I want something else, I always have.

Milla smiled, for thinking back she could not think forward beyond sitting on the table weeping. Milla wept.

IV

CHAOS

24

Arcanum Arcanorum – How, or What, on Earth?

An unquiet well-fed rat out there in the darkness. The darkness of the deserted Paris Grand. Sole occupant now of these vaunted vaulted corridors, soaring arcades of vacant ordered space, this exuberant stretching of a vast and daring imagination: the enigma that had been Edward Glass.

What genius it had been to take and twist, to trump up such perspectives. Deceptively solid walls flew into arches which reached out only to disappear back through their own ineluctable vanishing points, a troupe of acrobats springing from their haunches and dextrously turning five skewbacks at once in the air. How on earth had he done it? What precisely had he done? Men used to stand here hours at a time once, endangering vertebrae by also twisting and turning in frustrated attempts to work out whatever this is Sir Edward Glass has pulled off. Can that be a voussoir? An understood ring course? An unpronounced spring course? How could a span spring from the face to the crown then stretch back again unsupported, three times over? By rights such a structure had no right to stand up, yet here it still stood. Rumours that Glass must have sold his soul to the Devil were facetiously far-fetched, of course, but in the absence of any more rational explanation . . .

This is ridiculous! The man was a Genius and men, rightly suspicious of the jugglery of genius, were suspicious of Edward Glass. Glass had been able to draw straight lines without a ruler and draw to scale without first needing to measure. He could draw several symmetrical lines simultaneously, two pencils in each hand, four lines at a time symmetric about a rotational axis. He produced meticulous sections and flawless elevations with great speed straight from out of his head. He had an exact eye and exacting vision. He could create order out of chaos or chaos out of order with a few quick strokes of his masterly pen.

Lesser mortals stood with their heads thrown back, their mouths wide open, shrugging their shoulders in admiration tinged with disbelief. How? What? Which? Where? Mass education having encouraged the belief that to every question there is an answer handily printed upside-down at the back of the book, there'd been the feeling that a solution was somewhere, waiting only to be found. A thorough enough search and an elusive angle or some relatively simple, inspired equation would eventually be discovered to reveal at last the secret behind this grandest of Sir Edward's Grand Designs. Gradually people lost interest: enigmas are all very well but life is too short. Only a few still came to stand with their hands on their hips, to wonder and gawp. The novelty had worn off, Edward Glass had died and was pronounced *passé* . . .

Tomorrow, one cold wet day in April 1941, amid the fear and the dying in this the cruellest of cruellest months, a bomb will fall and everyone will say 'High time too!' The Paris Grand has been empty for years. No one got killed. No one who could not afford to lost property. The place was rat-infested, a menace to public health. Sucks-yaa-boo to the Luftwaffe, wasting their bombs and so harmlessly. Jolly good show – the ugly Victorian monstrosity wanted razing and the Germans have saved us the bother.

Even the plump rat made it to safety out of the collapsing network of spirally moulded downpipes, across the subtly contrasted tracery already precariously rocking, through the elaborate labyrinthine trellising, down endless galleries of toppling archways and tumbling twisting spandrels. Out in the nick of time as Sir Edward Glass's last great edifice crumbled completely: a complete and expensive disaster. The plump rat choked in the dirt, angrily flicking smuts from its whiskers, but otherwise displaying an English *sang-froid*, really rather calm at having made it niftily.

'The Paris Grand was Quintessential Glass' – that had been the thesis of one Delmé Hawkins. By 1941 Edward Glass had been dead fifty years, Glass was forgotten; in 1941 there were other more pressing concerns, the world had moved on. This had not been Delmé Hawkins's view but Hawkins himself had been dead now a decade.

'There's more to life than cleverness, mentions and mortar!' Back at the beginning of the Century, Milla Glass had laughed in Delmé's face. She was blowed if she was going to help her father's would-be biographer and she told him so. 'The world has moved on,' she said. 'I am a middle-aged woman, there are new fashions, new ideas, new people. The old certainties my father built for have been swept away and thank goodness!'

Delmé Hawkins, who had taken great pains to track down this daughter, was disappointed. He had expected more from Milla Glass and he, in his turn, told her so. He was writing a book on *The Life and Work of Edward Glass, Architect* and he needed her help: 'You can – and you must – in strictest confidence of course!'

Who was this spy, this nasty little sneak, this Hawkins? Not much of a mystery as it turned out. Delmé had been that unfortunate thing, a second son who could only be a nuisance to the family business, Hawkins Specialist Footwear (surgical-boot manufacturers in Bristol). When Delmé left school, old Mr Hawkins sensibly decided to solve the problem of what to do with him by paying the lad (who had been highly educated, though for nothing in particular, and had never shown any aptitude for the surgical-boot trade) a small honorarium simply for staying away.

'You should find an interest to pursue,' his father sternly advised and the sure-footed Hawkinses who were to remain in Bristol banded together to give the redundant and discarded son some suitable parting-presents to encourage him to go. They purchased a Kodak Box Brownie and a bicycle.

All through his youth Delmé Hawkins had wretchedly envisaged a life spent taking orders from his brother, ironing bank-notes, and getting under everyone's feet. Yearningly he had dreamed of studying in Oxford and becoming an eminent Art Historian. It seemed to him that John Ruskin's father could never have run a surgical-boot business in Bristol. Liberated unexpectedly from rumpled bank-notes and stumpy boots, this dream of the Aesthetic was the only interest Delmé could think of pursuing. He fancied he might make his way to Oxford after all. 'Delmé Hawkins, MA, Art Historian (Oxon.)' – it sounded good and would look good printed on calling-cards.

Soon Delmé Hawkins could no longer remember what had attracted him as an impressionable young man of independent means and transport to pursue the works of Edward Glass. Perhaps it had only been a random choice, one of the few subjects Professor Ruskin had not got round to. At first the ambitious youthful Hawkins made no secret of his aspiration to become the heir to Ruskin's greatness. He too would pronounce on all things Aesthetic

– and where better to begin than amidst the complex workings of the elusive Aesthetics of Edward Glass? There had been a lot of preparatory work to be done. For several years Hawkins had cycled the length and breadth of Britain with all his worldly goods including the Box Brownie strapped into his front basket, meticulously recording the great architect's scattered *Oeuvre*. Right along the South Coast he had pedalled, staying at cheap guest-houses and filing away careful descriptions of one Glass edifice after the other.

The venture had not been without incident. Once, a patriotic landlady had reported her peculiar guest to the police. She had searched Delmé's room while he was splashing in the bath and discovered his suspiciously detailed notes, spidery cryptic sketches and the photographs of strategic buildings. She was convinced her lodger must be spying for the Kaiser. That night the innocuous guest-house (exactly the sort of place someone careful to attract no attention might choose to stay) had been silently surrounded while an armed member of Special Branch shinned up a drainpipe and climbed in through Delmé's bedroom window. There was no doubt that Delmé Hawkins looked shifty as he cowered in bed wearing stripy pyjamas and evasively trying to answer questions his interrogators fired at him. The Detective Sergeant, furious at having ripped his best trousers on a down-spout outside, scoffed dismissively: 'Edward Glass? Never heard of the fellow!'

'My point entirely!' Despite the pistol that prodded him in the ear Delmé Hawkins sat up boldly in bed. Though only half-awake and without his spectacles he blinked beneath the bright searchlights they trained on him and passionately he protested his case: 'You *should* have heard of Sir Edward Glass, everyone should! The man was a genius.'

'Oh yer – who says so?'

'Well,' Delmé Hawkins sighed; surely his predecessor John Ruskin had never had this problem? 'I, for one. I do.'

The officials decided against taking Delmé Hawkins away with them on this occasion but they removed his files and photographs pending further enquiries and advised the landlady to keep her suspect under twenty-four-hour surveillance. You never knew. 'There are a lot of funny people about, odd goings on . . . Secret naval operations in the Channel, diplomatic activity behind closed doors . . . This one's guilty of *something* – stands out a mile!'

'Aren't we all, though?' The landlady winked and elbowed the nearest policeman who jovially elbowed her back.

A day or two later (during which time Delmé had had nothing to do but ponder on the nature of his guilt) Special Branch returned, returning his papers to him, somewhat the worse for wear. 'The silly sod' was harmless enough they said but commended the patriotic landlady nevertheless on her vigilance. Warily she unlocked the door and released a bewildered and hungry Hawkins. Delmé was delighted to see how interested the authorities had been in his work since all of it was dog-eared and had clearly been read many times. Despite Delmé's official clearance, the landlady remained tight-lipped but she allowed him a double helping of bacon and eggs with fried bread and limitless tea for his breakfast. The scholar meekly accepted these reparations, but as soon as he had finished eating she cleared away his plate and said pointedly: 'I'll be needing your room again *immediately.*'

Delmé Hawkins pushed back his chair and stood up. He wiped vestiges of egg yolk from around his mouth, then replaced the napkin on the table and bowed politely to the vigilant landlady and his fellow breakfasters. He paid his bill, packed his possessions into the wicker basket on the front of his bicycle and climbing on to the well-worn saddle he pedalled nobly, silently away.

Having completed his study of Glass's buildings on the South Coast, Delmé Hawkins hastened North and eagerly pursued the same magical hand at work in every manufacturing town he came to. There was scarcely an Edward Glass railway station, hotel, church, civic monument, factory, town hall or Public Building that Hawkins did not visit and write about in his copious notes. The fact that an armed member of Special Branch had climbed through his window in the middle of the night for a thorough examination of his studies and then later returned his papers in person lent, Delmé thought, official validation to the work he was doing.

Delmé Hawkins started to give lectures for small fees to Societies for Improvement. These Improving lectures proved very popular, especially in towns like Bingley and Batley, and suburbs of London where free entertainments were thin on the ground. Delmé now had 'Tutor in Art' added to the printed cards he kept proudly in his top pocket.

Soon Mr Hawkins was much in demand. The young man with the

amiably enthusiastic manner was known to have both relatively interesting subject matter and a lecture that didn't go on for too long. The Chairman would stand up at the end to thank our young Mr Hawkins for a thought-provoking talk; this Edward Glass were an enigma, no doubt about it, but we can't all be Great Artists, tea was ready in the adjoining room and please, *only one biscuit* per person and be sure to put a penny-ha'penny in the tin! By the way, did anyone have any questions?

Sometimes Mr Hawkins was asked if he had publications to sell. It was pleasing when an audience clamoured for more and made up for the unruly ignorant element who sat at the back nudging each other all the way through, sniggering and passing inaudible remarks. You might have suspected they turned up not so much for Improvement as for the free evening's sport the lecture and the lecturer provided. Most of the audience who had done a hard day's work sat appreciatively attentive and seemed to come awake at the end. Mr Hawkins on the platform, refreshing his raw throat with a sip of tepid odd-tasting water, shook his owl-like head and answered bravely. No, there was nothing in print as yet.

With the passing of years the smile with which he said this grew sadder and more defiantly brave in its fixedness. Despite enormous piles of notes and photographs that made his bicycle wobble perilously, Delmé Hawkins was beginning to realize that no, there was nothing in print, nor was it likely there ever would be. The problem was built into what had attracted him to pursue the architect Edward Glass in the first place: the searchlights were too bright, angles were too dazzlingly elusive to see, equations and principles too inspired to detect. The admiration he'd once set out with had become an unhealthy obsession and like the thwarted sorcerer's apprentice he pored jealously over the Master's Works. Edward Glass, it seemed to him now, held the secrets, if not of the Universe then of something in keeping with the earthly dimensions human beings are permitted to construct. Yet *Arcanum Arcanorum* kept the secrets selfishly, infuriatingly to himself.

The arcane complexity that had once excited him would, Delmé realized, eventually defeat him. His work had lost its youthful edge: he'd replaced enthusiasm with pedantic obsessiveness. He was as baffled as ever by the enigma he had no chance of solving; the further he went on, the less he understood. Edward Glass was quintessentially elusive. He no longer aspired to follow in Ruskin's footsteps: if he could only hobble together a short monograph with a few footnotes then that at least would be something. The swing had gone from Delmé's step, the lilt in his lop-sided walk was beyond any surgical-boot to correct. He trod this earth a doomed and shuffling shadow. He blamed Edward Glass.

In 1914, aged thirty-six, with little to offer and little to lose, Delmé Hawkins voluntarily queued up to enlist. The Regimental Recruiting Sergeant sighed, put a perfunctory stethoscope to the scholar's chest, pronounced him Unfit for Anything and sent him back to his books. Hawkins D., 36, of no fixed abode, limping from guest-house to guest-house, could be of no use to King & Country. The poor fellow might as well continue to give Improving lectures and the women who came for Improvement were kind to Delmé: no one ever mocked the man by bestowing on him a white feather.

Milla Glass had not been kind to Delmé. She remembered – for who having seen, could forget? – the vision of Delmé Hawkins on her doorstep late on a washday morning when she was already behindhand with her tasks.

'Whatever can I do for you?' she'd asked the gawky young man, so full of himself and wildly eager. Round owl-like spectacles perched on his nose and swathes of unruly papers spilled enthusiastically from his long ungraceful arms. Milla assumed the poor lad had been let out of a home for the day and sent round the neighbourhood to peddle scrubbing-brushes to soft-hearted housewives. Only when he mentioned Sir Edward Glass did she see that the papers he waved in the air resembled no ordinary order-book.

'There's so much I need to discuss with you,' Hawkins had gushed. He saw Milla Glass as his hope of salvation. He looked to this woman doing her weekly wash to illumine his intolerable darkness. In his nervous agitation, he craned and twisted his neck so ferociously as she stood with the spindle from the wash-tub in one hand and a pair of sopping wet trousers in the other, Milla wondered if the demented creature had damaged his neck gawping up at her father's trickery. 'Tell me, for instance,' he was saying. In which case, she decided with a ruthlessness born of self-preservation, it served the young fellow right. As soon as she could, she'd sent him packing. It had been foolish slamming the door shut; a man who had taken the trouble to track her down and had cycled so far to see her would not give up easily.

Milla told her sisters about the snooper.

'Don't you tell him anything, Milla!' Stacia and Helen both said at once. 'And don't whatever you do mention us. We're busy – we can do without being spied on!'

'He can't know very much if he doesn't even know Sir Edward Glass had *three* daughters,' Stacia concluded after a moment's consideration. 'I wonder how he tracked *you* down when *I* am the eldest . . .'

'Who knows how much the Snooper knows,' Milla said, recalling with a shudder the swathes of detailed notes that had once alarmed a patriotic landlady also. 'When he said Hawkins, I quite thought he was hawking brushes . . .'

Snooper Hawkins was disappointed in Milla Glass and he blamed her for heckling him from the back of the hall, for her lack of co-operation and her refusal to succumb to his charms. He'd had an idea that just as a wife may not give evidence to condemn her husband, by the same turn-about a wife could be forced to reveal anything her lawful wedded spouse might require to know. Even concerning her own father. Convinced that Milla was hiding something from him, Delmé Hawkins asked Sir Edward Glass's daughter to marry him and Milla had laughed. She knew what to say but did not say it: *You can't expect to become one of us just like that, you know*!

To return to the well-fed rat in 1941 enjoying the final hours of the New Paris Grand, about to be bombed by a youth who is not quite twenty and will never see *zwanzig* for he won't make it *heimwegs* across the English Channel. High over sleepy Rye *the dark dove with the flickering tongue* will pass *below the horizon of his homing* and go up in flames with his bomber and down with its ashes in a roller-coaster inferno all his very own. His freckled fair skin will grill quick enough for the *Junge* to still be alive *where no other sound was* to regret flecks of his own roasting fat bespattering the proud grey-blue of his immaculate Luftwaffe uniform. *Schade*! If the gods were fond of the New Paris Grand they could not have devised more cruel a revenge.

Our nifty rat, hearing the enemy in action, the approaching drone high above, instinctively understood the menace, and got out quick. Which was more than Delmé had done; one sunny almost carefree afternoon a long time back, the scholar had come to the Strand and let himself in. He had kept Edward Glass's last building till last for Delmé regarded the Paris Grand as *his* last chance to unravel the enigma and redeem himself.

It did not feel like trespassing. He'd been frightened only that there might be rats but if there were any rats they, like women during the War to End All Wars, were good to Delmé and kept out of his way. No serious attempt had been made to board up the building, it was hard to see that anyone would object to his presence. Besides, Mr Hawkins had his card ready in his top pocket, credentials in Garamond twelve point: '*Delmé Hawkins, MA (Oxon.), Architectural Historian. Tutor in Art. Official Biographer of Edward Glass*'. I am making a study. All my life I have been making a study; I am a Specialist, not in Footwear but validated by Special Branch. I knew the great man, he might add, since this was no more than one of the innumerable variations available on the truth, part of the complex geometry Edward Glass himself had been fond of. Ever since Delmé had left the comfortable home and the surgical-boot business of his youth to pedal his way valiantly uphill, Edward Glass had been the scholar's only friend and the inspiration that guided him as Virgil had guided Dante in Limbo.

Ah, Edward Glass! If only you could see your precious Paris Grand now! In latter years, Delmé Hawkins had come to take a scholarly, spiteful pleasure in what his old friend would have seen of his exuberant creations if he had still been around. The insolent willowherb, unmindful of the grandeur and the mosaics it desecrated, had planted its roots in every available crack. Unrestrained boys with no respect for Great Art had pitted the traceried windows with well-aimed stones. In places the intricate leading had caved in, sprinkling glittering fragments of finely tooled glass. Plaster peeled from moulded ceilings and chandeliers too vast to have been stolen or repossessed by the bailiffs hung in the centre of ripped out rooms, tarnished and hideous, their erstwhile grandeur foully exposed like wrinkled old women stripped naked. The sun danced in on the destruction as Delmé wandered rejoicing vindictively. Then quite suddenly he wished he had not come.

Delmé Hawkins was lost in the maze. The further he went on, the more impossible it was to return to the entrance he had forced to let himself in. All around in the silence he sensed there was someone other than himself disturbing the dust. He tried to pull himself together: it was a trick of the light, the dusty reflections in the great gilded mirrors, the obtuse elevations, the discrete circulation systems, the hollowness inside. Then he heard – or was it his own uneven breath? Then the echo of footsteps – or were they hollow, ungainly and merely his own? Anticipating the eternal fear some dozen years later in the punitive cold blazing high above Rye, he looked wildly about the misted glass of his cramped cockpit; above, below or in the shadows and the deepest recesses, hidden inside? Milla Glass had hidden something unspeakable, Delmé Hawkins thought, as he opened his mouth to scream but dared not. He cowered and covered his head with his hands. Chilled to the marrow yet with his cheeks burning, he was trapped: you should never have come this far, you should have left well alone and not concerned your miserable bookish self with what, after all, was none of your bookish business. Who was the man Edward Glass to you that you pursued his secrets into the shadows so relentlessly? Delmé Hawkins knew now that he was indeed guilty, of trespassing. Not in Limbo, but in Hell.

'Forgive us as we forgive them . . .' he cried noiselessly into the silence that was closing in. 'Thy will be done *on Earth* . . . ' Delmé yelped. He turned and fled, tripping over his clumsy feet, dropping his spectacles, his Kodak Box Brownie, the bundle of photographs he'd spent his life collecting. He clutched his pounding heart and felt the weight of an impounded brain that threatened to burst from its skull as he retreated nimbly, *rat's feet over broken glass* running now for his life. When he stumbled outside into the cheerful ordinariness of daytime in the Strand, he was free but he was a changed man.

'Hey, steady on, old man!' a passer-by said.

'You look as though you could do with a drink,' someone on the cadge whispered solicitously, grasping Delmé Hawkins at once by the arm.

'Had one or two already if you ask me!' a third man remarked to nobody in particular as the tottering scholar was firmly led away to sample the delights of the Ring & Goose.

Hawkins had done with Edward Glass and the nightmare of the man's imagination but he was utterly spent, and he spent then the remainder of his hollow days a hollow man in a home run by a Charitable Institution.

By chance, a young gentleman of the cloth, the Reverend Hubert Percy Blatt, had encountered the depleted Hawkins not long after the fateful visit to the Paris Grand, minus his owlish spectacles and entering a far from salubrious Public House in the Reverend Blatt's own parish. Blatt had attended a number of Delmé Hawkins's Improving lectures over the years and had even from time to time found inspiration for sermons from them.

'And how is the *magnum opus* coming along?' the Reverend Blatt enquired, trying to sound jovial, trying to sound as though he were not standing but five feet from the entrance to *this last of meeting places*, the Spotted Cow.

Hawkins looked blank.

'And what new revelations have you got for us, Delmé?'

'Revelations?'

'On the enigma that was Edward Glass?' Blatt persisted with affable impatience. He had spotted not cows but fallen parishioners through the iniquitous windows of the abhorrent establishment; he must do whatever had to be done to save yet another unfortunate sinner.

'Never heard of the fellow!' Delmé Hawkins tried to draw away. A case of mistaken identity, he explained. He had never spied for the Kaiser. 'I am innocent of any charges. *This is the way the world ends –* all I ask is a glass of good cheer . . .'

The Reverend Blatt had been taken aback to witness such a sorry decline. In his heyday Hawkins had often stayed at respectable guest-houses in Blatt's parish so when he returned to his rectory Hubert Blatt immediately put pen to paper and addressed the Board of a Charitable Institution that had been pestering him to send them likely inmates: Dear Sirs, I strongly Recommend one, Delmé Hawkins, sometime scholar, *quiet and meaningless as wind in dry grass*, probably . . .

The Reverend Blatt wondered after he had posted the letter whether he had not been over-zealous in his attempts to help Mr Delmé Hawkins, a man he knew little about. A man, moreover, too quick to protest his innocence and guilty at least of lurking in Blatt's own parish, preparing to slink through the swing portals of the Spotted Cow. For a week the conscience-stricken Blatt weighed a little well-meant dishonesty against an Act of great if undeserved Charity, found for the latter and preached to this end the following Sunday. This caused his Bishop, who was late with his Reports to the Archbishop and needed something to say about Blatt, to write:

'I notice a certain unorthodoxy in the otherwise competent sermons of the Reverend Hubert Blatt, but conclude that we live in worn-out times. The old ideas may not perhaps wear so well. Blatt takes a flexible approach which I really rather admire . . .'

The Archbishop, on receiving the tardy Report, at once sat down and wrote a rambling furious memorandum. He had inherited this wavering Bishop from the previous Archbishop and had no liking for or faith in the man:

*'Suggest immediately cease really rather admiring. Stamp hard on subver-*sion in the ranks. Direct attack, parry and return. *Make use of the flexible butt if a hit with the point on our flexible Blatt has failed. Heels together, and platoon in line!*

Is this man Blatt a Hun? *By God and St George, we will not harbour spies.'*

Blatt's Bishop, who had hoped to become Archbishop when this testy so-and-so had been appointed over his head, resented the archiepiscopal interference. Blatt's Bishop would really rather admire as he pleased, and responded with a prickly note to that effect. He had been at school with Hubert Percy Blatt's Papa which was why the admirably flexible Blatt Junior had been admitted into the Church in the first place. His Grace got carried away and begged to further point out how the Archbishop's own name was *Machen*, a word to be found in every schoolboy's shilling *Wörterbuch*. And had it escaped the Archbishop's own Graceful notice that we were no longer at war with the Bosche? (If our Bishop belaboured his point it was because he had once overheard Archbishop Machen remarking how his days of command in a trench at the Somme had been the happiest time in his life, cut short by an official carelessness which caused the tiresome loss of his entire platoon in less than ten minutes. The Honourable Mention he received in War Office Dispatches – given principally for not criticizing his superiors – had later helped him become the Archbishop.)

Delmé Hawkins meanwhile, blissfully ignorant of this vituperative chain of ecclesiastical correspondence, sank contentedly into Charitable Institutional life. You could have mentioned Edward Glass these days and Delmé, like the armed member of Special Branch, would have denied all knowledge. Had Milla Glass herself visited one afternoon to reminisce about the distant and the dead, Hawkins would not have been interested. Delmé sat staring into space: *the space on the blank page is the space in our heads and our hearts bounded forever by ourselves.*

The Reverend Hubert Blatt had attended many Improving lectures. His own life was not so interesting that he didn't find himself missing Delmé Hawkins and the talks the two of them had enjoyed in his rectory study over a game of draughts and a glass of respectably diluted port. The peculiar scholar had been a bit of a bore and had frequently outstayed his welcome but he'd been fascinating on his own subject: *the enigma that was Edward Glass.* What pleasant evenings they had passed when one of his parishioners, a guest-house landlady, had begged him to keep the man occupied while she rifled his possessions and tidied up his room.

Blatt called once or twice at the Charitable Institution only to find Delmé Hawkins, hunched and hurt, staring unblinkingly from his corner like a resentful dying owl. He refused either to acknowledge the Reverend visitor's presence or to eat the bunch of little green grapes Blatt had kindly brought. Blatt stayed a short time, picking distractedly at the grapes in their soggy brown paper bag and trying unsuccessfully to think of things to say to his friend.

When Hawkins was given a pauper's burial the Institution peremptorily summoned the Reverend Blatt to fetch away the poor man's effects. They held him responsible. Blatt duly emptied Delmé's locker which contained only a dishevelled heap of papers and some out-of-date railway timetables. He took Hawkins' possessions back to Parson's Hill and pondered what he might most profitably do with them. They were not worth enough to return to Hawkins Specialist Footwear in Bristol.

One evening over a solitary glass of good port, Blatt decided to advertise in the papers for Miss Milla Glass to come forward. If the Charitable Institution held him responsible for Hawkins's remains then he, in his turn and aided by good port, could equally well hold Milla responsible. This was the daughter Hawkins had spoken of. Surely she had some sort of filial duty to take care of these papers concerning her father? Besides, now Snooper Hawkins was gone and no harm could be done, the Reverend Hubert Blatt rather fancied meeting Milla Glass. Idle curiosity on his part, he supposed. Something to fill his vacant hours for Parson's Hill was a dull and comfortable parish full of good-natured hopeful spinsters, their pushy mothers, bossy landladies and besides . . . Who knows why we do the things that we do? (An edifying sermon for the eager behatted ladies next Sunday perhaps?) In any case, the Reverend Blatt diligently placed advertisements, at his own expense, in a number of national dailies:

Delmé Hawkins, Art Historian (d. 2–9–29)
Requiescat In Pace
(Miss Milla Glass, daughter of the late Sir Edward Glass, Architect, is requested to apply to the Rev. H.P. Blatt
of St Olive's, Parson's Hill,
where she will learn something to her advantage)

25

1929: To Every Question an Answer

Something to her advantage! Milla wrote to Helen in China: 'Snooper Hawkins has snuffed it. RIP.'

Helen, with Chiang Kai-shek's troops not far from the mission-gates, sent a postcard back with the simple exultant message: 'Praise be the Lord!'

Milla telephoned Stacia across London with the news of Delmé's demise but Stacia said: 'Who did you say? I can't chat now, Milla, we've got dozens of people coming this evening . . .'

Milla lived a quiet comfortable life with her two little dogs and felt herself greatly contented. She had married happily and been left widowed but well off, a fact that did not escape her nieces, Stacia's daughters, who called and dropped hints, and wrote and dropped hints. They were a new breed, these modern girls, so independent and always strapped for cash.

Milla had no intention of replying to the Reverend Blatt's announcements, but one of these dashing nieces, thinking sizeable legacies somehow involved, took it upon herself to supply the Rev. H. P. Blatt of St Olive's, Parson's Hill with her Auntie Milla's current address.

Thus one afternoon in 1929 the dogs alerted Milla to the figure of Hubert Blatt clearly visible, if fragmented and distorted, through the bubbled glass in the front door to her flat. She was forcibly reminded of a similar apparition nearly thirty years back when Delmé Hawkins had arrived fresh from an exhilarating bicycle ride, ranting and raving on the doorstep about the Genius that had been her father. Involuntarily she smiled.

'Whatever can I do for you?' She needed no scrubbing-brushes and resisted the urge to say: 'Not today, thank you!'

The Reverend Blatt saw a trim, well-preserved woman in her early sixties, and though living alone, clearly in the best of health. There was something rather selfish about women like this who looked only after themselves while the likes of poor Delmé were left to fend as best they could in Charitable Institutions. Milla's sleek little dogs compounded the impression; well-fed and well-kempt they snuffled around him, yapping at his shoe-laces, and the woman did nothing to stop them.

'I have come about Delmé Hawkins,' the Reverend Blatt said.

Milla realized at once who her clerical visitor must be. Now he was here he had better come in; a man who had taken the trouble to track her down would not give up easily. 'Delmé Hawkins was a friend of yours?' she asked sharply as she showed Hubert Blatt into her sitting-room. Hawkins had once told Milla that her father had been his one and only friend. Virgil to his Dante, was what the scholar had said.

'Why yes, indeed,' Blatt began, about to explain how he had attended the dear departed Hawkins's Improving lectures and gradually struck up something of an acquaintance over early evening draughts and glasses of suitably diluted port.

'Hawkins was a spy and a trespasser,' the woman said. Hubert Blatt tried not to look disconcerted. There were plenty of awkward ladies in Parson's Hill and Blatt was adept at dealing with them.

'A spy and a trespasser,' Milla repeated as though Blatt had not heard her the first time. Blatt recalled Delmé's confused account of how he had once been mistaken for a German spy. Blatt had paid little heed then and he ignored what Milla was saying now. Gingerly seating himself in a chair that was covered with dog-hair he patted his briefcase importantly:

'I felt by rights these things should be yours, Miss Glass, papers, lecture-notes really, the draft for a monograph . . .'

'A monograph?'

'Delmé's life's work.' The Reverend Blatt cast around inside his briefcase while Milla, spotting a rosy-red apple amongst the man's things, pressed two fingers into her cheek and tried to look suitably serious. The visitor produced a sheaf of large tattered papers crudely stitched together. On the worn cover in an erratic twisted hand was written: 'The Life & Work of Sir Edward Glass. An Enigma. A Monograph by Delmé Hawkins MA (Oxon.). Tutor in Art.' It reminded Milla of the battered scrap-book she had once possessed as a child. The Reverend Blatt handed the quirky volume across and, as if to impress on her the responsibility and the value of the gift, he tapped it repeatedly: 'Remarkable stuff, you know! Truly remarkable!'

'What, my father's Life? Dear Delmé's Work?' She looked quizzically at the dishevelled papers resting in the fine woollen Jaeger of her lap.

'The whole enigma, Miss Glass.' The Reverend Blatt was already exasperated. The woman was being genteelly obtuse. 'Delmé and I spent many happy hours in the study at my rectory discussing the enigma that was Edward Glass.'

'There was no enigma,' Milla said quietly. 'Only in the sponge of Hawkins's brain. My father was just a man like any other, a jobbing architect doing a job.'

'Surely not!' Blatt laughed.

Milla Glass looked across at the Reverend Hubert Blatt. He was struck by the brightness of the old woman's eyes; the eyes of a little girl who did not care to be laughed at. Over some port, less diluted than usual, Delmé had once confessed how he had proposed marriage to Milla Glass; not long after, he'd discovered she was already married. He had not known and she had not seen fit to tell him. There was no doubt the middle-aged woman had made the young Hawkins feel a fool. Recalling these semi-maudlin confessions, the Reverend Blatt considered that this afternoon he himself had not got off to a good start either. Surreptitiously he kicked at one of the dogs which was lifting its leg against his shoe.

Milla in her turn was struck by the boyish good looks of the Reverend Blatt, disconcerted by her dogs but trying not to show it. There would be plenty of young women in Parson's Hill suffering in silence for this man's unheeding smiles. Milla thought of her own darling son who had died heaving a bayonet over the top of some badly dug trench in the muddy Great War. And her nephews, Stacia's children: all gone as though the Pied Piper had come and piped the boys away. Only the rather dull nieces were left, organizing piano parties and writing inane chatty notes which said nothing but were basically asking Auntie Milla for money. She thought then of the rats that infested her father's derelict buildings. She had called her only child 'William' after a long-lost brother and now this second William had been lost also, and a long time ago for it was 1929 and the world had moved on again. She looked Hubert Blatt in the eye: 'You yourself, Father Blatt, could always take over where dear Delmé left off. Perhaps you would be able to solve the enigma that defeated your friend!'

Blatt beamed, immediately enthusiastic. 'Do you really think I could?'

'It might provide a little *divertissement* in Parson's Hill. I dare say Hawkins will have left you some clues . . .'

'He was a sensitive soul,' Blatt remarked, feeling something sentimental was called for. 'As you will remember, Miss Glass, Delmé Hawkins was an unusual man . . .'

'You can say that again!' Milla laughed.

'What?'

'Unusual. Delmé Hawkins was unusual all right; I can never forget his owlish stare!'

The Reverend Blatt did not like the old lady's attitude. He suspected her of flippancy. Milla Glass should have taken her father's would-be biographer more seriously. No wonder Delmé had found the daughter disappointing. He had been sure she was hiding something from him.

Piously Blatt drew himself up: 'Delmé's work, long hours in libraries or out on his bicycle, made him awkward in company. He had a peculiar way of standing and craning, he probably needed surgical-boots, his eyesight deteriorated and you will find his lecture-notes hard to read in places. He revised his thoughts all the time, the same lecture was never the same twice; I must have heard the same story told a dozen different ways, always saying something different. These will be his final thoughts, they are only really notes to expand on as he talked: *a heap of broken images*. When he spoke – remember, Miss Glass, I was privileged to attend many of his lectures, *I* took an interest, you see – he acquired a lucidity you will not find in these, his rambling random jottings. When he stood before his audience he didn't need surgical-boots. He became lavish and replete, articulate as honey; he shed that gawky owlish stare you yourself remarked on; the peculiar jerking and stuttering were gone. When he described the enigma that was Edward Glass, a grace suffused Delmé Hawkins . . .'

The Reverend Blatt paused. The dogs started nipping each other in play. It was impossible to decide what Milla Glass was thinking. He had not known he was going to make a speech and supposed it had been the truth.

'An admirable fellow!' Milla said too easily. The Reverend Blatt's encomium hung between them like wisteria in full bloom, imposing unwanted wanton luxury on a sorry summer evening. Blatt wondered if Sir Edward Glass's daughter hadn't been laughing at him as well as at Delmé – of course he himself could not take over. He had duties in Parson's Hill to perform. It was an absurd idea and besides, when he thought about it, the scholar had been more than a little unhinged: Delmé had been mad, certifiably insane, a real fruitcake; the guest-house landladies had wanted him out of the way so that they could search for dangerous weapons or incriminating evidence in his room. Blatt only invited the man to St Olive's rectory in the hope that wary parishioners would reward him in the collection-plate the following Sunday.

As if to hide what was on his mind, the Reverend Blatt slipped on a solicitous face. His coat was now covered in dog-hairs, he had not been offered refreshment, it was his turn to be agreeably malicious. He tilted his head and enquired in a voice redolent with clerical concern: 'Regrettably I know nothing about you, Miss Glass, except of course what poor Delmé told me.'

'*What poor Delmé told you?*' Sir Edward Glass's daughter immediately repeated and slapped down a dog which was scrabbling to join the manuscript on her lap. Milla regarded her visitor uneasily. She *has* got something to hide, Blatt thought.

'And what, pray, have *you* done with *your* life, Miss Glass?' he asked affably, pressing his advantage home.

'Why, Father Blatt, I have enjoyed myself. There's no enigma here for you to puzzle about over a glass of port and a game of draughts!' There was a pause and then the old lady's tone changed. She had regained her composure and was no longer flippant: 'Delmé Hawkins was a trespasser, trespassers are not easily forgiven. I am not surprised to hear he has perished. When I was a child I was taught not to spy.'

It sounded like a warning. Blatt said nothing. He did not correct her when she called him 'Father'. He wondered if Milla Glass was making fun of him but he refused to gratify the old lady by letting her see his discomfiture.

Milla meanwhile was surprised how much she was enjoying this unlooked for encounter. 'Tell me, Father Blatt' – how delicious to be calling this sweet young man 'Father' – 'Tell me, Father Blatt, what we can retrieve from the ruins . . .'

'I beg your pardon?' the Reverend Blatt blurted helplessly. The newspaper adverts had cost him dear, he was not at all sure his Bishop would approve. He'd hoped to find the woman contrite, or to make her so at least, but Milla Glass was not how he'd imagined the daughter of an enigma to be. 'I beg your pardon, Miss Glass?' he repeated abashed.

'I thought you were here to talk about my father, the genius of the voussoir, the ring course, the spring course, understood but unpronounced, *Arcanum Arcanorum* – Sir Edward Glass! I'm talking about him: what if anything can we retrieve from the ruins? That was what he asked me.'

'Retrieve from what ruins? I do not understand,' the Reverend Blatt admitted.

'I didn't know what to say,' Milla continued. 'Any more than you do now! The man was desperately dosed at the time; arsenic, strychnine, morphine, and my sisters, Stacia and Helen, would have nothing more to do with him – or her, our step-mother – and there was only me then in the stuffy dark house, and the two of them. I stayed on out of pity and perhaps *that* was wrong of me for pity seems a contemptible emotion, though not one of our worst, don't you think?'

'Well, I really don't know! I didn't even know you had any sisters.'

'You don't think I invented them, do you? Stacia and Helen!' Milla laughed. 'I was the middle one, Father Blatt. He was terrified; he thought his days were up and the reckoning was coming, which I suppose in a way it was – but then you, Father Blatt, Days of Judgement don't terrify men like you the way they might terrify a jobbing architect.'

Hubert Blatt glanced round the sparse but expensively furnished flat. The woman might earlier have been tippling, her cheeks were as rosy as the apple he'd brought to munch on the bus back to Parson's Hill. Apart from pampered dogs who were allowed up on chairs, he discovered only tidiness and order. He could see no half-empty decanters of port or bottles of Belgar Brandy like the ones in his rectory study. How dear and cosy that study seemed to him now. I am not *Father* Blatt, he wanted to shout but Milla continued.

'When people claimed my father had sold his soul to achieve the impossible, I would wonder whether poor old Faust had a daughter also and what she would have done when Mephistopheles turned

296

up for the reckoning. Perhaps she was a better person than I and offered to be taken in his place. I was never anybody's idea of the ideal daughter – "wilful" was what they called me, Milla the middle one. Can you imagine that, Father Blatt? Me being wilful?'

'Oh, I really think . . .'

'Yes, Father Blatt, what do you really think?'

'I am sorry I came. I did not mean to reawaken . . .'

'You cannot reawaken what has never been asleep, Father Blatt. All you have to do is turn the pages and peer underneath.'

The Reverend H. P. Blatt looked into Milla Glass's fiery eyes and felt himself scorched and his cheeks burning. He was now as convinced as the mad Hawkins had been that Milla Glass was hiding something. Maybe even from herself.

'Has Delmé Hawkins really gone?' Milla continued. She held up the scholar's notes. 'He can hardly have gone altogether if he can cause you of your own free will and at your own expense, Father Blatt, to advertise and come this afternoon unwelcome and uninvited to deliver his parting-present as though you were his glorified errand-boy.'

'Er . . . I . . .' The Reverend Hubert Blatt panicked. He wanted only to escape as politely as possible. In his desperate haste, he leapt up quickly and the rosy-red apple tumbled from his briefcase and rolled away across the floor. Too bad if he felt peckish on the bus home! Hurriedly he thanked the old lady for her time and commended her and her nasty little dogs to his God. (A God who was also the God of Archbishop, Lieutenant Commander Archibald Machen, in whose carelessly regimented platoon Milla's beloved son William had perished, direct attack, parried and returned, on the Somme. Neither the Reverend Blatt nor Milla Glass was aware of this comfortless 'coincidence'. There is no such thing as chance, Milla once screamed at her step-mother: many events commonly said to be 'mere chance' are in reality governed by rules. Long lists had been brought Back from that Other Side of the Channel itemizing the luckless Dead; you did not need algebra to calculate then that the second beloved William's number was up. *Rien ne va plus*: the pay-out was *you*.)

Out of the habit of his profession, the Reverend Blatt called up to Milla as he plunged gasping for breath down the stairs: 'If ever there is anything I can do, Miss Glass, you have only to let me know, you have only to call on me, St Olive's, Parson's Hill, you have only to drop me a note. If ever there is anything . . .'

'Why, thank you, Father Blatt, I'm sure there will be! Thank you so very much, Father Blatt, and for the papers and the apple. Do come and see us again, any time you are passing!' Milla closed the door on the world outside, distorted and fragmented by a bubble of glass. Her two little dogs were now chasing each other as they chased Hubert Blatt's rosy-red apple. Milla dived quickly into the fray to rescue the papers that had been poor Delmé Hawkins's life.

'You naughty dogs!' she exclaimed. 'Have you no respect for the distant and the dead?' She tucked the papers into a large envelope and put them away. Then she picked up the bruised apple and spun it across the room for her wire-haired terriers to whoop at (tails wagging, noses twitching) and retrieve.

Milla opened a newspaper and scanned again the Houses To Let columns. She had always moved on whenever Delmé Hawkins tracked her down and now she contemplated taking a house in the country where her dogs would have space to run. From beyond the pauper's grave, Delmé kept up his relentless pursuit. Milla smiled: the Snooper could not have told Father Blatt what he had not known, what nobody knew.

The Reverend Blatt meanwhile was surprised how light-hearted he felt. His coat had been covered in dog-hair, the advertisements had cost a few bob and he had received a mild reprimand from his Bishop, but it had all been worthwhile to shed the awful legacy of Delmé Hawkins's notes.

In the years that followed, the Reverend Hubert Blatt would recall Milla Glass's generous offer that he might take over where the worn-out scholar had left off. Waking alone in the middle of the night, Hubert Percy Blatt would start in his single bed at St Olive's rectory, Parson's Hill, listening intently. All was quiet, no member of Special Branch had climbed in through a window pressing a pistol butt to his ear but Blatt, breathless and covered in streaming sweat, would notice a constraining around his throat as though someone had attempted to strangle him. Then Blatt would sit bolt upright in his damp nightshirt and Give Praise indeed in the darkness and try to exorcize all thoughts of what he had perhaps only narrowly escaped. He bitterly regretted inviting Milla Glass to get in touch if there was ever anything he could do for her.

Whatever the enigma of Edward Glass, it had in no way been Improving. *Lips that would kiss Form prayers of broken stone.* 'Forgive us our trespasses,' the Reverend Blatt would intone fearfully into the hollow loneliness of his darkened rectory. 'Who knows why we do the things that we do? Who knows what if anything we can retrieve from the ruins? Only forgive us our trespasses, forgive Milla Glass, forgive us all . . .'

26

1941: A Resurrection

'We are too old,' Stacia wrote to Milla who in 1941 was living safely in the country. The letter was a direct consequence of the bombing of the Paris Grand. Stacia, reading the Late News notice in the evening *Telegraph*, felt sorry for herself and thought, not for the first time, but seriously now, of getting out of London. If Herr Hitler's bombs could do that to Sir Edward's New Paris Grand what couldn't they do to Stacia née Glass? She told Milla what a good war her daughters and grand-daughters were having and asked in a postscript: 'No news I suppose, from Helen?'

There had been no news out of China since the postcard 'Praise be the Lord!' which arrived as a consequence of Delmé Hawkins's snuffing it. Later Milla decided she had altogether imagined this connection. Helen would never have Praised the Lord for the Snooper's, or anyone else's, demise. It had been a last desperate communication, a cry from the gates of hell, a few words hastily scribbled and sent out before the postal system went down.

'I wonder if we'll ever know,' Stacia said. She had come for the afternoon to see how she liked the rural quiet. 'It's funny not knowing what's happened to Helen,' Stacia mused. The décor in this country tea-shop lacked somewhat and the waitresses were decidedly frumpy, but how nice to lick melting butter from one's fingers again!

Milla frowned. Milla had never known exactly how her own son William died and not knowing that, why would she want or expect to know about Helen?

'There are a great many things we don't know,' Milla said conversationally, for something was required. You couldn't just sit with your sister and gulp tea and nod your head stupidly.

'Oh! I've never understood you!' Stacia retorted impatiently. Milla lacked what it took to hold a conversation – but what could one expect of someone stuck down here?

'That's probably just as well, Stacia, darling,' Milla laughed. 'Shall we order more tea-cakes?'

'Isn't there such a thing as rationing? Really Milla, you always were terribly greedy! You always liked a nice cake. Whenever I see a tea-trolley, which with all the shortages I haven't for years, I think of you. They don't pile tea-trolleys high like they used to.'

'Mmmm.'

Stacia considered whether Milla would be the one paying. She, after all, had had the bother of coming and her train-fare to find. Milla meanwhile was wondering how she would manage if Stacia did decide to come and stay. It was all very well this getting out of London . . .

Stacia said, 'I saw Daddy's Paris Grand copped it.'

Milla glanced abruptly at her sister.

'Rather a shame, don't you think?' Stacia persisted.

'What?'

'All Daddy's work – a lifetime of work and so little left. Nobody's even heard of him. Which is one of the things I wanted to talk to you about. Lady Mountsier . . .' (this, Milla already knew, was the prospective mother-in-law of Mabel the youngest one's eldest). 'Even Lady Mountsier hadn't heard of him, she almost intimated that she didn't believe all I'd been telling her about Daddy. "I'll have to look him up!" she said in that sniffy way she has, as though she knew already she wouldn't find Sir Edward Glass in *Debrett*'s or wherever it is Her Ladyship checks up. Of course there'll be stuff buried deep in some dusty architectural library but you can hardly expect Desidera Mountsier to go to the trouble, and the girl is really rather plain with frankly not much to recommend her. Poor Mabel!'

'I always thought Mabel was the brightest.' Milla recalled a girl with an intelligently large forehead and protruding teeth.

'It isn't brightness that gets one a husband, Milla; if anything it's more likely to put them off. Hugo Mountsier is such an eligible young man, the Mountsier Belmont Estates more than make up for that dreadful stutter. If Mabel doesn't encourage the boy someone else will.'

'Oh dear!' said Milla distractedly.

'It's a shame Delmé Hawkins never finished his book,' Stacia said. 'A biography of Sir Edward Glass would be useful at times like this.'

'Would it?' Milla concentrated on pouring stewed-looking tea from the pot. Her hands jerked and threatened to make a mess of the table-cloth.

'I've often wondered about that,' Stacia continued, eyeing her sister's clumsiness irritably.

'Wondered?' Milla banged down the tea-pot. Tea dripped from the spout. She wished very much that Stacia had not taken it into her head to invite herself down here, disturbing the peace with talk about the Snooper. The dogs would be fretting at home. Why should they be locked in and she be sat here while Stacia talked of Lady Mountsier this, Lady Mountsier that and then resurrected Delmé Hawkins? To steady herself, she stared blankly at her sister and several times she silently asked the question they had all been told to ask: Was your journey really necessary?

'Yes, indeed!' Stacia went on. 'I've often wondered. I mean, if Delmé Hawkins had published a book on Daddy with lots of pictures and . . .'

'He never was "Daddy" to us,' Milla said shortly.

Stacia continued as though uninterrupted: 'It would make all sorts of things and not just dealing with dopey Mabel so much easier. There are books on all kinds of uninteresting people these days. I'd have thought Sir Edward Glass . . .'

Milla sensed with relief that the talk of moving to the country had only been a pretext to come and discuss the matter now in hand.

'I know you got Mr Hawkins's things from some interfering vicar a while back . . .'

'Twelve years ago,' Milla corrected her, establishing distance by her precision. 'I met the Reverend Hubert Percy Blatt in 1929.'

'Couldn't we get all the papers out again, it might be ever so jolly, and maybe Freddy or someone could . . .'

'Stacia, I'd gladly let you take them away with you this afternoon but they went on the fire years ago when I moved from the flat. What a pity you didn't say . . .'

'You *burnt* them? You burnt Delmé Hawkins's book on Sir Edward Glass?' It was Stacia who stared now. Milla could certainly pay for their tea.

'It doesn't do to rake over the past,' Milla said. 'You mightn't like what you find. Anyway, most of his buildings have gone, Edward Glass is *passé*, his style is out of fashion – if it ever was in fashion – and once again the world is at War, tearing itself to pieces . . .'

'You don't have to tell me, Milla! I'm the one who has to cower in the London Underground when the sirens go like an animal in a dark and dirty burrow, huddled up with all kinds of people one has never met. And there's always some dreadfully chummy person who gets up a frightful sing-song and they make it so hard not to join in. I, who used to play Chopin at soirées in Mayfair, singing *Knees Up Mother Brown* in a tunnel beneath Oxford Circus! Did you read the thing before you burnt it?'

'What?'

'The biography, Delmé Hawkins's book!'

'There never was a book. It was just an illegible pile of incomprehensible lectures. I didn't even look at it.'

'You didn't look at it!' Milla was the limit. Delmé Hawkins had only ever known about the one daughter. The three of them, Stacia, Milla and Helen, had agreed for some reason not to enlighten him. How Stacia wished she had stepped in earlier.

'I don't know why we didn't give the man every assistance. How nice it would be to have an illustrated volume to show people when they ask. I am always reminiscing about the past,' Stacia told her younger sister. 'It is a feature of London life these days and so important to be able to hold one's own. You'd have thought Sir Edward Glass could have held his own with anyone, though you notice the *Telegraph* didn't mention the architect by name. It simply said the "structure had been dangerous" – confounded cheek! No wonder no one ever believes me! I've written to the *Telegraph*, but you know what they're like, these newspapers, so terribly taken up with the war.'

'I don't care to think about the past,' Milla said quietly.

Stacia noted Milla's stubbornness. How stupid she was; at their age the past was *all* they had. If you didn't think about that, what did you think about? 'You were always so clever, Milla,' she said spitefully. 'And yet you did nothing with it. You were the one who had anything of Daddy's brains. I think you have wasted your life . . .'

'I wish you wouldn't keep calling him Daddy!' Milla snapped. 'You can rewrite the past if you wish to, Stacia. I prefer to leave it where it belongs, in the past and neatly buried.'

'Or burnt!' Stacia could not forgive her stupid sister for this thoughtless and selfish destruction. 'I think it too bad of you! Mabel will weep with aggravation when I tell her. Lady Mountsier and her son, Hugo . . .'

Milla stood up and fished her purse from her pocket. Lady Mountsier and her son, Hugo, could go to hell, Virgil could guide her and the whole of *Debrett*'s along with them! In a cold fury, Milla briskly paid for tea, said a scarcely polite 'goodbye' and, leaving Stacia to find her own way back to the railway station, she hurried home to let out her dogs.

Milla regretted the waste of an afternoon. Later she knew she would regret the quarrel too. Stacia returned to London enjoying feeling furious with Milla and sorry for herself. She had a little loud weep in the train and struck up a pleasant conversation with someone who might know Freddy's brother. There were not many people left one could quarrel with: one sister lost-and-gone in China (why had Helen needed to go to China when there was plenty of room for 'Good Works' and Improvement back home?), the other sister stubborn and silly as ever, stuck down in boring Kent greedily guzzling unfair quantities of creamy melting butter. It was most provoking! Sir Edward Glass might just as well not have been your father for all the good it did you in other women's war-time London drawing-rooms.

Milla meanwhile opened a drawer in her bedroom and took out a large grubby envelope. She had not burnt Delmé Hawkins's papers, though she'd often been tempted, but she had not read them in the dozen quiet years they had been in her possession. She sat on her comfortable eiderdown and looked bemusedly now at the envelope. In the distance the steady thud of London being relentlessly bombarded came to her over the fields. It was as though the world was being punished. Warring factions were bent on an all-out destruction that even the most awesome timepiece washed working from the ice could not allay. Milla shivered in the warmth of her room and, taking the papers out of the envelope, she saw again the familiar jumbled handwriting.

What could have happened to Delmé Hawkins's owlish spectacles? There had been something remarkable about those lenses. If you looked through them this writing would correct itself, rearranging the world as Snooper Hawkins had seen it. Delmé had had his own very particular way of looking at what he saw, yet lenses that gave Hawkins vision would probably diffuse and distort for anyone else, like the bubbled glass in the door to her flat where the Reverend

H. P. Blatt had been sent unwelcome and uninvited. Had the flexible boyish-looking Blatt appropriated the unique spectacles for wearing in church to give added authority when he stood up and preached? Could it be that Hubert Blatt thought the glasses would help him emulate the eloquent, authoritative Delmé whose style he so much admired? Maybe Blatt wore them in his pulpit to prevent himself being distracted by the bevies of scented females who cluttered the front pews at St Olive's every Sunday and gazed up at him with adoring eyes. Whatever the fate of Delmé Hawkins's spectacles, that afternoon in 1929 the Reverend H. P. Blatt had fled from her comfortable flat in a blind and sightless terror. What exactly had he seen?

Milla sighed gently.

Supposing back in 1900 Milla had asked the young scholar in, introduced Delmé to her hard-working schoolmaster husband and let little William sit on his lap? The child could have played with the Kodak Box Brownie while she herself talked to Delmé about what was gone. 'Don't waste your time on Edward Glass,' she might have said. 'You could sell scrubbing-brushes or grow prize dahlias,' she might have suggested. Perhaps she should have said: 'I have two sisters, Stacia and Helen, an authority on Edward Glass ought to have a word with them. After all everybody sees things differently, don't they, Delmé? There's no such thing as an ideal system of Memory, so don't waste a valuable shilling!'

'Show little William how the Box Brownie works!' she might have said and then in 1914 when they'd handed out jobs, instead of discovering that William was a dab hand with a cricket-bat they might have found he knew about photography and set him up in an indestructible darkroom way back behind the front lines.

If she herself had behaved differently back in 1900 and ordered a whole selection of the salesman's brushes, who knows how different the world might have been? Who knows, the Reverend Blatt had asked the good ladies of Parson's Hill one Sunday long ago, who knows why we do the things that we do? Who wants to know? Milla Glass might have answered if she had been wearing a hat and sitting in one of his pews. Some things are best forgotten, hidden away, pasted over . . .

Always one for sitting down and writing letters, she would write to dear old Stacia and spread some glue over their foolish quarrel.

Meanwhile, reluctantly, almost idly at first, she began to turn over Delmé Hawkins's tattered pages.

He may be requiescating in peace, Milla thought, but the owl-like Hawkins was as bent as ever on disturbing her peace. He had even managed to send Stacia now to visit her.

Stacia is probably right: we are too old. I am certainly too old to move house again just to get away from Delmé Hawkins, pedalling interminably, breathlessly peddling his brushes. There never was a salesman so determined to get an order!

Milla smiled – here before her again was Delmé's parting-present, his extraordinary order-book: 'The Life & Work . . .'

27

Never the Same Twice

Yes, Milla wept.

A girl sat on a table weeping. Rather a disconcerting sight to come across in an otherwise empty house.

'Excuse me!'

Milla, hunched over her tears, did not hear him at first. When she did she was flustered, caught weeping thus: 'Oh, I'm so sorry, I do beg your pardon!'

'I am the one – I beg yours! The door was open, I assumed the house was empty, I came straight in.'

Milla smiled. Hardly a cat after a canary.

'Have you come to live here?' she asked, brightening at the idea. She would like to think of someone like this living in York Street. Altering the past.

'No, no! I bought a table in an auction last week. Rather a useful item of furniture, I thought. I've got a cart outside. Lot 213. Is that it, by any chance? The one you are sitting on?'

Milla climbed off Mrs Curzon's table – there had been many housekeepers since but none that had stayed. Sure enough, stuck on the side when they looked was Mr Frewitt's label: 213.

'It's yours then,' Milla said.

Milla and Ted chatted. They walked together round the echoing house. She told him things because he was there and because he listened, and when at last Ted had to go (the man who had lent him the cart had said 'No more than a couple of hours, mind!'), Milla went with Ted and the table.

Eventually Milla found time to sit down (at the table) and write to Stacia. Stacia read the letter in disbelief. 'With the table!' It was unbelievable, and yet not untypical that Milla should wilfully have contrived to throw in her lot with an old scrubbed table: Lot 213.

'But we know nothing of this Ted,' Stacia said helplessly. Ted it seemed was a high-minded, impoverished schoolmaster who saw no future for the world unless the children of slum-dwellers were given the chance of an education. Milla doubted if her darling Ted would single-handedly make much difference to the world, but how she admired him for trying. It was only after he'd died leaving Milla with a little son, William, that Stacia discovered her brother-in-law to have been worth knowing after all. The family that came to Milla's rescue were well-connected and rich. Practically all the cousins had titles of one sort or another. 'How lucky for you,' Stacia said. 'You married well, after all!'

In 1941, when the New Paris Grand was hit, a splinter of thick glass cut the plump rat's foot as it escaped down the long toppling galleries of archways and tumbling twisting spandrels, out and out in the nick of time. The splinter came from Delmé Hawkins's owlish spectacles, now unrecognizably crushed, the frames bent, the lenses smashed. Never again would anyone look through the thick glass to see the world as Delmé Hawkins had seen it.

But Delmé Hawkins was a trespasser and a spy. It had not been his business to pry like the Preedys, to track down poor Milla like a persistent salesman, or to trail the country making detailed notes and taking photographs. The armed Special Branch Detective should have summarily dispatched the nosy traitor; plenty of men were to die in 1914–18, with far less cause. The vigilant, patriotic landlady owed no double helpings of bacon and eggs, she should have spared herself the expense though the purging of a guilty conscience was never meant to come easily or cheap.

How much had the Improvement Societies paid Delmé Hawkins to turn up at Batley, Bingley or wherever on his bicycle? How much had Hawkins Specialist Footwear, that astute company of surgical-boot manufacturers in Bristol, paid their redundant and duplicate son to stay away? Milla herself had been unable to make the man stay away.

Milla had been happy to regard the art historian, Delmé Hawkins, as a sycophantic, intellectual nincompoop, skinny and harmless in bicycle-clips and owlish spectacles. But now, turning the pages of his order-book, she thought again about the disturbed young man who claimed not to have been selling brushes. How gravely she had disprized the fellow. Of course he'd been right to be disturbed. But Delmé Hawkins had also been a nuisance. 'I have appointed myself Official Biographer' he had announced, presenting himself and presenting her with his printed card. He'd been determined to stop her pasting over the past.

Again now, years later in this mad world, where bombs whizzed out of the air destroying indiscriminately and sisters arrived from London licking butter from their fingers and recounting conversations in other women's war-time drawing-rooms, it was a madman who held sway. Delmé Hawkins had Returned from the Dead as surely as if Dr Lucius Morgan had summoned him Back, returning to disturb the comfortable peace she had spent fifty years constructing, coming back intent on disturbing her, making her weep. Ah yes, Milla wept.

Her tears and her reminiscences could do Delmé Hawkins no good now, five foot under in a pauper's grave, she knew not where, while this, his precious 'Monograph', lay in her lap at her mercy. It was 1941, a time of fires and destruction, what would it signify another little fire downstairs blazing cosily in her Kentish cottage grate, another little destruction which she'd given her sister Stacia to believe had already taken place? Why not throw Delmé's 'Monograph' on the fire like her scrap-book, and have done?

'I'm as much a human being as Edward Glass ever was!' Delmé Hawkins would reiterate but with less and less conviction as time went on. 'He was only a man like me!' he would say, but Delmé Hawkins no longer believed this. While Edward Glass loomed larger with the passing years, Delmé effaced himself until he was the *hollow man* as derelict as the deserted Paris Grand but with even less to him, for he had put down no foundations.

And yet the Living can have such power over the Dead – they can, if they choose, obliterate them entirely. Milla's father had looked at her at the last, fearing there was Nothing to be retrieved from the ruins, knowing that she could obliterate him simply by forgetting him, hating her for it. But for the ministrations, the interference, the spying and the trespassing of Snooper Hawkins, Edward Glass would have been obliterated. As *passé* when he passed on as a light wind passing by. Lady Mountsier herself had never heard of him.

But yes, there had been another version, less forgiving.

Nothing was ever the same twice in Delmé's lectures, wasn't that what the Reverend H. P. Blatt had averred, arriving on her doorstep munching an apple, telling her about the hordes of young ladies in Parson's Hill who pursued him as relentlessly as Stacia had stalked husbands for her daughters? There had been such a terrible shortage after the carnage of eligible men and no Government-issued coupons to ensure fair play. The motleyed piper had taken the boys but left lame beggars like Delmé Hawkins and greedy girls and rats to scrabble about as best they could. The nifty girls chased the Reverend Blatt and there had been rats in the trenches with death at the Somme, as surely as there were well-fed carefree rats enjoying life in Edward Glass's derelict buildings.

'A rat gnawed at my boot while I was asleep,' her own little William had written in the letter that had taken its time to arrive, arriving after they'd informed her officially of his death 'On Active Service'. *Thou shalt not escape the consequences of thy actions*, Mrs Curzon had cursed. A valiant young man, they'd said, as though she'd needed telling for her William had always been a *handful* and now (along with twenty thousand others that first day, one day alone, on the Somme) he was *dust*. His blood spilled like gold doubloons, such rich rich earth. He'd befriended the rat and let it sleep in his trenchcoat pocket. 'I rather think I have grown to love her, she shares my sandwiches!' he'd written and then gone on, protesting (as if the rat had been a girlfriend and he'd been anxious to reassure his mother of his unchanged feelings for her) that he loved Milla more than anyone else, and that whatever happened she was to be sure to take good care of herself. Silly boy; hadn't she, till then, been the one who had always taken care of him? Despite all she had done he had grown into a man who cowered in a muddy trench in Flanders, covering his head with his hands, chilled to the marrow, his cheeks burning, loving a rat he kept in his pocket and fearing the worst.

'Look after yourself, Mum, take good care!' (A cry from the gates of hell if ever there was one. Dear William! No green parrot there either, but what good times they had had together, what love and happiness there had been.)

'So this is Edward Glass's grandson!' Delmé Hawkins had appeared beside her in the kitchen. It was another of Ellen's afternoons off, the maid had left the front door carelessly unlocked and the trespasser had let himself in. 'Edward Glass's grandson!' he'd repeated, staring down through thick lenses at William who was singing to himself and playing with wooden bricks, piling them up, constructing something childish, nonsensical that could not stay standing.

Milla swept little William up, protecting him from the madman in bicycle-clips: 'What do you want, now?' she demanded.

'I was just passing,' he said.

Milla's husband, Ted, had made a few enquiries by this stage. He had discovered that *there was no Delmé Hawkins* registered amongst those who held MAs from Oxford. His credentials, though clearly printed on his card in a twelve point Garamond Bold, were hollow and fabricated. Delmé if taxed would have blamed Sir Edward Glass. An MA had been on the cards and his cards were printed way back in the days before an obsession with the man's inscrutable works had stifled his academic career. He had been forced to break from all formal study in order to concentrate: a study of Edward Glass defied any form of ordered regular examination by degree but he had acquitted himself well beneath the bright searchlights. Not every scholar could boast Special Branch validation so that his adoption of an MA was only in fact a variation, part of the complex geometry that had swept him along.

Milla turned the page:

So tonight, my last ever lecture on the Architect, Inventor and Innovator, Sir Edward Glass. An Introduction to perhaps one of the most remarkable thinkers in brick and stone of the 19th Century. Perhaps . . .

John Ruskin, a wine-merchant's son, ignored Edward Glass leaving the subject for me, a surgical-boot maker's boy, who knew no better. You will not find references to the architecture of Edward Glass in any of Ruskin's worthy writings. He had more sense than to waste his life as I have wasted my life. I am not a trespasser since I never found a way in, nor yet a spy for I never found anything out. I was only ever an innocent passer-by doing his best.

What is there to say of Glass's Life & Work? No more than one might expect, for there is little, it seems, to be known. He was secretive, he came out of Nowhere; we know nothing of his parentage, his early life, and little enough of the man after that. A glance at the extent of Edward Glass's Work will reveal how his days must have been spent in constant toil and travel, the man worked like the Devil; Edward Glass with no History behind him chased as all Artists chase after posterity. Timor mortis – *has Edward Glass a right to a unique posterity? To being the subject of this lecture this evening at Bingley or Batley or Parson's Hill? Should you be sitting forward in your chairs? Should I be wasting my time, and yours, describing the Life & Work of this particular man after all these years in this particular way?*

Edward Glass is out of fashion, his magnificent buildings are encouraged to crumble, the man is forgotten. His genius no longer disturbs, the Modish and the Literati do not want to know, I myself have been unable to interest any publisher. 'Passé!' *they say, repeating and barking the horrible word at me like some complicated step I'm unable to foot, in a dance I'm unable to master.* 'Passé!' 'Passé, old chap!'

After the building of his most soaring and daring creation, The New Paris Grand Hotel, Sir Edward Glass gave up completely and did nothing more. At the height of his powers the Genius lost interest and withdrew from the world. Like the most dazzling firework that climbs and with one last stupendous burst of energy – bang! – gives out altogether, and is no more. Perhaps he perceived his irrelevance, understood the limitations of human endeavour and retreated.

Edward Glass built for a confident World that is no longer with us, on a gargantuan scale in which we are now too timorous even to think. Brick upon brick, he built with a devilish ingenuity no one would countenance, let alone pay for, these days. The World has changed, and the shadow cast by the past is deep and dark. We live out our lives walking round in a ring in a Wasteland where long complicated shadows thrown way back by the endeavours of men like Edward Glass are upon us. They, who built for their own worldly glory (and knighthoods), regardless of their fellow men, and for their own Posterity at the expense of future generations, should be made answerable by us – we, whose lives are as blighted dust to their exalted sometime ashes.

No wonder there are so many Societies for Improvement, Gentlemen! As I cycle between engagements I often consider that there is plenty of room for Improvement on this planet where the spokes of the wheel never stop. No one can win, there is no pay-out; this keeps me going. It drives me on.

Glass never wanted to see my 'Monograph' written; he was a selfish man – he ruined my life and others' besides mine. A man of illusions, tricks and broken promises. Two planes meeting, equally brightly lit, no light and shade, only brightness and illusion. An unending interrogation. There was no edge, no corner, no meeting of the walls. I lost my bearings, over and over, and so perhaps did he.

Was it his intention to drive us mad? Did Edward Glass have any intentions at all? Or was he not a man like other men, fearful of the great zero at the centre which all the fancy brickwork, finicky turrets and soaring arches could not begin to hide? A world in reverse in which no conscious divinity guides, creates and constructs, a world of absences and disguise, hidden forces of trickery and illusion. We are all of us, each of us, insuperably alone, rolling through cyclical limitless space towards our own destruction.

In the end, and at the risk of a Special Branch bullet in my ear, am I to borrow Albert of Saxe-Coburg-Gotha's words: I do not comprehend what is this Arcanum Arcanorum?

Or, do I comprehend Edward Glass a little too well? Was that the crime of which I am accounted guilty? I must have done something to have been punished in this way, to have been hollowed out thus and reduced.

I call him a thinker in brick and stone, for whatever his thoughts they are only there now in the parabolas, those unending vistas of darkness and despair he constructed so eloquently in brickwork and stone. Hieroglyphs to take and tease the spectator, turn him around, befuddle him in his own relentless infinitude of ignorance, and then send him home sadder but none the wiser.

When Preedy's Fabbricotti factory in Chelsea collapsed and there could be no question of the Preedys being invited to Windsor, it was obvious to everyone that Charles Preedy, Architect and Copyist, had copied his designs from Sir Edward Glass. Copied them badly. Ignorant men did not make the distinction – Glass's buildings reminded them of the disastrous Fabbricotti that had cost lives in Chelsea. Glass's style went out of fashion: people wanted something safe, not something fantastical. They did not want to have to wonder if the building would stay up.

As I say, the man came out of Nowhere, content enough at first to strive in his buildings to express all that was triumphant in the human condition. Unbuilt Albert Memorials testify to that but when you consider Ruskin's venerable Seven Lamps of Architecture – Sacrifice, Truth, Power, Beauty, Life, Memory and Obedience – none *of these nobilities is applicable to the light that came to guide Edward Glass, the shadows the man cast over the Twentieth Century. Glass was a devious, deceitful man. The architect of our misery, the Architect of the New Paris Grand.*

With all the lovely forms in the Universe to choose from, the overweening Edward Glass dismissed such toys as child's play. He was not content. With the hubris of a giant, Glass turned cunningly to illusions. No longer satisfied with mortal proportions, measurements in feet and thumbs, he scorned configurations conceived in human dimensions and began at last to reach out beyond and seek to order the vast and vacant spaces.

Glass & Co. – ah, yes, the & Co. Never forget the & Co. Not common – though not unknown – for architects' practices then to be & Co. But what was this Company that Glass then kept? Even the punctilious Winnup who sat over the books for hour after hour never found out, but Winnup refused to acknowledge that a man may have assistance that cannot be reckoned up by an auditor or ever reckoned with properly afterwards. I have often felt Edward Glass laughing at me from the Shadows. The man was laughing in the face of time like a sewer-rat hidden in the shade. Watching and waiting, if only for sandwiches. Chuckling and amused.

We have walked through the neatly labelled Chapters of this fabrication. Here a gentle seemly entasis, a delicate straining below the surface, a modest façade. Note the detail thrown into the brickwork to interfere and distract attention from a man in mortal terror of the emptiness, the waste. See here, the central void in his own soul reached by countless steps to be climbed as strenuously as though one is actually going somewhere. But there is neither up nor down. A dead end. A mosaic of reconstructed scraps shored up. Datta. Dayadhvam. Damyata. *Just about.*

It was a fearful descent of Genius . . .

*

Delmé Hawkins gives out. Another scrap of the past pasted over the untold layers. Poor Milla must look again. Whatever his suspicions Delmé had not known everything . . .

*

314

Edward Glass sat and stared: not into vast vacant space but into a middle distance beyond the walls of the room he occupied. The second Mrs Glass lay crippled in her bed in the room next door. The house in York Street was a dreary place where servants refused to stay.

Helen lived at her Mission in the East End doing good works, her eyes ablaze with the fervour of her splendid intentions. Stacia had married the first man who'd asked her. He couldn't believe his luck when Stacia Glass, Lady Blouvier's one-time protégée, accepted his timid proposal.

Only Philip Eames still called at the house, arriving promptly and for old times' sake every Friday afternoon. He had found badly paid work elsewhere. Glass was rude but this was what Eames came for, returning the following week for more. When an ugly spate of killings took place in the streets of London Eames advised Milla to fasten the doors at night. 'I once had a canary,' he told her for no reason. 'A neighbouring cat got into the house – the bird didn't have a chance . . .'

Milla assured Eames that she bolted the doors firmly at night. Philip Eames visited York Street out of habit, out of need for habit, and besides, there was business to execute behind the closed doors of Edward Glass's study. Glass & Co. had been bankrupted. Countless, endless law suits were rife. Eames was sent to settle out of court: there was no money to make settlements with but there were scores to be settled anonymously. The famous diary had long since been disposed of, Milla knew not how or when. Occasionally she would notice fires had been lit in her father's grate, unburnt chunks of paper had been stoked amongst the ashes. She did not look too closely. She had not thought too closely, she let her mind drift, it had been the only way. Unlike Stacia and Helen she had not left the sinking ship.

One night some time in all those years, Milla had helped herself to a box of her father's pills. The doctor had not liked the surly arrogant Glass, but he knew about suicide rates amongst bankrupts. He would be failing in his professional duties if he did not take the daughter aside. 'Extreme care!' he'd repeated insistently, tapping the pharmacist's label on the box with a long bony finger. Milla sat in the cold empty room she had once shared with her sisters. With *extreme care* indeed she swallowed the little white lozenges, one by one. She had had enough.

She put her head down on her pillow. As her mind started to float she remembered a picture she and her sisters had seen, years ago, in the window of an art gallery during one of their walks. She had promised herself she would keep dogs, but Milla had promised herself many things. She had wanted to travel the oceans and dance with a tribal chief in darkest far-off Dahomey. She drifted, and drifted so she hazily thought towards the Other Side into sleep . . .

In the morning Milla woke a bit late with a deep and dulling headache. She could hear Mrs Glass calling and she climbed off her bed wrapping a cotton gown about her as she rushed downstairs.

'You're late!' were the first words Mrs Glass, who never slept at night, said. A mug of hot coffee was required.

Milla nodded. She went to the kitchen and set about preparing the coffee. So this was what it was like to be late, to be dead, she thought blearily, until it occurred to her then that the pills had not worked. Despite her 'extreme care' they (like life itself) had let her down.

She took Mrs Glass her drink and went back upstairs and was violently sick, expelling the vicious but ineffectual milky white poison from her body. She was shaken and shocked by what had happened, she felt cheated and betrayed. Nothing would be the same again: the walls had revolved. Everything, however slight or imperfect or short-lived, had been rendered mere bonus. She lived life after that at a slight remove; everything before her eyes was glazed over and distanced by the fact that she might so easily not have Returned from the Dead to see it. You could not waste time which by rights, by all the normal laws of nature and pharmacy you should never have had in the first place. You could not regret your boring life when the value your thoughts put on that life had been non-existent.

To Elizabeth, Milla seemed more incompetent and dreamy than ever. To Edward Glass, she was an irritating reminder of the long-gone Sarah, her mother, but most of the time he was too sunken into his own sunken world to consider Milla's shortcomings. Husband and wife maintained a silent politeness in adjoining rooms. They dignified each other with unspoken affection. An enduring mutuality that had endured, they travelled quickly and steadily towards death together, locked in this house, this trench, this embrace, this mausoleum: the web.

Anything of value was tacitly sold – Eames again, that oh-so-efficient operative. No wonder the valuer Mr Frewitt had been disappointed, confronted with only the stale left-overs to knock down to sewer-rats.

Eames ceased to come to the house. As three o'clock struck, another Friday passed and no Eames, Milla's anxieties grew. Then Flora Eames sent word that her son had taken his life, a terse note for she did not trust herself to say what she would like to have said.

'Eames?' Edward Glass appeared not to know who Milla was talking about.

'Yes, Philip Eames, three o'clock, Friday afternoons, rain or shine, year in, year out.'

'Oh yes?' Glass was incurious. He gazed into his middle distance. Sarah had had just such an infuriating way of trying to involve him irrelevantly. This man, Eames, he supposed must have had his uses. 'An operative, rather an effective one, if I remember.'

'Effective?' Yes, Eames had been effective all right. He'd made a better job *in extremis* than she had done. 'Shall I write to Mrs Eames?' Milla asked.

Edward laughed. Milla, the middle one, always did have funny notions: 'I wouldn't bother,' he said. 'These things only come back at you.'

Well-meant letters to Pasha, Mrs Ruby Smith, and the house-keeper, Mrs Curzon, had indeed only come back at her so Milla did not write to Mrs Eames in whose parlour a stuffed wire-haired terrier still sat rigidly still, still begging for a biscuit. Mrs Eames had outlived her husband and son and found certain satisfaction in that.

But yes, there had been one other conversation . . .

Snooper Hawkins had asked her, materializing – whoosh! – like a genie from an old brass lamp in her kitchen, Ellen's afternoon off, dear sweet Ted living but out teaching at the slum school, the front door left carelessly open, and Delmé Hawkins had let himself in. Edward Glass's grandson had been afraid: William had kicked over his wooden bricks and screamed so loudly that even Delmé had seen it was useless to persist. Before he had gone he tried to ask, shouting over William's bawling: 'Did you and your father ever have any conversation about his work?'

317

'About his buildings?'

'Yes. Didn't he talk to you? Tell you anything?'

Milla shook her head. William bawled. Delmé Hawkins departed, threatening above the child's din to return. Alone, in a street where doors were generally left open, Milla had kept hers permanently locked. After Ted died, she moved away.

She wondered if Delmé had known it was Ellen's afternoon off. Had Ellen left the front door off the catch deliberately? The girl denied it and took to her bed. She was upset that Milla thought so little of her, she said.

Later she had taken to her bed in earnest.

'Who is the father?' Milla enquired. Ted too was upset. He said they were responsible. *In loco parentis*, they should have kept more of an eye. The baby had sickened when Ted sickened. Scarlet fever from the slum notched them both up in its merciless tally.

'Who was the father?' Milla asked Ellen again after the funerals, something to take her mind off her own dreadful loss.

'Can't you guess?' Ellen laughed, hysterical with tears.

'Not . . .' It was unthinkable.

'You said to keep the biographer away from you at all costs – it was a high price, I can tell you!'

Milla was shocked. You could not think, at least she refused to think, of Delmé Hawkins as a real person, a man like her Ted, who could father a child. She would not have let Ellen's baby in the house if she had known, which was presumably why the maid had sensibly never told her.

'I was sorry for him, I suppose,' Ellen said. They had moved now to the comfortable house in the comfortable district, paid for by Ted's family. Later Ellen would marry and go to Australia and send a postcard. 'You were hard on him. He was harmless.'

'The man was a trespasser!' Milla stated firmly.

'Well, I know I should never have taken pity and let him in . . .'

'So you did leave the door unlocked!'

'I only meant . . .' Ellen pursed her lips. 'He was a lonely man, he was probably just passing and fancied a cup of tea and a chat.'

'A cup of tea and a chat!' Milla repeated scornfully. As though Delmé Hawkins could ever have wanted anything so straight-forward as a cup of tea and a chat!

'It's not uncommon you know.'

'I don't think we had better discuss this any more,' Milla said. Delmé Hawkins was not something rational that could be reasoned away.

Ellen, however, was determined to have her say: 'You might have told Delmé what he wanted to know. You might have told him about your father. I can't see there'd have been any harm. Poor Delmé, he had nothing else, apart from his Box Brownie and his bicycle . . .'

Milla turned her back on the girl. It was ridiculous how they had held a proper funeral like the one for dear Ted at the graveside of a baby cuckoo. A little Hawkins.

But yes, Delmé, yes, you suspected correctly. Her father had indeed talked to her about his work. Once, just the once, just before he died.

Milla had entered her father's room, assuming him to be asleep. It was late at night. A voice in the darkness stopped her in her tracks: 'Is the New Paris Grand still standing?'

'As far as I know, yes . . .' Milla faltered. She had only come in to check all was well.

'Of course it is, you silly girl, the New Paris Grand was built to last . . .'

She had nodded dumbly in the darkness. Edward Glass was a difficult patient. There's not much physically wrong with him, he could live for years, the doctor had told her. He was just weak at the moment with feeling sorry for himself. Milla watched as her father sat up and lit a candle, then he helped himself rather lavishly from the assortment of medicinal delicacies heaped high beside his bed. He might have been Lady Blouvier at her sweetmeats, Milla thought and smiled. Glass saw his middle daughter's smile. It was like a slap in the face.

'That building will be mocking me in the Strand long after I am gone!' Edward Glass said savagely as though the thought had just struck him and he blamed Milla for mocking him too. He seemed to have forgotten that the building already stood empty. It had been too expensive to run as a hotel, built on a scale – never mind Delmé's assertion that Glass built for a world that is no longer with us, on a scale in which we no longer think – the Paris Grand had been built on a scale that had never existed. A gargantuan order in proportion only to Glass's demonic imagination.

'Surely,' Milla tried to say to her father, 'that is the glory of architecture, you build in your lifetime for the future that comes after. It is your contribution to the world, you expect your work to outlive you.'

'You expect your daughter to outlive you,' she might have said the way he snarled. He thought of Elee and how Elee would come to see Milla when he was gone, bringing the truth about William Back from the Dead to haunt her. 'I'm a friend of your father's,' Elee who had never acted Shakespeare would say. *The evil that men do lives after them . . .*

'I have never been fond of you, Milla,' Glass said now.

'No,' Milla agreed sadly, accepting what she had always known. She wished he had not said it though. By speaking of these things it gave them form.

Strengthened by one of his lethal preparations, Glass turned and glared: not into the middle distance but directly at his irksome middle daughter. How dare the neglectful child stand there in her orange and gold birthday-party hat talking to him of the future! She who had giggled at her mother's funeral and stuffed her face with jelly had sneaked up on him like a rat and niftily stolen what was his! Not one of the draughtsmen at Glass & Co. would have had the nerve. It was true that he was not fond of her, nevertheless he had not meant to say so. She was the sort of child that you wanted to give presents to, to make up for who knew what.

'You can have the future, Milla, and much good may it do you!' Harry Withercott had been welcome to Lucy and to the diary of work he had snaffled. Milla the middle one was welcome to her present: the future. How he hated the New Paris Grand and all it once meant to him, the spans springing from the face to the crown, stretching back again unsupported three times over. What a contortionist he had been, Houdini-like the genius of the future had tumbled and twisted, vanishing ineluctably! But to what point? Had he not, like a child that opens its mouth to speak but who has nothing to say, merely been vacuously showing off? The thought was almost unbearable. He glared at Milla who had provoked it and his voice rose tremulous with fever: 'I hate you and I hate the New Paris Grand. If I could flatten the building I wouldn't hesitate. If I could fly through the air and drop some device straight down – whoosh! – on the whole infernal creation and see my Masterpiece go up in a vast flash with flames and acrid smoke billowing all over London, flushing out the rats, crippling them like my poor Elizabeth bending to examine the mosaics, I would not hesitate. Oh no, Milla, birthday-girl, one great bomb and I'd destroy the whole world if I could, I never wanted three daughters anyway!'

He fell back chuckling and amused, his eyes blazing full of his vast and overreaching invention, his mouth open like a dog's howling unrestrainedly in the flickering candlelight. He laughed like the devil at his heels as he pictured the chaos created by the order he'd imposed on the chaos. The muddle he'd be leaving for Milla, the middle one. Her legacy. His parting-present.

Milla trembled. She did not like being laughed at. She should have turned on her own heels then and left Sir Edward Glass to his own devilish company as Elizabeth should have left the chancer Henry Cathcart to sit in his deck-chair the cheap end of Ventnor, waiting for the rain. Milla paused. He could live for years, the doctor had told her. She thought of the disappointing Pasha who had invited her to tea but only diminished her and fed her unpleasantness. She should have got down from the big fusty chair, planted her feet firmly on the floor and, eloquent as Delmé Hawkins delivering an Improving lecture, she should have spoken up then; she spoke up now.

She opened her mouth: 'YOU . . .' the jelly-stained, foul-mouthed birthday-girl began to shout as she reached over and helped herself from the trolley of lethal sweetmeats heaped high beside the bed. Milla is usually quite quick, she thought, as she filled a shiny steel syringe with something benumbing from a stoppered blue glass bottle, three times the morphine needed to kill, unequivo-cally, the ghastliest of pain. I'm afraid Milla's mind is more with the *pâtisserie* and *confiserie*. Plunging the stumpy needle deep into her father's unresisting arm, Milla yelled at the top of her voice: 'YOU MISERABLE OLD BUGGER!'

Sir Edward Glass died laughing. More than a little surprised by what he had heard from Milla the middle one's prim little tongue and weakened by long years spent feeling sorry for himself, Edward Glass, the architect, died painlessly. If the second Mrs Glass knew or heard what had happened in the room next door she was hardly in a position to say anything. Step-mother and step-daughter, their story in a book specially written to accompany a grim wax tableau: a little unforgiving entertainment for Mrs Preedy to purchase from a bookstall and trill about over Afternoon Tea. What a charade, what a party-prank, what a dangerous oozing of filial glue!

He was an inventor, an innovator, Delmé Hawkins, Art Historian, with the dubious Oxford MA, had proclaimed. Milla, allowing herself now to remember, had of course to agree. Her own father it had been who, with an exact eye and an exacting vision, could create order out of chaos and chaos out of order with a few quick strokes of his masterly pen. Sir Edward Glass who, in the ghastly contortions of an imagination turned inside-out, and a vaulting ambition that fell flat on its nose, had single-mindedly, single-handedly envisaged merciless and mass destruction on the grandest of scales and without any measurements. A greater Oblivion by God and St George, neither Heroic nor Grandiloquent. You could not imagine the innocence of the world before bombs like the ones being dropped every night killing and maiming with total abandon. Human beings reduced to irrelevancies in time, time playing tricks with words and dimensions, discarded shadows that mattered not one jot.

Delmé had been right to be disturbed, his brushes were the best on the market: no wonder Milla had prized her forgetfulness. No wonder she had turned away from what she had done; her father had wanted her to know the facts but there is comfort in fiction, she had always suspected that. You could lose yourself.

'I accuse him as the architect!' the poor crazed Hawkins had raved, the sweat pouring down his face as he furiously pedalled uphill. 'Delmé Hawkins, Art Historian (d. 2–9–29) Requiescat In Pace' – so the Reverend Hubert Percy Blatt had said, printing it boldly at his own expense in a number of national dailies long ago.

'Snooper Hawkins, RIP,' Milla murmured in agreement. It was easier for you, Delmé, with your official validation, your bicycle and your Kodak Box Brownie than it ever could have been for me. When I turn round to accuse my father, Sir Edward Glass, it happens that I must also accuse myself . . .

28

Tea-Cakes

Always one for sitting down and writing unnecessary letters, Milla wrote now to the Reverend H. P. Blatt:

You said 'any time, if there was ever anything' so I trust you will forgive my troubling you. I expect you too saw the Late News notice in the Telegraph. *Edward Glass's New Paris Grand Hotel was bombed last week. Since then, Father Blatt, I have found myself thinking again about Delmé Hawkins.*

Hawkins investigated the parabolas, diabolas my father built. Vast giant structures we gaze back on across No Man's Land, the rat-infested emptiness that divides us from the past. Hawkins was awe-struck. It affected his judgement. Anglo-Saxons living in mud huts amongst the mosaics and hypocausts of the ransacked Roman Empire probably felt the selfsame wonder and perhaps some of them were as disturbed by what they saw as our dear friend, Delmé. Perhaps they too twisted their necks gazing up at the crumbling magnificence and wondered about the race of giants who built on such a scale and then went away, leaving only chaos, ruins and destruction behind them.

Father Blatt, my father was no giant. He was only a jobbing architect earning a living in a competitive market. Delmé Hawkins claimed too much for him. You cannot blame the piper for the tune, even if all the rats and boys do chase after him and perish in the quagmire he unthinkingly led them into. No, Father Blatt, Hawkins was the one who possessed the perilously overstretched imagination which unsteadied his grasp on reality.

She would not belittle Hawkins, deep in his pauper's grave, by telling the clergyman about the little Hawkins that had died in her own nest at the turn of the Century. A nest that had been a proper household, complete with a housemaid some smooth-talking itiner-ant brush-salesman got pregnant. Nor would she mention that Hawkins's MA, though printed in bold, had actually been bogus. Sir Edward Glass would have swept aside the deception as of no consequence. He had never enquired into the nature of Harry Withercott's training.

Miss Housecroft had taught the three of them nothing. Milla had learnt for herself by lifting the flannel covering a kidney-bowl and seeing a drop of Poor Mamma's blood on the end of a steel syringe: *Blood will have blood*. Milla could remember one occasion when the governess was in a frenzy, trying to finish some work to please her professor and Milla had asked her what could be so urgent. An Ode, by Horace, Miss Housecroft had said, and then read them some of the language that might have died completely with the ransacked Roman Empire but for the giant-like efforts of Emily Housecroft and Professor Arthur Fahey:

immortalia ne speres, monet annus et almum
quae rapit hora diem

'What does it mean?' cried Milla.

Emily Housecroft sighed: 'Life is desperately short, make good use of what little time you have; the moon may wax and wane but there's no coming Back from the Dead, no second chance for us. We merely crumble like over-ambitious cupolas to shadow and dust. Something like that! Now, girls, I really must get on . . .'

'It's sad,' Helen said – Miss Housecroft clearly had no idea what was suitable; no wonder a proper school wouldn't have her! Stacia had already turned away with an impatient shrug. What fresh nonsense was this?

'It's beautiful,' thought Milla, regretful that Latin lessons had not been included in Miss Housecroft's contract, though it was hard to say what had been included. Latin had been a book she made sure was open for William. Oh William, never mind *immortalia*! *Mortalia* itself you could not hope for. They taught him Latin (using School Editions edited by Professor Fahey in Marylebone, next door to Madame Tussaud's) but they taught him cricket too at the expensive school Ted's parents paid for. When boys went to enlist, ones good at bowling were given hand-grenades to throw, those who could bat were issued with bayonets. *Direct attack, parry and return*. And then when the point has failed, what then? *Dulce et decorum est* to make use of the butt, the inflexible butt. She and William had learned the drill together.

324

The night before William went away to join Archbishop Machen's platoon they had sat over his War Office *Manual of Infantry Training* as once they had sat together over his Latin verbs – *amo, amas, amat*: a rat – mothers tend to help children with their homework. When Mrs Glass came up to the school-room to lend a hand with the algebra she had screamed at Milla: 'Chance is the only factor in the whole equation!'

Could this, Father Blatt, be the elusive equation Delmé Hawkins was seeking? My step-mother and I disagreed about Chance – by all the laws of probability she should no more have been my step-mother than Edward Glass's buildings should have stood up. It was chance that brought her to our house one chilly afternoon, chance that made my father install her as a mainstay to keep the world from toppling about our ears, as now it topples. Every night I hear the distant thudding of incendiary and high-explosive bombs raining down on London and I think of Stacia in other women's drawing-rooms, I think of you Father Blatt upholding the church in Parson's Hill and I think of Helen the other side of the globe in China.

Dear Father Blatt, if there was any enigma about my father's work, it was in the way that Hawkins chanced to single him out in the way that he did. Even on Hawkins's own admission, John Ruskin himself never bothered with Edward Glass. I do not know how Delmé Hawkins knew I killed my father, a man who liked things understood but unpronounced. He never liked me, I do not know why he stayed for my birthday tea. I do not understand what the Improvers of Bingley and Batley could possibly have made of Delmé Hawkins's lectures. Why did they sit forward on their chairs? Why did they rush to enlist in 1914, why did they let themselves be ordered over the top to face the relentless German artillery? Why do men do the things that they do? I cannot now imagine the innocence of the world back then, before the dreadful inventions of the 20th Century. But you, Father Blatt, you talked to Delmé – over diluted port and a game of draughts. You went to his lectures. Perhaps you could tell me what, other than dear Delmé himself, was so intriguing? Or failing that, perhaps you could ask your esteemed Archbishop a question or two . . .

Milla's letter was returned to her unopened. St Olive's of Parson's Hill had been laid waste. A direct hit, no chance to parry, all mail returned for there were no survivors. *Enemy Action* stamped on the envelope, of course. (The Post Office had no rubber stamp to explain that Hubert Blatt had been dug out of the ruins more than half-alive but he'd been given a blood-transfusion with contaminated blood, septicaemia had set in and he'd died rather horribly several days later.)

Milla tore up her letter to the late Reverend H. P. Blatt. No wonder it had been returned, sent Back from the Dead – these things had a way of coming back at you. She had missed him, he'd been late, her timing had been bad: Not today, thank you! Return to Sender! and the door had been shut in her face.

Milla and Stacia met up again in the same tea-shop as before. On this occasion Milla did not ask her sister, silently or out loud, if her journey had been necessary. It was important in war-time to patch up a quarrel. Besides, Hugo Mountsier (the youngest one's eldest, Mabel's intended, intended by Stacia, at least) had been shot down. A hero's death dangling on the end of a parachute over France, or somewhere. The 'Monograph' was no longer necessary to establish poor horsy-toothed Mabel's credentials.

'Maybe Sir Edward Glass was nobody particular,' Stacia generously conceded. Stacia had enjoyed their quarrel while it lasted, but it was good to smooth things over: two pleasures for the price of one, an economy of which Mrs Curzon would have approved.

'You're wearing Poor Mamma's brooch; how clever to have kept it safe all this time,' Milla said.

'It's funny how it was given to me, though *you* were the one who always got on with Mrs Glass.'

'She kept trying to give me presents I didn't want. When she was dying she couldn't bear it when I didn't want her knick-knacks. I only ever succeeded in annoying her,' Milla said sadly.

'She was married before, wasn't she?' Stacia asked. 'Who to? I never wondered before.'

'I don't know,' Milla said, though she knew only too well. She was the one who had had to sit beside their step-mother as she raved about tartar emetic and hired deck-chairs. Milla was also the one who should be standing in wax beside Elizabeth Cathcart in a carefully reconstructed parlour packed with knick-knacks at Madame Tussaud's. If a bomb hit the Marylebone Road, would the wax melt and the people come alive? she wondered. Come Back from the Dead to accuse their accusers? Those who left the doors open and blindly pronounced on the innocent and the driven.

'At least you – I sometimes think I should have . . .' Stacia remarked. Lady Blouvier tried to send me home – if I had come she would not have gone to the Himalayas to get rid of me; Chopin would continue to have been played at soirées in Mayfair even though Stacia would not have been the one at the ivory keyboard. They had dressed her up like a doll and taken photographs of her. There had been something very odd about Lady Blouvier's photographs; even though she was the one in the picture, Stacia could never recognize herself. Had it been a trick of the light or the fickle chemicals Lady Blouvier employed in her patented darkroom? Stacia fingered the diamond brooch she wore on her lapel. 'Our father gave it to Poor Mamma when dear William was born,' she said.

'Our Father who art in Heaven!' said Milla with an impish grin.

'Or in hell!' said Stacia. 'For all we know . . .'

'The *depths* of hell, like Virgil and Dante,' Milla remarked. Like Edward Glass and Delmé Hawkins, she thought. Like Pasha's gloomy sitting-room.

'That what you call your latest dogs?' Stacia asked patiently. Virgil and Dante, indeed! Milla was already fretting about letting her dogs out. 'I never saw the attraction in dogs myself, but there you are! We all see things differently . . .'

'They're good company,' Milla said. She poured the tea.

'I suppose there is that,' Stacia sighed. Good company was increasingly hard to find. 'No news from Helen?'

'No.'

'One hears such horrid things from China. Live prisoners used for bayonet-practice . . .'

Some ladies at a nearby table turned their backs on the two peculiar old women chuntering loudly in the corner. This was the sort of conversation one would rather not overhear.

'I met someone,' Stacia went on oblivious. In an *uncertain hour* one dark night late in London, *in the waning dusk* she had thought it was leaves chasing along in the street and then Esther Szlabin, the Manchester chocolatier's daughter, had walked past her, a down-turned face loitering and hurried, pale and ancient as a ghost. 'The woman clutched at my sleeve and looked into my face. "Are you . . . Are you, forgive me . . . Edward Glass's daughter?" It was very strange, rather disturbing in a way though I did not think so at the time. But she . . .'

'Who was she?' asked Milla.

'Goodness knows! London is a strange, unreal city these days. One has such strange meetings. I denied it: "Never heard of the fellow," I said and hurried on. I thought afterwards I should not have turned her aside, but it was too late then – *In the disfigured street She left me* – I even wondered if it really happened and in any case, if Delmé Hawkins's "Monograph" is burnt . . .'

'Probably for the best, Stacia darling,' Milla said.

Stacia was enjoying their chat. 'Dr Morgan, you remember him, Milla?'

'No one ever forgets Dr Morgan!'

'He was Helen's godfather . . .'

'Was he?' Milla laughed.

'A man before his time. How well he'd have done for himself after the Great War, and now. I mean, Lady Mountsier, Desidera, would probably pay out a fortune to speak to her Hugo, even though the poor lad had such a terrible stutter, and I'm sure the youngest one's eldest, Mabel, is much better off with her new chap, even if his family do live in Peckham and aren't remotely concerned with the child's credentials, having none of their own . . .'

Stacia chatted on. Milla did not say much, which was odd when you recalled how she was the one who used to pipe up. Still, a quarrel patched; two old ladies companionably eating currantless, eggless, sugarless war-time tea-cakes in an unlit tea-room in Kent. And enjoying them very much although, since last they had come, supplies of butter down here had completely run out.

Milla munched and idly considered how these dry tea-cakes could be bracketed with the joys of her life: tea-cakes, little William and dear old Ted – such wonderful unexpected bonuses. She wet her finger and chased the crumbs round the plate; she smiled up at Stacia. Here she still was, the defiant middle daughter enjoying her tea. She straightened her hat. How precious and enjoyable life could be on time warred over and frozen, ticking demonically beneath the unquiet surface, hidden and perfectly preserved in an unforgiving translucency of ice. In any case, the tea-party wasn't over yet:

'Come on, Stacia, let's be really wicked and have a couple more tea-cakes, while we still can . . .'